D1247514

STRANGER
AT WILDINGS

Madeleine Brent

STRANGER AT WILDINGS

British Title:
KIRKBY'S CHANGELING

G.K.HALL &CO.

Boston, Massachusetts

1977

Library of Congress Cataloging in Publication Data

Brent, Madeleine.
  Stranger at Wildings.

  Large print ed.
  I. Title.
[PZ4.B8393St5] [PR6052.R419] 823'.9'14 77-9565
ISBN 0-8161-6495-9

Published in Large Print by arrangement with
Doubleday & Company, Inc.

Set in Compugraphic 18 pt English Times

British Commonwealth rights granted courtesy of
Souvenir Press Ltd., London

STRANGER
AT WILDINGS

ONE

My face no longer hurt much, but it was still a little swollen on one side from the slapping Strabo had given me the night before. I touched fingers to my cheek as I walked down through the woods to the stream, wincing at the memory. I had been quite helpless as he held me in one big hand and delivered those slow, deliberate slaps with the other.

For a moment I wondered if I would put myself to the same ordeal yet again. This would be the fourth time, and it was getting worse every day. I had thought at first that Strabo would soon become ashamed of beating me in front of all the others, but I knew now that his pride would never allow him to give up.

I had only to stop defying him, of course, and the whole business would end. But even as I was tempted to accept defeat, I knew with sick certainty that when the moment came I would go on with the task I had so foolishly begun. I would have no help. The others might murmur and protest halfheartedly, but that was all, partly because they were a little afraid to quarrel with Strabo and partly because it was their wise tradition never to interfere in disputes not of their making. Even Mr. Kayser himself took no part in squabbles between his people unless they became so serious as to affect our work.

I had half hoped, and feared at the same time, that I might goad Strabo into forgetting himself and beating me about the shoulders or legs, for everyone would have condemned him then, and Mr. Kayser would soon have taken a hand in the matter. With stiff shoulder or thigh muscles I could not possibly work, and that would have been serious. But although Strabo was stupid and a bully, he had enough sense to avoid that kind of trouble, and so it was only my face that suffered.

Inwardly I fumed at my own hot temper, which I knew would drive me on. It was only ten minutes ago that I had set out to walk down to a small clearing by the stream, where I could sit quietly with the long morning's work behind me and talk to myself sensibly. I would point out how ridiculous it was for me, a girl of just eighteen, to expect fair treatment for myself and others like me from a man such as Strabo. It was too much to hope for, even in these first years of a new century, when women were beginning to be held in higher esteem, and even among people whose ways were not those of the outside world, and who had never regarded women as lesser creatures. But I knew already that my good intentions would come to nothing. Instead of talking some sense into myself I would sit and brood about Strabo's behavior, growing more stubborn and resentful every moment, until my anger overcame my fears and I would go back determined to outface him again.

I sighed, and sat down on the sun-warmed grass near the bank of the stream, watching two small purple butterflies dancing in the air. I could not remember seeing this kind before, though we had traveled the same route the summer before last, moving west from Budapest to Graz. In their daintiness they reminded me of Maria, and this turned my mind from Strabo for a while. I was a little worried about Maria. She was fifteen now, and in the last year she had grown three inches. This in itself did not matter, for she was still light and beautifully proportioned, but if she continued to grow taller it might seriously affect her work.

I comforted myself with the thought that a year ago I had been afraid that I might grow too tall myself, but I seemed to have stopped growing now and I was still only an inch or two above five feet. A phrase jumped suddenly into my mind from the past, a memory from that other life in another world I had once known. It had been spoken in pity, not in malice, by the tall, sad, remote man I had believed to be my father, and I had overheard the words by chance. ". . . She's fat, white, spotty, red-haired, and bad-tempered. I shall never understand it."

If he had lived only another month he might have understood, at least in part, for he would have known then that I was not his daughter. I shivered, and quickly closed my mind against remembrance of those years when I had been another person. It had once been desperately hard to blot out such thoughts of the past, but now they rarely touched me, and even they carried no sense of reality. That other world was long dead, and the girl who had been myself was dead with it.

I stood up and moved to the edge of the stream. Here there was a small inlet where the water was almost still, and I tried to find my reflection in it, moved by a foolish desire to see myself as I was now, as if for reassurance. But I could see only a wavering and foreshortened shape of mingled green and black. I was wearing an old green shirt of Leo's, with short sleeves, and a black skirt of homespun, cut short so that it fell to only a few inches below my knees. This was for freedom of movement, and most of our womenfolk were similarly dressed by day, for we worked no less hard than the men and often at the same tasks. Beneath the skirt I wore a calico petticoat and what Maria and I always called our *petit caleçon,* which was a garment made by cutting the legs from a pair of woolen tights to form short, close-fitting drawers. My feet were comfortable in shoes Old Sven had made for me. They were of soft leather, like moccasins but with eyelets and short laces.

I thought ruefully that although I still had my red hair and bad temper, at least nobody could say I was fat, white, and spotty now. On the contrary, beneath what I wore my body was hard and lean. With my very short hair I could have passed for a boy, though Leo had roared with laughter when I said as much on one occasion, remarking that he thought my shape was entirely wrong for a boy.

Except for the hated freckles, my complexion was clear, and my bare arms and legs had long since been weathered, like my face, to an unladylike tan, despite the natural whiteness of skin that usually goes with red hair.

Sometimes I daydreamed that in yet another new life which I hoped to enter one day, I would have a beautiful pale complexion, no freckles, a serene manner, an elegant carriage helped by an extra few inches of height — when it was safe for me to grow again — and long hair piled in a chignon.

I gave a little laugh at my thoughts, and from somewhere close by a voice said in German, "May I share the joke, young lady?"

I turned quickly, startled. A man lay in the shade of a hornbeam, propped on an elbow as if he might just have woken from sleep. He wore a torn gray jersey, crumpled blue trousers, and rubber boots like short Wellington boots. Beside him lay a tattered topcoat bearing smears of tar and paint. His hair was thick, brown, and uncombed, and the beginnings of a beard showed that he had not shaved for several days. His face was gaunt and unnaturally pale. He might have been a vagabond, but for the voice. It was rather deep, pleasing in intonation, and held a quality hard to describe. I only knew that if I had heard him speak without seeing him I would have judged him to be of the gentry.

For all that, I was alone with him here in the woods, he was a stranger, and his appearance was certainly that of a tramp. I did not move, but was ready to pluck up my skirt and run, sure that I could outdistance him if the need arose.

He smiled and said, "I am sorry if I startled you. Please do not be alarmed."

I felt no surprise that he spoke in German, for I had discovered that almost half the people of Hungary did not know the native tongue but instead spoke German, Serbian, or Slovak. Because of my travels over the years past, and because our people spoke a mixture of tongues, I had learned a little of several languages. French and Italian I could manage quite well, especially Italian, since Maria and Leo had spoken it most of the time when I first came to live with them. In German and Spanish I could understand simple phrases, but had little practice in speaking.

Rather haltingly I said, "Good morning.

I am not alarmed."

"Good. I must look rather ——." The last word was unknown to me, though it was easy to guess his general meaning. He smiled again as he spoke. It was a good smile, and I felt less need to be wary. He got slowly to his feet and said, "You are not from these parts. Are you with the people up there?" He glanced up the wooded hill, and began to move towards me. Then he lurched suddenly, his legs seemed to give way and he half fell, half sank to his hands and knees.

I ran forward and crouched to take his arm, forgetting my German as I said, "Are you ill?"

"Damn," he said shakily, sitting back on his heels and wiping an arm across his sweating forehead. "Sorry, I'll be all right in a moment —"

He broke off, looking at me in surprise, and I saw now that his eyes were a curious dark blue. "Are you English?" he said.

"Yes. Are you?"

He hesitated for a moment, then nodded. "Yes," he said, thoughtfully, I'm English." It was almost as if he had been unsure about it, which was very strange, but no more so than the contrast between his scarecrow clothes and his manner. Although several questions came to my mind, I asked none of them, for it was not the way of our people to be inquisitive. In any event, curiosity was driven from my mind when I looked at him more closely, for I saw signs that I recognized, and said, "You're half starved. When did you last eat?"

"Well, it was quite a long time ago, now you mention it." He spoke solemnly, but there was a touch of laughter in his eyes, and I liked him for that. When things were bad I always became grim and surly, but I was not proud of it.

"Haven't you any money?" I asked.

"I can't deny that I'm temporarily embarrassed," he said with an air of humorous apology.

I pulled the little knapsack round in front of me, opened it, took out two thick pieces of coarse bread and a wedge of cheese, and said, "Here, you'd better eat this."

He reached out eagerly, then hesitated.

"I don't want to take your lunch."

"Oh, don't be stupid. Eat, and you'll feel better. I've got some pieces of sugar here, too. They'll help."

He blinked, then grinned and took the bread and cheese. I could see that he wanted to wolf the food down, but he restrained himself and chewed slowly, watching me with a blend of curiosity and what seemed a kind of amusement. I felt the color begin to rise to my cheeks under his gaze, and said, "Do you think I'm funny?"

He looked surprised. "Good lord, no. What makes you imagine that?"

"The way you were staring at me."

"I apologize. I wasn't laughing at you. I was entertained by your directness."

"What do you mean?"

He laughed. "There's an example. Most young ladies would say, 'I'm not quite sure I follow you,' or something of that sort. You say things like 'Haven't you any money?' and 'Don't be stupid.' I'm not used to it, and I find it refreshing."

"I see. I'm sorry I misunderstood you. What are you used to?"

"There you go again. I don't know . . . what would you imagine I'm used to?"

I thought for a moment, suddenly aware that I was enjoying my encounter with this stranger. "Well, you're hungry and you've no money and you're dressed like a tramp, but you're not one. You speak like an English gentleman. I should think you were used to morning calls and polite conversations with ladylike ladies in drawing rooms, over cucumber sandwiches and cups of tea."

He laughed and shook his head as if I surprised him. Then his face became quiet, and after considering for a while he said, "Yes. Yes, that conjures up a familiar picture."

"You'd better eat, not talk."

There was a silence for some time, and when he had swallowed the last morsel of bread he said, "I'd like to know your name."

I took a dozen pieces of sugar from my knapsack and put them in his hands, glad to see that there was a little more color in his face now. The sugar would quickly restore his energy, at least for a while. I knew that from my own experience. "I'm Chantal," I said.

"Chantal? That's surely not an English name?"

"It's my working name."

"Ah, I see. Very pretty, too. I saw the notices for Kayser's Giant Circus in one of the villages this morning, and I could see the top of your tent beyond the trees as I came over the hill."

"Yes." I hesitated. "We're not *really* a giant circus, but there are lots smaller, with a little one-pole tent and a few animals. And we do have a fifteen-meter ring, and a tent with four king poles, and eighteen wagons *and* electric lamps, so we're not really small, either. But we call it Kayser's Giant Circus to make it sound bigger."

He nodded, pursing his lips. "You could hardly advertise yourselves as Kayser's Medium Circus."

"There's no need to make fun of us," I said sharply.

He looked puzzled. "Is that what you thought?"

"Yes. Oh, I don't know. I did at first, but perhaps you didn't mean to. I'm sorry if I was touchy.''

"I'm sorry I made a weak joke. What part do you play in the circus, Chantal?''

"I'm one of the Flying Gallettis, the least important of the three. Leo's the catcher and Maria, that's his sister, does all the difficult tricks. I fill in the gaps while she's getting her breath.''

"And how do you fill in the gaps?''

I shrugged. "Well, it's a flying trapeze act. I can do single somersaults and pikes and pirouettes and open back somersaults, but Maria's much better and does all the big tricks. I'm sure she could do a triple if only we had enough room. She's been at it almost since she could walk, of course, and so has Leo. They were born in a circus, and that makes all the difference. If you start late, you can never catch up.''

"How late did you start, Chantal?''

"I was old. Over thirteen.''

"Elderly indeed,'' he said gravely, and ate the last piece of sugar. "You must have a name of your own, I imagine?''

"No. Just Chantal.''

"I mean in the time before you became Chantal.''

14

I said rather curtly, "I'm not interested in the time before."

"I'm sorry. I don't wish to be inquisitive." He paused. "It must be very dangerous. Aren't you sometimes afraid?"

"Well . . . no. I'm always keyed up, but not really afraid. There's a net below."

"Circus nets always look too small to me. Suppose you fell while you were swinging out beyond one end?"

"You'd have to be very silly to do that. All the catching and somersaults are done when the trapezes come close together, over the middle of the net. That's when you're most likely to fall."

"All the same, I'm sure I'd be terrified."

I shook my head. "It isn't like that. You don't begin by climbing up into the big top and swinging from one trapeze to another. When Mr. Galletti started to train me, I spent months doing exercises and gymnastics on the ground before I was even allowed to climb the ladder to the platform. Then for weeks I just did very simple exercises on a single trapeze, getting used to the height —" I stopped abruptly, surprised to find myself talking so freely to this stranger. It was unlike me.

"Please go on," he said.

I plucked a blade of grass, studying him. It occurred to me that his questions had given me the right to ask one of my own, so instead of continuing I said, "You haven't told me your name yet."

"No, that's true," he said apologetically, and scratched the stubble of beard on his cheek. "Would Martin do?"

I sat very still, looking down at the ground so that he would not see the quick suspicion I knew must show in my eyes. *Martin.* To meet an English stranger beside a stream in Hungary, and to have him speak a name I had tried to blot out of my mind these years past — surely this was too much for coincidence. And he had not exactly given the name as his own, he had said, "Would Martin do?"

I heard him laugh. "No need to give too much thought, Chantal. It isn't important."

I began to nibble the blade of grass, trying to collect my wits. After a few moments I realized how silly it was of me to be startled. Martin was a common enough English name. I got to my feet, brushed my skirt, and said, "You'd better come home with me, Mr. Martin. You need a decent meal, and I'm sure we can find you a bed for the night, even if it's only a pile of hay in the stables."

"That's extremely kind of you." The man stood up as he spoke. "Are you sure your colleagues won't mind?"

"They're circus people and you're an outsider. They won't talk to you much, but they'll be polite and they won't begrudge you a meal and a place to sleep — as long as you behave yourself. Don't ask questions and they won't ask you any." I hesitated. "If they catch you stealing, they'll give you a whipping you won't forget."

"I'll be good," he said meekly.

We spoke very little as we walked up through the woods together. I set a slow pace in case he still felt weak, and it was ten minutes later when we emerged from the trees and came in sight of the big top.

This was a quiet time of day for us, yet it must have seemed a busy scene to any stranger. Half a dozen men with sledgehammers were doing the rounds of the great guy ropes, making sure that the long steel anchors were secure. Mr. McLeod and his assistant were testing the traction engine which Mr. Kayser had bought only six months ago and which was his great pride. On the road, it towed the elephant wagon, which had previously needed a team of six horses, and when the circus was set up the engine provided electricity for over a hundred wonderfully bright lamps in the big top, though we always kept our old naphtha flares in reserve in case of a breakdown.

Mr. Albertini had finished his daily practice and was leading his liberty horses from the big top to the stables. Two carts from Sávár had just arrived, full of provisions which were being unloaded. Pepe, on tall stilts, was busy at his usual task of securing any loose rings and hooks where the canvas wall and the roof of the big top joined. Old Sven, who was in charge of all props and maintenance and who worked miracles every day, stood at his long workbench giving orders to one of his men who was repairing a row of seats.

The three little Khalaf boys were playing on a patch of ground thickly spread with straw, jumping from a roughly built platform about five feet high, and doing forward and backward somersaults. Their mother and father performed a springboard tumbling act, and one day the boys would join them.

As we passed nearby the man beside me said, "They're speaking English." He glanced back at the little boys. "Does everybody speak English?"

"Well, the families often use their own particular languages among themselves, but everybody can speak some English, and that's our common language. I think it happened because Mr. Kayser used to be the manager of Broadwell's Circus years ago, and that was an English-speaking circus. All the people like their children to learn English, so I spend some of my time teaching." I smiled to myself. "Most European circuses use French, and our people feel we're rather superior."

The living quarters lay on the far side of the big top, and to save skirting it we went through. Here a few men and women were working quietly, bringing in fresh sawdust and sweeping litter from between the rows of seats. At other times there might have been more noise and bustle, with several acts rehearsing, but Gustave was putting his three lions through their paces and it was important to have no distraction.

I saw Mr. Kayser in conversation with the tentmaster and made my way round the ring towards them, pausing when I found that the stranger had stopped and was staring up at the platforms and trapezes high in the roof of the big top. When he caught up with me he said, "It's strange. . . . I find it hard to think of you as a girl who wears tights and spangles and goes flying through the air on a trapeze. You're out of place, Chantal."

"I am *not* out of place," I said sharply. "I find it hard to think of *you* as a penniless vagabond, Mr. Martin. You're out of place, if anyone is."

We looked at each other, and after a little silence, he said, "Mr. Martin doesn't sound right. You'd better just call me Martin."

"Very well. Wait here a moment, please." I moved on and stood near Mr. Kayser and the tentmaster until Mr. Kayser looked at me and raised an eyebrow.

"Yes, Chantal?"

"I'm sorry to trouble you, Mr. Kayser. I found a man down by the stream. He's English, and speaks like a gentleman, but he has no money and he's half starved. May I give him a meal and find a place for him to sleep tonight?"

Mr. Kayser glanced past me to where Martin stood waiting a little way off, and said in his fluent but heavily accented English, "Do you know anything about him?"

"He says his name's Martin. I don't know anything else, sir."

"Seems a bit odd." He peered over his spectacles at me with a half smile. "But then you Engleesh are odd people, aren't you? I once met a snake charmer in Tunis who turned out to be an Engleesh baronet. No, he was Irish, now I come to think of it. Never mind. Your face is lopsided, Chantal. Why do you make Strabo angry, hey?"

"Because what he does isn't fair, sir."

"Fair? Dear Got, child, sis world was not made *fair!* You think you can change it?"

"No. Not really."

"Goot. So you will not make Strabo angry again?"

I was silent. It was useless to make a promise I knew I would be unable to keep. Mr. Kayser sighed and put a hand on my shoulder. "Lissen, Chantal. Perhaps I am on your side. But I will not intervere with my people unless I must. And please remember, if I must lose you or Strabo, I can better afford to lose *you.* Understood?"

"Yes, sir." I glanced over my shoulder. "What about this man?"

"What is he like? I don't want anyone who makes trouble."

"He seems all right, Mr. Kayser. Very quiet and pleasant."

"Well, give him a night's lodging. Tell Zammy I have agreed."

I had scarcely thanked Mr. Kayser before he turned back to the tentmaster and was deep in conversation again. We made our way out of the big top by the artists' entrance, passing under the arch on which the red-coated band played during performances. This brought us into the mounting place, where all kinds of props and apparatus for the different acts were kept in readiness — ladders, pedestals, gaily painted tubs, paper hoops, sections of cage, Pepe's exploding piano, and a mass of other paraphernalia.

Beyond the mounting place was a long canvas gallery running to left and right. This was the wild-beast gallery and formed one side of a big square with an open courtyard in the center. We turned left and walked past the cages in which Strabo's bears were having an afternoon sleep. The lion cage was empty, since Gustave was rehearsing, but the menagerie cats, the leopard and puma, were pacing impatiently, waiting to be fed.

Twice Martin opened his mouth and closed it again without speaking. It dawned on me that he was remembering I had told him not to ask questions, and I felt I ought to explain a little about this strange world of ours as we went along, so

I said, "The wild-beast gallery is always nearest to the artists' entrance, because the animals have to be brought into the ring through an enclosed runway leading into the cage, and the distance must be kept as short as possible."

"I see. Thank you."

We turned right, and I paused for a moment to make a fuss of Sunbeam as she thrust her trunk through the bars to nuzzle me in search of sugar. "I'm sorry, my beauty," I said to the gently, towering creature. "This gentleman's eaten all your sugar."

Beside me Martin laughed and patted her trunk gingerly. "I hope she won't hold it against me."

"Oh, no. Sunbeam has a heart of gold, haven't you, pet? I'll come back with something for you later, I promise."

We moved on past wagon horses, ponies, and the menagerie camel, and again turned right into the gallery forming the top of the square, where the monkey cages and the tank with the sea lions lay. Here, through an opening in the canvas, we could glimpse the courtyard where the living tents of the grooms and animal men were set up. I pointed across the open square and said, "That's the fourth side, the gallery where the liberty horses are kept, but we're going out to the living wagons now." I turned through an opening, and led the way across a stretch of grass towards the line of wagons.

Martin said, "It all seems very confusing."

"Yes. But you get used to it."

That was true. Although we traveled Europe from Spain to Russia, our world was in many ways unchanging. Wherever we stopped to build our little canvas city it was always the same, every wagon and every tent occupying its own allotted place. I think I could have moved blindfolded through the circus without so much as stumbling over a rope or steel anchor.

"I live with Maria and Leo and Mr. Galletti," I said. "He's their grandfather, and he was a great trapezist in his early days. Leo is a year younger than I am, and Maria's three years younger. Their mother and father were killed in an accident before I came to the circus."

"A trapeze accident?"

"No, on the road. There was a storm and their wagon team bolted. The wagon toppled into a river, and only Maria and Leo were saved. Look, there's Maria."

She was hanging some washing on a line at the rear of the wagon, and gave me one of her big warm smiles as we came into sight. I loved Maria, though she was always scolding me for one thing or another.

"Hallo, *carissima,*" I said. "This is Martin. I found him in the woods, and Mr. Kayser says he can have a night's lodging."

She gave him a quick glance and said, "How do, Mr. Martin?" Her English was better than Leo's, mainly because he was too lazy to practice, especially now that I no longer gave them lessons as I had done when they were younger.

Martin shook hands politely and said, "How do you do, Maria?"

"Where are Leo and Mr. Galletti?" I asked.

"Grandfather's in the wagon, reading as ususal, and Leo went into town with the band and some of the clowns. They're having a small parade through the park." She put her hands on her hips and looked stern. "Chantal, I told you to leave that torn costume for me to stitch, but you've done it yourself."

"I know. You can't do everything."

"But you are bad at sewing. You make big ugly stitches."

"Never mind. The audience can't see them when I'm in the ring." Mr. Galletti appeared at the door of our wagon and came down the steps, a book in his hand. He could read in three languages and was the most educated man I had ever known, for he was always studying books on every kind of subject, as well as any newspaper he could lay hands on.

He was a small man with gray hair, a brown face, and dark eyes that were kind but always rather sad, which belied his nature, for he was not a sad man, simply quiet and patient. He greeted Martin courteously when I introduced them, studying him a little but asking no questions, then said to me, "I think you should take your compatriot to the kitchen without delay, Chantal. He has a hollow look. You have spoken to Mr. Kayser?"

"Oh yes, Mr. Galletti."

Martin said, "I don't wish to be a nuisance, sir. Chantal was kind enough to give me her lunch, and I can well wait until your next mealtime if that would be more convenient."

I could tell that Mr. Galletti was puzzled at the contrast between Martin's appearance and his manner, but only because I knew him so well, for he was too polite to show it. He smiled and said, "You would have to wait a long time, Martin. The artists do not eat until the evening performance is finished. A full stomach is a bad friend to acrobats of any kind. Go with Chantal now, and perhaps you would like to join me here for a glass of wine this evening, after dinner."

"You're very kind." Martin rubbed his stubbly chin. "If I could borrow a razor at some time convenient to you, I'd be more than grateful."

"Certainly. Come back when you have eaten."

As we made our way along the line of

wagons Martin said, "You live with a remarkably nice family."

"Yes. I'm very lucky."

Old Solange, the fortuneteller, was sitting on the steps of her small wagon as we passed, and called to me in French. *"Holá,* Chantal. Come and talk to me. I will make a dish of tea."

We stopped beside her. "Later, Solange. I have some things to do."

"When are you going to let me read your palm, little kitten?"

This was an old joke between us, and I gave my usual reply. "When the elephant flies on a trapeze."

She chuckled, her brown face crinkling in a network of creases, then looked at Martin and spoke in English. "So you understand, eh, *Anglais?* Our Chantal does not wish to know her future but will wait for it to come."

"Perhaps she is wise, madame."

Solange stared at him from her little black eyes. "Perhaps. And what of you, young man? Will you cross my palm with silver to know what is to come? Or what has been?"

For a moment there was complete silence, and I sensed that for some reason Martin had been taken aback. Then he said, smiling, "I'll decide when I have the silver, madame."

"As you please."

When we had walked on a little way Martin said quietly, "How did she know I was English, and that I understood when she spoke to you in French?"

"I don't know. She's very good at noticing tiny things and making clever guesses, but I think she has the sight, too. It troubles Mr. Galletti."

"Why does it trouble him?"

"He says if someone can see into the future, then the future must exist already in some way. But that means — oh, now I've forgotten the word."

"Predestination?"

"That's right. And Mr. Galletti doesn't believe in it."

"Remarkable." Martin shook his head. "It's true that Sophocles' idea of man's life being woven with a 'shuttle of adamant' has its critics, but I never expected to find an ex-acrobat among the philosophers.''

"Don't make fun of him!"

Martin turned to look at me. "Chantal, I wasn't. I spoke with admiration. Please don't be so prickly."

"Oh. Well, I expect I shall always be prickly about anything anybody says about Mr. Galletti, but if you weren't mocking him, then I'm sorry I snapped at you."

We had reached the dining tent. It was not large, for many of the families had wagons with tiny kitchens, and cooked for themselves. Mr. Galletti had changed to a smaller living wagon since the parents of Maria and Leo had died, and we always ate in the dining tent with the others in the company who had no woman to cook for them. There were usually about thirty of us in the evening, for the grooms, tentmen, and animal keepers took their dinner at other times of the day.

As we passed through the canvas doorway I called, "Sammy, where are you?"

He came from the kitchen which adjoined the tent, wiping his hands on his apron, a wiry little man of about fifty,

31

with a bald head and bright cheerful eyes. Sammy had been born in Lambeth and traveled with tenting circuses for thirty years, working as a cook. He had come from Broadwell's Circus at the time when Mr. Kayser left to set up on his own.

"'Allo, Chantal," he said. "Watcher want, ducks?"

"A nice big plate of your stew for Martin." I indicated my companion. "Mr. Kayser said it's all right."

Dinner was rarely anything other than stew, except on Sundays, when we would have roast meat. After my first few days with the circus my stomach had revolted, but this had quickly passed and it was years now since I had thought it strange to have the same meal every day, especially when it was Sammy's stew, which was always wholesome and tasty.

As I had known he would, Sammy protested. "I can't serve meals all times of the day to any Lord Tom Noddy who just walks in," he said indignantly. "I got better things to do."

"I know you have, Sammy," I said soothingly. "I often wonder how you get through all the work. But just this once, please? And can you find me a piece of bread and cheese? Martin's eaten my lunch. Oh yes, and some sugar for Sunbeam. He's eaten that, too, and I promised her I'd take her some."

Sammy snorted, disappeared into the kitchen, and returned a few moments later with a big dish of stew and some bread and cheese, which he set down on the serving bench.

"Cutlery in the box at the end there," he said briskly to Martin. "'Elp yourself."

"Thank you very much," said Martin. He collected a knife, fork, and spoon from the box on the serving bench, and stood waiting for me.

I said, "Sit down and have your meal. I'm going to see Sunbeam, and then I'll be busy for the rest of the afternoon."

"Can I help in any way?"

I smiled. "No. I'll be rehearsing."

"Oh. May I watch?"

"I'm afraid not. You can see the show tonight, if you want to. I'll speak to Mr. Galletti and he'll show you where you can sit. Oh, and I'll arrange about a bed in the stables for you.''

''Thank you. What should I do in the meantime?''

''Whatever you like as long as you don't get in anybody's way. I'll see you here at dinnertime this evening.''

''Well . . . thank you for all your trouble, Chantal.'' He hesitated, then moved away to one of the benches by the two long trestle tables. Sammy watched him go with raised eyebrows. ''A toff, eh?'' he murmured. ''Don't often see the likes of 'im begging for a bite. Black sheep of the family and down on 'is luck, I reckon.''

I shrugged, picking up the bread and cheese and the little bag of sugar lumps he had brought me. ''Thank you, Sammy. I'll see you later.''

''''Old on a tick, Chantal.'' He placed his hands flat on the bench and leaned forward a little, looking at me sternly. ''We're not going to 'ave any more trouble tonight, are we?''

I felt my heart sink at his reminder, but managed to smile. ''I hope not, Sammy.''

He gave a sigh of exasperation. ''Blimey,

34

I dunno what gets into you, honest I don't."

I felt the old stubborn anger rising like a tide within me. "Nothing gets into me, Sammy. I just don't see why everybody has to wait for Strabo to come along and be served first. And I don't see why the girls and the young ones have to be served last. All we get is the skilly."

"Skilly!" Sammy stared at me in horror. "Are you calling my stew skilly?"

"I didn't mean that. But you serve from the bottom with your ladle and there's not much solid left by the time our turn comes. All the best bits have gone. It ought to be first come, first served. We're all working artists, and one's no more important than another."

"But Strabo's a *man*."

"There! You're as bad as he is! Auguste and Raoul and Pepe and the rest are men, too, but they don't behave like Strabo."

"I know. But they got enough sense not to cross 'im. Like one of 'is own bears, Strabo is. Nasty." He wagged a warning finger at me. "You'll only get another walloping, ducks, and you can't expect the rest to stand up for you. I mean, I know they don't like Strabo, so they may sort of sympathize in a way, but it don't seem proper for a bit of a girl like you to act cheeky with a grown man like 'im.''

"I'm *not* cheeky to him, Sammy,'' I said angrily. "I've never spoken an impolite word, even when he hits me.''

Sammy tugged at his ear. "All the same, it ain't proper,'' he said worriedly.

I made a wry grimace. "Well, it seems proper to me.''

He gazed at me with a baffled air. "I dunno. What does Mr. Galletti say?''

"He doesn't say anything, Sammy. You know he never interferes, it's against his principles.''

"That's what comes of 'im reading all them books. Gives 'im funny ideas, if you ask me. But I notice he stopped eating 'ere the last couple of days. Can't stand to see you get whipped.'' He shook his head sadly. "Still, no good talking. You can't talk sense into people with red 'air, I always say.''

"I must go now, Sammy. Thank you for the sugar. I'll tell Sunbeam it's from you.''

I had forgotten about Martin, and paused for a moment at the table where he sat to say, "You wanted to borrow a razor from Mr. Galletti. Can you find your own way back to our wagon?"

He smiled and nodded, his dark-blue eyes fixed on me with a rather curious expression. "Yes, I'm sure I can, thank you, Chantal."

Five minutes later I had given Sunbeam her sugar and was sitting with Solange in her little wagon, eating my bread and cheese while she put aside her sewing and made fresh tea.

"Has this been a good pitch for you, Solange? I don't think the menagerie has taken much money here."

"Pah. There are many peasants and few gentry here. Not so many merchants or shopkeepers, either. But every pitch is a good one for old Solange. Lord or peasant, they all are eager to know what the future holds. The peasants more than the lords, perhaps." She chuckled. "Not like Chantal."

"You didn't only ask the stranger if he wanted to know the future, you asked if he wanted to know what had been. Why did you say that?"

She settled down across the tiny table from me. "Who knows? Do you think those who have the sight can see the future set out in words or pictures, as in a book?" She gave a snort of contempt. "No. We do not see. We feel. And it is for a moment only, like a small light that flickers and is gone. Then you must find words for that feeling, and it is no easy thing, Chantal. It is like trying to tell of a half-remembered tune. You should know, for there is something of the gift within you."

"In *me?* Oh, Solange, nothing like that ever happens to me."

"It happens, but you are blind to it because your mind is not quiet, child."

I shrugged. "What made you say that to the stranger?"

She shook her head. "It is gone now. Perhaps I felt an emptiness in him, a need to fill it."

"I don't understand."

Her few remaining teeth showed in a grin. "Nor I. When the gift touches me, I speak as the words come, that is all."

"But you tell fortunes with cards and tea leaves and your crystal, Solange."

"Oh, surely. That is my trade. Tell a man or woman that good fortune will come before the moon wanes, and they will find cause to believe it has happened — even if it is no more than their hens laying better."

"But you don't just make it all up?"

She stirred her tea, gazing past me at the little window of the wagon. "No, child. I give what is in me to give, if it is good and will bring hope. And I hold my tongue if what I see is bad . . . except when the power grips hard, and I cannot help myself."

"I don't see how the cards or the tea leaves can tell you anything. I mean, whatever pattern they show is just an accident."

To my surprise, she nodded. "True. And I see nothing in the crystal. But the people expect these trappings, and since I must have something to aid me in my task, I am content to use what my customers like to see."

"What do you mean about having something to aid you?"

She chuckled again, and reached out to pat my hand as it lay on the little table between us. "Oho! We are curious today, heh? Well, I will tell you. The sight can come only when the mind is quiet. For the mind to be quiet, the eyes must be held, so that the inwardness of the mind may be opened. It is like mesmerizing a chicken by putting its beak to a line of chalk. I could as well work by gazing upon" — she looked about her, one hand still resting on mine — "a candle flame, or a raindrop on the window." She took a pin from the box at her elbow and held it up. "Or upon a pin. The crystal, the teacup, the cards, they are nothing in themselves —"

Her voice trailed to silence, and I saw her eyes become quiet and absent, no longer focused upon the pin, but looking far into space. She drew a long, slow breath and began to sway very slightly. Then she spoke, and her voice had become a strange, singsong whisper. I sat very still, longing to move but unable to do so.

"There are two in one," she crooned.

"Two in one, the wolf and another. The wolf sleeps, yet in sleep he walks, for he wears the mask of the other. And there is but one heartbeat. It lies beneath the ebony snakes where one is seven and seven are one. The ring is without light, and brings death with the sound of thunder. Within two furrows of the plow, one shall die and one shall fly and one shall fall. The actors wear masks, and the day when the lost ones stand face to face shall be heavy with fear. Have a care . . . have a care in the time when the sleeping wolf wakes . . ."

TWO

Solange's whispering voice faded, but her lips still moved as if she were struggling to form words. Then slowly her eyes lost their emptiness and began to focus again. The hand holding the pin fell limply to the table and lay trembling a little. A long breath sighed from her lips, and she croaked. "Gone. There is no more."

I said in a shaky voice, "Solange, are you all right?"

She gave a weary nod. "Well enough. I have not felt the gift so strong for many a day." She drew her hand away and rubbed her eyes, then looked at me with a troubled air. "Forgive me, Chantal. It was not intended. I know you do not seek to look beyond the veil."

"It doesn't matter, Solange. But . . . what did you mean? It was all so strange."

"What did I say, child?"

The words were fresh in my memory, and with a little faltering I was able to repeat the sense of them. She sighed again and shook her head. "This was as it came to me, but words are poor tools, and I cannot go back to try again. The way is closed." There was distress in the old face as she looked at me and tried to smile. "Fortuneteller's nonsense, little one . . . but it is always wise to be watchful, to take care."

I knew she did not truly believe that her words had been nonsense, but she seemed so troubled that I made an effort to hide my own uneasiness and treat the matter lightly. "I'm always careful, Solange, so don't worry. Anyway, you can't read my fortune properly until Sunbeam has flown on the trapeze. Now tell me about the time when you were with the big circus in Paris, and Napoleon the Third sent for you to tell fortunes at a soirée."

"Pah. I have told you that story many times."

"But you remember more every time. Tell me again, Solange. I have half an hour before I must go and change for rehearsal."

"Eh, *bien*. Well . . . I was young, and perhaps one might have said I was beautiful in those days . . ."

As she told the familiar story I could see the shadows lifting from her eyes, and at the same time the tinge of eerie dread I had felt when she had spoken those strange words slowly faded from within me. When the time came for me to go and change I could almost have laughed at myself for being so strongly affected by a pin and a few meaningless phrases. Certainly all memory of them had vanished from my mind as I climbed the long rope ladder in my practice leotard and pumps to join Maria on our platform in the dome of the big top.

The rehearsal went well that afternoon. Leo had enjoyed being in the miniature parade earlier, and was in a cheerful mood, which meant he did not indulge in his usual complaints that I was coming out of the somersaults too soon or too late or too fast, making it difficult for him to catch me cleanly. I never minded his criticism anyway, for compared with Maria I must have seemed heavy and awkward. Maria floated through the air like a gull, and her timing was perfect. Under Mr. Galletti's teaching I had acquired enough skill to please the audience with a neat and quite graceful performance, but to a catcher I was not in the same class as Maria.

When we had finished we dropped one by one into the net below, diving like swallows and turning at the last moment to land on our backs and bounce to our feet on the net. I loved the sensation now. It was hard to believe that in the early days I could not drop from as low as twenty feet without landing awkwardly and being flung into the air again, arms and legs thrashing helplessly as I tried to control my body.

Mr. Galletti was watching from his usual seat by the ringside, and when we had swung ourselves down from the net we stood in front of him together, as we always did, to hear what he had to say.

"Very good, children. Just one or two small things. Chantal, you were a tiny moment too slow with your release for the last back somersault. Leo had to reach for you a little. Maria, when you take the pike position after your first open single, you can afford to hold it a tiny moment longer." Most of Mr. Galletti's comments were concerned with "tiny moments." He looked at Leo. "Please do not slouch on the platform while the girls are doing their twin act, Leo. Stand up straight." He was speaking of the early part of our act, when Maria and I swung side by side on two trapezes and performed several gymnastic maneuvers in unison, a mirror image of each other.

"No stiffness or muscle strain?" Mr. Galletti always ended with this question.

"No, Grandfather."

"No, Mr. Galletti."

"Good. Off you go, then."

In the women's dressing tent Maria and I took off our practice clothes, sponged ourselves down in the tub of warm water there, and began to put on the scarlet jackets and blue trousers of our soldier uniforms, ready for when the people began to come streaming in from the town and the nearby villages. Almost everybody in the circus had more than one job to do, but artists were usually on what was called soft service, such as selling tickets or directing people to their seats. Maria and I would take money at two of the sideshows until half an hour before the show began, and then sell programs and sweetmeats. When the circus bandsmen struck up the overture we would go to our wagon and rest for twenty minutes before returning to put on our costumes and makeup in readiness for our performance, which came in the middle of the second half.

Maria, seated in front of the dressing tent's big looking glass, was chattering away in her usual manner while I brushed her hair for her, and I was as usual listening with only half an ear when she said, ". . . but I think he looks very nice now, don't you, Chantal?"

I could not think who she was talking about, and said, "Who looks nice now?"

"That *man,* of course, silly. He looks nice now he hasn't got a beard any more."

"Oh, you mean Martin. I haven't seen

him since I left him with Sammy."

"He's very handsome," she said excitedly. "I think he's an English lord, and he's seen you in the ring and fallen completely in love with you, Chantal, so now he's pretending to be a vagabond."

I was used to Maria's romancing, and smiled at her in the mirror as I said, "Why should he pretend that?"

"So that he can try to get a job with the circus, of course. He wants you to fall in love with him for himself alone, not because he's a rich English lord."

I burst out laughing. "Really, Maria, you're funnier than Pepe the clown."

"Well, he's surely not a vagabond, so he *must* be pretending. And if he's not an English lord, then who is he?"

"I don't know. And I'm not much interested."

"Oh, you! You're just a cold-hearted English girl."

"I suppose so. There, you look lovely." I took Maria's place on the stool and she began to brush my hair. After a few moments she paused and looked at me in the mirror, her face troubled. "Chantal, you won't make Strabo angry again tonight, will you?"

"Don't start scolding me again, *piccina*. You kept me awake for ages last night."

"I was nearly sick while he was hitting you." She slipped her arms round my neck and put her cheek against mine. "Please, dearest Chantal. Promise me you won't."

I sighed and patted her hand. "Maria, it's no use. Something comes over me and I just can't help myself."

She straightened up, blinking quickly as if to hold back tears, and began to brush my hair again with quick, brusque strokes. I did not dare tell her that it was really because of her that I had impulsively started the quarrel with Strabo three days ago. She had felt hungry that evening, and we had sat in the dining tent, waiting, waiting till that surly and arrogant man deigned to appear.

Maria was like a younger sister to me, and in my opinion the greatest artist in the circus. I was biased, of course, because it was impossible to compare her skill with that of a lion tamer or trick rider, but to me she was more perfect in her performance than anyone. To see her that night, waiting patiently to eat until the bearlike Strabo had been served, suddenly became too much for me, and a wave of fury had driven me to act. Looking back now, I still could not regret it.

Maria threw down the brush with a clatter. "That man! I hate him."

I shrugged. "He's not very nice, but he has a good act. Have you noticed he gets much more applause lately?"

Maria sniffed. "That's only because we are in Hungary. He comes from here, and the people know it. You always get more applause in your own country. Look how they clapped and cheered us in Italy. If we go to England you'll see — Oh no, they won't realize you're English, they'll think you're part of an Italian troupe. But perhaps Mr. Kayser will tell the ringmaster to make a special announcement."

I felt a stab of unease. "Are we going to England?"

"I don't know, but Sammy seems to think we'll make a tour there next spring, and he always seems to know everything.

It must be time for another English tour, we haven't been there for over three years now."

"Over four," I muttered, slowly buttoning my scarlet coat.

"Is it so long since you came to us? Yes, of course it is, I remember now. Leo and I had just made our first appearance. We could only do simple things, but people clapped because we were just children."

I felt strangely torn by the thought of going to England. In one way I longed to see my own country again, but at the same time I felt afraid, though I hardly knew of what. Perhaps I feared that memories would be revived, memories of all I had put behind me, the shameful bitterness I had felt for the mother and father I had never known, the misery and loneliness my own odious nature had brought upon me, and, at the end, the loss of home and anyone to call my own. I was another person now, and I did not want to be reminded of what I had been.

Maria was holding my arm, shaking me a little and saying, "Come *on,*

Chantal. We'll be late."

The first customers were trickling in through the gate in the fence to the north of the big top. A few came in carriages, but most were in farm carts or on foot. We had had the best of our time here, and would think ourselves lucky if the big top was three-quarters full this evening. Most of the gentry and the better-off townsfolk and farmers had come with their families in the past two weeks. Now the prices had been reduced and the audience would be made up of those with little money to spare. We could always tell when that moment came, because the money taken was in small coin. We had noticed the night before that there were fewer crowns, which were worth tenpence in English money, but far more of the little hellers and the old kreuzer, which was still in use although it was being withdrawn.

We gave an afternoon performance on only three days of the week, and this was one of our easy days. For an hour and a half we carried out our usual duties, then went to rest in readiness for our act. Maria and I slept in the front section of the wagon, Leo and Mr. Galletti in the rear section, with a wooden partition between. During the day our beds were folded back against the sides of the wagon, and we used the larger rear section as a sitting room.

A few minutes before it was time for us to dress and put on our makeup, Leo called from the other room, "Chantal! Someone to see you."

I pulled my dressing gown about me and went through the door. Leo lay on his bed. The rear door of the wagon was open, and just inside stood a man I did not recognize for a moment. Then I saw it was Martin, but clean-shaven now, and wearing a decent shirt that was almost too small to button across his chest. I guessed it had been lent to him by Sammy.

Despite what Maria had said, I did not think him handsome. His mouth was rather wide and his ears a little too large for his lean face, but it was a pleasant face, and the eyes were what I could only describe to myself as outward-looking, the eyes of a man less interested in himself than in all that was going on around him.

He said, "I hope I'm not disturbing you. I've been watching the circus, and I felt I must come and see you for a moment during the interval, to wish you —" He hesitated. "I don't know your traditions. It's not bad luck for me to wish you good luck, is it?"

Leo chuckled and lifted his round curly head from the pillow to look at me. I said, "No, that's an old story but it isn't true."

"Good. Well, I'll wish you good luck tonight. And every night."

"Thank you, Martin. Did Sammy give you enough to eat?"

"As much as I could manage on a shrunken stomach. He said I was to come back after the show this evening when the artists dine, so I'll see you then, I hope. I mustn't keep you now."

He dipped his head to me in a little bow, then backed out and closed the door. Leo propped himself on an elbow and looked at me. "Are you going to be a fool again at dinner, Chantal?"

"I don't know, monkey face. Wait and see." Leo hated me to use endearments to him, and I called him monkey face as a term of affection now, though there had been a time when I used to fling it as an epithet.

"Wait and see, wait and see," he mimicked angrily. "Why are girls so *stupid?*"

"Oh, be quiet. It doesn't matter to you, anyway."

"Of course it doesn't! Why should it matter to me if you get slapped? And if you go on like this, Mr. Kayser will dismiss you. Yes! Then you will have to go, and I will no longer have a great sack of potatoes flying through the air for me to catch, and that will be good!"

Just for a moment I was truly hurt, but then I remembered that Leo was only young, still not quite seventeen, and very much a boy. Deep down he was worried for me, and this had made him lash out.

I laughed and said, "Don't drop me on the outswing tonight, or you'll have mashed potatoes."

He turned on his face, and I was going back to my room when he said in a low voice, "Chantal . . . I didn't mean it."

"I know, monkey face. It's all right."

Twenty minutes later I was in the dressing tent again with Maria. We had powdered our legs and arms, put on the greasepaint and makeup which would prevent our faces looking like white blurs, and were fastening the last hooks on our costumes, which were in purple silk with glittering spangles sewn all over the bodices.

Leo was waiting for us in the mounting place behind the great curtain which hung from the bandsmen's arch over the entrance to the ring. He grinned at me and said, "Hallo, fat English girl." That was an insult from the past, and I returned it with another. "Hallo, monkey-faced Italian boy."

The curtain was drawn aside, the entr'acte clowns came tumbling out and we heard the blare of the ringmaster's voice as he announced in German the famous, the amazing, the breathtaking, the death-defying Flying Gallettis.

Then to a great fanfare from the band we were in the ring, skipping, bowing, curtsying, smiling, before running to the two rope ladders and beginning to climb, Leo on one side of the ring, Maria and I on the other.

I never failed to feel a surge of excitement each time I stood on the little platform. Above, the great canvas dome seemed a living thing, moving and dancing gently. Below was a sea of upturned faces, a pale blur in the light of our lamps, and in the center lay the yellow ring, very small from up here, with the long net stretched across it.

Maria and I unhooked our side-by-side trapezes, and as the band began to play a slow waltz we launched ourselves as one. The first time I had ever launched myself in training, after months of ground gymnastics and weeks of practice on a low single trapeze, I had immediately lost my grip and fallen straight into the net. Now, this part of our act seemed so easy a child could have done it.

We swept back and forth, hanging by our knees, slipping from knees to insteps to bring a gasp from the audience, swinging up to grip the bar again with resined hands and work up fresh impetus, circling the bar, balancing across it horizontally on our stomachs with arms outspread, always moving in unison, and at last returning to our platform and landing there unassisted, which looked the simplest part but was in fact the most difficult.

Now it was my turn. Leo was already in position, swinging back and forth, head down. I moved to Maria's trapeze, which was directly in line with Leo's, and waited. He clapped his hands sharply, and at once I made my launch. Four swings to gain height, and for Leo to judge that the timing of the two trapezes was just right, then he clapped his hands again. I soared up, and released my grip. The dome, the great circle of the audience and the tiny circle of the ring swooped about me as I made a good somersault, curled in a ball, then opened up and dived, reaching for Leo's wrists as he came curving up to meet me. There was the good smack of flesh on flesh as those sure hands of his took my own wrists. He grinned, looking down at me as we swept across the ring, and said, *"Bene!"*

I made the return to the empty trapeze with a simple pirouette, reached the platform and waved to acknowledge the applause. Maria, mouth smiling, eyes very serious, launched herself. Double somersault and return to her own trapeze. Single open somersault, a beautiful movement in which she made one long slow revolution, her lithe body fully extended and arched back like a bow. A plange pass, in which she took off over the trapeze bar, and a return with a marvelous double pirouette.

She came to the platform again, and I took the trapeze. A backward launch brought me into a forward somersault, and then I had to pirouette in the air to face Leo for the catch. Return to my own trapeze, and then my best trick, calling for good balance and strength rather than skill — a release from a handstand on the bar.

After the catch Leo returned me to his own platform, then began his solo, flying from one trapeze to the other and back again without a catcher. I was always most nervous at this point, for Maria and I had to take turns in setting the empty trapeze a-swing at exactly the right moment for whatever trick Leo was performing, and I was always afraid of misjudging.

At the end of Leo's solo I launched myself for him to catch me and swing me back to the other platform for our finale. There I held up a black velvet bag, then drew it over Maria's head and fastened it loosely with a drawstring, ready for her blindfolded double somersault. We were cheating a little, for Maria could see to some extent through a band of black gauze set in the bag, but it was still a very difficult trick.

She launched herself and began to swing, gaining height. The music stopped and there was a taut silence. Leo sat on the other bar, swinging, watching her carefully, then fell back to hang by his feet. One more swing, and he clapped his hands. Maria soared up, released her hold, made a perfect double, and met Leo for the catch as lightly as a butterfly coming to rest on a leaf.

The music blared. The audience roared. Another roar as Maria, still hooded, returned with a single pirouette to her own trapeze. I launched myself on the parallel trapeze, crossing Maria as she swung, then made my release and dived with arms spread like wings to the net below, turning in a half somersault at the last moment to land on my back. A high bounce brought me to my feet and I moved at once to the edge. Leo shot down and rose in a tremendous bounce, making a somersault before landing on his feet, then moved to the far edge.

Maria was still swinging, still blindfolded. She soared up and made her release into that peerless open somersault of hers, in which she revolved slowly, like the spoke of a wheel, seeming to hang weightless for a long second, a tiny purple figure poised head down in the center of the canvas dome. Then she dived, body straight as an arrow, hands by her sides, hurtling down with the speed of a stooping hawk.

At the last fraction of the last instant, her hooded head tucked inwards for a safe landing on her shoulders. She rose, plucking the hood from her head as she floated up and turned to land on her feet. Leo and I swung down from the net, leaving Maria to take the main applause she so well deserved. Then she swung herself down, and we frisked back and forth, smiling and making our bows first in one direction and then another. I never knew if it was the same for Maria and Leo, but at this point my smile was no longer fixed and artificial. I was always swept by exhilaration, breathless and half laughing with wonder, for it was now that all seemed a dream, and I marveled that this girl curtsying and tripping about the sawdust ring should be me.

We knew we had given a good performance that evening, and when Mr. Galletti met us in the mounting place after we had made our exit, he did not have even one "tiny moment" to mention. We had to remain in our costumes, to take part in the parade round the ring at the end of the show, and during this time Leo always went to the men's dressing tent, for he liked to gossip with the artists there and feel like one of the men. Maria and I preferred to put on our wraps and remain in the mounting place, watching all the bustle and seeming turmoil as act followed act, and listening to the response of the audience.

Later, during the final parade, I remembered that Martin was there, but as we marched round the ring I was unable to pick him out amid the crowd. In the women's dressing tent we chatted with Violette, the pretty blond bareback rider, and Fiama Khalaf, the springboard tumbler, while we waited our turn at one of the tubs, then we bathed the sweat from our bodies, hung up our costumes carefully, and took our leotards back to the wagon to wash them through.

I lit the lamp in our bedroom and lay on my bed, listening to familiar sounds: the distant thudding of the traction engine which lit the big-top lamps, the occasional cry of an animal from the wild-beast gallery, the sound of harness and hoof and moving feet mingling with the wordless murmur of many voices as the crowd slowly dispersed.

For an hour I studied my medical books, while Maria worked on her embroidery. This was almost the only time of day that she stopped chattering, while we rested after the evening performance. At last I closed my books and said, "It's dinnertime, Maria."

She bent over her embroidery. "Let's wait a little, Chantal."

"No, I'm hungry, and so are you. You're always hungry at this time."

She looked up at me, biting her lip. "All right. You go on, I just want to finish this piece."

I thought she had decided to come late to dinner, when the trouble with Strabo would be over, but to my surprise she caught up with me as we reached the dining tent. Only a dozen people were there, and my heart sank as I saw that Strabo was not among them. I had foolishly hoped that he might come early to avoid a repetition of the past three nights. Leo was there, fidgeting and looking very irritable as he he sat on a bench with his back to the table, talking to Martin, who sat beside him. I saw Martin start to rise as I came in, as if he were about to speak to me, but Leo quickly took him by the arm and drew him down again.

I stood still for a moment, telling myself not to be a fool, and cringing inwardly at the memory of Strabo's heavy hand. But that very thought brought the old anger boiling up inside me, and I walked doggedly past the tables to the serving counter. Everybody fell silent. Sammy, behind the counter, looked at me almost despairingly as I said, "I'm hungry, Sammy, and so is Maria. We'll have ours now, please."

He stirred the great copper stewpot beside him with the ladle, scowling, and said, "It's a bit 'ot yet, ducks. Why don't you wait a minute, eh?"

"No, we like it hot. Dinner for two please, Sammy." I was inwardly shaking with fright, but I could not have stopped myself now to save my life.

Sammy gave a huff of exasperation. "Awright. But you speak for yourself, Chantal. Don't bring Maria into it."

"No. I'm sorry. Dinner for one please, Sammy."

He filled a bowl with stew, put a wedge

of crusty bread on a smaller plate, and handed them to me. I collected my cutlery, sat down at the end of one of the tables, and began to eat, not looking at anybody. A murmur of forced and uneasy conversation began.

I had scalded my mouth, and began to chew some bread, looking blindly down at the table. Not far away I could hear Leo whispering to somebody, and wondered dimly if he was telling Martin what to expect. I knew when Strabo entered by the sudden silence, broken only by the scuff of his boots on the duckboards as he walked the length of the tent. Then he was standing over me, and I looked up to meet his glare. He was a stocky, powerful man with a shaven head and small, unintelligent eyes set in a big square face. His voice was deep and ugly.

He said, "So you eat before Strabo again, liddle girl?"

I think I would have run then, if I could have found the strength in my legs, but somehow I kept looking at him until a new surge of anger gave me the power to speak, and I said in a croaking voice, "I was hungry. Why should I wait, Mr. Strabo?''

"You think you bedder than everyone else?''

"No. I think we're all the same, so nobody should have to wait.''

His face took on a red tinge. "You are girl! Liddle girl!''

"Everybody here is a working artist. We're all the same.'' I was afraid my voice would crack with fear. "If you want to separate us into men and women, then it would be polite to serve the ladies first, Mr. Strabo.''

"You not lady!'' he roared, his little eyes narrowing till they almost vanished. A great hand took me by the shoulder, and I was jerked to my feet. His other hand swung ponderously in a slap which made my head ring. Fury flamed in me, and I tried to clear my blurred vision, watching for the hand to strike again. If I could, I was going to catch it and set my teeth in it.

To one side of Strabo a small figure darted forward. It was Maria. Her hand emerged from the folds of her skirt, and in it she gripped an eighteen-inch wooden tent peg. "Beast!" she screamed, and the tent peg cracked down hard on the side of Strabo's head.

It was an act of madness, and the shock made my stomach twist as if I were about to be sick. Strabo staggered back a pace or two, clutching his head. Maria was between us, poised like a cat ready to spring at him. Frantically I caught her from behind, spun round with her, and thrust her away with all my strength, crying, *"Run, Maria! Run!"* Then I whirled to face Strabo again.

From the corner of my eye I saw Leo up on the long table, running towards us, eyes glittering, shouting something in Italian. Strabo was lumbering at me. I crouched to hurl myself at his legs. At least I could cling to him until he beat me unconscious, which would give Maria time to get away.

And then, as if by magic, one of the long benches slid forward and caught Strabo across the knees. He sprawled over it and hit the wooden flooring with a thud. Next moment a new figure blocked my view, a man in a shirt too small for him. It was Martin. Moving forward, he said in an amiable voice as if nothing untoward were happening, "Please don't think me impertinent, Mr. Strabo, but I just wanted to say —"

He appeared to trip, and sprawled across Strabo, knocking him down as he tried to rise. Then they were tangled on the floor together, Strabo grunting with rage and Martin apologizing as they struggled to find their feet; but each time Strabo tried to rise, a thrashing leg or arm of Martin's would tip him off balance, so that it was almost as if two clowns were enacting one of their absurdities before us.

Leo had halted at the end of the table, staring down, and suddenly he laughed. It was infectious. In a moment the whole tent was filled with laughter. Strabo sat trying to disentangle his foot from where it had become caught in the crook of Martin's knee. He stopped and blinked dazedly about him, bewildered, a great red blotch on the side of his shaven head.

Martin was saying, "I'm sorry, do forgive me for being so clumsy."

Strabo glared about him, then bellowed, "Stop!"

The laughter dwindled and faded. Very deliberately Strabo disengaged his foot and stood up. But now Martin rose with him, grasping his hand, pumping it up and down with smiling admiration, still talking. "What I was about to say, Mr. Strabo, was how much I admired your performance this evening. Magnificent. Really magnificent. I realize my opinion means nothing to you, of course . . ."

With pounding heart I saw suspicion and menace creep into Strabo's little eyes as he glared at Martin. Suddenly he tried to fling away the hand that gripped his own, but again in almost clownish fashion the two hands remained joined, and Martin talked amiably on. ". . . I would be deeply interested to know what training methods you favor. I've no wish to be a nuisance, of course, perhaps we could talk during dinner?" He still smiled, but it now seemed to my fevered mind that there was a hint of wolfish menace in his look.

70

Strabo looked down at the two clasped hands, drew in a deep breath, started to raise his clenched free hand threateningly, then suddenly froze, staring. I was closer to the two men than anyone else, and could see the direction of Strabo's gaze. He was looking at Martin's right wrist, at the close-fitting black band which encircled it. As far as I could tell it seemed to be made of black leather thongs, skillfully plaited in a band an inch wide. I could see no clasp or fastening. When I had met Martin in the woods it must have been hidden under the cuff of his torn jersey, but now that he was wearing a borrowed shirt, with sleeves too short for him, it showed plainly.

The effect on Strabo was astonishing. His eyes grew steadily wider as he stared, and the color faded from his heavy cheeks. I knew he did not lack physical courage, for only a brave man could handle bears, the most dangerous of all the wild beasts, but there was fear in his face now. He looked up at Martin, then down at the strange black wristband again, and all the fire drained out of him.

Martin must have realized that the danger was past, for he let go of Strabo's hand and stepped back a pace, watching him curiously.

The bear tamer wiped sweat from his brow, wincing in surprise as he touched the big bruise made by the tent peg. It was almost as if he had forgotten it in the past half minute. Slowly, uncertainly, he began to move away at a shambling, sideways gait, like one of his own bears, half turned to keep his eyes on Martin. Then suddenly he crossed himself with a furtive movement and went lumbering down the length of the tent and out into the darkness.

Sammy said, "Blimey!" in an awed voice, and next moment the tent was filled with a buzz of excited chatter. I was still trembling inwardly as I said to Martin, "Thank you. Thank you very much."

I turned upon Maria. She was holding the tent peg she had carried concealed in the folds of her skirt, and her big eyes seemed bigger than ever. Mingled relief and anger almost choked me as I cried, "Are you *mad*, Maria? He might have killed you for that!"

"Me? I am the mad one?" She glared at me indignantly, eyes flashing. "What of you? Every night, *slap, slap, slap* with his great paw!" She dropped the tent peg so that she could gesture with both hands. "I *told* you it made me feel sick to watch! So I think, 'If Strabo hits Chantal again tonight, I will hit *him!*' And I did, and you can shout as much as you like, but I am glad I hit him!"

A moment before I had wanted to shake her, but now tears came suddenly to my eyes and I felt utterly wretched. I was sure there would be no more trouble with Strabo, so in a way I had won my battle, but I felt no sense of triumph. By my stubborn ill temper I had caused Maria to put herself in danger because she was fond of me, and that was the last thing in the world I would have wanted.

Tears began to run down my cheeks and I said miserably, "I'm sorry, *piccina*. I only shouted because I was so frightened for you."

She put her arms round me quickly. "Don't cry, silly. It's all right." She gave

73

a little giggle. "Wasn't Martin funny, getting Strabo all tangled up? He should be a clown." She glanced up at Leo, who still stood on the end of the table, and snapped impatiently, "What are you doing up there, stupid?"

Leo scratched his head. "I was going to jump on his back, but then Martin stopped him."

"Pouf!" Maria tossed her head contemptuously. "Trust you to be too late. Get down at once, and go and get me some dinner."

"Me?" Leo dropped to the floor. "Why can't you get it yourself?"

"Didn't you hear what Chantal said? A gentleman should always attend to a lady before he thinks about himself, and it is time you learned to be a gentleman."

"Oh." Leo looked puzzled as he moved away. He had never regarded Maria as a lady before, but I could see he did not intend to argue with his fiery young sister when she was in this mood. Sammy was serving busily now, and the atmosphere in the dining tent was fast returning to normal. I found I no longer wanted to eat, but I made myself do so, for I knew that otherwise Maria would start scolding me.

Gustave paused for a moment to speak with us. He was a quiet man with a very gentle manner, even when he was handling his cats. "So it ends well, Chantal," he murmured. "But please do not seek a new cause to fight for. Trouble is trouble, and best avoided, especially in the circus." He glanced to where Martin stood at the serving table, having waited to be last. "Did you see how the stranger handled him? He should be a tamer, that one. He has the gift."

When Martin had been served he came and asked if he might sit with us. "But of course," Maria said warmly. "We are very grateful to you, Martin."

He gave her a wide-eyed look of surprise. "For what?"

"Oh, don't pretend. It was very clever. Gustave thinks you should be a tamer, but I think you should be a clown."

He laughed and shook his head. "I don't think I'd be much good at either. But I'm a good spectator. I thought your flying-trapeze act was beautiful."

I warmed to him when he said that. I had heard people describe our act with such words as thrilling, amazing, breathtaking, but Martin had chosen the right word. I did not include myself in his compliment, for anybody who spoke of our act was really speaking of Maria's performance, which was the whole heart of it, and her performance was truly beautiful.

I felt drained of energy and said very little as we sat at table. Maria chattered away in her usual fashion, and Martin asked her many questions, but I noticed that they were all about her work and not one of them was personal. He had evidently taken to heart my warning that circus folk dislike inquisitive people.

Half an hour later Mr. Kayser walked in. I had never known him to enter the dining tent when the artists were at dinner, and I guessed that word of the quarrel with Strabo had already reached his ears, probably through one of Sammy's kitchen helpers.

We all fell silent and started to stand

up, but he waved us to be seated and moved to the end of the table where I sat with Maria and Martin. It was hard to tell whether he was angry, for his face rarely showed his feelings.

He said, "I abologize for intruding, ladies and gentlemen. Tonight there has been a zerious quarrel. I cannot permit trouble between my artists. Maria . . ." He looked at her. "You struck Strabo on the head?"

She stood up. "Yes, Mr. Kayser. He was hitting Chantal. He wouldn't let anyone be served until he had been served first. It wasn't fair, so Chantal took her dinner. Then Strabo began hitting her, and so I hit him."

Mr. Kayser looked at me sternly. "Chantal, I warned you about quarreling with Strabo."

I stood up, feeling cold inside. "Yes, sir."

"And yet you continued to make trouble?"

Maria said, "It isn't fair to say Chantal made trouble, sir. She has never quarreled with anybody here, only Strabo.

And he is a pig."

Mr. Kayser raised a hand to stroke his chin, but I felt that he was also struggling to hide a smile at Maria's words. After a second or two he frowned fiercely and said, "I am tired of little girls telling me what is not *fair!* Chantal, it is fortunate for you Maria was not hurt tonight."

"Yes, sir. I'm sorry —"

"Be quiet, and lissen. I have arranged for Strabo to be served in his wagon in future. Maria, you will lose one week's wages for striking him. Chantal, you will lose four weeks' wages for starting the quarrel, and if there is further trouble you will be dismissed! And please do not tell me I am not *fair!*"

"No, sir," I said meekly, "I wasn't going to."

"Goot." He looked round the whole company severely for a moment, then his eye turned to Martin, who sat quietly beside Maria. "You are the man Chantal brought from the woods today?"

Martin stood up, following our example. "Yes, Mr. Kayser," he said politely.

"I believe you prevented bad trouble becoming worse. I zank you for what you did. Call at my wagon before you leave tomorrow, if you please. There will be a sovereign to help you on your way."

"You're very kind, sir. Thank you."

"Good night, ladies and gentlemen." Mr. Kayser walked out to a chorus of response.

Later we sat on folding chairs outside our wagon under a starlit sky, the air of the summer's night warm about us, while Martin and Mr. Galletti shared a bottle of Tokay and talked. Nothing had been said to Mr. Galletti about the scene in the dining tent, but there was no doubt that he knew all about it. I could sense the enormous relief in him, and this made me realize how deeply anxious he had been before, which in turn made me feel guilty for having caused him so much worry.

The conversation was mainly about circuses, and Martin seemed to have a knack of drawing people out, for I had never before heard Mr. Galletti conjure up so many reminiscences of his young days in different tenting circuses.

I think the excitement had made Maria tired, for she was unusually silent, and at half past nine she excused herself to go to bed. "Don't wake me up when you come in Chantal, *mia cara,*" she said, yawning.

"I'll be careful." I took her hand and remembered how she had come to my rescue that evening. "Sleep well, Maria."

Leo followed five minutes later, and soon Mr. Galletti looked at his watch in the light of the lantern which hung from a pole where we were sitting. "Good wine makes an old man sleepy." He smiled. "I think I will also retire. You will show Martin where to sleep, Chantal?"

"Yes, I'll take him to the stables. I've arranged it with Mr. Albertini. May we sit a little longer please, Mr. Galletti? I don't feel a bit tired yet." That was true. I felt somewhat as if I were in a dream, but the drama of the evening was still working in me and my head was full of whirling fragments of thought.

"As you please." Mr. Galletti nodded. Martin had half risen, and I saw that he showed a touch of surprise as he sat down again in his chair. Mr. Galletti said good night and went into the wagon, closing the door. There was a door at each end, so I could go to my bedroom without passing through the room where Leo and his grandfather slept.

Martin said, "A young lady would never be left unchaperoned like this at home."

"Oh, circus people are as strict as gypsies. But I'm not one of Mr. Galletti's family, and when he first took me into his home he told me that he would never be responsible for me."

"Wasn't that a little hard?"

"No, of course not. It was wonderfully kind of him to give me a home."

"How old were you?"

"Thirteen." I spoke warily, for I did not want questions about my past. Perhaps Martin sensed this, for he changed the subject and said, "I can't tell you how much I enjoyed your performance this evening."

"Mine? You mean Maria's."

"Both. I've already told her how much I enjoyed hers. Now I'm telling you, Chantal."

"It's kind of you, Martin, but I know very well my work is nothing compared with hers."

He gave me the same look of interest I had seen before, and which I was beginning to find familiar in him. "How do you know?" he asked.

"Know what?"

"How do you know what you look like in the air, compared with Maria? You've never seen yourself."

I looked at him blankly, realizing that what he said was true. "Well . . . I suppose I can *feel* how I must look."

"Perhaps. But anyone with great skill is always very much aware of his own faults. I'm sure even Maria is seldom satisfied with herself."

That was true, too. She was forever trying to perfect tiny details which to me seemed perfect anyway. I was thinking about this when Martin went on, "Let me tell you what I saw this evening, as one of the audience. I saw Maria, skimming through the air as if gravity didn't exist, floating and twisting and turning like a leaf in the wind, but a leaf performing a dance of its own, not subject to the wind. It was truly beautiful. And I saw Chantal, hair glinting under the lights like a fiery helmet, different from Maria, not free from gravity but defying it, flashing through the air like a thrown spear, every movement clean and sharp as the crack of a whip. Not with Maria's elfin beauty, no. But with another quality . . ." He seemed to grope for words, then shrugged and smiled. "For Maria the band plays Mendelssohn's *Spring Song*. For you they play *Marche Militaire*."

Until he spoke those last words I had been ready to laugh in astonishment at his poetic fancies, but now I felt suddenly glum and said, "You mean I'm more like a boy than a girl?"

"No, Chantal, no. You're very much a girl."

"Well, what you said is all nonsense anyway. People who really know about trapeze work can tell you I'm not especially good."

"I've told you what I see."

"Yes. And I do thank you for saying nice things, Martin. I realize now that you

83

weren't flattering me. It was just ignorance."

He laughed. "Chantal, you have a knack of saying the most disconcerting things."

I scarcely heard his words. His head was in profile and tilted back a little. Beyond, Orion hung low in the sky, his starry sword belt and sword seeming to frame Martin's head, and it was as if I had lived this moment before. There was the smiling face — but was it a smile or was it the look of the wolf again? The look I had glimpsed when he faced Strabo? The lamplight cast strange shadows to trick my eyes, and I could tell only that his lips were parted and his teeth showed; but this did not always make a smile. I lived too close to the wild beasts not to know that.

The stars framing Martin's head against a background of dark sky made a picture which brought me recognition without memory, a sense of an experience repeated. But with it came a sharp stab of fright, as if something deep within me had given warning of danger.

THREE

Martin reached out to adjust the wick of the lamp, and the moment passed. All was normal again, and I could not recapture that swift sense of recognition even though I tried, but the impression had been deep and remained with me. I said, trying to keep my voice casual, "I was wondering if Martin is your surname or your Christian name."

He sat as if in thought for a little while, then seemed to come to a decision. "To be honest," he said ruefully, "I'm not sure that it's either."

Surprise made me forget the strange moment of alarm I had just experienced. "Not sure? Whatever do you mean?"

"I mean I can't remember. When you asked my name down in the woods I tried hard to think, and 'Martin' popped into my mind, so I said that. It seemed as good a name as any."

I stared at him, shaken. "You can't remember your own name?"

"No. And it's a very peculiar sensation." He seemed to reflect on it as if it were a matter which interested rather than disturbed him, then put a hand gently to the back of his head. "I had some sort of accident recently, and it included a nasty bang on the head."

"But this is awful for you, Martin! What sort of accident?"

"I've no idea. I can't remember anything."

"Nothing at all?"

"Just odd fragments, from different times in my life, I suppose. A few faces, a stretch of road, a school desk, a room which I think must have been my bedroom at some time, scenery — I mean mental pictures of places I've been to, and some I recognize. I know I've been to Rome, for example. Hundreds of fragments, but they don't really mean anything to me."

A shiver of sympathy ran through me as I tried to imagine how frightening it must be to have all memory wiped away, to be a stranger to yourself; and at the same time I felt quick respect for Martin's untroubled manner. He seemed intrigued by his plight rather than alarmed, as if he were standing aside and observing it.

I said, "But surely you had something in your pockets? Papers, letters, or . . . something."

He shook his head. "I woke up without any pockets. Without any clothes, for that matter. It was just before dawn, and I was lying under a pile of hay in a barn. I've a vague memory of crawling there from a river only a stone's throw away."

"And you don't know how you got into the river?"

"No. But I rather fancy I was put there, once I'd been stripped of everything."

"You mean somebody tried to . . . to kill you?"

He made a humorous grimace. "It does sound rather dramatic, but I can't think of any other reason for being hit on the head, stripped, and dropped in a river."

"Was it this river? Where I found you?"

"Oh no, something much bigger and about a hundred miles east of here. I woke up under the hay just before first light, and found a little boathouse along the bank. That's where I found those clothes I was wearing." He looked at me apologetically. "I suppose you could say I stole them, but I didn't think about that at the time. Then I started walking. I didn't do very well the first day, though. I was feverish, and I must have been suffering from concussion."

I looked at him in bewilderment. "It's a wonder you aren't dead! You should see a doctor, even now. Why didn't you go to the nearest farmhouse for help? Why haven't you been to the police?"

He nodded, gazing absently at the great white shape of the big top lifting above the line of wagons against the dark sky. "Yes, that would be the natural thing to do. But the trouble is, although I can't remember anything about myself, a very strong instinct keeps telling me to lie low and stay out of sight. I don't know what I was doing here in Hungary, but I'm quite sure it was something the authorities wouldn't like at all."

"You mean . . . something criminal?"

He gave a little shrug, and smiled. "Who knows? I suppose it must have been, since I can't think of an alternative. Mind you, I don't *feel* like a criminal, but for all I know most criminals don't feel like criminals." He half closed his eyes and squinted up at the stars. "It's quite an interesting question when you think about it."

"Surely you have more important things to think about." I spoke impatiently, for suddenly I found his calmness irritating.

He put his head on one side and said unexpectedly, "Why are you angry with me, Chantal?"

"Angry?" I glared at him. "I'm not angry. Why should I be?" He continued to gaze at me, smiling a little, and I felt suddenly confused. "Oh, I don't know. Perhaps I do feel annoyed. You haven't any food or money, you're a stranger in a strange land, you've lost your memory, and you're hiding because you might be a criminal. But you just sit there wondering whether criminals *feel* like criminals. It's enough to make anybody angry."

He nodded. "Yes, I suppose it is."

"No, it isn't," I said abruptly. "The real reason I felt annoyed was because . . . well, I always seem to rush at things like a bull at a gate, without thinking. And when you're impulsive it's very easy to get annoyed with people who take things calmly."

There was a silence, then he said gently, "You're a strange girl, Chantal."

"I suppose so. And you're a strange man, Martin. What are you going to do now?"

"Tomorrow I shall start walking again. Thank you very much for all you've done, I'm more than grateful."

"It was little enough. Where will you go?"

"I shall be glad to get out of Hungary, for a start, so I'll make for the Austrian border. But both countries are linked by the Crown, so I suppose I'll go on to Switzerland and perhaps go to a British consulate there. I'm hoping my memory will come back before then. Once or twice I've felt I'm just on the verge of breaking through the veil, especially in the first few moments when I wake from sleep." He grinned and shrugged. "But it hasn't happened yet."

I said, "What will you do for food and shelter?"

"I'll just have to manage somehow as I go along. Once I'm over the border I might be able to do some casual work on farms here and there. Anyway, I'm lucky it's not winter."

He was watching a moth as it danced about the lamp, and I said, "Can you see that moth clearly, Martin?"

"Yes." He glanced at me with a raised eyebrow. "That's an odd question."

"If you were still concussed, your sight would be blurred. Do you have a headache?"

"Hardly at all, but I had a very unpleasant one for a couple of days."

I got to my feet and moved to stand behind him as he sat. "I'd better have a look. Can you hold the lamp up for me, please? No, a little more this way. That's right."

There was a bump as wide as my palm

beneath the hair at the back of his head. I felt it as gently as I could, and turned his head first one way then the other, to see if he had bled from the ears. Then I moved round to peer at his eyes. With his face close to mine, he smiled at me and said, "You seem to know what you're doing."

"We get quite a lot of accidents in a circus. All kinds. Not so much with the artists, but with the tentmen and roughnecks and wagonmen. I often help Mr. Brunner, and I've got some medical books that I read. Hold the lamp higher, please." I tilted his head to see better, and was relieved to find that the pupils of his eyes were normal.

"Is Mr. Brunner a doctor?" he asked.

"Well, he's really an animal doctor, but he's quite good with people, too. Did you have any nose bleeding?"

He shook his head. "No."

I took my hands from his face and sat down again. "Good. I'm sure your skull can't be fractured. All the same, you'll be worse than stupid to try walking hundreds of miles without any money and sleeping rough."

He did not answer, but sat looking quietly at my hands, which lay in my lap. After a moment or two he said slowly, "You have magic hands. I couldn't touch that bump without it hurting, but you seemed to draw the pain away. Isn't that extraordinary?"

"Oh, you talk such nonsense!" I exclaimed, and felt the color come to my cheeks. "When are you going to stop thinking about things that don't matter and start thinking about what lies ahead for you?"

"I've already thought about that," he said simply. "I don't suppose I'll make any progress by thinking about it over and over again."

Before I could be angry I found myself laughing. "You're quite impossible, Martin."

"And you should laugh more often, Chantal. It's a joy to see." His manner was in no way serious, yet I knew that he meant what he said, and for a moment I was so pleased that I felt my eyes swim a little, though I could not think why his words should affect me in such a way. We were silent for a while, but it was a pleasant silence without any feeling of awkwardness.

A thought came suddenly to me, and I said, "Martin, can you remember if you know anything about horses?"

"Horses?" He closed his eyes for several seconds, then opened them again. "I can't exactly remember, but I know I'm at home with horses. Why do you ask?"

I was already pondering the same question, wondering why I should be anxious to help this man, who by his own admission was probably a fugitive from the law. He had saved me from Strabo less than two hours ago, which put me deeply in his debt, but that was not the whole of it. Criminal or not, he needed help badly, and I wondered why this in itself seemed reason enough for me. Then I remembered the time when I had sat under a tree in an English woodland long ago, a stranger to the gray-haired Italian beside me. I had been the one who needed help then, and it had been given.

I said, "Mr. Albertini needs a groom

for the wagon horses. He's using a local man for the time being, but he really wants somebody to travel with us when we move on. You'd have to help with all sorts of other jobs, of course. Everybody in the circus does."

Martin's eyes sparkled with interest. "What other jobs?"

"Well . . . dozens of things are happening all the time in a circus, when we pitch and when we strike and while we're on the road. You could find yourself doing anything from driving in a tent anchor to helping scrub down Sunbeam. She's our elephant."

"Yes, you introduced us, and I saw her perform later." He smiled. "I'm almost sure I've never bathed an elephant before. I think I'd enjoy the experience." He sat considering for a moment, but his face was placid and showed no anxiety. "When do you move on, Chantal?"

"The day after tomorrow. We go to Graz first, then on to several smaller towns and up the Danube Valley into Bavaria. If you don't want to be found, you couldn't choose a better way of traveling than with a circus." I gestured towards the line of wagons. "We have people of all different nationalities, you've seen that for yourself, and there's never any trouble at the borders when we cross from one country to another."

"That might be very convenient," he said. "Where do you go from Bavaria?"

"Into France. We have bookings there for several weeks, and then we go into winter quarters near Rheims." I looked at Martin curiously. "It's all very slow, of course. We work for a week here and two weeks there, sometimes longer, but you could go to a British embassy anytime, once we're out of Hungary and Austria. I suppose it all depends on whether it's urgent for you to reach England."

He shook his head. "I don't know whether it's urgent, Chantal. I don't know who I am or what I'm supposed to be doing. I'm not even sure about going to a British embassy for assistance. There's a very strong instinct urging me to stay hidden, tell nobody, and hope for my memory to come back."

"You've told me," I pointed out.

He gave me a long, rather puzzled look, then reached out slowly and picked up my hand. He studied it for a few seconds as if it were an object he had never seen before, then looked at my face with the same deep interest. At last he said, "Yes, I've told you, Chantal. That's another instinct at work."

I was looking at the strange black band about his wrist. My first impression had been right. It fitted closely and was made of black leather thongs woven in a plait of seven strands, but there was no join that I could see. It was as if the plait had been ingeniously woven from a single continuous thong, with the two ends hidden beneath the band in some way.

He saw the direction of my gaze, put my hand down gently on my lap, and looked at the black wristlet himself, touching it with the fingers of his other hand.

"Curious, isn't it?" he said. "I wonder what it is, and how it was put on."

"You mean you don't know?"

He shook his head. "I've no memory of it at all. I only know it doesn't seem in any way familiar to me. I imagine it must be made from rawhide of some kind, and was put on the wrist wet, then shrank to fit snugly."

"Do you think *you* put it on? Or was it put on by whoever attacked you?"

"I can't imagine any good reason for either."

"It meant something to Strabo. I think he was going to lash out at you, but then he saw that wristlet, and it frightened him."

Martin looked at me quickly. "So you noticed, too? I thought I'd imagined it."

"No. It frightened him badly, and I've never seen Strabo show fear before."

"Would it be possible to find out what it meant to him?"

"I doubt it, Martin. Strabo hardly talks to anyone. He certainly wouldn't talk to me, and I don't think anybody else would be willing to ask him questions."

Martin nodded placidly, still studying the wristlet. "I think I'll take it off," he said. "It's rather conspicuous. I'll try soaking it in water, and if that doesn't work I'll just have to cut it away, but that would be a pity. It's beautifully made."

A yawn took me unawares. He saw me stifle it and stood up at once. "I'm sorry, I'm keeping you from your bed. Will you speak to Mr. Kayser tomorrow about finding me a job as a groom?"

"Yes. I'm sure it will be all right." I rose to walk with him to the stables, feeling quick pleasure at knowing that he had decided to travel with us, though I could have given no reason for such a feeling. "Mr. Kayser was grateful for what you did, and so am I. If Maria had been hurt, I'd never have forgiven myself."

He turned his head to look down at me as we walked, and said softly, "Maria wasn't in danger. You were barring the way." He chuckled. "You looked like a red vixen protecting her cub."

"I'm not a vixen!" I said hotly. "I — well, I just have a quick temper sometimes, perhaps."

"I intended a compliment, Chantal. You weren't in a temper when you stood between Strabo and Maria. It was something very different. Perhaps I should have said 'she-fox' instead of vixen. It's the same thing but sounds nicer."

We entered the stables, and I lit the lamp which hung there, whispering to soothe the horses. In an empty stall was a pile of dry hay and two blankets. Mr. Albertini had been as good as his word.

I said, "You can come to our wagon in the morning to wash and shave. If Mr. Kayser gives you a job tomorrow you'll be able to have a bed in one of the sleeping tents with the other grooms. Be sure you put the lantern out properly before you go to sleep."

"I'll be very careful."

I hesitated, then said, "May I tell Mr. Galletti you've lost your memory and don't know anything about yourself? He won't gossip, and I don't like having secrets from him. It doesn't seem fair."

"I'm sure you're right."

"I'll speak to him tomorrow, then. Good night, Martin."

"Good night, Chantal."

I walked back to our wagon and undressed in the dark to avoid waking

Maria. Usually I slept as soon as I was in bed, but although my eyes were very tired tonight I could not quite lose myself in sleep but hovered in a half-waking state, with the events of the day drifting through my mind.

It had been an unusually crowded day. The meeting with Martin, the eerie moments when Solange had gazed with sightless eyes and crooned strange words of prediction, the scene in the dining tent with Strabo, the astonishing effect on him of the mysterious black wristlet, and now the revelation that Martin was a man with no knowledge of himself or his past — all this made a slow-moving tangle of thoughts in my sleepy head.

I tried to concentrate on one thing in the hope of lulling myself to sleep, and set myself to recalling what Solange had said. It was easier than I had expected, for I could almost hear that husky voice whispering in my head.

There are two in one. Two in one, the wolf and another. The wolf sleeps, yet in sleep he walks, for he wears the mask of the other. And there is but one heartbeat.

It lies beneath the ebony snakes where one is seven and seven are one. . . .

Suddenly it was as if a darting sliver of light made a connection between two thoughts, and I found myself sitting upright in the narrow bed, heart beating quickly.

The ebony snakes where one is seven and seven are one. . . .

Within the last hour I had seen something where seven were one — the black wristlet Martin wore. It seemed to be woven from seven black thongs plaited together, but there was only one continuous thong. Black thongs were not ebony snakes, but Solange had said that what her mind saw — no, what her mind *felt* — when the gift came upon her was hard to translate into words.

But what came next? . . . *There is but one heartbeat. It lies beneath the ebony snakes* . . . Nothing lay beneath the wristlet except Martin's wrist. I drew in a quick breath. His pulse, His heartbeat.

Two in one . . . the wolf sleeps, yet in sleep he walks, for he wears the mask of the other. What other? Was Martin two

102

men in one? And was the wolf in him sleeping?

Two days later we were on the road for Graz, and I had long since decided that it was only tiredness and strain which had caused me to read so much into old Solange's cryptic words. Before we left I had asked Martin to join me in watching the big top come down. It was a sight I never ceased to enjoy, and I felt sure it would fascinate Martin, who seemed interested in all things new.

He was free from his stable duties for half an hour that morning as we stood watching the tentmen at work under the direction of Captain Lefevre, the tentmaster. Nobody was sure that he was really a captain, but he was a fine tentmaster. I noticed that the black-thonged band was gone from Martin's wrist, and wondered whether he had soaked it off or cut it off, but something held me back from voicing the question. I only knew that the disappearance of the sinister black wristlet brought me a sense of relief, and I did not want to think about it any more.

The caged wild beasts were already in their wagons, the liberty horses and Violette's rosinback in their traveling boxes, the sideshows and living tents dismantled and stowed in the baggage wagons, together with tiers of seats and all the ring equipment. Sunbeam, resting from her labors with Rama Singh perched on her back, was stuffing hay in her mouth and occasionally turning her great head to look with contempt at the chugging traction engine as it rumbled on its way to the road, towing a loaded wagon. Only the big top remained, the huge canvas dome itself, for the sidewall panels had been dismantled, rolled, and stowed before the seats with their supporting framework were cleared.

Captain Lefevre called a command in his penetrating voice to the men on the pulleys, and the billowing dome began to descend, heaving like a great harpooned whale. The waiting group of tentmen in felt slippers raced forward, treading the canvas down, then starting to unhook the seams before rolling up the long strips of canvas which together formed the big top. We would see more of that canvas when we were on the road. Each night two or three panels would be unloaded and examined to see if they were damaged, for keeping the canvas in good repair was a never-ending task.

Now only the four king poles were left, great tubes of steel sixty feet high, each in three sections bolted together. The men moved to lay hold of the thick stays, and there came a clank of iron on iron as the pawl on the pulley was knocked free. The men on the ropes moved slowly forward, and the two king poles on our right came swaying down together, settling gently to the hard-beaten ground. A rush of feet, the clank of another pulley, and the third king pole leaned over to begin its descent, supported by the one that remained.

Beside me Martin said wonderingly, "How on earth will they manage the last one? They have no mechanical advantage for it."

There was no need for me to answer. Already Rama Singh was moving Sunbeam into position with her back to the king pole. A chain attached to the harness she wore was hooked to the back stay, and a word from Captain Lefevre sent men running to lay hold of the side stays. Rama Singh glanced over his shoulder and spoke casually to Sunbeam in his own tongue. She moved back slowly, still munching, and the great mast swung gently over in a quarter circle to touch down neatly on the ground.

There came the ring of metal as the section bolts were knocked out, and Martin gave a laugh of sheer delight. "It was marvelous!" he said. "And all done so quickly." Then he looked thoughtful. "It must be very difficult in the rain, surely? The canvas would be twice as heavy, and the ground slippery — no, it would still be dry where the big top stood, of course."

I thought how swift he was to see the problems in something entirely new to him, and said, "I've seen them do it in a raging storm."

"Wouldn't there be a danger of the king poles attracting lightning?"

"Captain Lefevre says it's happened to

him once. The pole was damaged but nobody was hurt because he always uses rope stays, not wire, so the lightning goes down through the pole and not through the stays."

"Yes. There's a lot to think about. I shall look forward to seeing the big top go up when we pitch again."

Mr. Galletti came strolling to join us, a folded newspaper under his arm, greeting Martin with the gentle courtesy he used towards everyone, from Mr. Kayser to the youngest circus boy.

"Do you have everything you need, Martin?" he asked.

"Yes, thank you. Mr. Kayser was good enough to give me a sovereign, so I was able to go into the town and buy these clothes and a few items of toiletry."

"Excellent." Mr. Galletti touched the newspaper he carried. "I think it as well that we are moving on. When political troubles arise, the people grow cautious and are unwilling to spend their money."

Martin's head came up and he gave Mr. Galletti an alert glance. "What troubles have arisen?"

Mr. Galletti unfolded the newspaper, and I saw that it was printed in German. "This is a Budapest paper a week old," he said. "There has been an assassination. One of these anarchist groups threw a bomb into the carriage of von Dreyer, the Austrian envoy, and killed him."

I said, "A bomb? Oh, that's horrible!"

"The destruction of the man is horrible," Mr. Galletti agreed. "The method makes it worse only to the extent that a bomb may claim other victims, as it did in this case."

Martin was standing with eyes half closed, as if concentrating on some difficult problem. "Is the motive for this assassination known?" he asked.

Mr. Galletti shrugged. "If it was indeed an anarchist group, then the motive is simply that they wish to destroy all forms of government. If not, there could be a dozen different reasons in this mixture of a country, with its long history of strife. The Magyars feud with the Pan-Germans, the Serbians with the Croats. There are some who approve the Customs Union with Austria and others who hate it. The same may be said for the Dualist System and the Hapsburg Monarchy. There are riots over language, education, and taxation . . ."

I stopped listening, for after a while I always became confused when Mr. Galletti spoke about politics. This was something in which I was not alone, for most circus people lived in their own little world and had no great interest in happenings beyond. Mr. Galletti was an exception.

It was a relief when Martin interrupted politely to say, "Only one man can throw a bomb. Have the police caught him, Mr. Galletti?"

"No. They say they expect to do so, for what that is worth." He lifted the paper, running his finger down one of the columns, and began to read, translating as he went along. "It says here . . . the authorities have reason to believe that a foreign — er — hireling was guilty of this — er, yes — this barbaric crime." He looked up with a grimace of doubt. "That is a favorite thing for governments to say in such cases, of course. It helps them divert attention and pretend that all their problems are caused by foreigners."

A little shiver touched my spine. For a moment I could not think why, and then I found that some words were running through my head. *The ring is without light, and brings death with the sound of thunder. . . .*

They were Solange's words, spoken when the gift was upon her. She had not known their meaning, and they were still obscure to me, but I was thinking that the black wristlet could have been a *ring without light,* and that *death with the sound of thunder* had come to that poor man in Budapest, when the bomb destroyed him. It was a coincidence, of course. As Solange had said, you could always find something to fit a vague prediction.

In the days that followed, as the long line of wagons moved steadily westward, I saw little of Martin while we were on the road, but on most evenings he fell into the habit of coming to our wagon after dinner to sit chatting for an hour. He slept and took his meals with the grooms, but I learned from Sammy that he had settled in without difficulty and seemed to be well liked by the men.

One evening, when Leo was away with his friends and Maria had gone to bed, we were sitting outside the wagon in the warm dusk when Mr. Galletti said in a low voice, "Have you had any signs of your memory returning, Martin?"

"No, nothing at all." Martin spoke as if it was a matter of little importance. "Occasionally I have an odd feeling that something's just about to come back to me, but then it doesn't happen. The feeling fades away." He shrugged idly. "No matter."

I had a sense of disappointment. Somehow it seemed feeble of Martin simply to accept his situation without trying to do something about it. I felt he ought to be making every effort to discover who he was, not traveling as a groom with a circus and letting the world go by. What of his family? Suppose he was married, what of his wife? The thought that he might be married came as a slight shock, even as the question formed in my mind. It had never occurred to me before, probably because Maria was still enlarging on her romances about him, in which he was an English lord who had fallen desperately in love with Chantal, the trapeze artist.

Mr. Galletti said absently as he puffed at his pipe, "You know, Martin, it is fortunate that blow on the head did not affect you in other ways. I was remembering . . . it must be thirty years ago now. A big pulley fell and hit one of the tentmen on the head. They put many stitches in his scalp. He had always been a quiet, fellow, but after that he became different. Very quarrelsome, always seeking to make trouble. Reckless and wild."

Martin said tranquilly, "Yes, I suppose it's better to lose your memory than be changed to a different person. At least that hasn't happened to me."

"One cannot be entirely sure." Mr. Galletti's eyes twinkled. "Perhaps you were wild and reckless before, my young friend."

Martin smiled lazily. "I hadn't thought of that."

We opened for two weeks at Graz, and then began to move north, working the smaller towns for a few days at a time. Martin's duties usually prevented him seeing the Flying Gallettis perform, but every day he attended our rehearsals, and often snatched a few minutes to watch us at ground practice, when we would spend at least an hour daily in exercises and acrobatics to keep our muscles strong and supple. Because I needed to train more than Maria and Leo, who had been at it almost since they could walk, I often joined the little Khalaf boys to help them at their tumbling practice. There, too, I would sometimes find Martin watching when he had a few minutes to spare.

In a circus it was seldom that anyone had much time to be idle, whether we were on the road or working, for to make sure that everything ran smoothly was a huge task in which everybody had a part to play. When we were making short stops the work became doubly hard, for there was the constant pitching and striking of the whole circus to keep us busy.

Even at night there were always some men on guard duty. The artists were excused from this, but the grooms, tentmen, and roughnecks took turns to patrol the perimeter each night. Trouble was rare, but I remembered a few occasions which could have become dangerous, when two or three boys tried to creep into the animal gallery by night for devilment of some sort, and when a group of drunken young men were bent on stealing some horses.

The worst occasion I had known was when the alarm bell sounded while we were pitched outside Seville, two years earlier. There was some long-standing trouble between a factory owner and his work people, and one night it flared into violence. Some fifty men marched on the factory, threatening to burn it down. They were stopped by the police, who charged them with truncheons. It was a brutal affair by all accounts, and the men became enraged. Our circus was pitched on a field nearby, rented from the factory owner, and the infuriated mob turned on us, perhaps because we were foreigners.

The police were concerned only with protecting the factory, and for two hours that night we found ourselves engaged in a pitched battle to save the circus. The men fought with belts and cudgels in the darkness, while the women and children waited in the big top, wondering if the attackers would break through, each one of us gripping a weapon of some kind, an iron stanchion or a heavy tent peg, for we knew that if the worst happened Mr. Kayser would use us as a last hope to stem the mob. Nobody thought this shameful of him. A canvas city is only too easily destroyed, and the circus was fighting for its life. Old Solange could even remember a time long ago, in another circus, when the women and children had in fact been used to save the day.

Martin was content to sit for hours when the day's work was done, listening to such tales told by the circus folk, and again this annoyed me. I could not imagine why a young man should be content to dwell on the past instead of looking to the future.

I even asked him about this once, when

he had watched our rehearsal as usual and we were sitting on the ringside to chat for a few moments before I went to change. Instead of answering me he said, "Do you have plans for *your* future, Chantal?"

"Of course I do. I don't want to go on being a trapeze artist until I'm too old for it. I want to be a doctor." The moment I had said those words I regretted it, afraid he would laugh at me, but I was wrong. The smile vanished and for long seconds he stared straight through me, the lines of his face changing and hardening. I felt an aura of danger, and with it came a strange sensation, partly fear and partly elation. It was as if this was in some way what I wanted to see in Martin, yet at the same time I found it frightening.

"Doctor . . . ?" he whispered. His head moved from side to side, eyes narrowed, as if trying to peer through the veil that hid his past, and for a moment his lips tightened and drew back from his teeth. Then he gave a little sigh, the tension drained out of him and he was himself again, quiet and untroubled. "Doctor . . ." he repeated softly. "For a moment something almost came back to me. Oh well . . .'' He shrugged carelessly and looked at me with interest. "How do you hope to become a doctor, Chantal?"

At least he had not laughed at me, and I said, "I have some books I study. I mean, medical textbooks an Italian doctor recommended when Mr. Galletti asked him, and I help Mr. Brunner with everyday doctoring in the circus."

"Does Mr. Galletti think you can learn to be a doctor in that way?"

"No, of course not. I shall have to go to a medical school somewhere, and be properly taught, and take examinations. I know that, and I know it's very difficult for a woman because most men doctors are against them, but anyway, the more I can learn now, simply by reading and looking at diagrams, the better. I've just learned all the bones in the hand, twenty-seven of them."

Martin looked across the yellow ring at the tiers of empty seats. "So you'll be giving up the circus eventually?"

"Yes, in two or three years, when I've saved up enough money to keep myself while I go through medical school. I expect that will be in Rome."

"You'll need quite a lot of money."

"Circus artists are paid quite a lot of money. Mr. Kayser pays my living expenses to Mr. Galletti, and except for a little pocket money he puts the rest into a bank for me. That's almost two hundred and fifty pounds I save every year."

He whistled softly in surprise. "Five years' wages for a butler!" Then, gazing up at the great canvas dome, he added with a smile, "Not that you don't earn every penny of it, Chantal. But won't it break up the Flying Gallettis if you leave?"

"Oh no. They can easily get somebody as good as I am, if they need anybody."

"Won't you miss the circus life? Miss being with the Gallettis?"

"Yes." The shadow of the parting in time to come pressed down upon me, and I shook my head as if trying to thrust it away. "I hate to think about leaving the family, and I'll miss them terribly, but it can't be helped. You see, Leo and Maria are going to become better and better, as long as she doesn't grow too tall, but I can't improve any more because I haven't their natural talent, and I started late without any experience. So one day I won't be good enough for the act."

"Is that what they say?"

"No, but they all know it, and so do I, so I'll go before that time comes. I don't want to become just a general worker in the circus. Most people would think it silly of me to try to be a doctor, but Mr. Galletti doesn't."

"I expect that's because he knows you. It couldn't be harder than joining the circus at thirteen and becoming a trapezist." Martin's dark-blue eyes dwelled on me so intently that I felt uncomfortable. "I'm quite sure you'll do it, Chantal. You come of a rare breed."

The quick pain of memories revived brought stinging tears to my eyes, and my voice was unsteady as I spoke. "Don't say that, please. I'm ashamed of my breed." I stood up quickly. "You'd better get back to work, Martin. I must go and change."

Five days later, on a road that wound down into a valley and crossed a tributary of the Enns, our long line of wagons came to a halt. This was not unusual, but after an hour had passed with no movement I went to the head of the column with Maria to see what was wrong.

Mr. Kayser, Captain Lefevre, the wagonmaster, and a little crowd of men were gathered on the small bridge. Mr. Kayser was arguing with two Austrian policemen, who kept shaking their heads. Martin stood by the stout wooden parapet with Rama Singh, pointing and talking earnestly. When we joined them and looked down, the trouble was clear.

A huge tree trunk had been carried down the river and was jammed across two of the old stone piers which supported the bridge. Other branches and debris were piling up against the trunk. The two policemen kept insisting that our heavy wagons must not cross the bridge while the piers were under such strain.

This was very serious, for a detour would take us far from our planned route and throw our bookings into chaos. It was little wonder that Mr. Kayser looked almost haggard with anxiety, for the policemen were shrugging and saying that they did not know how soon something would be done to shift the logjam.

Martin greeted us a little absently, then turned back to Rama Singh. "All it needs is a heavy rope round the trunk, running out at an angle to the bank there." He pointed. "With Sunbeam on the end of it, you can soon haul the tree clear."

I looked down. The river was running very fast, foaming as it piled up against the obstruction. I said, "You'll need someone who can swim well to get a rope round the trunk, Martin."

He gave a brief smile. "I can swim well. Let's see what Mr. Kayser says."

Ten minutes later Sunbeam stood on the bank some fifty yards or so upriver. One of our heaviest ropes was attached to her harness, and the other end had been brought to the middle of the bridge, where three men were paying it out over the wooden parapet. Martin, barefoot and stripped to the waist, clambered over and went hand over hand down the rope until he sank into the water beside the logjam.

Three times he dived beneath the surface, trying to thrust the end of the rope between a crevice in the jam so that it could be made fast round the massive tree trunk, but each time he failed. I watched anxiously, knowing how exhausting his efforts must be, for I was a swimmer myself — it was perhaps the one small talent I had brought to the circus with me. Hardly any of our people could swim, but I had learned as a child, on holiday with my nannie at Frinton. It had come easily to me, I enjoyed the water, and whenever the circus pitched near the sea or by a lake I never missed an opportunity to go swimming.

Martin was resting for a moment, clinging to a thick branch to prevent himself being swept away. I pushed my way through the little crowd by the rail to Mr. Kayser and said, "He needs somebody on top of the trunk to take the rope when he pushes it up, sir. May I go down?"

Mr. Kayser dragged at his chin worriedly, then nodded. "Zank you, Chantal. But be careful."

I had been playing with the little Khalaf boys for a while when we first halted, and had quickly put a dress on over my leotard before going with Maria to find out what was amiss. Now I slipped the dress off, handed it to Maria, and was sliding quickly down the rope before she could begin to argue.

Perched on the great tree trunk, I could feel the powerful thrust of the river grinding it against the pier. From beyond the growing mass of debris around it Martin called, "A little to your left, Chantal . . . yes, there. Now wait." For a moment I saw the wolf look on his face, the smile that was not a smile, then he drew in a long breath and disappeared beneath the foaming water, to begin clawing his way towards me beneath the debris. I was almost quivering with anxiety when at last I saw his hand thrust up between the trunk and a thick branch. Crouching, I snatched the end of the rope from him and drew it swiftly through. Seconds later I heard a great indrawn gasp from behind me, and turned my head. Martin had surfaced under the bridge, and was clinging to a branch jutting from the main trunk, the confined water battering against him.

"All right . . ." he choked. "Make fast."

Quickly I passed the end round the

standing part of the rope and made a timber hitch, then looked up at the row of anxious faces staring down from the parapet. "Made fast!" I called. "Let go and haul!"

As I lowered my gaze I saw Martin wave, grin, then release his hold. At once he was swept from under the bridge. Unable to climb out, he had realized that it would be dangerous to cling on when the jam started to break up, and so he was letting himself be carried downriver.

A great exhilaration swept through me as the slack of the rope splashed into the water. I looked up, called to Maria, "Don't worry, *piccina!*" and dived into the boiling water on the downriver side of the jam. For the first few seconds I was swept along like a cork on a millrace, but then the torrent grew calmer and I was able to swim comfortably as the strong central current carried me on.

Martin appeared beside me, pushing wet hair back from his eyes. "Didn't know you could swim," he panted, still grinning. "I think we've done the trick, my little red vixen."

I splashed water in his face, and he laughed. "Don't fight the current. We'll just edge in towards the left bank as we go down."

Three minutes later we dragged ourselves up a low bank by the exposed roots of a tree. Laughing and breathless, Martin gathered me in his arms and hugged me for a moment, then we fell panting on a patch of thick, sun-warmed grass. "That was good," he said at last, and lifted his head. "I enjoyed it." He reached out to put his hand companionably over mine. "What else can you do besides fly on a trapeze and clear logjams?"

"Nothing, Martin." I made a laughing grimace. "You've exhausted my talents now."

He sat up and pointed. "Look, there's all the debris floating down. Sunbeam must have hauled the tree trunk clear."

"Yes." I felt an extraordinary happiness. Together Martin and I had fought a little battle, and won, but I was uplifted in a way that seemed out of all proportion to what we had achieved. I said, "What else can *you* do, Martin?"

He shook his head, smiling. "I've no idea. But it doesn't matter, anyway."

125

Before I could say more there came the sound of Maria's voice calling me, and the next moment she appeared, hurrying along the bank, carrying my dress.

"Chantal! Ah, there you are. *Mio Dio,* you might have drowned! Martin, I'm cross with you, why do you encourage her? Mr. Kayser is almost dancing with delight and is going to give you both a present of money." She turned to me. "You must take off that wet leotard and put your dress on, *carissima,* just to get back to the wagon. Go *away,* Martin. We have to hurry. The wagons are starting to move."

Three weeks after we crossed the border into Bavaria, Martin was still with us and had made no attempt to go to a British consulate in one of the larger towns. Only Mr. Galletti and I knew of his lost memory, but I spoke impatiently about him to Maria as we were going to bed one night, saying how ridiculous it was for a man like Martin to be working as a groom in a circus.

She looked at me in surprise and said, "But he's only doing it while he waits for you to fall in love with him, Chantal. I don't know why you haven't already. He's very nice.''

''Oh, stop romancing, Maria. It's not like that at all.''

''Now you're cross with me.''

''No I'm not.''

She climbed into her narrow bed and drew up the blankets. I smiled and bent to tuck her in. ''I'm cross with him, *carissima,* not you.''

She looked at me over the top of the blankets with her big dark eyes. ''If he isn't an English milord, perhaps he's content to be just a groom in a circus. Not everybody is like you, Chantal, struggling and striving all the time.''

''Is that really what I'm like?''

''Of course it is, and I'm glad you're like that. When you first came I didn't like you much, and when you started exercising and trying to do ground acrobatics on the practice rope, I wanted to laugh. Everybody did, except Grandfather, and Leo was horrid the way he mocked you. But you kept on and on for months, just to learn an easy back flip, and I started to feel proud of you.''

"I remember you spent hours every day helping me."

"Yes, but even then I never thought you'd be able to work on the trapeze, and look at you now. You're really exciting when you fly, Chantal."

I laughed. "That's not what Leo says."

"Oh, he's a boy and stupid. All I mean is that you've done something impossible just by struggling and striving, but you mustn't expect other people to be the same. Not everybody is so stubborn."

I was touched by her words, but shook my head as I said, "It's not much of a virtue. I just get angry with myself, and that makes me keep on." I patted her cheek. "You were so good at tonight's performance, *mia cara*. I've never seen you better."

"Truly?"

"Truly. Now sleep well and have good dreams."

I blew out the lamp and climbed into my bed.

In the darkness Maria said, "You have good dreams, too, Chantal. Remember those horrible nightmares you used to have when you first came to us?"

"Yes, I remember."

"Was it because you were frightened to be with us?"

"No. I'd had them all my life. When I was small, the woman who was my nannie used to tell me stories, but they were dreadful stories of goblins and giants and all the horrible things they did. I used to try to keep awake because I was too terrified to sleep."

"That was a wicked thing to do."

"Perhaps she didn't understand how children feel. A lot of people don't. Anyway, it's all over now."

"Except for that, do you sometimes wish you were back where you came from?"

"No. Never. Go to sleep now, Maria."

"All right. Good night, Chantal."

Two weeks later we were working at Regensburg. An uneasy atmosphere hovered over the circus, for two things had occurred to disturb us. The first was that a young bandsman who was also a tentman was found dead one morning. He was lying face down in a big water trough, and had drowned. His name was Hans, and he happened to be a surly young man whom nobody liked much, but this did not lessen the shock, for he was still one of us. The general opinion was that he had got drunk and blundered into the trough, perhaps hitting his head on the side and losing consciousness for a few moments — long enough to drown before he could recover his senses.

And then, the next day, Martin disappeared. The first I knew of it was when Mr. Albertini came to our wagon just before the evening performance, asking for him. Martin had been absent from his duties in the stables that morning, but then it was learned that he had been told by Mr. Kayser to join the commissary party going into town with the supply wagon, because they were shorthanded for loading, so Mr. Albertini had thought no more about his absence for a while. Nobody in the commissary party could remember for sure whether or not Martin had returned with them, but the fact was that he had not been seen anywhere in the circus since.

I was surprised to find how upset I was, and realized for the first time that I had much enjoyed Martin's company, even though I often felt impatient at his placid acceptance of his situation. I was partly hurt and partly worried by his sudden disappearance. If he had gone away deliberately, then to do so without saying goodbye to us was deeply wounding, for we had given him our friendship. But if not, then any alternative was cause for anxiety. Perhaps his memory had returned and he had run away because . . . there my imagination failed me, and I could not think why.

If he was afraid of the police, and knew the reason now, the circus was still the best place to remain hidden. Perhaps what troubled me most was remembering Solange's cryptic words: . . . *Have a care . . . have a care in the time when the sleeping wolf wakes.* I did not know why those words should ring in my ears now, for I had put them out of my mind long ago.

I knew from my medical books that loss of memory was called amnesia. There were different forms of it, but it seemed to be an obscure condition about which little was known, and nothing I had read was of any help to me in trying to decide whether or not Martin's memory might have returned. Maria did not help my anxiety that day by concocting a new and enlarged romance, while we were dressing for our act, to explain Martin's disappearance. He was still an English lord who had seen me perform, fallen desperately in love with me, and pretended to be a vagabond so that he could be near me. But he had a wife, whom he had married reluctantly on the orders of his father, who was a duke. Torn between love and duty, he had at last chosen the path of honor and given me up forever, to return to the wife who wept and waited for him.

If she had not been Maria, I would have shaken her till her teeth rattled. As it was, I waited until I could bear it no longer and then said, "Don't keep talking about him, *piccina*. It upsets me, and I don't want to give a bad performance."

She looked startled, then horrified, and flung herself into my arms, hugging me. "Oh, Chantal, I'm sorry! I'm such a fool. I wouldn't upset you for worlds. Did you love him very much?"

"What? No, no, of course I didn't. It's

just strange that he didn't say goodbye, and I hope nothing bad has happened to him."

She stared at me, round-eyed. "What sort of bad thing?"

"I don't know. That's exactly what I don't want to think about."

She gave me a puzzled look, then shrugged, and a few moments later began to scold me because I had let my hair grow an inch longer than she thought it should be. I did not mind this. For nearly five years I had mothered Maria, but she liked to pretend that it was the other way round, and frequent scolding was her way of showing this.

We were doing well at Regensburg. Every seat in the big top had been filled since we arrived a week ago, and tonight was no exception. They were good audiences, too, which was always stimulating for the artists and made them produce their best.

When I stood on the platform with Maria beside me all thought of Martin had been wiped from my mind, and the familiar feeling of elation came welling up within me. Below, in increasing circles round the sawdust ring, were a thousand upturned faces. Here, in the dome of the big top, we were the center of two thousand eyes. It was a sensation few people could have known, and it never failed to bring me a sense of joyous wonder.

To say I was never afraid is not to boast. As with Leo and Maria, my nerves were finely tuned and every sense was alert, every part of my mind focused to a pinpoint upon what I had to do. But we were not afraid. It was impossible to work at all on the flying trapeze in a state of apprehension.

Maria and I smiled and waved to the audience below, then unhooked our two trapezes. Maria said quietly, "Now," and we launched ourselves as one into our twin act. We had been performing our series of acrobatics in unison for perhaps thirty seconds when it happened.

We were both hanging by our hands and swinging hard to gain height for the next move, when I heard a small crack and felt the bar above me give way. It was as if a rope had broken, or the bar had snapped at one end, but I had no time to wonder.

At one moment I was swooping forward with Maria beside me on her trapeze. A split second later, with a jerk and a lurch, I was swinging out and away from her, trying frantically to cling with one resined hand to a bar that hung vertically from a single rope, and knowing that I must fall.

FOUR

Apart from one numbing moment of shock, as if an icy spear had been plunged through my stomach, I had no time to feel terror. I knew I must fall, for with the first lurching drop as the end of the bar came free, the grip of my right hand had been broken and my left had begun to slip. I felt one fleeting instant of relief that whatever had broken was on my left, on the side nearest Maria, for I was swinging out sideways now, away from her, and if the other end had broken we would surely have collided.

The impetus of my swing, together with the great wrench sideways, sent me flying out towards the edge of the net, near one corner of it. I tried furiously to cling on for the return swing to bring me back, but then the end of the bar slid through my hand and I was a-sprawl in the air, twisting to look down, and seeing at once that I had been swung out to the very edge of the net below.

No more than a second had passed since the instant of disaster. I was dimly aware of a great sound coming up at me, the explosive gasp of horror from a thousand throats, but there was no thought in my mind, for instinct had taken charge of my senses and muscles. The return swing had begun just before I lost my grip, and I was moving slightly inwards . . . but not enough. My body snapped into a ball and I made a quick forward somersault, then opened into a swallow dive that was not quite vertical, a position which would give me a tiny forward movement.

The net hurtled towards me. I was going to miss it. . . . I was going to hit the edge. . . .

I folded at the hips, revolving, arms spread, head tucked in, and hit the net hard with my back, head only inches from the outermost edge. Here the ropes of the net were tauter than in the middle, and the impact harder. I was flung up and back, hovered head down in the air for an instant directly above the outer stay, then fell again. My hands caught the stay, my body swung down in a circle and up underneath the net; then I lost my grip once more, and fell the last few feet to the sawdust. In that final moment the years of training in ground acrobatics served me well, for I fell limply and with every muscle relaxed to avoid strained sinews or broken bones. Even so, the impact of my landing drove the breath from my body in a great gasp, and I lay sprawled in a daze with the light of the big top whirling dizzily before my eyes.

Then, incredibly, the lights were blotted out, and I was looking into Maria's face as she knelt over me, her eyes huge with alarm. An instant later and Leo's head was beside Maria's. In my stupor I could not think how they came to be there. It was only later I learned that they had dived for the net before I hit the ground, and had flung themselves out on the first bounce, to reach me before anyone else could move.

Maria had a hand on my brow and was saying in a shrill, wavering voice, "Chantal? Chantal? How is it, *carissima?*"

"I'm all right," I wheezed slowly. "Help me up." It was difficult to hear against the enormous noise from the audience, but she must have read my lips. I rose gradually to my feet, testing each muscle carefully, trying to keep my mind a blank. There was no pain. I was shaken, but apart from a soreness of the palms where they had slid from the bar I was unhurt. Maria pressed her hands under my ribs, lifting and lowering rhythmically to help me get my wind back.

Then Mr. Kayser was there, sweat trickling down his cheeks, and Mr. Galletti, relief breaking over his face as he saw me stand. Mr. Kayser looked round, gestured, and shouted, "Pepe!" The next moment Pepe had swung himself up into the net, a grotesque figure with his great red nose, bowler hat, and enormous trousers. He began to bound along the net, making ridiculous swimming motions as he soared in the air, turning somersaults, coming out of his flapping trousers and landing in them again on the next turn. The band had struck up a cheerful march, and the people were beginning to settle back in their seats.

We moved away from the net, and Mr. Galletti put his hands on my shoulders and looked into my eyes. "No strains, Chantal?"

"No . . . no, I was winded for a moment, but I'm all right, Mr. Galletti."

"Show me a back flip."

I stepped away, stood breathing deeply for a few seconds to compose myself, then performed three back flips in succession. Mr. Galletti, Maria, and Leo were watching me like hawks. When I moved back to them Leo took my hands and looked at them. They were trembling. He glanced at his grandfather and said, "Better if she goes up again at once."

"Yes." Mr. Galletti looked at me. "Can you do it, Chantal?"

I would have given anything to say no, but I knew that if I refused now I might never had the courage to work on the flying trapeze again. I nodded, and Mr. Galletti said, "Quickly, then. Up with you, children. Chantal begins her solo as soon as you are in position. Hurry!"

Leo, grinning at me, said, "Don't worry, fat girl. I will catch you." He turned and ran for his rope ladder while Maria and I moved to ours. Twenty seconds later, at a signal from Mr. Kayser, the music stopped and Pepe swung himself down from the net. Every face was upturned again, and my own music began.

Maria squeezed my arm. I took the main trapeze, looked across to where Leo was already swinging head down, heard him clap his hands in the signal, and launched myself out into space.

That night I gave the worst performance I had ever given, but only the sharp and experienced eyes of the circus folk would have known it, for Leo performed miracles. My timing was bad, and I was inches out for the catching, but always Leo was there, reaching for me and finding me, seeming almost to alter the speed of his swing to adjust for my errors. And each time that we met and I hung from his hands, he would talk to me, his dark monkey face split in a grin. "Good, good! That's my clever little fat girl! Nicely. Don't reach for me, *piccina,* leave it to Leo. Smoothly now. *Bene! Bravo!"*

My second and final solo was a little better. The need for complete concentration had held back the dangerous onslaught of fear, and now, with every moment that passed, this pent-up fear waiting to seize me grew steadily more feeble, for it had only to be contained and it would die. The Galletti family, in their wisdom and experience, knew this.

Maria performed her wonderful blindfolded finale, and returned with a pirouette to her own trapeze. Now was the time when I would normally launch myself on the parallel trapeze for the swallow dive into the net, but this trapeze was broken, and hung hooked back beside our platform, useless. I was about to start down the rope ladder when I saw Maria circle up into a sitting position, take off her hood and toss it away, then swing down again and sweep towards me, landing lightly on the platform. Keeping her hold on the trapeze, face glowing with excitement as she spoke, she said, "You're to come down last tonight. Be ready with the hook." Then she turned and was gone.

Puzzled, I reached for the long light cane with a hook on the end which was clipped to the side support of the platform. Leo swung out from the far side and dived to the net, followed a moment later by Maria. It took me a few seconds to catch Maria's empty trapeze with the hook as it swung back towards me, and to draw it into my grasp. By then Leo and Maria were standing beside the net in one of our well-rehearsed poses, each with one hand on hip, the other raised. They were looking and pointing up, drawing every eye in the circus towards me.

Then the light dawned, and I understood that they were giving me the pride of place which had always been Maria's. A lump came to my throat and for a moment my eyes blurred at their warmhearted generosity. I blinked to clear my vision, took hold of the bar, and launched myself. At the top of the swing I made my release and performed the best open somersault I had ever made before plummeting down headfirst to the net. It was a finish almost as good as Maria's worst, and I felt truly pleased with myself as I swung over the edge of the net and dropped down between them.

Maria should have been in the middle as we made our bow, but they each took one of my hands for the first bow, then skipped away and turned to face me, pointing, clapping, and focusing all the cheers and applause of the audience upon me. I was smiling and curtsying with the tears trickling down my cheeks.

We ran off at last, and the moment we were beyond the curtain and in the mounting place we hugged and kissed each other in a great outburst of relief, all chattering incoherently.

"*Benissimo!* Eh, Maria?"

"Chantal, you were —"

"Oh, bless you, monkey face —"

"— *wonderful,* wasn't she, Leo?"

"— I don't know *how* you caught me!"

"You frightened us to death!"

"Fine finish, fat girl!"

"Don't *call* her that!"

"I don't mind, Maria —"

"Listen! Listen!" Leo shouted us down, eyes shining with glee. "Did you hear the audience? It brought them out of their seats! So why not do it by *arrangement?* Not every night, but once each time we pitch. Chantal swings, the trapeze breaks — *pfft!* There must be some device for that, and careful rehearsal — oooh!"

The last word was a startled gasp of pain,

for Maria had stamped furiously on his toe with her slippered foot. "Imbecile!" she cried. "Is your head made of bone? Chantal comes close to being killed and you say she must do it again?"

"But it would be different, stupid! A well-rehearsed trick —" He jumped back, fending her off as she tried to stamp on his other foot. I began to laugh. When our gentle Maria lost her temper she was even worse than I — as Strabo had once found.

"Maria, please! *Mio Dio!* Stop her, Chantal!"

"Idiot! Better to keep a pig than have such a brother! One can always *eat* a pig!"

I was laughing and crying at the same time when a voice said sharply, *"Children!"* It was Mr. Galletti, and with him was Mr. Kayser. Maria gave up her attempts on Leo and came to slip her arm through mine, still scowling. Leo ran a hand through his curly hair and blew out his cheeks, bewildered.

Mr. Galletti said sternly, "Leo, did you examine the apparatus after rehearsal today?"

That brought us to our senses. A trapeze

had broken, and this was something which must never be allowed to happen. Our apparatus was of the finest materials. The ropes were not of hawser-laid hemp or jute, but consisted of many plaited strands of cotton cordage, for strength and flexibility. The bars were of close-grained ash. The end of each rope was eyespliced and whipped, and set very tightly in a groove encircling the bar close to each end, with a short L-shaped sleeve of soft leather covering each point of attachment to give protection when we hung by our ankles. Every day all the apparatus in the dome was examined by one of the rigging men to make sure it was secure, but trapezists and high-wire walkers always tested their own equipment, too.

Leo said quickly, "Yes, Grandfather. All three trapezes. I never forget to do that."

Mr. Galletti looked at the circus proprietor. "We do not yet know precisely what happened. When the performance ends I will go up myself and examine every shackle, every attachment, every strand of rope."

Mr. Kayser nodded. "Goot. Please report to me immediately what you find." He looked at me. "Chantal, I zank Got you were not hurt. It was very well done, young lady. Leo, I congratulate you. Only the best of catchers could have nursed Chantal through her solo. I am very pleased with all of you. Now run along and do not quarrel. I will see you later."

Long after dinner that evening we sat in Mr. Kayser's big wagon in horrified silence, staring at the bar and the length of rope which lay on the table. Even Maria had no word to say, and her hand held mine so tightly that it almost hurt.

"Dear Got," said Mr. Kayser softly, and looked at Mr. Galletti. "There can be no doubt?"

"None at all. It was deliberate." Mr. Galletti's face was very pale, and his hand shook as he picked up the bar and a small round piece of wood which had once been part of it. "The ropes and the eye splices are intact, but the bar has been cut more than halfway through with a fine saw blade," he tapped with his finger, "cut here, very close to the inner side of the eye splice, so that it would not be seen."

There was another awful silence, broken

at last by Leo, his eyes glittering like chips of jet. "Who?" he said hoarsely. "I will take a knife and kill him!"

"Let us have no wild talk." Mr. Kayser spoke firmly but not unkindly. "However, Leo has asked a question we must answer. *Who?*"

My hand was like ice, and Maria began to chafe it gently. "It was meant for Chantal," she said in a shaking voice. "She is the only one to use that trapeze."

Mr. Kayser looked down at the table. "I do not wish to point a finger of suspicion, but I am bound to ask you if you have in mind . . ." He raised his head to look directly at me. "Strabo?"

I was startled, and said, "No, Mr. Kayser. Oh, no."

I looked at Leo and then Maria. Both shook their heads in turn. "No," I repeated. "I know we quarreled, but I'm sure Strabo would never do such a dreadful thing."

Mr. Kayser gave a sigh of relief. "I am of the zame opinion. Strabo is ztupid, and can become a bully when he is afraid of losing face. But he is not a bad man, not a man to

148

do zis." He gestured with disgust at the broken bar. "So let us conzider who had the opportunity to use a saw upon the trapeze, and when it might have been done."

Mr. Galletti rubbed his eyes. I had never seen him look so old and tired. "It would have to be done at night," he said. "The bar held during rehearsal this afternoon, therefore it is hard to know for how long it has held. Not more than two or three nights, I think."

"Hans was the rigging man on duty zis week," Mr. Kayser said slowly, "but we cannot question him now." Hans was the young man who had drowned himself in the water trough while drunk.

"He could do such a thing," Maria said slowly. "He was the man for a vendetta, that one. The tentmen will tell you."

Mr. Kayser raised an eyebrow at me. "Chantal? Did Hans ever ask you to walk with him?"

This was the way we spoke of courting. In the circus, a young man might ask a girl to walk with him, and if her parents had no objection it was for her to say yes or no. If she said no, that was the end of it. A man who made a nuisance of himself with any circus woman would be harshly dealt with.

I said, "He asked me once, sir, but that was last year when we were in winter quarters, and I don't think he expected me to say yes. All the young men know I'm not interested in walking out. I hardly knew Hans and I didn't like what I did know, but we never exchanged a cross word."

"Only a madman kills for no reason," said Mr. Galletti, "and Hans was not mad."

Mr. Kayser nodded. "Who else, then?"

My mind was a blank, and I felt so tired I could have put my head on Maria's shoulder and wept. The strain of the performance had drained much of my strength, and the knowledge that somebody hated me with such bitterness that they had tried to kill me was so terrible that it left me an empty shell.

Then Leo said, "Martin disappeared today."

My nerves jumped and I felt sick. It was an effort to speak as I said, "But . . . but Martin was my friend."

"I wasn't saying he did it, Chantal. But

he was a stranger, and a mystery." Leo shrugged. "I don't know. I just remembered that he vanished today, that's all."

There was another silence. Mr. Kayser looked round the table at us and sighed. "I see no way of arriving at the truth," he said heavily. "If we except Strabo, we can think of nobody who might be Chantal's enemy. And not one of us believes that Strabo would do zis." He looked at Mr. Galletti. "You and the children must be very careful, old friend. If the man is still with us he may ztrike at Chantal again, but not by the zame method, I think. And if . . ." He hesitated, then went on. "If he is dead, or has left us, zen we will have no more trouble, zank Got." He looked at me. "Will you be nervous about using the apparatus, Chantal?"

I thought for a moment, for this was important. If I mistrusted the apparatus my performance would go to pieces and I would make all kinds of mistakes. At last I said, "No, sir. I won't be nervous. I'm sure it will never happen again."

"All the zame, I will make sure in future

to have one of the night guards always in the big top." He dipped his head a little to peer at me closely. "Take her to bed now, Maria. The poor child is exhausted."

I was barely able to reach our wagon without help, and was only vaguely aware of Maria undressing me and getting me into bed. That night I had bad dreams. They were not dreams of falling from the trapeze, for I had dissolved that fear by continuing with the performance. I dreamt that I was standing by the curtain which separated the ring entrance from the mounting place. The big top was in darkness, but I could see a figure climbing steadily up the white rope ladder to the platform which served the twin trapezes. He was no more than a faceless black shadow.

I must have moved the curtain, for a narrow strip of light seemed to filter into the great tent. Then I saw that the ring enclosure was no longer a low parapet of gaily painted, curving sections which encircled the sawdust ring. It was black, and formed of monstrous ebony snakes intertwined, a giant replica of the strange wristlet which had made Strabo afraid.

I shuddered and tried to cry out, but my throat was locked. Unwillingly, but helpless to prevent myself, I lifted my head slowly to look up again. The shadowy figure was on the platform now, and faintly to my ears came the sound of a thin saw blade on wood. His head turned, and a pencil of pale light seemed to play upon it. Then my mouth opened wide in a silent scream, and I woke to find myself sitting up in bed, heart thundering wildly, sweat on my face, and hands clasped over my mouth to stifle the scream before it could burst from me. The head of the figure on the platform had not been that of a man, but of a wolf.

It was an effort for me to behave normally in the days that followed, for I was heavyhearted and felt a gray bleakness pressing down upon me. Perhaps it was partly the shock of my narrow escape from death, but if so this was only a small part, for I knew my trapeze work had not suffered and I was in no way nervous in the air. What lay heaviest upon me was the knowledge that somebody, for some unknown reason, had tried to kill me in cold blood.

The mood began to lift when we left Regensburg for Ingolstadt, but that day had left its mark. For the first time in years I felt a tiny sense of estrangement, as if I were not quite one with the great family of circus folk among whom I lived. This was no fault of theirs. I knew that it lay somewhere within me. Perhaps it arose from an obscure feeling that something from the outside had reached into the secure little world I knew, and laid cold fingers upon me.

It was while we were on the road to Ingolstadt that Strabo came to our wagon when we had made our halt for the night. Dusk was gathering, and I was sitting on the steps of the wagon. Mr. Galletti and Maria had gone to see Old Sven about some new boots she needed, and Leo had disappeared on his own pursuits as usual.

I half guessed why Strabo had come. Mr. Kayser had told us not to talk about the incident of the trapeze, but by the next morning everybody in the circus knew exactly what had happened, probably from the men who had watched Mr. Galletti bring down the broken trapeze. Strabo stood scowling and fidgeting uneasily, not quite knowing how to begin.

I said, "Good evening, Mr. Strabo. Will you sit down? I'll fetch a chair."

"No, no," he grunted, and waved a huge hand impatiently. "I come to say . . ." He ran a hand over his shaven head. "Somebody make your trapeze break. People know we have fight. Maybe they think Strabo do it. I come to ask if you think this."

I shook my head, feeling genuinely sorry for him in his obvious distress. "No, Mr. Strabo. I've never thought that for a moment, and neither have any of the Galletti family."

His little eyes were puzzled as they stared at me. "You say this truly?"

"Truly. I know we quarreled and I'm sorry about that, but I don't believe anyone in the circus would suspect you of damaging the trapeze. I'll speak to Mr. Galletti, and he'll make it known that we're sure you had nothing to do with it."

He puffed out a gusty sigh of relief, and rubbed his head again. "You not so bad liddle girl."

"I'm glad you spoke to me about it."

He nodded, frowning. "Is true the bar was cut?"

"Yes, but Mr. Kayser doesn't want it spoken about."

He spread his hands in a baffled gesture. "Who could do this thing?"

"I don't know, Mr. Strabo. I just want to forget all about it now."

"*Ja*. But you find him one day, you tell Strabo." He glowered and hunched his great shoulders. "I break his back."

On an impulse I said, "Mr. Strabo, what did that strange black wristlet of Martin's mean to you?"

"Nothing," he muttered, and blinked at me warily.

"Please, Mr. Strabo."

He looked down for a while in silence, then gave a shrug and jerked his head to indicate the way we had come, from the east. "Is nothing but what I remember from a little boy. When we did a bad thing they would say, 'The wolves will come for you!'"

"Wolves?" I tried to hide a sudden uneasiness. "What has the wristlet got to do with wolves?"

He shook his head. "Not animal wolf. It is men. In my country, in Transylvania, there is" — he groped for words — "men who are secret, like brothers but not of the blood. It has been for many, many years. Two, three hundred years, I think."

"A secret society? A brotherhood?"

He nodded agreement. *"Ja.* So. Brotherhood of the Wolf."

"What do they do, Mr. Strabo?"

He stood frowning at the ground. "I was peasant boy. I do not know these things well. I think in old time they were of the great families of the Magyars, the true Hungarians. They fight in secret against foreign people who come. The Turk, who hold our country for hundred fifty year. Then come the Hapsburgs of Austria." He looked uneasily over his shoulder and lowered his voice. "But that was in old time. Is different now, these men of the Brotherhood."

I felt a great urge to know as much as I could discover about the strange black wristlet Martin had worn, and felt that this was probably the only chance I would have. Once Strabo fell silent on the subject I was sure he could never be persuaded to speak of it again. I said, "How is it different now?"

He moved a little closer. "It is for money now," he whispered. "Money, land, power. In my village was a farmer with forty *hold* of land. It joins the land of the Count. One day the Count wishes to buy. Kuthen will not sell." Strabo held out a thick wrist and ran a finger across it. "Later comes a man wearing the sign of the Brotherhood. The seven black thongs. He smiles much, and tells Kuthen it is better to sell. Kuthen is hard. Brave. Make his dog go at this smiling man." Strabo paused, and sweat beaded his forehead. "After three days I am little boy walking through forest and I find Kuthen. He is tied to tree. Dead. What they have done to him before he die is very bad. I run to my father. He say I must not speak. I have seen nothing. He is much afraid. So is all village." Strabo shook his head and wiped a hand across his lips.

I said, "But Martin wore the wristlet, and he's English. He couldn't be part of a secret society in Hungary."

Strabo shrugged. "Who can say? Today

it is by *die Politik* that men take money and power. The secret men use fear and death. The knife, the garotte, the bomb. Who can say that they will not pay money to a foreign man to do some bad thing?"

"You think Martin was —?"

"Nem!" he said quickly. Then, "I think nothing. I am fool to speak so much. I say only I do not make enemy of man who wears the mark of the wolf." He tapped his wrist with a thick finger, scowling again.

I said, "You can be sure I won't repeat what you've said to anybody, Mr. Strabo, I promise."

"Good." His brow cleared. "Is better so." He looked blank for a moment, then seemed to remember why he had come to see me, and began to fidget awkwardly again. "You will speak to Mr. Galletti, so he tell the people you know it was not Strabo who try to make you fall from trapeze?"

"Yes, I promise that, too. *Jó éjszakát,* Mr. Strabo."

He was surprised to hear me wish him good night in his own language, though in fact I scarcely knew a dozen words of it, but he seemed to take it as a friendly gesture and came as near to a smile as I had ever seen him as he answered, *"Jó éjszakát, Chantal."*

I sat with a confusion of thoughts turning slowly in my head. Muddled memories of Martin, the black wristlet, Solange's obscure prophecy, and all Strabo had just told me, were twined like a tangled skein. Strabo had said that the wristlet was the mark of the wolf, and Solange had warned me to have a care when the sleeping wolf woke. Was this Martin, then? If so, what had he done that made instinct rise above his lost memory and warn him to hide?

The knife, the garotte . . . the *bomb?* A man called von Dreyer had been assassinated by a bomb only a few days before I found Martin. *The ring is without light* . . . Was that the circus at night, when someone who wished me dead had climbed to the trapeze? Or was it the black circle of the wristlet?

I felt suddenly impatient with myself for brooding on these silly questions. Perhaps Solange had the gift, but she was a circus fortuneteller and much of what she said was mumbo jumbo which could mean anything. Of all she had said, only one thing was in any way real, and that was her description of the black wristlet . . . *the ebony snakes where one is seven and seven are one.* But before that she had seen Martin when we passed her caravan on the way to the dining tent. Her old eyes were keen and well trained to observe every detail. Perhaps without even knowing it she had glimpsed the woven thong on Martin's wrist, and it had emerged from her memory later. Now that I thought about it, I realized that apart from a warning about the sleeping wolf there had been no prophecy in her words except —

My heart jumped and I caught my breath. *Within two furrows of the plow, one shall die and one shall fly and one shall fall.* Solange studied the stars for compiling horoscopes. Perhaps *two furrows of the plow* meant two appearances of the constellation called the Plow. Two nights. And within that time Hans had died, Martin had flown, and I had fallen from the trapeze.

Mr. Galletti was strolling towards me,

and I felt quick relief. Telling him about Strabo would help to turn my mind from the foolish business of matching chance events with Solange's prophecies. I had been a little worried about Mr. Galletti, for during the past two days he had seemed deeply preoccupied, as if he carried some heavy burden he was trying to conceal.

He sat quietly while I told him of Strabo's visit, then nodded a little wearily. "Yes. I will do as he asks."

"Is anything wrong, Mr. Galletti? You seem troubled."

"Oh . . ." He gestured vaguely and looked at his pipe. "Sometimes the world seems out of joint." He shrugged and gave a little smile, holding out the pipe. "And this tobacco will not draw."

"You never fill it properly, Mr. Galletti." I took the pipe and his pocketknife, teased out the tobacco, then tamped it into the bowl again as I had so often done for him before. "There. Now try."

He smiled again, and this time it was not forced. "I have often wondered where you learned that."

"It was long ago." I sat down on the

162

bed locker facing him. "There was an old man who tended a big garden, and he was my best friend. My only friend, really. I often watched him filling his pipe. He had a way of packing every shred of tobacco just so. And when he was ill, the winter before I . . . before I came to you, I used to fill it for him."

He nodded, sitting with eyes closed, drawing gently upon his pipe. After a little while I said, "Will you excuse me if I go to my room and study for an hour, Mr. Galletti?"

"Of course, child, of course." He opened his eyes. "Are you making progress?"

"I think so, but there's so much to learn. Still, I have at least two years before I start trying to find a place in a medical school."

"Yes."

His voice sounded strange, and for a moment I saw grief in his eyes. I was soon to learn that he was grieving for me, and for the ruin of my hopes. But before that moment of discovery came there was to be a new and startling twist of fate which even he had not dreamt of.

We pitched outside the town of

Ingolstadt, and on the afternoon of the day following our second performance there, while I was helping to exercise one of Mr. Albertini's horses, Maria came racing across the field, calling to me.

"Chantal! Chantal! There's a *visitor* for you, an Englishman with a lady! Oh, he's so handsome, Chantal, and she's not his wife but his sister, and they have beautiful clothes, so they must be *very* rich!" She paused for breath, gazing up at me excitedly.

"And you think he's seen me in the circus and fallen madly in love with me? It's not Martin, is it?" I laughed as I spoke, but at the same time I felt a touch of unease.

"No, it's another Englishman, and he did see you perform last night, and he thinks you're somebody he's been *searching* for! He's with Grandfather now, and they're waiting for you. Who do you think it is, Chantal? He says you don't know him."

"Then I can hardly guess who he is," I said shortly, my uneasiness growing suddenly sharper. "Oh, I'm sorry, *piccina*, I didn't mean to be crabby with you." I reached down a hand to her. "Come up behind me and we'll see."

FIVE

Maria took my hand and floated up into the saddle as lightly as a thistledown. I put the horse to an easy canter until we reached the stables, and there gave him into the care of a groom. My foreboding must have communicated itself to Maria as we made our way to the wagon, for she walked beside me in silence except when she broke it to say anxiously, "You don't think they have come to take you away?"

I shrugged. "Whoever they are, they can't make me go away with them."

But there were butterflies in my stomach as I climbed the steps of the wagon and entered our little sitting room. Mr. Galletti sat on the long bed locker. The two visitors had places of honor on the folding chairs set against the partition, and when I saw that their faces were strange to me I felt a surge of relief.

The woman was in her middle twenties and very beautiful, with dark hair drawn back behind her neck. She wore a walking costume of fine navy tweed with a three-quarter-length skirt, and a pretty round hat with tiny fabric flowers clustered on it. One gloved hand rested on her parasol.

The man had risen to his feet as I entered. He was perhaps four or five years older than the woman, also dark, but with a rather hawklike face where hers was oval. It might have been a forbidding face, except that his smile was warm and his eyes the merriest I had ever seen. He wore a light-gray suit of fine worsted, beautifully cut, a gay fancy waistcoat, and carried a short thick cane.

It was a long time since I had worn clothes as fine as the young woman wore, or even seen clothes of such quality as the man wore. In my old skirt and jersey I might have felt at a great disadvantage, but I did not, and was pleased by that.

The man said, "Good afternoon. My name is Gideon Sumner, and this is my sister, Belinda."

I bowed slightly to the lady and said,

"How do you do? Please sit down, Mr. Sumner."

"Thank you."

I moved to the other bed locker and Maria followed. Mr. Galletti said to me, "If a private matter is to be discussed, perhaps you prefer us to leave you with this lady and gentleman, Chantal?"

Because I knew him well I could tell that beneath his usual calm manner he was nervous, so I smiled and said quickly, "No, please stay, Mr. Galletti. It can't be anything private."

Belinda Sumner said, "It may well be private, if you are who we think you are, my dear." Her voice was soft and rather deep, her eyes friendly. I felt my stomach tighten at her words, but shook my head stubbornly and said, "I want Mr. Galletti and Maria to stay."

Gideon Sumner took something from his pocket, an oblong of white card, looked at it carefully, then lifted his eyes to study me. I realized he was holding a photograph. After a moment he leaned forward and handed it to me with an apologetic smile. "It isn't very much like you now, but the features are quite distinct."

I looked at myself as I had been six years ago, and remembered the photograph being taken. Mr. Taylor, the vicar, had called to take tea with my governess. I could not remember which governess it was at that time, for there had been a succession of them. Few could put up for long with a spoiled creature likely to throw an inkpot when she flew into a temper. On that day the vicar had brought his new camera, and we had gone into the garden for him to take some photographs. I could remember the dress I wore. It had been of pale-yellow watered silk with pleated shoulders and cuffs. I was standing beside an oak tree, one hand resting against the trunk, and I was scowling. The picture did not show that I was pale and spotty, but it showed clearly enough that I was fat and unpleasant.

Beside me Maria stared down at the photograph and said in a surprised whisper, "Why it *is* like you when you first came, Chantal. I'd forgotten."

Mr. Galletti said, "Please do not interfere, Maria."

I handed the photograph back and said, "What is it you want, Mr. Sumner?"

"I would like to confirm that you are the girl in the photograph," he said politely.

"I'm another girl."

A sparkle of enjoyment showed in his eyes, and he exchanged a quick glance with his sister. It was as if they had realized that their task was not to be made easy, and in some strange way they rather respected me for it.

"Yes," he agreed amiably, "I realize that in a sense you're a different girl now. Let me put it another way. Your real name is Roberta Armitage, is it not?"

"No."

He glanced at Mr. Galletti, who said quietly, "I have no answers for you, sir. I do not know them. But I know Chantal does not lie."

Gideon Sumner looked at me again. "Will you tell me your name, please?"

"My name is Chantal."

He smiled. "But that is a stage name, I believe?"

"Everybody calls me Chantal."

"I see. And do you say that your true name is *not* Roberta Armitage?"

We were fencing, and I knew that I must lose in the end, but I was stubbornly determined to put up a struggle. "It is not my true name," I said.

For a moment he seemed startled and at a loss. "Will you tell me your true name?" he asked at last.

"I have no true name, Mr. Sumner."

"Ah!" The dark eyes in the hawk face sparkled again as understanding dawned. "Would it be better to say that for thirteen years you *believed* your true name to be Roberta Armitage?"

Belinda Sumner gave a little laugh of delight. "Well done, Chantal! It's not often I see my bumptious brother even briefly put out of countenance, as he was just now."

Her brother rested his hand on her arm and said, "Don't be a wretch, Belinda." But he was still looking at me with a question in his lively eyes, waiting for my answer.

The silence grew heavy and at last I said, "Mr. Sumner, if I were the person

170

you think I am, what would you have to say to me?"

His face became serious. "If you are the girl who once believed herself to be Roberta Armitage, only child of Charles Armitage, of Farleigh Hall in the county of Surrey, then I would have much to tell you."

I said slowly, "Perhaps this girl would not wish to know, Mr. Sumner."

"Perhaps. But part of what I have to tell concerns a false belief she has held for the past few years. I think she would wish to know the truth."

"A . . . false belief?"

"Yes. Concerning herself and her parents. It's a very remarkable story. Perhaps it would help if I told you what I know about the girl in the photograph, and then you can decide whether or not you are the same girl."

I nodded and said from a dry throat, "Yes, if you please."

"Well . . . let us begin not quite at the beginning. Roberta Armitage came to Farleigh Hall when she was a few days old. Her parents were Charles Armitage, a wealthy landowner whose hobby was to travel a great deal, and his young wife, Lucille, who had most tragically died in childbirth. It seems clear that Roberta grew up a lonely child. She had everything material she could have wished for, plenty of servants to attend upon her, but no family love or affection. Charles Armitage spent much of his time abroad, and when he was at home he paid little attention to his daughter. Some say that he could not forgive her for being the cause of his wife's death."

Gideon Sumner's hand moved in a little questioning gesture. "You will understand I have spent considerable time making inquiries of those who knew or served Charles Armitage and his daughter?"

When I did not speak he continued. "The nannie who had charge of her in early childhood was monstrously unfit for such an occupation, by all accounts. Roberta Armitage grew up lonely, spoiled, and rebellious. Without friends, and generally disliked."

"There was Adam," I whispered without thinking, and then realized I had made an admission, but Gideon Sumner did not seize upon it. He nodded and said, "Yes. The old man in charge of the gardens was her one friend, it seems, and the only person for whom she had any affection."

Belinda Sumner said, "Dear Gideon, is it necessary to paint such an unpleasant picture?"

"I'm sorry." He gave me an apologetic smile. "I feel bound to paint the picture as it was revealed to me, for this explains what came later, when Roberta was thirteen and her father died of malaria in India."

The barriers were down now, and the gates of memory I had closed upon the past were open. I sat looking into myself, remembering the day when Miss Lipton had come to the stables to tell me that my father was dead, remembering the shame and self-loathing I felt when I realized that I had been more greatly moved by old Adam's death, six months before.

Gideon Sumner was saying, "Perhaps in some degree Charles Armitage had been aware how neglectful he had been of his only child, for at least he did not fail in making ample provision for her in his will. His whole fortune was left to her in trust, with the Trustee Department of a bank appointed to act as executor and trustee. He had other relatives, a brother and two sisters, but Roberta had rarely if ever seen them. The brother was an Army officer serving in Egypt, one sister had married and emigrated to South Africa, the other was married to a man in the Colonial Service, in Kenya."

Gideon Sumner reached into the inner pocket of his jacket and drew out a stiff brown envelope. 'It was several weeks later, while the will was being proved, that a letter arrived for Charles Armitage and was passed unopened to the solicitor who was winding up his affairs. It had been sent by another solicitor, practicing in Canterbury, and with it was a document written by a woman called Daisy Minchin, with instructions that it be sent to Mr. Charles Armitage in the event of her death, which had just occurred."

I was gazing at the envelope in his hands as if mesmerized, and within me I could feel every nerve growing so taut that it was like physical pain. The envelope was long and bulky, large enough to contain the five thick, laboriously written foolscap sheets I had once held in my hands and which had shattered my life — or so I thought then. It had been a life scarcely worth living, but that realization had come later. I felt now that if Gideon Sumner drew out those foolscap sheets, everything within me would snap. It seemed suddenly very hot in the little room, and I could not get enough air.

He said, "Perhaps for a moment I should go back to the very beginning now, to the time when Roberta Armitage was born. It happened when Charles and Lucille Armitage were completing their return from a journey abroad. They had landed at Folkestone and were traveling home by the night train. Soon after leaving Folkestone, Mrs. Armitage was seized by labor pains. The baby was coming earlier than expected."

He hesitated and looked at Mr. Galletti. "Your granddaughter is young, sir. Perhaps you think this subject indelicate for her ears?"

"Maria is of circus stock," Mr. Galletti said simply. "We do not consider the birth of a child indelicate, Mr. Sumner." He looked at me. "But if Chantal wishes, my granddaughter and I will withdraw."

"No," I said quickly, finding my voice with an effort. "You have the right to hear everything, Mr. Galletti. You've never asked, but now I want you to know."

"As you wish, my dear."

He looked at Gideon Sumner, who said, "Well, to make a long story short, Charles Armitage stopped the train at a small station in Kent. It was well past midnight. A carriage was found to take his wife to a hospital, but there was no time to complete the journey. They stopped on the road, by a small farm, and there in one of the bedrooms with a local doctor who had been hurriedly summoned from the village, the daughter of Charles and Lucille Armitage was born. A baby girl."

It was very quiet in the wagon. Even the background noises of the circus seemed to have dwindled to silence, and it was as if we were alone in the world. Belinda Sumner sat with head bowed, her face grave now. Mr. Galletti had closed his eyes, as if to see more clearly the story that was being told. I was holding Maria's arm, and her hand was clasped over mine as she sat tensely beside me.

Gideon Sumner said quietly, "Mrs. Armitage was very ill and could not be moved, neither could she feed her baby. A wet nurse was needed, and now at last came a stroke of good fortune, for in that same farmhouse, in another room, was a young woman named Elizabeth Martin who had borne a child only the day before, also a girl baby." He paused, and looked at me steadily. "One of those babies was you, Chantal."

There was no doubt in his face now, and I nodded reluctantly. It was pointless to fence with him further. He inclined his head and said, "Thank you. And now I think the rest of the story is best told by this letter." He drew the folded sheets of paper from the envelope he held, and as he did so I came to my feet, saying breathlessly, "Please. I know the letter."

He looked up quickly. "Lord, you're pale as a ghost, young lady. Do you wish me not to read this out?"

"Yes. I mean, no. I want Mr. Galletti to know, but I — I must go outside for a little while." I was rubbing my chest with the heel of my hand, almost gasping with the effort of dragging sufficient air into my lungs. Gideon Sumner, his sister, and Mr. Galletti all started to rise as if to help me, but I whispered, "No! Please, *no*. I'll be all right, if you'll just excuse me for a few minutes."

"Of course," Gideon Sumner said gently. "But, Chantal" — he held up the folded papers — "remember that this tells the story as you know it. My sister and I have come to tell you more, and what we have to tell is a far happier story."

I scarcely took in his words, but mumbled, "Yes," then turned and almost ran down the steps from the wagon, gulping air. Somehow, in that crowded little room with everything pressing in upon me, I had felt that it must be dark outside, and now I was foolishly surprised to find the afternoon sun still shining down. Maria was with me, standing in front of me as my chest heaved, her hands under my ribs, lifting rhythmically in the manner we used in ground practice if one of us took a hard tumble and was winded.

"It's all right," I panted as the stricture of my chest began to ease. "I'll just walk for a little while. You go back in, *carissima.*"

"No," she snapped fiercely. "I don't care about who you were or anything they say. I don't understand it anyway. You're our Chantal, that's all. Why must they come here and make you so upset?"

"I don't know why they've come. Please don't talk to me for a little while, Maria. I just want to walk and think."

"I won't talk."

I turned to move slowly away from the wagons, and as I did so all awareness of my surroundings faded. Time rolled swiftly backwards, and I was thirteen again, wearing my dark dress with the jet mourning brooch pinned to it, and sitting in the musty-smelling office of Mr. Blythe, of Carstairs, Blythe and Carstairs,

Solicitors and Commissioners for Oaths.

Mr. Blythe, a thin man with a very long face, sat at his desk, looking at me over the top of his pince-nez spectacles. To my left and a little behind me sat Miss Lipton, my latest governess, hands folded on her lap, uttering no sound and looking straight ahead with pursed lips, pretending not to hear all that was being said. To one side of her stood a young man who had shown us into the office. He wore a dark suit and a wing collar, like Mr. Blythe, and I vaguely imagined him to be an assistant or junior lawyer of some kind.

A lean man with thinning hair and a sallow face stood with his back to the coal fire. Although the day was warm he had not taken off the Prefect he wore, a single-breasted overcoat with side pleats, but had unbuttoned it and stood with his hands linked beneath it behind his back. This, I had learned, was Major Armitage, on leave from India to attend to family matters arising from the death of his brother. He had been the only one of the family able to attend the funeral of Charles Armitage, who had been buried where he died, in India.

Mr. Blythe was saying, "You suggest, then, Major Armitage, that I now give the Minchin statement to Miss — ah — to the child so that she may read it?"

The lean man nodded, fingering his small mustache. "Certainly," he boomed in a penetrating voice. "Don't like verbal orders. Get 'em on paper, have 'em read, then call for questions. Simplest way. Same thing here. All on paper. No need to waste time with a lot of jabber."

"Very good, Major." Mr. Blythe reached a long arm across the desk and handed to me some sheets of foolscap pinned together at one corner. "You understand, Miss — ah — young lady, that you are of course a minor, and therefore have no entitlement to read this document or to ask questions. However, in the — ah — very unusual circumstances, Major Armitage, as representing the Armitage family, has very kindly suggested that you be permitted to do so, in order that you may understand — um — certain matters which will — ah — drastically affect your future."

181

He got up, unfolding his long form slowly, and paced across to the fire, where he and Major Armitage engaged in a low-voiced conversation. I glared at the papers. I had been glaring ever since we entered the office, because I was nervous. The top sheet was dated December 14, 1897. The writing was poorly formed but had evidently been inscribed slowly and with great care, for it was very clear and with few misspellings. I guessed that many of the longer words had been looked up in a dictionary. After one quick glance down the page I closed my ears to the background murmur of conversation between the two men and settled down to read, apprehensively but with no idea of what to expect.

I am Daisy Minchin of Five Elms Farm near Barham, Kent. I was a housemaid to Mr. and Mrs. Leonard Martin in Chatham for ten years, and I knew their daughter Elizabeth from when she was small. Then I got married and my Husband rented this farm. Elizabeth came to us becorse she was going to have a baby and there was nowhere else to go. Her mother and father never wanted to see her again after she ran off with John Kirkby. It was in July 1885 she came to us and she was Twenty Two. John Kirkby was in the navy and he was at some foreign place called Malta I think but he was going to leave the navy and do something else so he could be with Elizabeth she told us. She did not tell him about the baby becorse she did not want him to wory.

It was a girl and the day after it was born sombody woke us up in the night. It was Mr. and Mrs. Armitage. His name was Charles and her name was Luceel it sounded like. They had come from Folkestone on their way home and she was having a baby too only it was early. So they stopped the train at Barham and took a carriage to go somwhere to a hospital I suppose but the pains got close and they nocked at our door for help. We took her in and she had the baby.

It was her first and it was a little girl too. Mrs. A. was not a strong lady and took it very bad. We got the doctor and he said she must not be moved and he kept coming and doing all he could for her but she kept getting weaker. He asked Elizabeth to feed the baby until Mr. A. could get a wet nurse becorse she had plenty of milk and so she did that. Dr. Foreman said Mr. A. would pay her and she was glad of that becorse she did not have much money but she would have done it anyway.

Then a letter with a foreign stamp came for Elizabeth. She had wrote and told John Kirkby she was staying with us but not saying about the baby. This letter was from an officer who said he was sory to tell her John was dead of some fever they called Malta Fever. Elizabeth went funny like in a dayze and kept saying What shall I do? and the same day Mrs. A.s baby died. I think something was wrong with it but I dont know what. It was dredful with everything hapening at once and Elizabeth so hart-broke with her baby's Father dead. I tried to comfort her and then we talked about what to do and we told Dr. Foreman it was the other baby that died I mean Elizabeths baby. He did not know the diference becorse he had hardly seen them what with being so busy trying to save Mrs. A. I know it was a bad thing and God forgive us but I said Its better than the baby going into a Home. I was in a Home and it is very hard so that was what we did. Two days later Mrs. A. died and Mr. A. took her home to be burried and a Nannie and a wet nurse came to take the baby he thought was his. Elizabeth cried something terrible. While Mr. A. was here he did not hardly ever speak and did not look at the baby once becorse he was so taken up with his wife I think. When they took the baby I was afraid in case he did not like it becorse of his poor wife dying but it was too late to do anything then. When Elizabeth got better she went away and we did not see her again but we had a letter from her nearly every Christmas and it was from somewhere foreign but diferent places. Then last Christmas she never wrote and after that my Husband read in the paper about that ship being sunk in a storm when it was coming from Eegypt I think. It went down and lots of people drownded and Elizabeths name was in a thing called a Casualty List.

What I have wrote here all hapened over twelve years ago and it has been on my mind ever since. The doctor says I have got bad lungs but I will be alreight but I know I wont and he is only saying that. I have not got long to go so I am writing this now and I will tell my Husband to give it to a solicitor to send to Mr. A. when I am dead. I keep thinking and thinking and I hope I am not doing another bad thing but I dont want to die without telling the truth. I will get Mr. Davis and Mr. Tucker to witness my signature on this so it is all done proper but I will not let them see the letter. All this is true and I swear it by Almighty God. Amen.

Long after I had finished reading I sat staring blindly down at the papers in my hands. My mind was in chaos, and through that chaos stabbed a red-hot skewer of pain such as I had never known. Elizabeth Martin, my mother, had given her newborn baby away forever. All my life I had clung to the thought that if only my mother had not died when I was born she would have given me the love and care I craved. Now I knew that the young woman in the portrait which hung in the great drawing room at Farleigh Hall was not my mother, any more than Charles Armitage was my father. I was the natural child of a man my true mother had "run off" with. She had lived, but had abandoned me.

Mr. Blythe was saying, "Have you finished, Miss — ah — young lady?"

Vaguely I realized that he had been avoiding the use of my name because it was not my name. I was not the child of Charles and Lucille Armitage. When I lifted my head the room was a blur. I could not speak but managed to nod. A booming voice said something about "... bit of a shock," and then, "thimbleful of brandy in half a glass of water, Blythe."

The document was taken from my hands and a glass was held to my lips. I drank a little, then pushed the glass away. With the greatest effort I had ever made in my life, I slowly collected my scattered wits. The room came into focus again, and I saw the young assistant or clerk put the glass down on the desk before moving away behind me to his place in the background. Mr. Blythe had not moved from his desk. Still standing with his back to the fire, Major Armitage brayed, "Feeling better, girl? Nasty business, I must say. Can't be helped, though." He switched his gaze to Miss Lipton. "Now see here, young woman, I've got a question for you and I don't want coy blushes or any nonsense of that sort. Does this girl understand what's meant by an illegitimate child?"

Behind me I heard Miss Lipton give a little gasp. It was several seconds before she said in that tight, disapproving voice I knew so well, "I am very much afraid she does, Major Armitage. Roberta has been most unwisely permitted free use of her father's library, and has always been allowed to read the daily newspaper uncensored. Also, since the servants are undisciplined, she will have heard all kinds of unsavory gossip from the housemaids. In my opinion, her knowledge of unpleasant wordly matters is far too extensive for so young a girl. I have made every effort to discourage her but she is extremely headstrong —"

"Thank you, Miss Lipton, we needn't bother with all that," Major Armitage broke in brusquely. He looked at me again. "You understand that you are illegitimate and a changeling? That you are not the daughter of my brother or his wife?"

The words hit me like sharp stones, but now a fiery anger was boiling up within me. I was able to keep my head and meet his gaze as I said, "Yes. I understand."

"Good. Good." He fingered his mustache again. "All right, you carry on, Blythe."

Mr. Blythe lowered his lanky frame into the chair and took off his pince-nez, looking cautiously at the Major. "Quite so," he said. "But I require your instructions, Major Armitage."

"Eh? I'd have thought it was obvious enough. Poor Charles died without issue. This unfortunate girl isn't his daughter and isn't Roberta Armitage, so she can't inherit. Has no standing at all. Bank trustees aren't going to act for the wrong person, are they?"

"Indeed no, Major Armitage. That would be quite out of order. Of course, there is the point that your brother *believed* her to be his daughter, but I fancy this would carry little weight. Also, the Minchin document could be challenged."

"By whom? This girl? Damn costly business, and who's going to act for her?"

"Well, she has nobody, of course. I am simply pointing out the possibilities."

"And what would the outcome of a

challenge be, in your view?''

Mr. Blythe tapped the document with his long bony finger and shook his head. ''I am certain it would fail. The Minchin confession will stand up.''

''Then stop splitting hairs, man. Tell the girl what her position is.''

''Am I to take it that you see no reason for the Armitage family to assume any responsibility for her? I am not suggesting that you should, Major, merely inquiring.''

Major Armitage stared at him with a baffled air. ''I suppose a fellow has to expect stupid questions from lawyers. This child was foisted upon poor Charles for thirteen years. Why the devil should the family continue to have her foisted upon *us?*''

I stood up, keeping my eyes on the solicitor, and said furiously, ''I don't want to be foisted upon anyone! Will you please tell me what my situation is?''

I heard a snort from Major Armitage. ''Hoity-toity!'' he boomed indignantly. ''You were right, Miss Lipton. She's a damn sight too uppity. Girl of thirteen?

Never heard anything like it."

I did not look at him. Mr. Blythe rested his elbows on his desk and steepled his fingers. "I am bound to tell you," he said reprovingly, "that from this moment you are — ah — without family and without resources of any kind, Miss — ah — young lady. Charles Armitage's estate will be divided between his brother and two sisters, as provided in his will in the event of his daughter predeceasing him. Major Armitage would be quite within his rights if he turned you out into the street as you stand. However" — he glanced sideways — "I do not imagine he will take such precipitate action as that."

"Certainly not," Major Armitage grunted. "Officer and a gentleman, I hope. Wouldn't do a thing like that. Matter of fact, can't help feeling sorry for the girl, even if she is damned insolent. Tell you what, Blythe. I'll give you a month to find some sort of home or orphanage who'll take her in. Out-of-pocket expenses on my account. Meantime she can stay on at Farleigh Hall. Can't say fairer than that."

"Most generous of you, Major." Mr. Blythe nodded obsequiously.

"Must do the decent thing. Not her fault, I suppose. And you'll give the staff a month's notice, as instructed?"

"Quite so."

"Well, that's about all then." He moved to take his hat and gloves from the rack in the corner. "Funny business, eh? Poor old Charles. Remember him saying to me once that he never could understand about the child's red hair. Thought it must have been a throwback. Well, there you are. Get in touch with me at my club, Blythe. No, no, I'll see myself out."

I was still standing with my eyes on Mr. Blythe when I heard the door close behind me.

From somewhere nearby sounded the ponderous thudding of a traction engine, and I came back to the present to find myself walking slowly over the thick grass in the field where the horses grazed. Maria was beside me, holding my hand tightly. I stopped, blinking a little and staring about me, then said, "How long have we been walking?"

"Only twice round the field. But I'm glad I was with you, Chantal. You'd have walked into the ditch, I think."

"I'm sorry, *piccina*. I was miles away. Years away."

"Yes. But you look better now."

"I feel better." It was true. Reliving that scene seemed to have purged much of the tension from me. In a way it was like the occasion when I had fallen from the trapeze and then continued the performance. I drew a deep breath, smiled, and said, "We'd better go back."

Mr. Galletti was waiting for us outside the wagon. He looked at me anxiously, then relief showed in his face as he said, "You are feeling more yourself, Chantal?"

"Yes, Mr. Galletti. You know what's in the letter now?"

"Mr. Sumner read it out."

"I did tell you the truth that day, when I said nobody would care if you took me with you."

"Of course, I have never believed otherwise. It is of no interest to me to learn the reason now. I find it only sad."

"It's all long ago. Has Mr. Sumner said anything more?"

"No. He is waiting for you. I have made tea for him and his sister."

When we entered the little sitting room Gideon and Belinda Sumner were sipping tea from our best cups, the ones we used only at Christmas and Easter. I felt quite calm now, and apologized for my behavior. Gideon Sumner set down his cup and smiled. "We can well understand. And now are you ready to hear the rest of my story? The part you don't yet know?"

"If you please."

"Well, it's quickly told. John Kirkby, your father, came of a wealthy family. His grandfather built up a substantial shipping line, and his father, James Kirkby, continued it. John was the youngest of three brothers, and the only one who refused to enter the family business, much to his father's anger. He joined the Navy, and in Chatham he met your mother, Elizabeth. They fell in love . . . and they married."

"Married?" I echoed the word wonderingly. "But I thought . . ."

195

"Yes. They were married in London by special license, and nobody knew except two young naval officers, friends of your father, who were witnesses at the ceremony. You were not born out of wedlock, Chantal. You have nothing to be ashamed of in that respect."

He had misunderstood the quick happiness which must have shown in my face, and I said quickly, "I never felt ashamed, Mr. Sumner. I felt hurt and angry because I thought my father didn't care enough about my mother to marry her. Why did they keep it a secret?"

"For several reasons. Elizabeth Martin was not quite twenty-one, and her parents were opposed to the marriage. So was John Kirkby's father. And a young naval officer was not permitted to marry without permission from his commanding officer, which would never be given in the face of parental opposition. But I think we have to understand that this young couple were very deeply in love. Also, that your father was not a man to be deterred from a course he had decided upon."

Gideon Sumner's eyes glinted with quick

humor. "He had red hair, like his daughter, and a similar temperament, I imagine. He did not intend to wait two years, until he returned from his tour of foreign service, before marrying the girl who had captured his heart."

"Why did she have no money?" I asked.

"Most officers need a private income to augment what they earn. John Kirkby had nothing. And it was his intention to save every penny during his two-year tour, so that he could buy himself out of the Navy. Elizabeth had assured him she would need no money, since she had learned to work a typewriting machine and was certain she could find work in London to support herself."

"I see." With one part of my mind I was trying to picture my mother and father at that time, and to imagine their feelings as they faced such problems. It seemed to me that they had been foolishly impulsive not to wait a little while. Clearly they had not meant to conceive a baby during the brief days or weeks they were together, but such intentions could easily fail. Then I remembered that I had yet to learn, if I was ever to learn, how strongly people in love could feel. In any event, I was the last person in the world to judge anyone as foolishly impulsive, for this was my own greatest fault.

Another part of my mind was puzzling over the mystery of how Gideon Sumner had uncovered all these secrets from the past. But this question could wait, there was something more important I wanted to know.

I said, "What did you mean a little while ago, Mr. Sumner, when you said you had a far happier story to tell? I'm glad my mother was married, but it makes little difference." My voice began to shake a little. "I was her baby, and she gave me away to other people. Oh, I know she thought it was best for me, but I still can't understand. I'm not a very good person, but if I had a baby I would never let anyone else take it. I might steal, or do anything, I don't know . . . but I'd care for that baby myself, whatever happened. When I discovered she'd given me away I . . . I think I hated my mother for not wanting me. I know that's unfair, and I'm ashamed of it, but I couldn't help myself. And ever since, I couldn't bear to think of it."

Gideon Sumner sighed and shook his head. "Poor Chantal," he said. "And poor Elizabeth Martin. I'm afraid Daisy Minchin was to blame. She was able to read and write, but had no gift for clarity." He took out the foolscap sheets again and unfolded them. "She has been speaking of Elizabeth and herself, and goes on, '. . . then we talked about what to do and we told Dr. Foreman it was the other baby that died . . .'"

He looked up from the letter. "But when she says 'we' she isn't referring to herself and Elizabeth. She is referring to herself and *her husband,* who hasn't been mentioned since the early part of the letter. The fact is that Daisy Minchin and her husband made that decision to change the babies . . . *and Elizabeth did not know!* Newborn babies are much alike, and your mother was dazed by the news of her husband's death, remember."

My throat seemed to have closed up,

and it was hard to speak. At last I managed to whisper, "How do you know this, Mr. Sumner?"

"Very simply. I've talked to Albert Minchin, Daisy's husband. He's in his sixties, but still hale and hearty. I hope one day soon you will talk to him yourself. I gather that it was Daisy who really made the decision, and she certainly carried the burden of it for the rest of her life. But you have to remember she believed Elizabeth's baby to be illegitimate, and that may well have affected her decision. Whether or no, Albert is quite adamant that neither then nor till her death at sea twelve years later did Elizabeth Martin ever have the slightest suspicion that her own baby had lived."

SIX

I sat with eyes closed, feeling the tears well from under my lids and run down my cheeks. Then Maria drew my head down on her shoulder and I heard Mr. Galletti say, "Perhaps we might leave her with Maria for a little while. Would you and your sister care to stroll with me for a few minutes, Mr. Sumner?"

"I think it better still if we took the matter no further today," said Gideon Sumner, and I heard the sounds of him getting to his feet. "Chantal has heard enough for the moment, and needs time to collect herself. Belinda and I are staying in Ingolstadt, so perhaps we could return tomorrow, Mr. Galletti, if that would be convenient. Would you care to walk with us to our carriage?"

They left without disturbing me with

polite goodbyes, for which I was grateful. Maria had her arms round me and was patting my back, murmuring words of comfort in mingled English and Italian as if soothing a baby. After a minute or two the tears stopped. I sat up, dabbing my eyes, exhaled a long breath, and said, "Oh dear. I don't know what they can think of me. I hate girls who snivel."

Maria was looking at me with wide eyes. "I've never seen you cry like that before, Chantal. Never. Is it something good or something bad? I was so confused I gave up trying to understand."

"It's good, *mia cara*. I mean, it's good in a lot of ways, if you're as silly as I am. I thought my father had run away with my mother and then just left her without marrying her, and I thought my mother had given me away as a baby. Oh, I know it was all in the past and didn't really matter, but . . . well, the man I always thought was my father didn't want me, and then when I found out about my real mother I thought she didn't want me either, and I couldn't bear it."

"I don't think that's silly. If nobody

wanted me, I think I'd die."

I smiled at her. "I'm glad I didn't do that. I ran away instead."

"Yes. And Grandfather found you. How did that happen, Chantal?"

"Has he never told you?"

"No. I remember we were on the road to some English port to cross the Channel, and Grandfather went for a walk when we stopped after the day's journey. When he came back you were with him. He just said, 'This little English girl is going to live with us. She has no name, so we must find one for her."

"I'd run away two days before, when the circus was at Somervale, not far from where I lived. I just took some breeches belonging to the gardener's boy, and my oldest coat, and I hid in one of the baggage wagons."

Maria said, "Wasn't it horribly frightening for you?"

"Yes, I was terrified. It was so noisy on the move and so quiet when we stopped, and dark all the time. But I was more terrified of going back to the people I'd left." I gave a shaky little laugh. "I was such a fool I hadn't even taken any food or water with me. That afternoon, when your grandfather found me by the brook, I'd climbed out when nobody was looking to find something to drink.''

Maria giggled. ''Grandfather called you 'this little English girl' but you didn't seem little to us, you were fat. Leo only called you Chantal as a joke, because it was the name of a famous trapeze artist in Grandfather's day.''

''Yes. He told me so later, when he'd learned a little English and I'd learned a little Italian, and we were having one of our quarrels. I think that's what made me more determined than ever that one day I'd work on the trapeze.''

''Did Grandfather bring you to live with us so Leo and I would learn to speak good English?''

''No, he was glad of that but it wasn't the reason. He took me in because . . . well, I suppose because he's the kindest man in the world and because he's not like other people. He's a philosopher and he has strange ideas. You know what I mean.''

I had not thought about that day for several years, but it came back to me sharply now. I saw myself sitting near the brook with my back against a tree, miserably afraid, hunger gnawing at my stomach. I was dirty and my hair hung in tangled lumps. The white-haired old man with the funny accent sat beside me, slowly filling his pipe. We had been talking for several minutes. When he asked a question he did so diffidently, almost apologetically, and would then sit considering my answer patiently.

"To where are you running, signorina?"

"Anywhere. I shall have to find work. I thought of asking for work on a farm, but I'm afraid they'll send for the police to take me home."

"That is probable, I think."

"Please . . . could I work in your circus?"

A pause. "It is not my circus, and I do not think you are accustomed to hard work, signorina."

"I'll have to learn." My voice was shrill with desperation. "I don't care if I work till my hands are raw. I *won't* go back! If they make me, I'll run away again."

He looked at me for a long time, then began to light his pipe. "Children sometimes become angry with their parents, but these things pass. To run away is not a good answer."

"I haven't any parents and I'm not running away from anyone." I wiped my grimy face with a handkerchief that was scarcely less grimy. I felt tired, and ill, and breathless, and frightened, but I knew I would not go back. I would go on till I died of hunger or exposure rather than that.

The old Italian beside me said, "Will you tell me why you are running away from nobody?"

"Because they're going to put me in a home."

"Who are 'they'?"

"The solicitor and a man who's the brother of the man I thought was my father. He thought so, too. Everybody did, but he wasn't my father, and now they've just found out, so they're going to put me in a home. I'm nobody at all, and

I haven't any parents or relations or friends, so there isn't anybody to care about me running away.''

There was a very long pause, then my companion from the circus said quietly, ''Are you telling me the whole truth, signorina? Are you saying that nobody will even trouble to look for you?''

I was about to say yes, but those gentle dark eyes were looking at me, and after a moment I said reluctantly, ''I suppose they must have told the police I've disappeared, but that's all. They won't search for me, any more than they'd search for an orphan girl who ran away from a home. That's what I am now, really, except that I ran away before they put me in a home.''

There was another silence, lasting for several minutes. I did not feel any waning of hope, for I had not truly held more than a shred of hope that this old foreign circus man would help me. I sat there numbly, no longer even feeling despair, for hunger and weariness had taken me past that now. The stolen breeches were too tight, my blouse was like a dishrag, the folded coat on which I sat was too warm to wear now but too light to keep me warm at night. My hands and hair were smeared with black grease picked up from the axle when I had crawled out under the wagon to avoid being seen. My soft body was bruised from sleeping on a hard box in the baggage wagon. I felt like some battered toad crouching under a leaf — fat, ugly, spotted, and slimy, the most unattractive human being in the world. But I was not going back. There was nowhere to go back to.

The man beside me knocked out his pipe on the heel of his shoe and murmured as if thinking aloud, "The plant needs soil in which to grow. To a child, the family is the soil. Without it he grows stunted or badly shaped. To permit this is a sin against life, a sin which will not be forgiven. And a man must accept what is laid before him."

He rose to his feet. "My family is smaller than it once was. Come and eat with us, signorina, with little Maria and Leo. Then let us see what can be done."

Old Adam had been a friend, but Mr. Galletti was the first person in my life I had ever loved, and Maria was the second. As I came out of my reverie she was saying eagerly, ". . . and think how exciting it is, Chantal! Now you will be able to find your real mother, and —"

"No, *piccina,* no. Didn't you hear? Oh, of course, you weren't there while Mr. Sumner read the letter. My mother isn't alive now. She was on a ship that sank in a storm."

"Oh, Chantal, I'm sorry."

"Yes. It would have been wonderful to find her. At least, I suppose so . . . I mean, if we liked each other. It's hard to tell, isn't it?"

"Poof! Why are you always so unromantic, Chantal? I could make a beautiful story about you finding her and throwing yourself into her arms and —"

"Yes, Maria, yes, I know you could. You make up splendid stories."

"I'll make up one tonight before I go to sleep. How does Mr. Sumner know all about you and what happened? And why has he come here, do you think?"

"I've been wondering the same thing. I expect he'll tell me tomorrow."

The performance I gave that evening was far from my best. I made no bad mistakes, but my timing was poor and my twin act with Maria would have been very untwinlike if she had not been quick and clever enough to match her movements to mine instead of setting the time herself, as she usually did.

Long after she had chattered herself to sleep that night I lay awake thinking about Gideon Sumner. Now that I had time to reflect, I realized how kindly and well he had managed his difficult task. Quite apart from what more he might have to tell me, I looked forward to seeing him again. He was from my own country, which I had not seen for nearly five years now, and I liked the humor that so often sparkled in his eyes.

It was odd, I thought, that in only a few weeks two Englishmen had come into my life. Suddenly I realized just how much I had missed Martin since his disappearance. I had tried not to think about him, because I could not do so without being touched by the horrible suspicion that he had been responsible for my fall from the trapeze. It was an unwilling suspicion, for I had never been able to imagine why he might do such a thing, unless his mind had been in some way unbalanced by the blow which had taken his memory. In his placid way he had been the best of companions and had seemed to like me quite well. The day we battled with the logjam together had been one of the happiest I had known.

Now, after closing my mind to remembrance of Martin since he had so mysteriously left us, I found as I lay in the darkness that I could not get him out of my thoughts. I began to wonder if I should speak of him to Gideon Sumner, though for what purpose I was not at all clear. It was long after midnight before I slept, and then I woke several times during the night from troubled dreams which faded from my memory even as I opened my eyes.

During the last few minutes of Gideon Sumner's departure that afternoon it had been arranged that he and his sister would not come to the circus to see me next day, but that Mr. Galletti would take me into Ingolstadt, to the hotel where they were staying, for there we could talk in greater privacy and comfort. This had been Mr. Galletti's suggestion, and Gideon Sumner had agreed at once, saying that he would send a carriage for us.

Next morning at nine, with Maria fussing round me anxiously, I put on my best clothes. There was a long skirt in pale gray I had bought in Barcelona a year ago, a wine-colored velvet jacket from Milan, with sleeves puffed and gathered at the shoulders, and kid bootees with high heels and buttons at the sides, rather too tight for me after the comfortable moccasins Old Sven had made, which I used all the time. Beneath the jacket I wore a pretty white blouse belonging to Maria, with a broad ribbon tied in a bow at the neck, matching the jacket. Maria had brushed my short hair till it shone, and on my head was perched a small grey felt hat shaped like a man's Homburg, with a little spray of gray and black feathers pinned to the front. Maria had borrowed this for me from young Mrs. Albertini.

"You look lovely, Chantal," she said, full of excitement as she danced about me, straightening my neck bow or touching a fold of the skirt into place. "Here, put the gloves on. That's right. Oh dear, I do wish we had a parasol for you to carry. Never mind. Now remember to walk with little steps like this — *watch* me, Chantal! Like this. You mustn't go striding along as if you're just about to do a handspring. What are you wearing underneath?"

"My best petticoat and my gray stocking and my *petit caleçon.*"

"Oh dear." She put fingertips to her mouth in distress. "You ought to have corsets and proper drawers."

"The only one with corsets is Solange, and you could get both of us in hers. I don't think I could breathe in corsets my size, anyway."

Maria nodded reluctantly. "We could borrow some drawers for you, though."

"I don't want to. I used to wear them long ago, and they're not nearly as comfortable as *petit caleçon*. Besides,

213

nobody's going to know what I'm wearing underneath, so it doesn't matter."

"I know! I'll borrow the parasol Pepe uses on the slack wire! Ladies are supposed to carry parasols to avoid the sun and keep their faces nice and pale."

I giggled nervously. "Mine's nearly as brown as Rama Singh's. I don't think carrying a parasol will help much now, *carissima*."

Ten minutes later I was in the carriage with Mr. Galletti beside me. He was wearing his best suit. As the carriage rattled down the long winding road, I asked if Gideon Sumner had said anything to indicate what he might have to speak to me about this morning.

Mr. Galletti shook his head. "No, my dear. I did not presume to ask." He smiled. "I think you know it is not my habit to pry or to interfere."

I slipped my arm through his. "Yes. I wish I could say the things I want to say, Mr. Galletti, but words don't seem enough to tell how grateful I've always been to you. Most of all for believing me that day by the stream. I didn't dream you would."

"I believed your eyes, Chantal. They told me your words were true."

"Can you always tell by a person's eyes?"

"Usually, but not always."

"Mr. Sumner has nice eyes. They're so friendly, and they sparkle a lot, don't they?" When Mr. Galletti did not answer I looked at him and said, "Don't you think so?"

"Perhaps. I have a fancy they might look otherwise at other times."

I was a little startled. "Do you mean he's only pretending to be friendly?"

"No, no, child. I did not say that. I meant only that I judge him to be a man of some depth, but what the nature of those depths might be I cannot tell." He paused, then added thoughtfully, "And I would say the same of his sister."

I did not ask Mr. Galletti what he meant, for I knew he would not say anything definite but might well drift into one of his long discourses about the character of the human race contrasted with the characteristics of its individual members, or something of that sort, so I

215

said, "I know you never interfere, but will you give me your advice if I need it?"

"Of course. I am always willing to do that." He smiled again. "Though it is something you have rarely asked. You have a way of meeting your own problems in your own fashion, my dear."

Gideon Sumner and his sister were staying at a fine hotel set on the Danube, and occupied a suite with a pleasant drawing room between their bedrooms. They were waiting in the hotel foyer for our arrival, and greeted us with an easy warmth which helped me to feel less nervous. Their suite was on the second floor, and the drawing room had a large window which opened onto a balcony with a wrought-iron balustrade. Beyond lay the Danube, with boats of all kinds, from little sailing boats to huge barges, passing steadily on their way up or down the river.

On this second meeting with Belinda I found myself a little overawed. She was wearing a rather daring yellow dress with the neck cut in a small V, but without a chemisette of lace or net to cover the top of her chest. She looked very elegant and had an air of easy confidence, but was very friendly toward me. Complimenting me on how well I looked in my nice clothes, she said with a smile that it was hard to believe I could really be the trapeze artist drawn on our circus posters she had seen throughout the town.

I explained that the girl on the poster was just a drawing, and that if it represented anybody it would be Maria, who was the principal performer in our act. Belinda laughed, saying it was still a quite marvelous thing that I had become a circus artist, and asked however long it had taken me to learn how to do tricks on the flying trapeze.

I saw that Gideon Sumner was chatting quietly with Mr. Galletti on the sofa, seemingly in no hurry to come to the point of our visit, and I guessed that he wanted to allow time for me to settle down and feel at home, so I gave my attention to Belinda Sumner and said, "It was almost eighteen months before I became good enough to work before an audience."

"Heavens above! And did you practice every day?"

"Oh, yes. For several hours every day, Miss Sumner."

"Do tell me about it."

"Well . . . at the very beginning Mr. Galletti fixed a long bar at about the same height as my shoulders, and I had to practice turning somersaults round it, and doing simple gymnastics. At the same time there were lots and lots of exercises to make me supple and to get rid of all my fat. Then I moved on to the handsprings and back flips. Maria was a wonderful help."

"Didn't you have a lot of tumbles and bruises?"

"Heaps of them, but nothing serious. I used a safety rope and a waist belt at first, until I learned how to control my body. After that it's really a matter of confidence. Mr. Galletti is the best of all teachers, so I was able to start practice on a low trapeze fairly quickly. But altogether it was nearly a year before I was allowed even to go up the ladder to the trapeze platform in the big top, and another three months before I flew for the first time, with Leo catching me." I paused, then added ruefully, "Except that he didn't. I judged so badly that I simply crashed into him and fell into the net."

"Dear heaven," Belinda Sumner said softly. "Weren't you terrified?"

"Not of falling. I'd spent two whole weeks practicing how to fall into the net. I was terrified of what Leo would say, and Mr. Galletti, but they were both very nice about it. Then I tried again, and Leo caught me. After that it was just a matter of practicing the somersaults and pirouettes in flight, to get the timing right."

She looked at me from beautiful gray eyes in which there was almost a hint of envy, and said, "It must be a wonderful sensation, like nothing else in the world."

"Yes. In the moments when you're flying it is. But there are things that people watching never realize when they see something beautiful, like Maria doing her double. They don't know how much the bar hurts the back of your knees, or how your wrists smart from the catch, and ache from Leo's grip, or how the net stings your back when you dive. I thought about that when Mr. Galletti took us to see some ballet in Rome last year. The dancers seemed to float on their points and made everything look so easy and effortless, but Maria and I kept thinking how their toes must hurt and how their muscles must ache —"

I broke off, suddenly aware that Gideon Sumner and Mr. Galletti had stopped talking and were listening to me. Embarrassment made me flush a little and I said, "I'm sorry. I didn't mean to talk about myself."

"Trust Belinda to pounce on whatever is fascinating," Gideon Sumner said with one of his quick, merry smiles. "I only heard the last part, and I'm longing to hear what went before, but I must be patient. In any event, you mustn't apologize, because you're the very person we're here to talk about, Chantal. Oh, do you wish us to call you that, or should we call you Roberta now?"

"No," I said quickly. "That's a borrowed name. I wasn't given a name by my true parents, so I just want to be Chantal."

"Very well. Now, I've no doubt you have many questions buzzing in your head, but I expect you're wondering above all why I've been searching for the young girl who vanished from Farleigh Hall five years ago. Shall I deal with that first?"

"If you please, Mr. Sumner."

"It's very simple in essence, though not quite so simple in detail. I came because your family asked me to find you."

"My family? But you said both my mother and father were dead."

"I'm speaking of your father's family now. John Kirkby's family. As I said yesterday, he had two brothers. They would be in their late fifties now, since they were considerably older than John, but both died in Hong Kong of food poisoning, so we must go further back, to the father, James Kirkby, who was your grandfather. His brother, Rupert, married a minor member of the European nobility, a Hungarian lady in fact. They produced two sons, who are of course your father's cousins. Do you understand me so far?"

"Yes. I think so. Are these cousins still alive?"

"Very much so. Benedict is a bachelor of fifty odd. Arthur, a year or two younger, is married and has two children. They all live in a very fine house in Dorset, called Wildings. Having sold out the family shipping interest built up by James Kirkby, they are very wealthy indeed. Now, do you remember the name of the solicitors where you were shown Daisy Minchin's letter?"

"Yes, Mr. Sumner. Carstairs, Blythe and Carstairs. It was in Mr. Blythe's office that I first learned I was . . . not who I thought."

"Do you recall a young man who was present in the office during your visit?"

If I had not relived the scene only yesterday I might have had to think hard before answering. As it was, I said, "Well, yes, but he just stood somewhere behind me. I didn't know his name, and I don't remember his face."

"His name was Quillan, an articled clerk who later became a partner in the firm, when Blythe died. It seems that young Quillan was rather moved by your plight, Chantal. He felt that fate and the

Armitage family had been less than gentle with you. There was nothing he could do, of course, but he never forgot that scene. Sympathy apart, it was a strange story, an interesting anecdote to tell at table, perhaps, or at his club, and one that he would sometimes recount during the years that followed."

Gideon Sumner stood up and paced slowly across the room. "Some time ago," he went on, "Quillan happened to tell it when a certain retired naval officer was among the company — and it was then that the fact of your mother's marriage to John Kirkby was revealed."

I said, "You mean the naval officer had known my father, Mr. Sumner?"

"More than that. This man had retired from ill health, not age, and he had been one of the two friends who were witnesses at the marriage. He was no longer bound to secrecy, of course, since both your father and mother were dead. As you can imagine, Quillan was greatly intrigued by this new light on the story. Being a lawyer, he was experienced in ferreting out information, and next day he went along to Somerset House, where records of all births, deaths, and marriages are kept. There, sure enough, he was able to obtain a copy of your parents' marriage certificate, which confirmed the truth of what the naval officer had told him. There was no doubt whatsoever that your mother and father had been married almost a year before you were born, Chantal.''

I knew I would be glad later, but at that moment I could only feel ashamed for all the years through which I had thought myself to be the result of a casual union between a foolish young woman and a man who had used her.

Gideon Sumner moved to the open window and stood leaning against the wall with his head turned to gaze out upon the river. He said, ''Quillan then set about tracking down any close relatives of John Kirkby. Again, it was a simple task for a lawyer. John's father and brothers were dead. His wife, your mother, had been lost at sea. But you, Chantal, his daughter, had run away from Farleigh Hall believing yourself to be an illegitimate outcast without a family. You were lost, but you might well be alive, and by now Quillan felt almost a personal responsibility for the girl he had felt sorry for that day in Mr. Blythe's office, so he determined to take the matter a step further."

I wished now that I had been more aware of the young Mr. Quillan that day. It seemed to me that he had been an unknown friend. Gideon Sumner went on, "He made a careful memorandum of all the facts, and took it to the people who were now your closest relatives, Benedict and Arthur Kirkby. It was a revelation to them, of course. They were amazed, but they were also deeply concerned to think that their cousin's daughter, if she lived, might be . . . well, might be anywhere, living under quite terrible conditions perhaps." He looked towards Mr. Galletti and smiled. "They could not know that in fact she had been well cared for during the years which followed her disappearance."

Mr. Galletti bowed his head slightly in acknowledgment. "Please tell them that to care for Chantal has been a pleasure to me, sir, not a burden."

"Yes, I can see that, Mr. Galletti. Well, to go on with my story, the Kirkby brothers needed no urging from Quillan to decide that every effort must be made to find John's lost daughter . . . and it was then that I came into the picture, almost three months ago now."

Belinda gave me a quick smile and said, "Forgive me for interrupting, dear brother, but I think you should explain your own position before you continue."

"Exactly my intention, dear sister," Gideon Sumner said with a small, mocking bow. "Though I confess I find myself a somewhat difficult man to explain."

"Then I shall do it for you." Belinda looked at me. "Gideon is a fool. We have a London house in Melton Square, and we live very comfortably there during the season, usually wintering abroad. Our parents left us an inheritance sufficient to ensure that Gideon has no need to work. If he were a sensible man, he would marry one of the nice girls I have introduced him to, and settle down. But Gideon is stubborn. He jibs. And he has a fund of restless energy which drives him to undertake what he calls 'interesting little jobs.' Then he's likely to disappear abroad for weeks at a time, leaving me to languish alone at home."

"Oh, come now, Lindy," her brother protested. "You've never languished in your life. And anyway, I brought you along with me on this trip, didn't I?"

"Only because I solved the mystery for you, and insisted, Gideon." Then, to me, "He's hunted for buried treasure on some wretched island. He's carried out what he calls 'a delicate mission' for De Beers, the diamond people in South Africa, about which I know nothing. He's recovered a large sum of money for an American lady who lost it to card sharpers while gambling on an ocean liner. He's been responsible for putting at least three criminals behind bars, to my certain knowledge. And he's — but never mind the rest. To come to the present, Mr. Quillan knew something of Gideon's reputation, and recommended him to Benedict Kirkby for the task of finding you." She looked with laughing challenge at her brother. "Is that a good enough summary, Gideon?"

"Fairly good, Lindy. Except that you're the one who jibs at marrying and settling down. But we can quarrel about that another time." He turned to me. "However, it's perfectly true that Benedict Kirkby asked me to call upon him, told me the story of John Kirkby's marriage to Elizabeth Martin and all that had happened since, and asked me to seek their lost daughter."

I found I had screwed my gloves into a ball, and began to straighten them out as I said, "It must have been hard to know where to start."

"Well, yes. But I began with the newspaper files. There was a report of your disappearance in the local newspaper at the time, and the general belief was that you had run away and come to an unfortunate end, either by accident or, as the journalist put it, by foul misdeed. I sought out and talked to the last of your governesses, I talked to the vicar, to everyone I could find who had known you, even your old nannie — a monster if ever I saw one. And I began to build up a picture of you in my mind."

"Not a very nice picture," I muttered, tugging at my gloves.

"No," he agreed frankly. "But I found myself seeing many reasons to explain the way you had grown up. Then I went to Barham and spoke to Albert Minchin, as I told you yesterday. It was from him I learned that Elizabeth, your mother, had never known that the two babies were changed and that it was her own baby who had survived."

Gideon Sumner moved from the window and began to pace slowly across the room again, head bent, hands deep in his trouser pockets. "This was another startling discovery, but it gave little help in finding you. I went back to Farleigh and explored the district, trying to think which direction you might have taken in running away, and where you might have planned to go. I also returned to the local newspaper files of that time." He shook his head with a rueful smile. "I scarcely knew what I was looking for, Chantal. It seemed unlikely that you had been able to travel a long distance, for you had taken no money. I had to assume that you had come to no harm and were still alive, but in that case why had you not been found within a few days? I suppose I was looking for some hint, however slight, which might be helpful, and I failed. But fortunately Belinda was with me on this occasion, and she succeeded."

He smiled at his sister. "You go on, Lindy."

Belinda Sumner said, "Perhaps a woman's instinct is better than a man's logic, dear brother." She looked at me and fluttered an eyelid. "In a local newspaper, a week before you disappeared, there was a big advertisement, half a page, for a circus at Somervale, only a few miles south. The circus closed and moved on its way the same day that you ran away from Farleigh Hall. As soon as I saw that I said to Gideon, *'The circus! She must have gone with the circus!'* So then we set about tracking down Kayser's Giant Circus, though I hope Gideon will confess that he had doubts about my inspiration."

I said, "Well . . . you were right, Miss Sumner. That was how it happened."

"And Mr. Galletti took you in?"

"Yes. I told him there was nobody to care what happened to me, and that I would be put in a home, and he believed me."

Gideon Sumner nodded. "You were fortunate, Chantal," he said quietly. "And I must agree with Belinda, I did doubt her inspiration, right up to the moment when we saw you in the ring the other evening. We had the photograph I showed you yesterday. Quillan found it in the case file with the other documents when he first began his investigation. I found it hard to recognize you myself, but Belinda was quite sure. A woman's eye, I suppose. Anyway, that's really the end of our story. We learned that Kayser's Giant Circus had moved across the Channel and been touring Europe ever since. It was surprisingly difficult to find out exactly where it was, or was likely to be, at any particular time, and we've spent the last two weeks chasing across Europe and following you up the Danube. But we've found you at last, Chantal."

Mr. Galletti said, "You have been very kind, sir. This Mr. Quillan must also be a very kind gentleman, I think, to have taken so much trouble over a child he barely knew."

I said quickly, "Oh yes, please let me have his address, Mr. Sumner. I'd like to write and thank him."

Gideon Sumner and his sister exchanged a glance, then she said, "I'm so sorry, Chantal. The poor man lost his life in a boating accident on the Thames, only a few weeks ago. It's so sad that he died without knowing that you would be found. I'm sure that would have given him such pleasure."

"Oh," I said stupidly, and sat grieving for the man I scarcely knew, truly heavyhearted to learn that he had died. There was a silence in the room. On the river a barge sounded its siren. My gloves were beautifully straight now. Gideon and Belinda Sumner were looking at me. I felt I ought to say something, but hardly knew what to say. I glanced at Mr. Galletti. He nodded at me encouragingly and made a little gesture with his hand.

Slowly I began to pull on my gloves, and said, "I'm very grateful to you and to your sister, Mr. Sumner. What you have told me has made me very happy — except about poor Mr. Quillan. I hope Mr. Kirkby will be pleased with all that you've accomplished. I've never met him or any of my family, of course, but I hope you'll give him my warm regards when you return."

Gideon Sumner rubbed his chin. "But, Chantal, we've come to take you home. Your own family, the Kirkbys, are longing to welcome you among them."

I looked up, startled, and said, "Oh no, Mr. Sumner! No!"

There was an awkward silence. Mr. Galletti rose and moved to rest a hand on my shoulder, a strange blend of sorrow and relief in his eyes. "You do not want to leave us, Chantal, but there is something I must tell you now, something which has greatly troubled me." He gave a little sigh. "Last week Mr. Kayser told me that he has financial difficulties. Part of a loan has been called in earlier than he expected, and we know well enough how large the daily costs of a circus are. Well . . . there must be economies, a hundred small economies, to save a little money here, a little there.''

He hesitated, but I knew what was to come, even before the words were spoken. "Dear child, Mr. Kayser can continue to employ you as one of the Flying Gallettis only for the next few weeks, until we go into winter quarters. After that, it must be Maria and Leo alone.''

The pain was like a sword in me. I had known this must come one day, known that I was not truly needed in the act now, but there had seemed no reason why I should not carry on for a year, perhaps two years, until I had saved the money I needed. Even then it would hurt bitterly to part from the family I loved, but I would be braced for it. Now my time had shrunk to a few weeks.

Mr. Galletti said, ''It hurts, child. I know. But all things must end.'' He glanced at Gideon and Belinda Sumner. ''And perhaps now there can be a good new beginning.''

We sat up late that night in the wagon. My first instinctive feeling had been that the Gallettis were my family now, and I would stay with them even if it meant working in Sammy's kitchen for my bare keep. But Mr. Galletti voiced his opinion firmly when the four of us were gathered in our little sitting room that evening, with the oil lamp casting its mellow glow. We had postponed all discussion until after the evening performance, in which I had acquitted myself far better than I had dared to hope with so much to distract me.

"But I can't bear for Chantal to leave us," Maria was saying, her lips trembling.

"It is Chantal we must think of, little one," Mr. Galletti said patiently. "Consider now. We know that in a few weeks she will unfortunately no longer be a part of the act. When that happens, it will be harder for her to stay with us than to go, for she has the proper pride of a fine circus artist. Better for her to return to England, to her family, now that the opportunity has come."

Maria held my arm and said, "But you wanted to be a doctor, Chantal. How can you do that if you go away to England?"

I was feeling close to tears myself, but smiled as I patted her hand. "I can do it more easily there, *piccina*. Mr. Sumner said the family is rich and has influence. He's sure they will arrange for me to go to medical school there."

Leo said gloomily, "I don't like it that Chantal leaves the act, Grandfather. It may change our luck. After Maria, she is like a dead donkey to catch, but the people do not know that, and she looks good when she flies, very good." He just managed to snatch his hand away before Maria slapped it hard.

"Don't you *dare* call her a dead donkey!" she cried.

"I only said —"

"I heard what you said! Be *quiet,* monkey face."

"Don't call me that!"

"Chantal calls you that!"

"I don't mind with Chantal. She says it nicely. But it is not for you!"

Mr. Galletti said, "Children, children,

please. This is not a moment to squabble. Whatever we may wish, Chantal's circus career is ending." He looked down at the table. "I shall miss her . . . more than words can tell. But I have been greatly troubled in wondering what would become of her when she left us. Now there is a fine opportunity for everything to be made easy for her. It is better for her to return with Mr. Sumner and his sister. I am sure of it."

Maria said, "But . . . but that means tomorrow, Grandfather. They are leaving *tomorrow,* you said!"

With an effort I shook off the nervous reluctance I felt at taking this sudden plunge into a new life. There could be no doubt that Mr. Galletti was right. I put my arm about Maria and said, "It's better that way, Maria. A slow parting is a sad one. I'll come and see you when the circus tours in England, I promise."

Leo got to his feet, glowering. "So much talk has made me hungry. I will go to the kitchen for a bowl of the night guards' soup." He sighed, gave a wry shrug, then grinned at me. "I shall miss you, Chantal. At what time must you leave?"

"The train leaves for Augsburg at four o'clock, and we change to the Orient Express there. I have to send a message to Mr. Sumner at the hotel, to say I'm going with them, so he can reserve a sleeping compartment for me — oh!" A new thought struck me. "Can you manage the performance with just the two of you tomorrow, monkey face?"

"Yes, I think so." He looked at Mr. Galletti. "I can do two solos for a few days, until we have worked out the best arrangement."

Mr. Galletti nodded. "I had the same thought myself. It is certainly not a matter which can be allowed to hinder Chantal in any way."

Leo went to the door, then looked back. "If Maria and I rehearse early tomorrow, we can come and see you off, Chantal."

"No, I'd rather say goodbye here." I did not want Maria upset by a prolonged departure. "But thank you, Leo dear."

He rolled up his eyes comically, and said, "Now you begin to call me nice names." He went out into the darkness. Maria sat with her elbows resting on the table, her hands cupped over her eyes. After a moment she said woefully, "I cannot believe we shall never fly together again."

"You really mustn't be miserable, Maria. Listen, we'll fly together once more, tomorrow morning. We'll go right through our usual performance. There won't be any audience, so we'll be doing it just for ourselves. Would you like that?"

She took her hands away from her face. "Yes. Oh, yes. That would be something very special to remember."

"Good. We'll have to ask Leo if he agrees."

"Oh, he will agree." She wiped her eyes with a finger.

"Well, he's funny sometimes. You can't be sure."

"Yes, I can. He'll be afraid of me stamping on his feet and twisting his ears if he refuses. He hates that."

Mr. Galletti sighed. "Sometimes you are quite naughty Maria. In his own way he is very fond of Chantal. You will have no need to bully him."

I was wrong in thinking that our last performance on the flying trapeze would be for ourselves alone. Word had spread quickly through the circus, and when we stood on the trapeze platforms next morning, wearing our proper costumes and not just practice leotards, almost everybody in the circus was gathered there to watch, even Strabo.

Maria's performance was breathtaking, her finest ever, and this must have inspired me, for I could feel every muscle and sinew working easily and smoothly in a way I had never quite known before, and my timing brought glowing praise even from Leo.

We dived to the net at last to the cheers and applause of our circus friends, and then it was all over. I left the sawdust ring for the last time.

The next few hours were very busy. I bathed, and put on the clothes Maria and I had decided I should wear for the journey, some of them provided by womenfolk in the circus, for there had been no time to go shopping. Soon after midday I managed to force down a special lunch Sammy had kindly prepared for me, then began to go from wagon to wagon to say my goodbyes. Mr. Kayser had given me a fine suitcase, and this was already packed with my few belongings, including my medical books. I had also packed my leotards, tights, boots, and both my spangled costumes, for I could not bear to throw them away or leave them behind.

It was almost a relief when I was told at last that a carriage was waiting for me. In our tiny sitting room I kissed a glum Leo, then Mr. Galletti, whose pipe I had just filled for the last time and who tried to smile but could not hide the sadness in his eyes. I hugged Maria, urged her not to cry, started to cry myself, begged them not to come and wave me off, and almost ran from the wagon.

Of all people, Strabo was waiting there at the foot of the steps beside my suitcase, ready to carry it to the carriage for me. "The people say to tell you they don't come to see you go because it is sad for you, Chantal," he said.

"Yes. Please thank them for me."

"You fly good on trapeze today. Is pity you go."

"It can't be helped. Mr. Strabo, I'm sorry we quarreled."

"Was my fault. All finish now. Goodbye, Chantal."

He put my case in the carriage, shook hands solemnly, then stood back. The driver shook the reins and clicked his tongue. The wheels began to turn, and a moment later we were on the road which led down into Ingolstadt. When I looked back I saw the burly figure standing alone with one hand lifted high. I waved, and then the curve of the road took me out of sight.

I closed my eyes and leaned back, feeling confused, nervous, and close to tears again from the pain of parting. Kayser's Giant Circus, my home for five years, was behind me now, and I wondered what the new life ahead would bring.

SEVEN

For most of the journey to England I seemed to be existing in a void, my mind blank, my feelings numb. I was neither happy nor unhappy, neither looking forward nor looking back. I was vaguely aware that Gideon and Belinda Sumner must have guessed at my state of mind, for after some early attempts to chat pleasantly with me they left me alone, and for this I was grateful.

I slept poorly, with muddled dreams, and it was not until the Channel ferry from Le Havre brought us into Southampton next day that my mind threw off the strange lethargy which had dulled it ever since the journey began. Suddenly all was real to me again. I had left my old life and my friends behind me. Soon I would be living with my own family, but they would be strangers. I felt a little afraid, and to conceal it I smiled brightly at Gideon and Belinda as we waited to go down the gangway.

I was in England, my own country, yet at this moment it seemed more strange to me than any of the countries I had known during the past five years. I realized that this was a false feeling, for throughout those years I had always traveled with the circus, which had been my home no matter what the country. If I had come to England with the circus I would have been full of excitement, feeling secure and at home in my own little world. This was different, for now I was alone.

During the train journey from Southampton I began to feel better. More than once Mr. Galletti had remarked that the English countryside was different from any other he had known, and now I saw that he was right. The lanes that wound their way from village to village were different, seeming to ramble aimlessly between fields and hedgerows with little rhyme or reason. Everything seemed smaller, the farms, the village churches, the streams, the fields. Autumn had come, and great patches of woods were turning to gold, because here the broad-leafed trees had not been ousted by quick-growing evergreens.

I was so taken up with gazing from the window that I had almost forgotten Gideon and Belinda, as they had now asked me to call them, until I heard him say, "Is it good to be home, Chantal?"

I turned to look across the compartment at him as he sat with his long legs sprawled, smiling at me. "Yes," I said. "It's good . . . in a way. I'm going to miss my friends, though."

He shrugged, still smiling. "There's always something."

"Yes. I would have had to leave them in a year or two anyway."

Belinda said, "You really should tell Chantal about the Kirkby household, Gideon. If she's about to be introduced to them all at once, I'm sure it would help to know who's who."

"Ah, now there's a wise thought," said Gideon. "Would you like a description of your family, Chantal?"

"Yes, please. I didn't realize you knew them well."

"When I first undertook the task of searching for you, I had a number of discussions with Benedict Kirkby, and for the sake of convenience he invited us to stay at Wildings for a few days, so at least we've some small acquaintance with them. Benedict is the head of the family, and a bachelor. Then there's his brother, Arthur, who is married to Prudence, the proud mother of two children."

"How old are the children?" I asked.

"I'm not quite sure, but Adrian would be about twenty-two, and Theresa sixteen."

"I do hope they like me," I said fervently. "Gideon, how do you think I ought to address everybody?"

"Well, Benedict and Arthur Kirkby are cousins of your father, but I think it would be appropriate if you addressed them as Uncle. Then you could call Arthur's wife Aunt Prudence, and the young ones simply by their Christian names."

It was less than twenty-four hours since

I had left Kayser's Giant Circus, and already I was beginning to feel the first pangs of homesickness. My new family might not like me. I might not like them. And what would my life be like in future? How would I spend my time? Try as I might, I could not begin to imagine what ordinary people did with themselves all day long.

Ordinary people. To me, that had come to mean people outside the circus. But I was to be one of them now, and I felt completely at a loss. I tried to remember how I had spent my days at Farleigh Hall, in the years before I had run away. There had been schoolwork with my succession of governesses, of course, but apart from that I could scarcely remember doing anything with a sense of purpose.

I had spent much time outwitting governesses, avoiding piano practice, making deliberately clumsy samplers of embroidery, and causing the servants as much trouble as possible. But that was all. I felt sick at heart and ashamed as I remembered.

Gideon said, "Is something wrong, Chantal?"

I came back to the present with a start. "No, I'm quite all right. Well . . . not really. I think I'm anxious about meeting my new family, that's all." A thought struck me. "Oh! Will you and Belinda be going home to London, once you've taken me to Wildings?"

"No, we shall be close neighbors for a few weeks." Gideon smiled, and glanced at his sister. "When I'm not busy, Lindy and I like to spend a little time in the country. We've taken a cottage in the village of Osburne, so we'll be seeing quite a lot of you, I hope."

I felt my heart lift with relief. "I'm so glad. I'm just beginning to realize how different everything is going to be for me."

"I don't think that will trouble you for long," Gideon said reassuringly. "After all, you were brought up in the same style as the Kirkby children until you were thirteen, so it won't be new to you. I'm sure you'll soon settle in comfortably." He gave a little grin, and glanced at his sister. "At least it's much safer than flying on a trapeze, isn't it, Lindy?"

Belinda lifted her head from the magazine and looked at him for a moment or two, unsmiling. Then she gave a little shrug and said, "You can never tell."

It was a strange remark, for she did not seem to be joking. While I hesitated, wondering whether to ask what she meant, Gideon gave an easy laugh and said, "You think all the young men will be paying Chantal a lot of attention, but surely that's exciting for a young lady, not dangerous?"

"As long as she keeps her head and isn't taken in by some self-seeking scoundrel." Now Belinda smiled as she looked at me. "And I'm sure Chantal is much too sensible to allow that."

I still felt there had been some undercurrent of meaning in her words, but I had no time to puzzle over it, for the train began to slow down, and next minute we were drawing into Pellridge Station.

Gideon looked at his watch and said, "Right on time. I sent a telegram yesterday, so I'm sure some of the Kirkbys will be here to greet you."

I jumped inwardly, then struggled to compose myself. The moment had come when I was to meet my family, people whose names I knew but who as yet were faceless to me, and I desperately wanted to make a good impression. Two minutes later we were walking along the platform of the small station, a porter behind us pushing a trolley with our luggage.

I remembered Maria's instructions, and tried to walk with small feminine steps and a ladylike carriage. In fact, I was concentrating so hard on this that I was aware of nothing else until I heard Gideon say, "Ah, there you are. Good afternoon, sir. A pleasure to see you again, Mrs. Kirkby. You've brought Theresa along, I see. How are you, young lady?"

He was speaking to a middle-aged lady and gentleman accompanied by a girl with dark hair and friendly brown eyes set in a plump but pretty face. I guessed that the man was Mr. Arthur Kirkby, with his wife and daughter. He was of medium height, rather portly, with thick hair turning from red to gray. His face might once have been handsome, but was now rather fleshy. He wore a vague smile, as if he were pleased to see me, but I had the feeling that his thoughts were elsewhere at this moment. Later I was to find my impression had been right, for Arthur Kirkby's thoughts were invariably elsewhere. He wore a tweed jacket belted at the waist, with matching knickerbockers and a cap which he had taken off as we approached.

His wife was as tall as he, with beautiful dark hair framing a broad face. Her eyes were gentle, almost timid, and she was smiling at me in a kindly manner, but again I had the feeling that half her mind was occupied with other matters at this moment, though not in quite the same way as her husband's. He seemed to be preoccupied by some weighty matter, while his wife had the air of one constantly distracted by a multitude of small problems.

She wore a brown walking costume of coat and skirt, and a velvet toque. The coat reached to her knees, and had a collar and cuffs of astrakhan. I was sure the clothes were of fine quality and tailor-made, but she did not carry them with the elegance and style Belinda Sumner gave to whatever I had seen her wear. Fleetingly I wondered which I would be like if ever I had fine clothes, and decided sadly that I lacked elegance and would probably be like Mrs. Kirkby.

The girl wore a straw boater and a white blouse beneath a long jacket, with a flounced skirt of pale-blue wool serge. She was smiling, but unlike her parents she seemed to be living in the present moment, and her smile was meant for me rather than being no more than a polite expression.

Although all these impressions came to me during the few seconds while Gideon and Belinda were shaking hands in greeting, it was not until later that I was able to sort them out in my mind, for at the time I was so nervous that everything seemed confused. Then Gideon said, "Well, here she is, sir. This is Chantal." He turned to me. "Chantal, this is your Uncle Arthur and your Aunt Prudence, and the beautiful young lady is their daughter, Theresa."

Theresa giggled as I murmured, "How do you do?" and shook hands with each in turn.

Uncle Arthur said, "Ah, yes. Excellent. Well done, Sumner, my dear fellow. Safely home, eh? Jolly brown, aren't you, m'dear? A circus, eh? Extraordinary." His voice tailed into silence but he continued to smile, though he was looking past me rather than at me.

Aunt Prudence said, "Welcome home, Chantal. What a pretty name. I'm sure you'll be very happy with us at Wildings. Theresa, you did say I'd told Dixon to let Mrs. Foster know that —"

"Yes, Mamma," Theresa broke in hastily. "I heard you tell him three times. He knows Chantal is arriving this afternoon and that Mr. Sumner and Miss Sumner will be dining with us this evening, and he's told cook so." She rolled her eyes at me comically. "Shall we go now? I'm sure everybody must be dying for a cup of tea."

Uncle Arthur woke from his daydream and said, "Two carriages. Bit of a crush."

"We brought two carriages," Aunt

Prudence said. "Otherwise it would have been rather a crush. Arthur, tell the porter where to put the trunks. Now, how shall we travel?"

"I'm going with Chantal," said Theresa, and took my arm with such a vigorous movement that I dropped my handbag. In the months to come I was often to find Theresa irritating, for she was boisterously clumsy and had the tactless ways of a feather-brained schoolgirl, but I never forgot the warmth of her welcome nor ceased to be grateful for the friendliness she showed from the moment of my arrival.

In a little while I found myself sitting beside her in a fine carriage, with Belinda and Aunt Prudence facing us, while the men waited for the luggage to be loaded on a second carriage in which they would travel.

"I've been *so* excited since Uncle Benedict told us you were coming," said Theresa. "It was only yesterday, because he kept it as a surprise, and today I just couldn't stand still, could I, Mamma? Oh, you must have hundreds of stories to tell,

Chantal — fancy being with a circus! Was it very thrilling? I've seen two circuses, and I just had to hide my eyes when the people were on that wire, high up above the ring. Have you done that? I liked the clowns best, I think. Papa went to sleep, didn't he, Mamma? He hated the music, though, because he's very musical, you see, so he hated it. Did you ride round the ring standing up on a horse, Chantal?"

"No, I —"

"They had some monkeys, too, didn't they, Mamma? They were so funny. Perhaps I liked them better than the clowns, really. Your room's next to mine, Chantal. I'll show you as soon as we get home. I've got a horse called Jericho, and I tried standing on his back after I'd seen the circus, but I couldn't do it. I nearly fell off. I expect you have to practice for hours and hours, don't you?"

She paused to draw breath, but I was unready to say anything, for I had given up hope of having a chance to reply, and it was Belinda who said, "Chantal wasn't a bareback rider. She was a trapeze artist."

"A trapeze!" Theresa cried, her voice rising to a squeak. "Oh, you must be so brave! Did you never fall off?"

"Well, I —"

"We saw a lady on a trapeze, and I just couldn't look because I was so afraid she'd fall. She wore a pink costume with spangles, and just a tiny frilly skirt. Mamma thought it was rather vulgar because of her — well, her limbs, but I thought she looked quite nice really. After all, she couldn't be on a trapeze with a proper skirt, could she? Oh, did *you* have to wear tights, Chantal? Well, I suppose you must have done it you were on a trapeze . . ."

On this occasion Theresa's habit of asking questions and then chattering on without waiting for an answer was a relief to me. I was well content to give half an ear to her stream of words while I took in my surroundings. We had left the small town of Pellridge and were moving along a winding road between pastures where sheep were grazing. To my right the land rose in a series of low green hills. To my left the pasture soon gave way to woodland. A gentle upward slope took us past a farmhouse and a cluster of small cottages to a triangle of green where three roads joined, then we crested the hill and continued down into the village of Osburne.

The High Street was narrow at first, but widened into a great cobbled rectangle with an open market in the center. On each side narrow houses of stone were huddled together with a few small shops, and at the far end stood an old Norman church. We had just passed the smithy on the outskirts of the village when the coachman brought us to a halt.

"This is where I must leave you for the time being," said Belinda, preparing to alight. "Thank you for inviting us to dinner, Mrs. Kirkby, we shall look forward to it very much." I had forgotten that she and Gideon would not be coming straight to Wildings with us. A moment later he was opening the door and helping his sister to descend. Behind us the other coachman was lifting their trunks and cases from the second carriage. Now I saw the large, white-walled cottage set back from the road. Gideon leaned into the carriage and said, "That's our little home for a few weeks, Chantal. I hope you'll visit us often. Mrs. Kirkby has recommended an excellent cook-housekeeper who'll be coming in daily, so we'll be very comfortable."

Rather haltingly I thanked him and his sister for all they had done, a task made more difficult by Theresa, who kept talking all the time about the hunting season which would begin in a few weeks. When the coachman had carried their luggage to the cottage, with Theresa still talking and everybody ignoring her, Gideon smiled, touched my hand, and said, "We'll see you this evening, Chantal. Welcome home."

The two carriages moved on, and in only five or six minutes turned into a drive which ran between clipped yews. On each side, beyond the yews, was a stretch of fine lawn hemmed by tall limes and elms. The house faced south, with the autumn sun slanting down upon its stone walls and the gray-green tiles of the long roof. I was to learn later that the Kirkbys had lived here for only fourteen years, and were still considered foreigners by the local folk, but the house itself had first been built in Tudor times. There had been a good deal of renovation over the centuries, but much of the original structure still remained. Before we reached the porch, the door was opened by a butler, a tall, lean man with graying hair.

"Look!" cried Theresa, jostling me in her eagerness as she pointed to a small cupboard door of ancient timber set in one side of the porch. "That's our dole cupboard, Chantal. Isn't it funny? There's a passage leading to it from the kitchen, and they used to put bits of food in the cupboard for passing wayfarers."

"Oh, do stop bouncing up and down, child," Aunt Prudence sighed. "You're so *big* for that sort of thing now. It's like having a dancing bear in the house."

"It's not my fault I'm big, Mamma," Theresa said, quite unabashed. "I just happen to have big bones. Look, Papa's still sitting in the carriage, I don't think he knows we're here yet. I expect he's composing something in his head. Papa!

259

Papa!'' She gathered up her skirt and went bounding away to fetch her father just as he emerged slowly from the second carriage. As they reached the porch together Uncle Arthur said, ''Ah, yes. There you are, Dixon. Good man. This is — ah — now let me see. Chantal. Yes, Miss Chantal.''

The butler inclined his head as we entered. ''Welcome to Wildings, Miss Chantal.'' His manner was polite, but I caught an intonation, or perhaps saw some almost imperceptible expression in his eyes, which made remembrance come rushing back to me. For five years I had not seen a servant, but I remembered the staff at Farleigh Hall, where I had spent my childhood. They had been bad servants, because for much of the time their master was absent and because I, their young mistress, had been a detestable creature who deserved nothing of them. But I had learned to detect contempt in a polite word, or see it in a bland look, and I could read Dixon well. He knew that I had been a performer in a circus, and this set me among the lower classes, far lower than the servant class. As such I was beneath his dignity as a butler, a man who ruled perhaps a dozen servants.

He would not dare to show his feelings, of course, and if he were a good butler he would not even hint at them to his staff. But the other servants would be aware, as I had been, and they would probably take their attitude from him.

There was nothing to be done about it. I might not be well served, but I had not been served at all for the last five years, so it would scarcely trouble me. I was pleased, and a little surprised, to find that I did not immediately feel hot resentment towards Dixon. Perhaps I was beginning to outgrow my quick temper at last.

Theresa was already halfway up the broad stone treads of the curving staircase, leaning over the wrought-iron balusters and calling, "Come on, Chantal, I'll show you your room! Oh, do send up Miss Chantal's luggage quickly, Dixon, and tell Molly to come and unpack for her."

My bedroom looked out over beautifully kept grounds and was at least twice the area of our living wagon and half as high again. Theresa, knocking over a candlestick as she moved to point out the bell pull beside the bed, said that she hoped I didn't mind having a rather small room, but she had chosen it for me because it was nice and cozy, and next to hers, and it had an iron radiator which was heated by hot water from the boiler in the kitchen and which could be turned on or off as I pleased.

A footman brought up my case, and a parlormaid arrived to unpack it. Theresa was astonished that all my belongings were contained in a single suitcase. "Wherever are all your evening gowns?" she said as Molly began to unfasten the leather straps. "Surely you didn't leave them behind? And what about your hunting clothes? You do ride to hounds, Chantal, don't you?"

I could not help smiling at her concern. "I've ridden horses quite a lot, but I've never hunted. And we didn't need clothes for evening wear in the circus."

"Oh, I suppose not. How silly of me not to think of that. But you must have worn something for riding. I'm allowed to wear knickerbockers. Mamma thought it wasn't quite proper, but when Uncle Benedict said she was being absurd she didn't protest any more, of course. Oh, perhaps you rode sidesaddle?"

"No, bareback mostly."

"Oh, then you must have had knickerbockers, too."

"Maria made us some breeches for when we might be exercising a horse for a long time, but otherwise we'd just pull up our skirts a little."

Theresa's eyes grew round. "Oooh! It must be *ever* so different, living in a circus."

"Yes, it is very different, but you soon get used to it."

"Uncle Benedict will be so pleased to know that you ride. He likes hunting better than anything else. He and Squire Mortinger keep a pack a hounds, but we have our own stables with some beautiful horses. I was blooded last year. It was all tremendously exciting." She bounced towards the door. "I'll just tidy myself while you're settling in, and then I'll show

you round Wildings before we have tea."
She went out, and a few moments later I
heard something crash to the floor in the
room next door.

Molly was holding up one of my
practice leotards, staring at it in
bewilderment. "Whatever's this, Miss
Chantal?"

"It's called a leotard. Just leave the
unpacking, please, Molly, I'd prefer to see
to it myself. Perhaps you'd pour some
water into the washbasin for me."

She looked at the big china jug. "But
thaat's cowld, miss," she said with her
soft Dorset drawl.

"I don't mind."

"But — but you muzn't wash in cowld
water, miss! Alfred's fetching some 'ot for
you." She gazed at me in alarm.

"Yes . . . yes, of course," I said slowly,
and thought to myself that one of the first
things I would have to do in my new life
was to realize that young ladies were born
to be pampered and waited upon. I had
begun to smile when suddenly the thought
no longer seemed amusing, and I felt a
shadow of unease.

Molly was saying, "I made zure there's plenty of 'angers in the wardrobe, miss, and re-loined the drawers. The 'ip bath's in the bottom of the big cupboard 'ere, an' you don't waant to worry about matches for the gas, 'cause it loights itzelf when you pull the little chain. Ah, 'ere's that Alfred with the water."

I had washed, changed my dress, and tidied my hair by the time Theresa returned. During the next hour I found myself growing a little weary of the sound of her voice, but then, perhaps like the rest of the family, I learned the knack of regarding it as a natural background of noise, like the rattle of train wheels or the drumming of rain on a wagon roof.

When she had shown me her bedroom she pointed out the rooms occupied by the other members of the family. "That's where Mamma and Papa sleep, and Adrian's in a room at the end of the passage. Oh, he's my older brother, and tremendously clever, well, he's a poet, so he has to be. I expect he'll come down for tea. Now we go along here . . . ."

Uncle Benedict's room was in a passage

265

on the other side of the balustraded upper hall, and his study adjoined it. To my surprise we tiptoed past, Theresa with a finger to her lips. "Uncle Benedict always works in his study during the afternoon," she whispered as we reached a small staircase leading down to the servants' hall, "and we never disturb him. But he said he'll join us for tea today, because you're here."

"What does he work at?" I asked.

"Oh, writing letters and adding up figures and things," she said vaguely. Then, with awed pride, "And he speaks on the telephone, too! We've had a telephone for almost a year now, and they had to lay a wire all the way from the telephone exchange in Dorchester."

I was greatly impressed by this, for I had never yet seen a telephone, and could only imagine how strange it must seem to talk to somebody who might be many miles away. I thought Dixon the butler showed a hint of disapproval that Theresa should have brought me belowstairs, but he presented the cook and the servants to me politely, and I sensed a general atmosphere of contentment here, very different from the atmosphere which had emanated from the servants' hall during my empty childhood.

We mounted to the ground floor again, and I heard the sound of a piano. A few rather strange-sounding chords were played, then came a pause before they were played again and yet again, each time with a difference so slight that my ear could barely detect it.

"Papa's in the music room composing his symphony," said Theresa. "That's what he does most of the time, really, but he only actually plays on the piano between three and four o'clock, because Uncle Benedict says we'd all go mad otherwise." She opened a door, still talking, and led the way across a rather untidy room with a grand piano in one corner and several tables on which piles of paper were scattered. Uncle Arthur sat at the piano with a sheet of music manuscript propped in front of him, eyes closed, hands hovering over the keys, a pencil held in his mouth.

"We'll go through this way to the

library," said Theresa, stumbling as she almost tripped over a stool, and not troubling to lower her voice. "Don't worry about disturbing Papa, he's very good at concentrating. Hallo, Papa. You see? He can't hear us. Now this is the library . . ."

We toured the drawing room, the sewing room, a small private parlor where Uncle Benedict talked with people who came to discuss business affairs, and came finally to the great hall, as it was called from earlier times. This was the dining room, and was not as large as its name suggested but was still a lofty room of handsome size with a splendid arch-braced roof and a fireplace whose lintel was carved from a single block of beautiful stone, which I later learned was Ham stone.

As we entered, a maid and a footman were putting newly cleaned cutlery away in baize-lined boxes. I caught my breath at sight of the gleaming silver, remembering the days at Farleigh Hall. Each evening I had dined with my governess, one of us at each end of the great table with a full array of cutlery. On the rare occasions when my supposed father was at home, there had been three of us. And even more rarely, when he had guests, who were always men, there might be as many as eight or nine place settings. But for the last five years I had eaten from an enamel plate, using one knife, one fork, and one spoon.

We made a tour of the gardens, and at five minutes past four returned to the drawing room for tea. Aunt Prudence was there when we arrived, and Uncle Arthur entered a few moments later. He showed a touch of surprise at first sight of me, but then gave a misty smile as he remembered who I was. "Ah, Chantal. Have some tea, eh?" He settled himself in a chair opposite his wife, who was arranging and rearranging cups and saucers on the little table at which she sat, turning a cup slightly, altering the angle of a spoon in the saucer, and adjusting the position of the sugar tongs.

The next five minutes were an extraordinary experience. Uncle Arthur uttered random comments from which all the important words were omitted, and Aunt Prudence proceeded to translate his cryptic phrases as if they were her own remarks.

"Moved a bit," said Uncle Arthur, glancing at the window. "West tomorrow."

"I think the wind is shifting a little," said Aunt Prudence, adjusting the position of the silver teapot. "We could well have some rain coming from the west, I fancy."

Uncle Arthur's head began to wag slightly, as if he were beating time to music running through his mind. "Leaving for — er — you know, next week, they say," he remarked. "Don't know who's coming in."

Aunt Prudence glanced at the mellow old grandfather clock. "I hear the Dennisons are moving to America very soon now. I wonder who will be moving into White Lodge when they go?"

After a little more of this curious procedure, Uncle Arthur and Aunt Prudence went their separate ways in conversation. He continued his baffling remarks, while she began to recount a number of domestic problems which were troubling her.

"New hymnbooks, his wife told me," Uncle Arthur informed us.

"I'm sure I spoke to Molly about turning those sheets side to middle," Aunt Prudence sighed, "but she's done nothing about it."

"Says the eighty-four's running short. Don't believe it."

"We simply must have new curtains in the sewing room, Arthur. I suppose I shall have to go into Dorchester."

"Plenty. Cellar myself. When I can find time."

And through all this Theresa talked to me with scarcely a pause. "We're paying a morning call on the Bentleys tomorrow. Do you like paying calls, Chantal? I like it most of the time, well, except at the Manstons', because old Mrs. Manston is rather a dragon, and she keeps telling me to sit still. I hope Roger Bentley will be there. You'll like him, Chantal. He's not very handsome, but he's a simply marvelous rider."

So it went on, until the door opened and a young man with rather long fair hair came drifting in.

"Ah, there you are, Adrian dear," said Aunt Prudence. "Come and welcome Chantal."

Adrian Kirkby crossed the room, a rather sad smile on his lips, and offered me a drooping hand. "My dear Chantal, I do apologize," he said in a languid voice. "Forgive me for not welcoming you earlier, but I was in the toils of creation."

I was startled for a moment, but then remembered that Theresa had told me Adrian was a poet, and very clever. I took an immediate dislike to him now, was angry with myself for doing so, gave him the friendliest smile I could manage, shook hands firmly, and said, "Hallo, Adrian." His hand felt limp and squashy in mine, and he winced visibly, then said with a curious snuffling laugh, "Angels and ministers of grace, defend us! You have a formidable hand for a young lady, dear Chantal."

I felt myself flush with embarrassment. At the station I had been careful to shake hands in a very ladylike fashion, and also I had been wearing gloves then, for I was well aware that my hands were far from soft and gentle, as a lady's should be. I said, "Oh, I'm sorry!"

"Not at all." Adrian waggled his fingers, then drew back his head a little to study me carefully. "Lustrous," he said after a moment or two. "Your hair, your crowning glory, is lustrous, dear Chantal. That is the word. Lustrous. But you must allow it to grow, of course."

"What do you mean about her hands?" cried Theresa indignantly, taking me by the wrist. "Oh, my goodness, the skin's all hard and leathery! However did that happen, Chantal?"

I liked Theresa, but it was hard to keep all sharpness from my voice as I said, "It comes of spending so many hours on a trapeze every day during the last few years, Theresa. That's all."

"But — but whyever didn't you wear *gloves?*"

I made an extraordinary sound as I tried to choke back an explosion of laughter at Theresa's words, and I had just managed to transform it into a fit of coughing when the door opened again. The man who entered was gray. This was the color of his suit, his eyes, his receding hair, and it even seemed that there was an undertone of gray in the complexion of his hollow-cheeked face. Despite this, I judged him to be a fit man, for he moved lightly and looked to me to be of sufficient height for his weight, with no useless fat.

I realized, in a momentary thought, that if anyone could have read my mind they would have thought this a most peculiar appraisal, but in the circus nothing was more important to the artists than physical fitness, and I had yet to lose the habit of unconsciously assessing people in this way. Uncle Arthur was too fat. Aunt Prudence was too thin. Adrian was soft. Theresa was a little heavy but still had some puppy fat to lose. At this moment she was patting me on the back and saying, "Are you all right, Chantal? Would you like a sip of water?"

"No . . . no, thank you. I'm sorry." I recovered my breath, feeling very foolish, and smiled at the man who had just entered. This must be Uncle Benedict. I was aware that everybody had stopped talking now, even Theresa, and I was sure of something I had already begun to suspect — that Benedict Kirkby was very much the master of this household.

"Welcome to Wildings, Chantal," he said, and took my hand, studying me. "I'm Benedict Kirkby." His manner was amiable, but there seemed to be something wrong with his eyes, and his voice was as gray and unemotional as everything else about him.

"How do you do, Uncle Benedict," I said, dropping a small curtsy. "It's wonderfully kind of you and your family to take me into your home."

"You are one of the family, too, child," he said, still holding my hand. "We're delighted that you've been restored to us. Come and sit down." He put an arm lightly about my shoulders as he guided me towards a deep sofa. It was an affectionate gesture, yet I felt a quick chill run through me at his touch.

"We'll have a chat in my study later," he said, and looked about the room as he sat down. "Good afternoon, Prudence. Will you pour now, please?" His gaze moved to Theresa. "Have you been looking after your new cousin, young lady?"

"Yes, Uncle Benedict. I've shown her over the house and gardens. Oh, and she's ridden quite a lot, but she hasn't hunted before —"

"Excellent," Uncle Benedict broke in, lifting a hand to stop the flow of words. "Then we can have the pleasure of initiating her." He looked at Uncle Arthur, who said, "On time, Benedict. Coming to dinner, you know."

Aunt Prudence, pouring tea, said brightly, "Chantal's train was quite punctual, and we've arranged for that nice Mr. Sumner and his sister to dine with us this evening, as you suggested, Benedict."

He nodded. "I shall look forward to meeting that nice Mr. Sumner again." His gaze turned to Adrian, who was leaning back in an armchair, eyes half closed, stroking his chin slowly with an air of profound concentration. "Well, Adrian. Have you completed your current masterpiece?"

Adrian opened his eyes, frowning a little. "Not quite, Uncle Benedict. I'm still polishing it."

"All fine gems require polishing." Uncle Benedict took a cup of tea from Aunt Prudence and handed it to me. As I murmured my thanks he said, "May one know the nature of the present work, Adrian?"

"Well . . ." Adrian gestured widely, seeking for words. "It's about . . . I suppose you could say it's about Life."

"An ample subject indeed. But into which category does the work fall? A play in blank verse, after Shakespeare? A narrative poem? Something Miltonian or Homeric, perhaps?"

"It's a sonnet, Uncle."

Benedict Kirkby stirred his tea. After a few moments of silence he said, "It must be almost two months since you began this creation, if my memory serves."

"Adrian is such a perfectionist," said his mother fondly.

"A nonpareil, Prudence. Am I correct in believing, my dear boy, that a sonnet consists of fourteen lines?"

"Yes, of course, Uncle." Adrian looked pained.

There was another silence. I waited, gripped by a growing bewilderment. Nobody seemed to grasp that Benedict Kirkby's words were heavy with irony. At last he spoke again, thoughtfully, "Almost two lines a week. You must be careful not to drive yourself too hard, Adrian." Then, though he did not raise his voice, there was suddenly a razor edge in the tone of it. "Do you think you have enough energy left to pass the cucumber sandwiches?"

Aunt Prudence jumped, and dropped a lump of sugar from the tongs. Theresa looked up sharply, and smiled a feeble smile. Uncle Arthur blinked. Adrian came quickly to his feet, no longer languid, and said hastily, "Yes, of course, Uncle Benedict."

It was a curious scene, but one I was to see repeated with various small differences during the days to come.

I had always regarded myself as being one of nature's fools, for throughout my life I had rarely made a wise decision on anything. But at Wildings I was made to appear quite intelligent, for with the exception of Uncle Benedict, all the members of the Kirkby family seemed slow-witted to the point of stupidity. It was not, I discovered later, a matter of Uncle Arthur and Adrian being absentminded because of their artistic gifts. They were simply absentminded because their minds were absent. Aunt Prudence was always too busy worrying to have time to think, and Theresa did not worry at all but had no inclination to exercise her brain.

Caustic remarks from Benedict Kirkby would pass over their heads, and they responded only when he spoke with the whiplash in his voice. Then they became anxious and a little afraid, uncertain where their offense lay.

The first example of the Kirkby family's ways embarrassed me for a few moments, but then Uncle Benedict began to talk amiably about Wildings and the surrounding countryside, about the Osburne Hunt, the local gentry, and his own stables. Occasionally he brought one or other of the family into the conversation by inviting a comment, but in the main they sat quietly listening. It was during this time I realized what it was that seemed wrong with Uncle Benedict's eyes. The lids were almost lashless, and could hardly be seen at all when his eyes were open, so that when he blinked it was like the quick blink of a lizard.

At last he looked at his watch and said, "Thank you, Prudence. Now I think perhaps Chantal and I should have a chat in my study. We'll only be ten minutes or so. Theresa will wait for you here or in the sewing room, Chantal, and then you young ladies can amuse yourselves as you please until we dine at seven."

"We can have a game of Ludo," said Theresa eagerly, "or Snakes and Ladders."

Uncle Benedict looked at her. "Yes. But don't make Chantal overexcited on her first evening with us. Perhaps, if she's very fortunate, Adrian will read her some of his poems. Come along, Chantal."

I felt suddenly low in spirits, though I would have found it hard to say why.

Perhaps it was Uncle Benedict's sarcasm. Even if there had been a measure of humor in his remarks I would have disliked them, for in the days when I had been fat, white, spotty, and unpleasant, I had been much given to sarcasm myself, and was still ashamed of the memory of it.

We passed through the ancient hall with its fine linenfold paneling, and as we mounted the great staircase Uncle Benedict said, "We're a small community here in Osburne, and by this time everybody knows of your coming to Wildings, gentry and village folk alike. I'm afraid you'll find yourself the object of some curiosity at first, Chantal."

"Oh. You mean because I come from a circus, Uncle Benedict?"

"Well, any newcomer attracts attention, and your background makes you a particularly tasty morsel for gossip, but it will soon die down as you settle in with us." He opened the door of his study, led the way in, and sat down behind a large desk of beautifully carved oak, waving a hand to a leather chair facing the desk.

"Sit down, my dear."

I looked about me as I took the chair. The floor was richly carpeted, the walls paneled in dark wood and hung with many sporting prints showing scenes of the chase. Along one wall stood a bookcase and several tall roll-fronted cabinets, of the kind I had seen on that dreadful day five years ago in the office of Mr. Blythe, the solicitor. There were no papers on the desk, only a leather-cornered blotter, a note pad, and an object I had not seen before — a telephone.

In the wall opposite the big bay window was a wide recess with glass shelves on which were set out many small and sometimes strange objects or ornaments in pottery, glass, carved wood, stone, and other materials I could not name. My first impression was of a collection of curios, perhaps from different parts of the world since many of them did not seem to be native to this country.

I had barely seated myself when there came a shrill whistling sound from the wall behind the desk. Uncle Benedict frowned in annoyance, rose from his chair, moved to the wall, and picked up a speaking tube which hung there.

"Yes?" He listened, and I saw his face change. "Lame? How the devil did that happen? . . . No, never mind, I'll talk to Harridge myself. Has he sent for the vet? . . . Good, I'll come down and see him at once."

He hung up the speaking tube, looked at me, snapped his fingers with a gesture of irritation, then moved to the bookcase. "I have to leave you for ten minutes, Chantal. The vet's coming to attend to one of my horses, and I'm going to the stables to have a look at the animal myself. Here, you can amuse yourself with this history of Wildings."

As he handed me the large book I said, "I'm sorry about the horse. May I come with you, Uncle Benedict? I've often helped Mr. Brunner in the circus when —"

"No, no," he broke in impatiently. "Pegasus is a high-strung creature, and I don't want strangers about her at a time like this." He moved quickly to the door.

I felt oddly out of place, alone here in

Benedict Kirkby's study. This new family I had joined seemed very strange to me, but perhaps it was I who was strange, a girl who had forgotten what it was like to live in an English household. However that might be, the thought of living with the Kirkbys permanently made my heart sink a little. I pushed the feeling away, annoyed with myself. Idly I opened the book on my lap and began to run my eye down the first page.

I gathered that Wildings was so called because the slope on which the house stood had once been an uncultivated area of self-sown crab apple and other plants known generally as wildings, and that the house had first been built in 1534 by Sir William de Varre. It occurred to me that I was something of a wilding myself, carried far from my home pastures by the winds of fortune to put down roots in the unfamiliar soil of a traveling circus. And now, by the strangest freak of chance, I had been transplanted to my native fields again. Truly I was fortune's wilding.

I read another half page, then my interest flagged, for I found I was reading words without taking in their meaning. I felt restless. I had spent most of the day sitting down, which was most unnatural for me, and the muscles of my arms and legs were beginning to twitch. I put the book down on the desk, moved well away from the window, looked about me rather furtively, then began to go through what Maria and I had always called our "prelims." These were exercises to warm up and loosen our muscles immediately before a performance, and consisted of swinging the arms and legs in turn, doing knee bends, rotating the trunk, and gently trotting on the spot.

It was an awkward business, dressed as I was in a long skirt, and I could not help giggling at the strange figure I must have cut if there had been anyone to see me, but a few minutes of this made me feel more myself, and then I began to move round the study to look at the sporting prints which hung on the wall. Each one showed a hunting scene of some kind, but to me the horses seemed stiff and without any feeling of movement. It was already obvious that Uncle Benedict had a passion for hunting, and I had gathered from Theresa that it would please him if I rode to hounds. I was eager to do so, for at least it meant that I would have one active recreation to follow.

Moving slowly round the room, I came to the recess with the glass shelves, and began to study the little objects on display. I thought I recognized two pieces of porcelain. One was a tiny needle case from Meissen, and the other was a statuette in unglazed porcelain, perhaps from Sèvres, which Mr. Galletti had once told me was called Sèvres biscuit.

There was a watch on a small stand, its silver case so thin I could scarcely believe it could hold any mechanism, and several boxes which I took to be snuffboxes, two of them with enameled lids depicting Oriental figures. On another shelf were little bottles, scent bottles perhaps, of jade, rose quartz, and other stones I could not name. There were one or two big ancient coins, and several pieces of carving in wood or stone which looked primitive. With some of the objects it was hard to know whether they had been made for use or ornament — a strangely wrought piece of bronze, an ivory filigree ball with what seemed to be a smaller ball inside, a flexible silver fish with scales.

I bent to look at the bottom shelf, and saw a piece of very old embroidery framed behind glass, an early playing card similarly framed, two slender sticks of finely carved bamboo, a hollow stick which looked like some crude musical instrument —

I caught my breath and it seemed that my stomach rose into my chest in the way I had once known during my early days of dropping from the trapeze to the net below. There on the shelf lay something I had seen only once before in my life, a wristlet intricately woven in black leather from a single thong. It was exactly like the band which had been on Martin's wrist that day when I had found him by the stream below the circus, a man without a memory.

He had not known what the wristlet was . . . or had pretended not to know, it was hard for me to be sure now. But that mysterious black ring had entered into

Solange's words of prophecy, and the sight of it had frightened Strabo. He had recognized it from his boyhood in Hungary, and knew it as a symbol of the Brotherhood of the Wolf.

EIGHT

For a time I could not think at all, but simply stood staring at the seven-stranded wristlet with my mind a blank. Then slowly I collected my wits.

How did this object come to be among Benedict Kirkby's collection of curios? Did he know what it was? I shivered, a confusion of memories jostling in my mind . . . Solange crooning her prophecy about the ebony snakes: *where one is seven and seven are one;* Martin's head in the moonlight, framed against Orion, with that fleeting look of the wolf on his face; Mr. Galletti reading from the newspaper about the dreadful bombing assassination. Solange had said that one would die and one would fly and one would fall, and so it had come to pass. I remembered the moment of hearing the news that Martin had vanished, and the heart-stopping moment when the trapeze had given way above me, the bar sawn almost through by an unknown hand.

And now, here in Wildings lay that sinister black band which in some way seemed to be woven into my destiny. I was still gazing at it when the door opened and Benedict Kirkby came in. For no good reason I felt guilty, and said, "I was just looking at your collection of curios, Uncle Benedict. I hope you don't mind."

"Eh? No." He spoke rather tersely, and moved to join me with a preoccupied air. "You haven't touched anything, have you?"

"Oh no, I wouldn't do that. I can see you have some very precious pieces here."

"Yes. They come from many different parts of the world."

I hesitated, then pointed to the wristlet and said, "That's a strange thing. What is it, Uncle Benedict?"

He lost his preoccupied manner and turned towards me. "Why do you ask?"

The whole truth was too complicated, so I avoided it, though feeling somewhat guilty again. "Well . . . it looks like a bangle of some kind, but they're not usually of leather, and there isn't any clasp to hold it on."

He picked up the wristlet and studied it, frowning a little. "This was given to me by a Hungarian nobleman. There's no intrinsic value in it, but I understand it's a rather rare funeral object."

"Funeral?" I echoed wonderingly.

"In certain remote areas it used to be placed on a dead man before burial. It was a symbol with some sort of meaning, of course, but I've no idea what that meaning was."

I watched uneasily as he set the wristlet down in its place. To me it seemed there was an aura about the strangely woven black ring, as if it had a malignant life of its own. Certainly it held a mystery, for what Uncle Benedict had said did not tally with what Strabo had told me, except on one point — that it was from Hungary.

Suddenly I did not want to think about it any more, and said, "How was Pegasus, Uncle Benedict?"

"It's not serious. A split nail when she

was reshod yesterday." He moved away to his desk. "Sit down, Chantal."

Settling his lean gray figure in the chair behind the desk, he looked at me from those seemingly lidless gray eyes. "Now that you've joined the Kirkby family we must make proper provision for you, and I suggest we deal with the matter methodically." He took a folder from a drawer of his desk and opened it. Inside were some sheets of paper, and on the top sheet I could see a heading written in rather cramped handwriting. "What is the state of your wardrobe, child?" he asked.

I was taken aback for a moment, then said, "Well — I have enough clothes, Uncle Benedict."

"One suitcase cannot possibly hold sufficient wardrobe for a young lady in your position. Will you please make a list of what you have, and give it to Aunt Prudence. She will then let me know what you need." He took a pen, wrote a word or two on the paper, then put the top sheet aside. "Theresa receives an allowance of four shillings a week for personal spending on small items. Since you are older, I suggest five shillings. Will that be satisfactory?''

''Oh . . . yes, of course,'' I said, floundering. ''I mean, I didn't expect —''

''Five shillings, then,'' he said, and made another note. I had been about to tell him that I had savings of my own in a French bank, in a special account Mr. Kayser had opened for me, and that I intended to write and ask him to transfer this money to a bank in England, but before I could say more the telephone rang. He drew the instrument towards him and picked up the earpiece.

''Hallo? Yes.'' A long pause. ''Benedict Kirkby here.'' A longer pause. ''Very well. Buy five thousand, and sell when they have risen four points. . . . Yes. Goodbye.'' He put the earpiece back on its hook, scribbled on the note pad, then returned to the folder and said, ''I'm delighted to hear that you ride. As soon as I've seen how you shape, we'll have you properly fitted out for riding to hounds.'' For the first time I saw a spark of enthusiasm in his face. ''The best hunting is in the Shires, of course, but we do very well here. I hope we shall be proud of you.''

The spark faded, and he turned another sheet. ''Now, to what extent have you been able to attend church regularly during your — ah — absence?''

''I've been to Catholic churches mostly, Uncle Benedict.''

His eyebrows shot up as he said, ''You haven't become a Catholic?''

''No. But Mr. Galletti's family were Catholics, and so were most of the circus people. When there was an opportunity to go to church, they used to take me with them, but I just used to . . . well, *be* there. Mr. Galletti said it would be wrong to try to make me change my faith, but he thought it was better to sit in any church rather than no church at all.''

Uncle Benedict frowned. ''I think we'd best forget that. You attended regularly at Farleigh, and know the Church of England services, I take it?''

''Yes, I still have the prayer book I took with me when I — when I went away.''

''Very well. The family custom is to attend matins, so you might refresh your memory before next Sunday." He turned another page. "Occupations. Apart from riding, what are your usual pastimes?"

"In the circus there wasn't much time for anything like that, Uncle Benedict. I'm not very good at sewing, but I like to read, and then of course I have my studies."

"Studies?"

"My medical books." I was glad that the chance had come so soon to explain my plans for the future, though I was apprehensive about the way they might be received. Luckily I had rehearsed this speech in my mind several times, for otherwise I would surely have told my story in a very confused fashion.

"I want to become a doctor," I said. "I know it's very, very difficult because lots of people don't like lady doctors, and I know it means going to a medical school for several years, but more and more women are doing it, and at least it's easier than it used to be, because now there are ten medical schools which take women students in the British Isles alone, and six universities where women can take their degree as Doctor of Medicine." I saw Benedict Kirkby's eyebrows climbing steadily, and he drew a breath as if to interrupt, but I plunged on hurriedly. "I know I'm not very clever, but I can make up for that by working hard. I started studying medical books two years ago, so I've learned a little already. I realize nobody can learn enough just by reading books, but at least it's a beginning. I planned to study in Rome, in about two years' time, when I'd saved enough money, because Mr. Galletti introduced me to a doctor there who's a friend of his, and he said he would help me, but I suppose now I'm in England it would be better if I went to medical school here."

I ran out of breath with the last few words, and stopped, watching Benedict Kirkby anxiously. He had recovered from his first surprise and was now looking at me without any particular expression.

"This is an extraordinary ambition," he said. "Why do you wish to become a doctor?"

"Well . . . partly because I'm interested in medicine, and partly because I think it must be very satisfying to heal people of their ills, Uncle Benedict." I hesitated. "There's another reason. I'm ashamed to say this, but . . . well, I'm not a very nice person if I have nothing to do. Before I joined the circus I just wasted all those years, and I hate to remember what an unpleasant creature I was."

"And you're different now, of course?"

The rest of the Kirkbys might be oblivious to Benedict Kirkby's sarcasm, but I was not. I controlled a quick flare of temper, smiled briefly, and contrived to use politely the same mocking word he had applied to Adrian as I said, "Oh, you're teasing me, Uncle Benedict. I didn't mean that I'm a nonpareil now. But I'm different, yes. I've found out that I can do quite difficult things if I keep trying very hard, and at least I've discovered that if I don't keep myself occupied I'm unhappy and unpleasant."

The lizard eyes blinked twice while I was speaking, and when I had finished he sat looking at me with something different in his expression, a hint of wariness, as if he were measuring me anew. I could not read his thoughts, but looking back much later I realized that this was the first and last occasion on which he attempted sarcasm with me.

At last he said, "How did you propose to finance your medical studies?"

"I worked out that I'd need about eight hundred and fifty pounds altogether —"

"How much?" For the first time he looked startled.

"Eight hundred and fifty pounds. But that wouldn't be just for the fees and my board and lodging while I'm at medical school. The fee varies with the hospital, but in England it's about one hundred and thirty pounds, and I've allowed five hundred pounds to keep myself for six years with all expenses, so there should be enough left to buy a share in a practice when I qualify."

"I see." He made a note on his pad. "How did you hope to accumulate such a sum?"

"I've been saving hard. I didn't earn any money in the circus at first, but in the last three years I earned quite a lot, so first I paid back Mr. Galletti for keeping me all that time, and then I saved. I have almost five hundred pounds in a French bank."

Again he gave me that measuring look. "Remarkable. Where were you expecting to find the balance — I mean now that you're no longer earning?"

"Well . . ."

"Go on, child."

I felt awkward and at a disadvantage now, but could only plunge on. "Gideon Sumner said you . . . said he thought perhaps you would help me."

"Did he now?"

"Please don't think I expect you to, Uncle Benedict," I said quickly. "I shouldn't have mentioned it. If need be I can work and save up the rest." I spoke on impulse, for I was thoroughly unsettled now. No doubt it had been foolish of me to take for granted Gideon's belief that the Kirkby family would agree to my plans and help me, but I had given no thought to what I might do if he was wrong.

"Work?" said Benedict Kirkby. "I hardly think that would be becoming for a young lady of your position. In any case it's not possible. What work could you do?"

For a moment I was all at sea, then suddenly everything became clear. I looked at the gray man behind the desk and said firmly, "If need be I could find work with a tenting circus in England when they go on the road again next spring. I wouldn't earn as much money as before, because I was part of a flying-trapeze act with Maria and Leo then. On my own, I'd have to work on a single trapeze, and I'd only be considered by one of the smaller circuses. But I am *quite* a good trapeze artist, and the fact that Mr. Galletti trained me would count for a lot, so I'm sure I'd find work without too much difficulty."

I stopped. Benedict Kirkby was gazing at me with dull eyes, his complexion like gray paste. I was to discover in time to come that this was how he looked when he was angry, which happened only rarely. I did not realize it at this moment, for there was no hint of anger in his voice when, after a long silence, he said, "Are you serious?"

"Well . . . yes." I was puzzled. "It's all quite possible, Uncle Benedict, really it is."

"I see." He closed the folder. "I would have thought that to be in the bosom of your family ought to mean more to you than anything else."

I looked down at my hands in my lap, realizing that I could never hope to make him understand. "I'm sorry. I must seem very ungrateful, but it isn't so. I can't tell you how much I appreciate all the trouble you've taken to find me and bring me —" The word stuck in my throat for a moment. "Bring me home."

"But you still wish to pursue your ambition?"

"I can't do anything else," I said wretchedly. "I'm sorry, if I've hurt you, but I don't know what will become of me if I haven't something to — to struggle for. I can't bear the thought of becoming what I used to be again."

"Well, there's no need to be so downcast," he said, and I looked up in surprise to see that he was smiling a little. It was a strange smile, in which his lips stretched like rubber but remained closed, so that no teeth showed. "I understand ambition, Chantal, and although I think you expect far too much of yourself, I certainly don't wish to stand in your way. So the first thing to be said is that you'll have no need to find work in a circus. As Gideon Sumner suggested, I shall provide whatever funds you may need."

"Oh! Thank you, thank you so much, Uncle Benedict."

He waved a hand. "This is what I suggest. Allow yourself time to settle down here in England. We shall be at Wildings until just before Christmas, and then we shall move up to our house in London and remain there till spring. There will be parties, balls, trips to the theater, all the things young ladies enjoy — and we have friends in Kent with whom we spend most weekends hunting. Then, with the spring, if you're still of the same mind, I'll do what I can to help. No doubt you'll have to pass some sort of preliminary examination before you can hope to become a medical student, but that will be up to you, of course."

I felt quite weak with relief, and mingled with my relief was surprise that this gray, emotionless man seemed suddenly to have understood my inmost feelings. I had to blink back tears as I faltered my thanks.

"No need to make a fuss, child," he said amiably. "This is a new century and a new era, and I fancy a new breed of woman is growing up among us, so we older folk must learn to accept it. However, I suggest we keep this a secret between ourselves for the time being. Your Aunt Prudence and most of our local friends are going to be startled, if not shocked by the idea, so let us give everybody time to — ah — get used to you a little, Chantal. Then perhaps they won't be so surprised." He smiled his odd rubbery smile again. "I've had to get used to you rather quickly myself."

"Yes. I'm sorry, Uncle Benedict. I know I must seem peculiar. You're very kind not to be angry with me."

"No such thing. Well, I think we've settled all immediate matters. You'd better run along and find Theresa now. Oh, and

Aunt Prudence asked me to say that she thinks you must let your hair grow.''

''Yes, I will. It was only like this because of working on the trapeze. Thank you again, Uncle Benedict.''

I spent the next hour and a half playing an unending game of Snakes and Ladders in the drawing room with Theresa, giving only half my attention to her cries of excitement and constant chatter about horses, the school she had recently left, the friends she had known there, various happenings in the village, and how she was looking forward to the beginning of the hunting season. It was a pleasant relief after my difficult talk with Benedict Kirkby, for with Theresa I did not have to think. It was enough just to put in a word or two now and again to show that I was listening. I liked Theresa, in fact I almost envied. her, for I thought how lucky she was to be happy and content with so little to occupy her.

Before dinner we went up to change, and I put on the last of my three dresses, the pale-green silk with the pouched bodice and flared skirt. I could not remember when I had last worn three dresses in one day, and realized that Benedict Kirkby had been right in saying that my wardrobe was far too small for my life here at Wildings.

We were all gathered in the drawing room when Gideon and Belinda arrived. She looked very beautiful in dark-blue velvet, and was in a sparkling mood, completely at ease with everybody and quick-witted in conversation. Once again I felt a touch of envy, and thought how lovely it must be to have such easy confidence and so attractive a manner.

When we went in to dinner and I saw the long table laid with shining silver and sparkling glass, I felt a sudden inward gladness. My time with Kayser's Giant Circus had been the happiest of my life, but now I realized that there were some things I had missed. It was good to see the comfortable elegance of an old English dining room again, to take my place at table and draw a snowy napkin from a silver ring, to hear the slight clatter of dishes from the sideboard where Dixon and Alfred prepared to serve a wonderful meal of five courses, beginning with a consommé and fillets of salmon followed by saddle of mutton, roast duck, and apricots in chartreuse.

I thought of the dining tent in Kayser's Giant Circus, and of Sammy's famous stew, and I wished that Maria could have been with me at this moment, for I knew she would have been excited beyond all words at such wonders. I took only small portions, and even then left some on my plate, for I knew I could never eat as the others were eating. I had lost the habit of eating for pleasure, and ate only to satisfy hunger.

Benedict Kirkby, Gideon, and Belinda shared most of the conversation. Theresa was very restrained, as she had been earlier in the drawing room when Benedict Kirkby was present. Uncle Arthur made a few cryptic remarks, translated by Aunt Prudence, who was a-twitch with anxiety and spent most of the time needlessly watching the servants, who performed their duties with unobtrusive excellence.

I said little myself, except when drawn into the conversation, and was relieved not to be plied with questions about my days with the circus, for that was another part of my life which no ordinary person could understand and which I wanted to keep in memory for myself alone. In fact, nobody spoke of my past at all, until towards the end of dinner, when we were waiting for coffee to be served.

Adrian was sitting across the table from me, and for most of the time had been wearing a dreamily distant manner, but now I saw that he had begun to take notice of his surroundings, and was gazing at me. After a few moments he began to laugh. It was a silly, snuffling sort of laugh, and not very loud, rather as if he were giggling through his nose. Everybody stopped talking and looked at him.

"What's amusing you, Adrian?" It was his uncle, sitting at the head of the table, who put the question. "Have you conceived a witty poem? A sparkling ode of Gilbertian satirical quality?"

"Eh? Oh no, Uncle Benedict." Adrian snuffled again. "I was just thinking how absurd it is, you know. Quite ridiculous, really."

I saw Gideon look across the table at Belinda and roll his eyes upward. Benedict Kirkby said, "Ridiculous? I'm sure you're well qualified to judge, Adrian, but don't keep us in suspense. What exactly is it that you find ridiculous?"

"Yes," said Aunt Prudence fondly, "do tell us, dear."

"Well, you see, there's Chantal sitting at table with us in a nice dress and looking, you know, absolutely normal, just like any other young lady, except for her short hair and being a bit brown, but really quite normal." Another giggling snuffle. I wondered what was coming, and so, I think, did everybody else, except perhaps Uncle Arthur, whose mind was elsewhere. Adrian went on, "And then suddenly it came to me, you see, that only a day or two ago she was right up in the top of one of those big circus tents, actually swinging about on a trapeze and just wearing those sort of spangled things, and . . . well, it just seems quite ridiculous, doesn't it?" Snuffle, snuffle, snuffle.

Surprisingly, I was not annoyed. Adrian

could hardly have expressed himself more tactlessly, but I could see what he meant. Before anyone else could speak Theresa said indignantly, "Oh, I do think that's a moldy thing to say, Adrian. You're horrid, saying Chantal's ridiculous."

"Eh? I didn't mean that. I just meant that the *idea* was ridiculous. I mean, she's a young lady of good family, and how many young ladies of good family have ever gone swinging about on trapezes with a lot of unwashed gypsies in a circus? It simply doesn't seem possible."

It was then that fury swept me. My cheeks turned to fire and I must have looked like the red vixen Martin had dubbed me as I snapped, "It can't be impossible if I did it, Adrian. And they weren't unwashed gypsies, they were good, clean, decent people, and they were my friends and my family. Maria was lovely in every way, and Mr. Galletti was the best-educated man I've ever known." I took a grip on myself, looked at Benedict Kirkby, and said rather shakily, "I'm sorry. I beg your pardon."

"Not at all, my dear." He smiled his

rubbery smile. "Impertinence is bound to provoke plain speaking."

"Oh, I say," Adrian began to protest, but Gideon Sumner interrupted with a laugh and said pleasantly, as if trying to smooth over the situation, "Really, Adrian, I think if you'd ever had the good fortune to see Chantal's performance, as Lindy and I have, your only feeling would be one of admiration and respect."

"Yes, I suppose so, but I didn't mean —"

"I agree," Gideon went on, "that what Chantal achieved is very rare, probably unique for a girl of her background, which is all the more to her credit. Society today may regard such an achievement as undignified and unladylike, but that's because today's society is itself a thoroughly ridiculous and hypocritical animal."

Adrian said, "Oh, well, yes . . ." in a rather meaningless way, then relapsed into silence with the hurt air of one who had been misunderstood.

Uncle Arthur shook his head gloomily and said, "Radical. Ruination."

Belinda, eyes sparkling, said, "Oh come now, Mr. Kirkby. You mustn't call my brother a radical. He's a devout anarchist, aren't you, Gideon?"

"Hardly that, dear sister," Gideon replied amiably.

"Good gracious, I should hope not," Aunt Prudence said with a nervous titter. "I'm sure you don't throw bombs at people, do you, Mr. Sumner?"

"Very rarely, dear lady," he answered gravely. "And never when I'm with friends."

The awkward situation had passed, thanks to Gideon. I gave him a grateful look and made up my mind to hold my tongue for as long as possible, but this was not to be, for Theresa said, "Did you never have an accident, Chantal? I mean, did you never fall when you were performing?"

"I sometimes fell into the net when Mr. Galletti was training me, but never during a performance, except once, and that was because the trapeze broke." I could not bring myself to say that the bar had been cut, for it would seem unbelievable.

Looking back now, I could scarcely believe it myself.

"Ohhh, how awful!" Theresa gasped. "Were you hurt?"

"No, I was lucky. I managed to land near the edge of the net." All the Kirkbys were gazing at me with varying degrees of wonder, even Uncle Arthur, and I realized anew that Adrian's clumsily expressed notion had been very true. It was almost impossible for them to imagine, as a reality, that the young woman sitting at table with them had flown on the high trapeze. I wondered what they would have thought if I had told them of the time when the circus had been attacked by a mob of rioters, and even our womenfolk had been armed with cudgels in case the mob broke through our line of men.

Benedict Kirkby said, "Were there any English people in the circus, Chantal?"

"Very few, Uncle Benedict. There was Sammy the cook, and Mr. McLeod with his traction engine, and one or two tentmen and keepers — oh, and Martin was with us for a little while, just before I left."

Across the table, Belinda looked up quickly from the cup of coffee she had been lifting to her lips, and said, "Martin?" At the same moment Theresa said, "I think Martin's a nice name. The Dennison boy's name is Martin, isn't it, Mamma? What a pity they're moving away. What was your Martin's other name, Chantal?"

I had not intended to speak of Martin, and when the name slipped out I hoped that Theresa would go prattling on in her usual manner until the topic of conversation had changed. Now I said reluctantly, "I don't know his other name."

Belinda gave a little laugh. "That sounds rather odd. What did he do in the circus?"

"He wasn't really a circus man. He just joined us one day at Sárvár, and helped out in the stables for a few weeks."

"Still more odd," said Gideon with a smile, idly stirring his coffee. "Who would expect to find an English casual laborer wandering in Hungary?"

I remained silent for a few moments, as

if thinking it was one of those questions which did not call for an answer, but when nobody else spoke I realized that it would seem I was making a mystery of the matter if I did not reply. "He wasn't a casual laborer," I said. "I think he was a gentleman. I found him in the woods one day, and he'd lost his memory after hurting his head in an accident. He wasn't even sure of his own name, but he thought it was Martin."

"Oh, how exciting, Chantal!" exclaimed Theresa. "Whatever did you do?"

"I took him to our pitch, to have something to eat, and then Mr. Kayser said he could work in the stables."

"Did he carry no papers?" Benedict Kirkby asked.

"No, Uncle Benedict, there was nothing to tell who he was."

"A mystery indeed. And his memory did not return?"

"Not while he was with us. One day when we were working at Regensburg he went into the town and just didn't come back. Perhaps his old memory returned, and he forgot his new memories of being with the circus. I don't know."

I had been looking at nobody in particular as I spoke, but now I saw that Belinda had put down her coffee untasted and was looking across the table at Gideon. Perhaps it was a trick of the gaslight, but it seemed to me that her face had lost color, and certainly the sparkle had vanished from her eyes. I glanced quickly at Gideon, beside me. His hand still held the silver spoon in his coffee, but was motionless, as if he had stopped stirring without realizing it. He was looking at his sister hard, with lips slightly pursed, as if warning her to be silent.

"A fascinating tale," Benedict Kirkby was saying. "But how disappointing never to know the outcome of it. Perhaps Adrian could use the notion for a splendid narrative poem. You could possibly have the first verse ready by Christmas, my boy." He looked down the table. "Prudence?"

Aunt Prudence started, then stood up with a great rustling of satin and said, "Yes, of course, Benedict. Shall we leave the gentlemen, ladies? Oh, you haven't finished your coffee, Miss Sumner. Never mind, Dixon will bring it through to the drawing room for you."

Port and cigars. I had forgotten this until now, and thought wryly of Sammy's dining tent. It had not been the custom there for the ladies to withdraw and leave the gentlemen to enjoy their port and cigars.

It was a relief to me when, an hour later, Benedict Kirkby suggested that Theresa and I might like to retire. I had suddenly become so tired that I could scarcely keep my eyes open, for it had been an exhausting day. It was strange to undress in such a spacious bedroom after the cramped quarters I had shared with Maria. The featherbed was soft and warm. I had already turned off the gaslight, and now I pinched out my bedside candle and let my head sink thankfully down into the pillow. Yet sleep did not come at once. I found myself trying to remember the moment at table when that silent message had passed between Gideon and his sister. It was as if my story of Martin had carried some special meaning for them, and I was sure it had startled Belinda, perhaps alarmed her. But why? If they knew who Martin might be, why had they not spoken?

Yet Martin was just a name, and I had not even described him, so how could they know him? The more I thought about it, the more unlikely it seemed. Perhaps . . . perhaps I had been strung up by the events of the long day, and had only imagined what I thought I had seen at table.

Usually my sleep was sound, but when it came to me on my first night in Wildings it was uneasy and disturbed. Once I woke because I was too hot, and threw off some of the covers. Twice I was half roused by troubled dreams I could not recall, and once by a horrid dream of Martin lying dead in the sawdust ring, with the woven black band on his wrist.

At six o'clock I was wide awake. This was my usual time for getting up, and I lay wondering what to do. Breakfast was not till nine. Occasionally I heard faint sounds from below. The servants would be up and busy by now, clearing grates, laying fires, cleaning, polishing, scrubbing.

After a little while I got out of bed and gave the bell pull a tug. Two minutes later Molly tapped on the door and entered, looking startled. "What is it, miss?" she asked in a whisper. "Be you all roight?"

"Yes. I just rang because I want to take my bath now."

"But it's 'ardly gone six, miss! Oi don't think waater's 'ot yet!"

"It doesn't matter. Alfred can fetch it up as it is."

"Oooh, you muzn't, miss, you'll catch your death!"

"No, I won't, Molly, I promise." I had a sudden recollection of the way I had bullied the servants at Farleigh Hall, and said quickly, "But if it's going to upset your usual routine, I'll wait."

"Oh no, doan't you worry 'bout that, miss. If that's what you waant, I'll see to it."

A quarter of an hour later I stood in the hip bath, washing myself in barely lukewarm water. It was a long time since I had sat down to bathe, for our tub in the

318

wagon had been too small. I would have to get used to it again.

As I dressed I decided to spend the time between waking and breakfast each day in studying my medical books, but on this first morning I found it hard to concentrate. I kept imagining what Maria would be doing at a particular moment, and again and again my thoughts turned to Martin.

I was very glad when at last I could go down to breakfast. The Kirkby family greeted me pleasantly, but it was a rather silent meal, for Benedict Kirkby occupied himself in studying the morning newspaper, and the others were careful not to disturb him.

I would not have thought it possible to spend three hours with Aunt Prudence and Theresa discussing clothes for my new wardrobe, but that was how the entire morning was spent. After luncheon I went for a walk with Theresa to the village, so that some of the shopkeepers might be introduced to me, and we returned to find that Gideon and Belinda Sumner had been invited to tea.

It was one of those freak autumn days when the sun shines almost as strongly as in high summer, and Benedict Kirkby decided that we should be served outdoors on the lawn. After the ritual of tea we played croquet. I had never played before, and found it a dull game, probably because I was so bad at it or because Adrian was surprisingly good.

We played in pairs, and there came a time when Adrian and his father were matched against Gideon and Theresa. Aunt Prudence sat watching, and Uncle Benedict had withdrawn to his study. When Belinda said she felt like taking a stroll to the stables, to see the new foal, I asked if I might go with her. As soon as I had spoken I had the feeling that she wanted to be alone, but if so she concealed it quickly and said, "Yes, of course. Haven't you seen the horses yet?"

"No, but I'd like to very much."

"Come along, then. You will excuse us, Mrs. Kirkby?"

"Yes, dear. Don't be too long, though, in case it suddenly becomes chilly." Since the stables were only three or four minutes' walk away, I thought this hardly mattered, but Aunt Prudence always had to have something to worry about.

The stables were splendid. They had been built round a rectangular paddock, and no expense had been spared to make them perfect. The loose boxes, stalls, washhouse, saddle room, coach house, granary, and straw house were all immaculate, and the horses themselves were a joy to look upon.

Two grooms and a boy had charge of eight horses, two mares, and the new foal. Belinda introduced the head groom to me, a stocky, slow-spoken man called Harridge. I had learned much about horses during my time in the circus, and was delighted to have a chance to talk about them. At first Harridge was not very forthcoming, but it took him only a few minutes to realize that I was not talking without at least a little stable experience, and then he warmed to me. "Right you be, miss. We never wash 'em, not even their legs. Used to when I was a boy, mind, an' that's what give 'em mud fever if you ask me. No, we just 'and-rub 'em, we do, then wrap their legs in flannel if they bain't showing 'ot."

I nodded. "We used to wet the flannel with vinegar and water if the legs were hot."

"Same as I do meself, miss."

I would have been happy to spend a long time in the stables, but after fifteen minutes or so Belinda said, "I think we should be going back now, Chantal. Mrs. Kirkby will be getting agitated."

I said goodbye to Harridge and we began to walk slowly back. Belinda was silent, frowning a little, her thoughts seemingly elsewhere. On a sudden impulse I said, "Belinda, last night when I spoke about a man called Martin, who had lost his memory, I felt . . . well, I felt it was almost as if you and Gideon knew something about him. I can't think how that could be so, but if it is, I — I would like to know."

She did not answer at once, but came slowly to a halt and stood absently prodding a leaf with her parasol, as if trying to come to some decision. At last she said, "We used to know a man called

Martin Verne." She stopped, as if that were all.

"Oh," I said rather blankly. "But why should you think it might be the same man?"

She shrugged, her lips twisting in an odd smile. "That's hard to say. There can't be many Englishmen traveling about Hungary, and even fewer who meet with an accident there. But you could well find Martin Verne wandering anywhere in the world, and he's the kind of man who . . . invites an accident."

I had never mentioned that Martin had been attacked and left for dead, yet Belinda seemed to assume that whatever had happened to him had not been a natural accident.

I said, "Surely nobody invites an accident."

"A man like Martin Verne does." She lifted her head and looked at me. "Tell me what he was like."

Before I could finish describing him fully Belinda nodded. "Yes. It must have ben Martin Verne."

I shook my head, amazed. "But it's

such a strange coincidence, Belinda! Did you know he was in Hungary?"

She hesitated, then said slowly, "Gideon thought he might be."

"I don't understand. You said you *used* to know him, not that you know him now."

She sighed and looked at me almost pityingly. "Do you want me to tell you about Martin Verne?"

"Well . . . yes. He was a mystery, and I'd like to know more."

"Did you fall in love with him?"

"Oh, no!" I said indignantly. "It wasn't like that."

"You're fortunate, then. He has great charm. I was in love with him myself once, and he with me. But that was long ago, before I knew the kind of man he is."

"What kind of man is he?"

She began to move slowly on, and I walked beside her. "I first met him three years ago, during the London season. Nobody quite knew where he'd come from. Society matrons were fascinated by him, but careful to keep their daughters in the background when he was about." She gave a little shrug. "Society likes to have one or two men of wicked reputation to provide gossip, but Martin was the only man I ever knew who genuinely deserved such a reputation."

"Do you mean he was dangerous with women? A seducer?"

Belinda looked startled. "I advise you not use such indelicate words in front of your family."

I tried to hide my annoyance. I had not grown to maturity as a sheltered schoolgirl but in a traveling circus, where we spoke simply of natural matters, including human nature. Maria and I had known the would-be seducers among the young men, and were not shocked. Together we had soothed a mare being covered, and watched lion cubs born. I had helped Solange deliver Rama Singh's wife of her first baby when it came earlier than expected, and I had nursed sick men. It was depressing to think that from now on I would have to watch my tongue and pretend such things did not exist.

When I made no reply to Belinda she

shrugged and said, "I imagine Martin is a womanizer, but that wasn't what I meant when I said he was dangerous. I simply meant that he's a bad man."

"Bad? In what way?"

She stopped, gazing ahead of her with unseeing eyes, and said a little wearily, "Martin Verne is a man without a conscience. An adventurer. A swindler, a thief, a trickster. A hireling for anybody and anything, if the price is high enough."

NINE

If ever I had heard the ring of truth I heard it in Belinda's voice at that moment, yet I could not keep a note of challenge from my own voice as I said sharply, "How do you know?"

"Because Gideon told me so," she answered quietly, turning to look at me. "My brother is an adventurer himself, but in a very different way. Some men explore unknown parts of the world, some hunt big game, some find adventure as soldiers or sailors. Gideon chooses to amuse himself by engaging in enterprises which intrigue and challenge him. The latest was to find you, Chantal, but some have been more dangerous than that. When Gideon goes hunting, his quarry is usually a criminal."

"Do you mean he works for the police?"

"No . . . though he has friends in high authority among them who value his work. Most criminals are poor, stupid people. A few are clever, educated, and move in the best circles. Often the law is powerless to act for lack of evidence, and to Gideon this is a challenge."

Belinda shook her head and began to move on again. "He tells me little, but I know he has gone down into the worst thieves' kitchens in London, ragged and unshaven, to seek a hint which might lead him to his quarry. Yes . . . my brother is an adventurer who knows the dark world of criminals. That is his hunting ground. And when he says Martin Verne is a scoundrel of the worst kind, you can be sure it's true."

I felt horribly shaken. It was hard to imagine the Martin I had known as a criminal. A wave of sadness swept me, followed at once by sudden anxiety.

"Is Gideon hunting Martin?" I asked.

Belinda shook her head. "No," she said abruptly.

I wanted to ask if this was by her wish, but did not dare. After a long pause she said in a low voice, "If ever you see Martin again, don't fall in love with him, Chantal."

"Me?" Through my unhappy confusion I felt vague surprise. "I wouldn't. I mean, I didn't before. And I — I don't know about falling in love, but I couldn't do it with somebody bad."

"It's possible. And it isn't easy to stop being in love because a man is bad. Women are fools."

I tried to recapture a question which had risen in my mind while she was speaking earlier, and then it came to me. "Belinda, why did Gideon think Martin might have been in Hungary at the time when I met him there?"

"I don't know," she muttered, but there was no ring of truth in her voice now. "I don't want to talk about it any more." She quickened her pace, and at that moment Theresa appeared in the distance, coming towards us at a lumbering gallop, calling and waving her croquet mallet. The sight of her was almost as much a relief to me as I sensed it was to Belinda, for suddenly I too wanted to talk of Martin no more, and bitterly regretted that I had ever begun to question Belinda about him.

I was remembering, and trying not to remember, that Martin had avoided going to the police or to a doctor because an instinct had warned him to remain hidden. I was remembering how Mr. Galletti had read a newspaper report about the assassination of von Dreyer, the Austrian envoy, which had occurred a few days before I found Martin. The authorities had reason to believe it had been committed by a foreign hireling. And now, only a moment or two ago, Belinda had told me that Martin Verne was a hireling — for anybody and for anything, if the price was sufficient.

"I say, you've been ages, you two!" cried Theresa. "Did you like the horses, Chantal? Mine's Jericho, the bay with the black points. I expect Uncle Benedict will put you up on Tamarisk. She's a fine jumper, if you just leave her to it for timber and hold her in for water. Mamma says it's turning cool, and you should come in now."

She chattered on as we walked up the slope to the lawn, and in that time I decided I would not speak of Martin again to Belinda or Gideon. I wanted to shut him out of my memory. During those days with the circus his past had been a blank to him, so he had not deceived me, but it still hurt to remember that I had caused Mr. Galletti to give his friendship to a man who was a scoundrel, if not worse.

To my relief, neither Belinda nor Gideon mentioned Martin Verne in the weeks that followed. Most of my thoughts were concerned with trying to adjust to my new life at Wildings. During the first week or so I was desperately homesick and unhappy, though I did not say so in the long letter I wrote to Maria. I had a list of the circus bookings for the rest of the season, and could send my letters *poste restante* until the circus reached winter quarters. Then, in February, Maria would send me a list of the next season's bookings as soon as they had been arranged.

It was not easy, learning to become a

young lady again. I might have settled to the task more cheerfully if Theresa had not been the only one of the Kirkby family I felt at ease with. Nothing caused me to alter my first impressions of the others, and again I wondered why they had troubled to find me and bring me home. Certainly it did not seem to have sprung from any warm family feeling.

I got on well enough with the servants, in fact Aunt Prudence thought it necessary to warn me not to be too friendly towards them. Even Dixon, the butler, discarded his early coolness towards me and changed his manner from insolent politeness to amiable politeness.

Each day I would spend a quarter of an hour doing my "prelims" when I first woke, and would then read my medical books or a book borrowed from Benedict Kirkby's library until it was time for me to ring for my bath. The next event was breakfast, and when this ended I would find the long idle day stretching ahead of me.

It seemed unbelievable that so much time could be spent on so many things of so little importance. Apart from Sundays, when we went to church, the mornings seemed endless, particularly after the first two weeks, when I had made several trips by train into Dorchester with Aunt Prudence and Theresa to go shopping for my wardrobe.

Most afternoons were spent in making morning calls, or being "at home" to receive them. This was a very complicated matter. There were several ladies of lesser rank than Aunt Prudence in the district, one or two or equal rank, and only the Squire's wife, Mrs. Mortinger, of higher rank. Benedict Kirkby and John Mortinger were Joint Masters of the Osburne Hunt, so Aunt Prudence was on calling terms with Mrs. Mortinger, which meant that when we called it was not just a matter of leaving cards. We would ask if Mrs. Mortinger was "at home," knowing that she would be, and then we would be received and take tea with her.

There were other ladies on whom we did not call but simply left cards, one for Aunt Prudence and one for Uncle Arthur, who was never with us. This meant that the lady might repay the compliment, but was not expected to make a call. To return a card by a call was a grave breach of etiquette, unless made by a lady of higher rank.

When we were "at home," ladies who called were expected to turn down a corner of the cards they left on the hall table on departure, to show that Theresa and I were included in their call. At my old home, Farleigh Hall, I had been carefully instructed in all this by my governesses, but had not reached the age when I could put it into practice, and I found it very confusing now.

The calls themselves were painfully tedious to me. We would sip tea and nibble thin cucumber sandwiches while the ladies chatted politely about the weather and sundry happenings in the county. Sometimes, when a young man was present, either of the family or paying a call himself, the occasion was more interesting, for he would be expected to chat with the young ladies.

I found to my relief that nobody ever mentioned my past with the circus. This was evidently something to be completely forgotten, though on several occasions I noticed people studying me very curiously, particularly the young gentlemen, as if trying to convince themselves that I could ever have worn a spangled costume and swung on a trapeze in the big top.

Our evenings were spent playing little games, doing needlework, reading, compiling a scrapbook, and talking. Gideon and Belinda Sumner were frequent visitors, for which I was glad, since they were much less formal than the local people, and sometimes Theresa and I would walk across the valley and down the hill, dressed in our best, to visit them at the handsome cottage they had taken.

As the days went by I slowly came to realize that Gideon was unobtrusively courting me. He did not ask Uncle Benedict officially if he might call upon me, but in many small ways, with a look, a word, a smile, he quietly made his interest plain. Only Belinda seemed aware of it, and I had a very strong impression that she was annoyed with her brother on this score.

For myself, I found it hard to know my own feelings. Certainly Gideon was a man who intrigued me greatly, particularly when I remembered all that Belinda had told me about him. It was as hard for me to imagine him playing the role of some ragged footpad in a thieves' kitchen as it was for Adrian Kirkby to imagine me on a trapeze.

He was good company, an excellent and interesting talker, and I had to admit to myself that it was exciting to have him paying me such attention. I enjoyed it, but did not know whether this was because of a growing response within me or simply because it helped to ease the everyday tedium of life at Wildings.

As time went by I learned little more of Uncle Arthur, Aunt Prudence, and Adrian, perhaps because there was little more to be learned. But I discovered that Benedict Kirkby had two ruling passions. They were hunting and money. He divided his time between the stables, the kennels on the Mortinger estate, and his study.

In his study he devoured the financial pages of newspapers, foreign as well as

English, company reports, stock-market prices, and all kinds of items which were far beyond my understanding. There were frequent telephone calls to and from his stockbroker, and sometimes at dinner he would give a dissertation on his recent financial activities which I was sure nobody understood — except perhaps Gideon, if he were present.

I concluded that his passion for money arose mainly from his passion for hunting, which was an enormously expensive hobby. On one occasion Belinda told me that to run a kennel of hounds, and to hunt three days a week during the season, would cost many thousands of pounds a year. When I heard that, I felt less troubled at the thought of Uncle Benedict paying something towards my medical training, for this was a matter of only a few hundreds.

The stables were my great salvation, and I spent even more time there than Theresa. I learned that the cub-hunting season had already begun and would continue until the first day of November, when the fox-hunting season would start. Theresa explained the purpose of cubbing to me. "Well, you see, the fox cubs are at the right age now to be scattered, I mean separated from the vixen. So that's part of it, but you also want to blood the new entries."

"What are the new entries?"

She gazed at me, astonished. "Why, young hounds, of course. At about eighteen months, they have to be taught their business. Oh, and so do the fox cubs. They learn all sorts of tricks from the vixen before they're scattered and make earths of their own. Uncle Benedict and I don't go cub hunting because it starts terribly early in the morning, about seven, and it's not really the same, anyway. Chantal, do you *honestly* mean you didn't *know?*"

As November drew near, more and more of the dinner-table talk was occupied by Theresa and her uncle on the subject. Uncle Arthur, Adrian, and Aunt Prudence would withdraw into their own worlds of music, poetry, and anxiety. I would listen, not understanding the language but striving to get the gist of what was said.

When Benedict Kirkby and Theresa discussed the progress of the cub hunting, or recalled last season's hunting, it reminded me of the days when I had only a smattering of Italian and Maria would chatter away to me in that tongue.

"They've found a babbler in the new entries, Theresa."

"Oh, what a pity. I suppose you'll have to draft it, Uncle Benedict. Harridge was saying that George Felton came down at a rasper this morning."

"He's a fool. Hurt himself trying that hairy bullfinch below Tanker's last season."

"Yes, I remember that meet. It started badly when the pack chopped a fox in the turnips. But then we began a cheek-wind draw up by Gullet's." Theresa turned to me, eyes sparkling. "The hounds were sniffing round the covert, and suddenly one of them threw his tongue, dashed into the break, and out came the fox. We lost the view after ten minutes, and the pack started taking the scent heelways, but Old Tom gave a screech to stop them, and off we went again. There was a check on the downs, because the wind blew the hounds off the line, but Old Tom turned their heads upwind, and after they'd feathered a while they began running mute, and we got a tallyho just beyond the Tilney crossroads, where there's that long oxer. The stragglers couldn't take it because the ground was simply poached by the time they arrived. . . ."

And so it went on.

When Gideon and Belinda dined with us it was a little better. Gideon rode to hounds, but he was not fanatical about the sport, and would usually contrive to steer the conversation in other directions after a while.

My hunting outfit was ready now, made by a tailoress in Dorchester. I had two jackets, two pairs of riding trousers, a pair of boots, a top hat, a crop, and two pairs of gloves. The jackets were black, for only a man could wear the bright red which was called hunting pink. The trousers were a rare triumph for my powers of persuasion. I had never ridden sidesaddle, and was determined not to do so, for except at gentle trot I thought it highly dangerous. Theresa agreed. She had always ridden astride, her mother's objections to this being overruled by Benedict Kirkby, who pointed out that in these modern days of bicycling and bloomers it might be rare for a lady to wear knickerbockers on sporting occasions, but was nevertheless quite acceptable.

I had a secret loathing for knickerbockers, which to me seemed comical, and I begged to be allowed to have riding breeches made for me. Aunt Prudence was shocked, but Theresa proved an unexpected ally, for it seemed that she also disliked knickerbockers. Aunt Prudence wavered, wondered what the neighbors would think, refused firmly, wavered again, suggested we should wear calf-length coats over them, which produced a most uncharacteristic fit of sulks in Theresa, and finally appealed to Benedict Kirkby for a decision, who told her curtly to do as we asked.

"But Benedict, it means such a display of — of limbs!"

"Rubbish. The girls won't wear them to

a ball. And when men are riding to hounds they've something better to occupy them than women's legs."

"Benedict! Really!"

The upshot was that I got my trousers, and so did Theresa. I also had a jacket to wear for exercising the horses and riding practice. I could not be allowed to hunt until Benedict Kirkby was satisfied with my ability, and during my time with the circus I had done very little jumping, but Theresa was an excellent teacher and very patient. During the last two weeks of October we spent hours every day in the larger paddock or out riding across country. Tamarisk, the mare chosen for me to ride, was a beautiful creature, nicely spirited but responsive to a firm hand.

Sometimes Benedict Kirkby rode with us, watching me with quick gray eyes, and sometimes Gideon would also join us. Gideon rode well, but Benedict Kirkby was superb, and when one day he commended me after a jump I flushed with pleasure. His praise was worth having. Theresa on a horse was a different person. All her clumsiness vanished, and she rode as if she were part of the animal. I knew I would never make as good a rider as she, but I tried with everything in me to do my best, and thought ruefully that it was the same pattern as with Maria. By trying twice as hard I might become half as good.

I had one great asset which Theresa admired and which I had to make use of on an occasion when Uncle Benedict and Gideon were present at jumping practice in the paddock. Harridge had set up quite a high jump, and I misjudged it slightly. Tamarisk balked at the last second, when I had committed my whole body to the jump, and I went sailing over the fence alone.

I was vaguely conscious of Theresa shouting, "There she goes! Now watch!" My hands touched the ground, I tucked my head in, body curling in a ball, and made a quick forward somersault, coming easily to my feet with the impetus. I had done the same sort of thing a thousand times in ground practice, and it seemed as natural to me as breathing, but to Theresa it always seemed like magic.

"You see?" she crowed. "I told you! Isn't it marvelous how she takes a fall, Uncle Benedict?"

Gideon, sitting a big sorrel, was laughing, and I even saw a surprised look of approval on Uncle Benedict's face as I moved round the fence to mount Tamarisk again.

Gideon said, "If only you could teach the hunt that trick, there'd be fewer bruises and broken bones at the end of the season, Chantal."

"When she took a toss the other day, she somersaulted in the air and landed on her feet!" Theresa cried proudly. "Go on, Chantal. Show how you do it."

Uncle Benedict stopped smiling, and gave her a cold look. "We're concerned with hunting, not acrobatics," he said sharply. "I don't wish to see Chantal take falls, I wish to see her stay on the horse. Now, again please, Chantal, and let your mount gather herself properly as she comes to the timber this time."

These were the best days I had known at Wildings. The early misery of homesickness was almost past, and I felt I had found my feet again, that I could begin to look forward and not back. There was much to look forward to. The hunting season lay ahead, and after that, Christmas and the winter season in London, with parties, balls, theaters, new faces. I told myself I would enjoy it to the full, and then, with the spring, I would think again about my plans for the future.

Those good days were sadly short-lived. On a crisp November morning I rode to hounds for the first time. . . . and the last.

Feeling very smart in my jacket and very comfortable in my fine new trousers, I rode with Theresa, Benedict Kirkby, and Gideon to the meet at The Bell, a tavern on the road which ran west from the village.

This was not my first sight of the hounds, for I had visited the Mortinger kennels. There were ten couples in the pack today, and the scene on the small green in front of the old tavern made a colorful picture, with the huntsman, the whippers-in, and well over thirty riders. Many of the faces were known to me now.

Theresa and I brought the number of females to five, one riding sidesaddle, two in long divided skirts. Despite what Benedict Kirkby had said, I noticed that the trousers Theresa and I were wearing brought many a glance.

There was a great atmosphere of excitement. People were calling greetings. Horses stamped and snorted. The hounds frisked eagerly. Everybody was delighted that there had been no frost, for this apparently was the enemy of a good scent. The excitement was infectious, and I felt my blood quicken as I made up my mind that I would be up with the hounds when the end came. At eleven o'clock the huntsman touched his horn and set off with the pack, crossing the road and starting up the slope of a big pasture to some woods at the crest of a low hill.

"They're hoping to find in Gullet's," Theresa called as we rode at a gentle canter. "Old Biggs was out at crack there, putting to." I had heard enough hunting talk to know what this meant. Old Biggs, the earth stopper, had been out before dawn, blocking fox holes in Gullet's

Wood, so that the creature had no earth to hide in when he returned from his nightly prowl.

When we reached the covert, the huntsman had already put the hounds in to draw it, with the two whippers-in positioned on either side. If the hounds found and broke, the man on that side would go with them while the other would ride through the covert roaring "Away!" to bring on any hounds left there.

We sat quietly a little way off, waiting. Gideon smiled at me, but I did not speak. I had realized that this sport was very formal, with its own peculiar and complicated etiquette. I was not yet familiar with all the rules, and was anxious to avoid making mistakes.

Suddenly it came, the sound of the huntsman's horn and a loud *"Hue-eye-ee!"* from one of the whippers-in. Uncle Benedict said, "Steady, ladies and gentlemen, steady. Don't press the pack, if you please. Wait till we see them strike the line."

Even as he spoke I saw the pack break from the far side of the covert and begin racing down the hill towards a patchwork of fields below. "Enough fences and water on that line, Kirkby!" grunted Mr. Mortinger with satisfaction, and set heels to his horse. Then we were away in a headlong gallop and I took up station behind Theresa, for she knew every inch of the country, and would choose the best places to jump.

The next fifteen minutes brought me the greatest exhilaration I had known since the day I had given my very first performance with Kayser's Giant Circus. All around me was the drumming of hooves, the fierce snorting of horses at a gallop, and the strange whoops and cries of the field. The wind was on my face, and I was already spattered with mud from the hooves of Theresa's mount. From ahead came the wailing of the horn, and everywhere were the strong colors of horses and riders and countryside, red and green, brown and chestnut, gray and white.

I wheeled through an open gate on Theresa's heels, followed her over a low hedge, across a narrow path, then on through a stand of trees, weaving in and out, lying low in the saddle, mud on my face and jacket from a soggy patch we had crossed.

Now a low rise, with the pack breasting the top a furlong ahead of me. I glanced briefly back, and saw the hunt was well spread out now. No more than eight riders in front of me, Gideon and Uncle Benedict well to the fore. As I reached the crest there came the urgent sound of the horn, and the cry of *"View halloa!"* The fox was in sight.

I started down the hill, staring ahead, trying to pick out the quarry, but I could see only the pack and the riders who were before me. Theresa dropped back and panted. "River at the bottom. He's going to cross water. Be careful — it's fifteen hands deep and a muddy bottom. We'll have to cross at the ford." She touched her crop to the horse, and was away again.

When I reached the foot of the hill I found some confusion. The river wound sharply here, and the view had been lost. It was uncertain whether the fox had crossed or taken a line along the deep bank. Several hounds had separated from the pack as they sought to pick up the scent, and the whippers-in sat ready to bring them together again when they found. While we waited, keeping well clear of the hounds as they made a cast, some of the slower riders began to arrive.

I had the feeling that Tamarisk's girth needed tightening a little, and slipped from the saddle to attend to it. Even as I did so there came a cry from some way along the bank. I looked up to see the pack racing round the curve of the little river to vanish from my sight, and next moment the field was after them. I heard Theresa shriek, "Hurry, Chantal!" Her voice was almost lost among the shouts and noise of hooves. Within a few seconds the whole field had disappeared round the river bend, and I was alone.

I had only imagined the girth was slack, for I could tighten it no more. Furious with myself, I set foot in the stirrup to mount, and it was then I saw the fox break from the cover of some low bushes on the far bank. He was running beside the river, coming from the direction in which the field had disappeared, and no more than a stone's throw from me. The distance shrank swiftly as he came on, keeping to the edge of the bank. I froze, half mounted, standing in one stirrup.

The fox was running steadily, low to the ground, tongue lolling, moving with a seemingly leisurely gait yet covering ground fast. He swung towards me, and I guessed that having crossed by the ford he now planned to recross the river and double back on his tracks, for Theresa had told me that a fox could take to water like an otter. But now he saw me, and stopped on the very brink. I was the enemy barring his way. Or *her* way? Only the male had cheek ruffs, Theresa had told me, and I could see none on the creature facing me. The eyes in the pointed mask showed no fear. For a long second she stared, then turned and streaked away at an angle up the steep slope on the far side of the little river.

I stood down, my heart in my throat, shaken and confused. In that moment when our eyes had met, everything changed for me, and it was as if I had become a part of her. A phrase from the past sounded in my head. *Red vixen*. Martin had called me that, and for me this small red creature fleeing from the rending teeth of ten couples of hounds had for a timeless moment become myself.

The hounds came into my view along the far bank, then the huntsman and the rest of the field. I heard a medley of sound, the challenge of the hounds, the wail of the horn, the shouts of the riders. Theresa turned a startled face towards me and mouthed something I could not hear. Then the field was away after the pack, with the stragglers still rounding the curve of the river from the ford.

One rider had reined in his horse. It was Gideon, and he walked his mount to the water's edge, calling, "Are you all right, Chantal?"

"Yes. Yes, I'm quite all right."

"I'll come back."

"No! Please carry on, Gideon, please! I'm quite all right." I swung up into the saddle. He stared for a moment, then nodded and said, "Better hurry if you want to be in at the death." Next moment he had swung round and was putting his horse to a gallop in pursuit of the field.

I shivered. I did not want to be in at the death. I did not ever want to ride to hounds again. I knew that a fox was vermin, a destroyer. Let him find his way into a henhouse and he would leave a dozen dead. But this was not why men hunted him down with dogs. If a farmer shot a fox it was a crime in the eyes of those who rode to hounds. They wanted him to live, to breed, to grow cunning in the chase, until the day came when they chose to kill him for sport.

Poor red fox. Poor red vixen.

With sinking heart I wondered what I should say to Benedict Kirkby. Simply to announce that I hated hunting would make him think I had lost my reason. Tamarisk fidgeted beneath me. I looked about me, and realized I had lost my bearings, but felt sure that the river passed close to the village of Osburne. If I followed it in an easterly direction I would surely come in time to the outskirts, and then I would know my way home. I clicked my tongue, and set Tamarisk to a walk.

Ten minutes later I saw the church tower rising behind a low hill to my left. I turned in that direction and began to move at an angle across an open field bordered by thick woodlands on my right. I had covered only half a furlong when from far behind me I heard the faint sound of the horn. I stopped and turned. For a moment there was nothing to be seen. Then a moving patch of brown and white broke the crest of the green ridge beyond the river, and I heard the music of the pack in full cry.

My eye slid down the far slope, and now I picked out the small red shape of the quarry. She was heading for the water again. My heart began to pound with anxiety as I watched her ripple down the hill. The river was wider at this point, but very shallow. I lost her as she slipped into the water, but followed the faint line of spray as she splashed her way across. There would be no check for the hounds this time, nor for the following field. They were moving down, red jackets bright against the green background, riding hard.

As she came from the river I saw that

her speed had flagged and her head was low. It seemed to me that the hounds were steadily closing on her, for already they were pounding through the shallow water as she toiled up the slope towards me. And now the leaders of the field were pressing the pack, eager to be in at the death. I sat still, doing nothing, my mind blank with distress.

Tamarisk whinnied. I saw the red vixen's mask come up, and in the same moment she swerved, passing me close on my left and making for the fringe of the woods. Abruptly a shallow dip hid her from my view, and less than twenty seconds later the hounds were all about me, snuffling, panting, thrown into momentary disorder by my presence. Now came the huntsman, red-faced and glaring, roaring strange cries. *"Yut-yut — yut! Try! Try! Yo-hote!"*

For a few moments all was confusion. The hounds were scattering. Then one found a scent, and again came the huntsman's cry to bring the rest of the pack on to him. With a pounding of hooves, the leaders of the field came up. I heard shouts of indignation as they reined in, and then came a sense of panic, for all about me was an air of shocked hostility. Suddenly Benedict Kirkby was in front of me, breathing hard, sweating, eyes burning, his face a pasty gray with fury.

"Good God, you've headed the fox!" he cried as if I had committed murder. I saw Gideon, his face impassive, and Theresa, staring at me aghast. "You've headed the fox!" she echoed incredulously.

The horn sounded by the trees, and with a great panting and scuffling, cheering and cursing, the riders were away again. Benedict Kirkby lingered, but only for a second. "Get back to the house!" he choked. "At *once!*"

He wheeled his horse and launched it in a furious gallop after the field. I sat in a daze, feeling as if the sky had fallen upon me and realizing that by sheer mischance I had committed a dreadful sin in the eyes of huntsmen. Behind me Gideon's voice said, "I'll ride back with you, Chantal."

I turned and saw that he was sitting a few paces away, watching me with a rueful air.

"What did I *do?*" I cried despairingly.

"You headed the fox. You got in front of him and turned him from his line. It confuses the hounds, so he'll probably get away now."

I turned my head to hide the quick pleasure I felt, and said, "But it was an accident! I — I just happened to be here."

"My dear, you should have been with the field. In any event, a rider who heads the fox can expect neither justice nor mercy." He made a smiling grimace. "The noble Lord Scamperdale once said, 'Hanging is too good for him.' "

I had never heard of Lord Scamperdale, and his opinions had no interest for me, but I was now well aware that Benedict Kirkby held the same views. As we set off up the hill at a walk I said, "Do you think Uncle Benedict will forbid me to ride any more?"

"He's very angry. I doubt if he'll let you ride to hounds again."

"Oh." I had no intention of riding to hounds again, and comforted myself with the thought that I would now be saved the awkward problem of trying to explain why. It was a small comfort, but any was better than none, for I was dreading my next meeting with Benedict Kirkby, and foresaw that I would be under a very black cloud at Wildings for some time to come.

I was lost in my thoughts, scarcely aware of Gideon riding beside me as we made our way slowly through a stand of trees, and I jumped a little when he reached out and gently took my hand.

"I'm sorry, Chantal," he said. "It's a stupid business, but your Uncle Benedict is a fanatic, of course."

"I know. It can't be helped."

He continued to hold my hand, and after a little silence said quietly, "I was about to ask him if I might call upon you."

I was annoyed to find my cheeks growing hot, and said lamely, "Oh . . . were you?"

He smiled. "The correct thing for a young lady to say at such a moment is, 'Oh, Mr. Sumner, this is such a surprise.' Or something of that sort."

"I'm sorry. It isn't really such a

surprise, and I'm afraid I'm not a very correct young lady."

"Do you want me to call upon you?"

I hesitated, and at last said unhappily, "I don't know, Gideon."

He blinked, then laughed aloud. "Well, nobody could accuse you of flattery. You're uncommonly direct, aren't you?"

Martin had said the same thing to me, the first time we met. Why should I think of that now?

"Chantal?"

With an effort I gathered my thoughts. "I didn't mean to offend you."

"You haven't." He pressed my hand, then released it as we emerged from the trees. "I think I'll wait a little while before speaking to your uncle. He's inclined to be disobliging when he's in a bad mood, and I fancy he's going to be in a bad mood for some time to come."

That was something of which I had no doubt.

TEN

I had bathed and changed into a dress by the time Benedict Kirkby and Theresa arrived at Wildings. Theresa banged on my bedroom door with her crop and came stomping in, still in her mudspattered jacket and breeches, her face a picture of woe. "We lost him," she said. "He must have gone to earth somewhere up by Cranwood. The hounds struck another scent but it petered out down towards old Beecher's farm." She flung out her arms and gazed at me with baffled sorrow. "Why did you *do* it, Chantal? I just can't understand!"

"It was an accident," I said wearily. "Oh, I know that's no excuse, Gideon told me. I just hope they won't hang me."

"Oh, goodness, no! Nothing like that!" Theresa cried, shaking her head vigorously. "But I'm afraid Uncle Benedict's very angry. It *reflects* on him, you see. I'm to tell you not to mention the subject at luncheon, and he'll see you in his study before tea, at ten minutes to four."

At luncheon the only member of the family to speak to me was Uncle Arthur, who beamed mistily and said, "New chap. Cat among the pigeons, eh?" Aunt Prudence did not translate on this occasion, so I had no idea what was meant, and just nodded with a feeble smile. It was clear that everyone except Uncle Arthur was aware of my disgrace. Benedict Kirkby, when his cold gray eye turned in my direction, looked through me rather than at me, and for once there was no talk of hunting, which made the meal unusually silent. I withdrew into myself and began to recite mentally the names of the bones in the hand.

. . . *The human hand is composed of twenty-seven bones, namely the eight bones of the carpus or wrist, the five bones of the metacarpus forming the palm, and the fourteen phalanges of the fingers. The bones of the carpus are as follows: scaphoid, semilunar, cuneiform, pisiform . . .*

I set myself to repeat the list six times, which kept me occupied for a good part of the meal, and I was only distantly aware of Adrian catching the edge of his uncle's sarcastic tongue, and of Aunt Prudence being in a state of agitation because it was rumored that the new occupant of White Lodge would shortly be moving in. This was the house recently vacated by the Dennisons, and it lay only a mile away, its land adjoining Wildings land.

. . . *Os trapezium, os trapezoides, os magnum, unciform . . .* When I completed my mental recitation for the sixth time, Aunt Prudence was saying, "It's only gossip, of course, but Mrs. Denby's cook said *she* had heard, through her daughter, who is in service in Dorchester, that a *titled* gentleman had leased White Lodge for a few months."

"I should be interested to know how a kitchen maid in Dorchester is so well informed about a tenancy thirty miles away in Osburne," said Benedict Kirkby.

"But it's true, Benedict, I'm sure of it. The girl is employed in the house of the agent who acted for Hubert Dennison. Perhaps he is making a short let while waiting for a buyer. I really must talk with Josie Mortinger about the question of leaving cards. If he is titled, it will be for him, or rather his wife, to make the first call, even though they are newcomers . . ."

I withdrew again, and began to repeat to myself part of a chapter I had learned almost by heart, beginning with the introduction. *Different modes of percussing; recognition of healthy pulmonary percussion note; qualities of sound; duration, pitch, and volume; tympanistic sounds . . .*

Beneath the flow of my thoughts I felt a sudden sadness as I realized that I had not practiced sounding a chest since leaving the circus. There I had practiced on so many people that it was a joke. I remembered one of the little Khalaf boys saying plaintively, "Anyone has only to stand still for a moment and Chantal starts to sound his chest." Such a thing could never happen at Wildings.

When luncheon ended I went to my room and read until it was time to present myself at Benedict Kirkby's study. The interview was very brief. He had long since recovered his temper, and was his usual emotionless self as he said, "I've come to the conclusion that you have a great deal to learn before you can be allowed to ride to hounds again, Chantal. Perhaps — I repeat, *perhaps* if you show signs of adapting properly to our ways, I may review the situation next season."

"Yes, Uncle Benedict." By next season I intended to be at medical school, with or without his help, but I was not going to raise that point now.

"Well, is that all you have to say?"

"I'm sorry I embarrassed you at the hunt."

He waited for me to go on, and I realized he was expecting me to ask if I might continue simply to ride, though not to hounds. Stubborn pride kept me silent, but I was careful not to show defiance, and stood looking at him patiently. It was then I saw a flicker of anxiety deep in his eyes, an uncertainty that seemed strange in such a man. It was almost as if he had some reason to be afraid of me.

He looked away and said, "Very well. Let us hope the whole unfortunate matter will soon be forgotten. You may go, Chantal."

That night I dreamt I was in the big top again, flying high above the ring with Maria and Leo. Like most dreams, it had an element of fantasy. My body weighed nothing at all, and I floated like a thistledown. Waking to the reality of Wildings made a cold aftermath, and brought me close to tears. Once again I had to lecture myself angrily on the folly of pining for the life I had left and the friends I had known.

It was a cold and miserable day. I spent hours at the stables with Harridge, wearing my topcoat and cotton head scarf, longing to help with the stable duties to keep myself warm and occupied. But this was out of the question, for young ladies could not soil their hands with such tasks. I could only watch, and talk to the horses. At luncheon the atmosphere was normal again, which meant that most of the conversation was dominated by Benedict Kirkby and Theresa talking about hunting. I spent my time recalling what I had reviewed before breakfast about the physiology of the female generative organs in the gravid state. Maria had sometimes tested me on that chapter. I wondered what Aunt Prudence's response would be if I asked her to test me on such a subject, and doubted that she could ever have withstood the shock.

At a quarter past four that afternoon, as we were taking tea in the drawing room, Dixon appeared with a card on a silver tray. Only a few minutes earlier Aunt Prudence had said she was not expecting any morning calls, and now she looked up fretfully from the tea table as the butler approached.

"Who is it, Dixon?"

"Commander Sir Robert Wayman is inquiring if you are at home, madam."

A cup clattered in a saucer, and Aunt Prudence jumped as if stung. "Commander? *Sir* Robert —?"

"Of White Lodge, madam."

She took the card in a trembling hand. "Oh! So it was true! But — but surely he's not yet in residence?"

"I gather from Molly that the gentleman took up residence yesterday, madam. A single gentleman, according to village gossip, with a small living-in staff, a manservant and a cook-housekeeper." I could see that Dixon was torn between respect for the gentleman's title and disdain for the inadequacy of his staff.

"And he inquired if we were at home?" Aunt Prudence asked breathlessly. "He did not simply leave cards?"

"He is waiting in his carriage, on the drive, madam."

"Show him in at once, Dixon." Aunt Prudence pressed a hand to her breast. "Arthur! Wake up! Theresa, call Uncle Benedict on the speaking tube, quickly now! Tell him our neighbor has called —" She looked at the card again. "Sir Robert Wayman, Baronet! Chantal, whatever you do, don't *yawn* as you did at the Pooleys' last week. If it happens willy-nilly, convert it into a gay little laugh. Arthur, are you listening? You'd better stand up, dear, you always take things in better when you're standing up."

I felt quite sorry for Aunt Prudence in her anxiety. Theresa finished shouting into the speaking tube and now stood looking excited as she waited for further instructions. Uncle Arthur got to his feet and said, "New chap, eh? Sudden."

"White Lodge was let furnished, Arthur. He had only to arrive with his personal belongings. Oh, dear. I do wish we'd known. Ah, there you are, Benedict — isn't it extraordinary? One would think he would surely have called first upon the Mortingers. I wonder —"

"Stop wondering, and compose yourself, Prudence," Benedict Kirkby said sharply. He rubbed his chin. "Wayman . . . ? I don't recollect having seen the name in *Horse and Hound.*"

At that moment two things happened. The door was opened by Dixon, who announced, "Sir Robert Wayman." And Theresa, returning to her seat with her usual lumbering walk, caused her skirt to brush against a delicate cloisonné vase, perched on a low pedestal. I saw the vase topple, and instinctively I lunged from my chair, sprawling almost full length as I reached to catch it. If I had been a well-brought-up young lady I would have sat still and uttered a little scream, but I was from a circus, where to act on the instant was second nature, and to throw oneself about was an everyday thing for many of us. Next moment I was resting at full stretch on my knees and one hand, the other hand holding the dainty vase only an inch above the polished floorboards between two rugs, where it would have shattered; and from behind me the voice of Sir Robert Wayman was saying, "Good afternoon, Mrs. Kirkby. How good of you to receive me."

I lifted my head, flinching. Aunt Prudence stood with eyes tightly closed. Benedict Kirkby's face had gone gray. Adrian snuffled. Theresa had both hands pressed to her mouth and stared with horrified eyes. Rather bitterly I realized I had disgraced myself again. I came to my feet, put the vase down carefully, smoothed my skirt, and turned to face our visitor. He was a man of fifty or a little more, clean-shaven, with a square face beneath thick graying hair and the weathered complexion of a farmer. He wore morning dress, and was carrying his top hat, gloves, and cane in his left hand. I saw that he limped, swinging his right leg stiffly as he moved forward to shake hands with Aunt Prudence, who was smiling weakly and fluttering her other hand in my direction as she said, "Sir Robert, how kind. Pray excuse — ah . . ."

"I'm hoping to be excused myself, dear lady, for calling upon you so soon, but since we're to be neighbors I thought I'd pay my respects without delay."

Benedict Kirkby said, "We're delighted, Sir Robert." But though he smiled I could detect the undercurrent of anger in his voice, and I watched dully, wondering how much more misfortune could befall me, as he introduced his family to our visitor, leaving me to the last. ". . . And this is Chantal, a young relative we have taken into our home."

As I took Sir Robert's hand, dropping a small curtsy, he shot a glance at the cloisonné vase and then grinned at me suddenly. "That was splendidly held, young lady. Pity you won't be in Sydney for the first test, come December. Plum Warner could put you in the slips and we'd be bound to win the ashes."

I gave a nervous smile, wondering if I had lost my comprehension of the English language. Then I remembered a day when Mr. Galletti had read out a long article from *The Times,* about cricket and test matches and the ashes. He had asked me to explain it, which I had been quite unable to do, but I realized now that our visitor had made a little joke about cricket. His manner towards me was so genial that at once the atmosphere in the room lightened. I think he must have seen my gratitude, for he gave me a friendly little nod before turning to Aunt Prudence and saying, "May I be permitted to sit down, ma'am? I've a stiff leg which plagues me a little at times."

"Oh, please, Sir Robert. Where will you sit? The sofa is comfortable, I think. Do have some tea." Aunt Prudence fluttered her hands and beamed anxiously.

"Thank you, ma'am." Sir Robert

settled himself on the sofa with one leg stuck out in front of him, putting his hat, gloves, and cane on the floor. "I much enjoyed the ride from White Lodge. We came by way of the village, but no doubt there's a footpath across the ridge and down over the river?"

Benedict Kirkby said, "There is indeed, and it's a very pleasant walk. Will you be settling here in Osburne with us, Sir Robert?"

"I've no definite plans at the moment. It's ten years now since I retired." Sir Robert tapped his stiff leg. "This put me out of the Navy, and I've lived mainly in London since then. However, I fancied a spell in the country, so I've taken White Lodge for a while. I hear you're a great hunting man, Kirkby?"

"I'm Joint Master of the Osburne, yes." Benedict Kirkby smiled. "You're already well informed, considering how recently you arrived, Sir Robert."

"Not really. My manservant spent an hour in The Bell last evening and picked up a few scraps of gossip." Sir Robert turned to me. "Used to be with a circus, eh?"

"Yes, sir, for several years." I said no more, for I knew the Kirkbys wanted my past to be forgotten. Sir Robert must have sensed something of this, for he simply nodded and turned to ask Theresa how old she was and if she had left school yet.

For ten minutes or so there was some general conversation. Sir Robert tried at first to include us all, but soon desisted. Aunt Prudence could chatter well enough with other ladies but was out of her depth with him; Adrian and Uncle Arthur had as little to say as usual; Theresa could talk only when she could give free rein to her tongue, and always kept herself well in check when Uncle Benedict was present. And I was being cautious, for once.

"I suppose," said Benedict Kirkby, "that your leg prevents you riding to hounds, Sir Robert?"

"Oh, it doesn't stop me riding, but I've never been one for chasing a fox."

I saw Benedict Kirkby stiffen, but he managed not to frown, and even smiled as he said, "Well, each to his taste."

"As you say, my dear fellow. Whenever I've been a-hunting I've always preferred a more dangerous quarry."

"Ah. Big game?"

"Of a sort," Sir Robert said vaguely. "Of a sort."

"That's for the much-traveled man, of course. Africa, perhaps, or India. A very different sport. I imagine you use human trackers rather than dogs for running down quarry in the jungle."

"It depends on the jungle." Sir Robert's mouth twitched in a brief smile. "But my personal choice is a wolf-born hound." I had the feeling that there was a hidden meaning in his words, as if he had made a joke which only he understood, and from the puzzled look on Benedict Kirkby's face I was sure he felt the same, but before he could say anything Sir Robert continued, "And what about you, Chantal? Do you enjoy hunting?"

There was an awkward silence. This was hardly the moment to say I was in disgrace and had been forbidden to hunt again. Then I realized that if I told the truth it would appear to the Kirkby family as a diplomatic white lie, so I said, "No, I'm afraid I don't enjoy the sport, Sir

Robert. Yesterday was my first meet, and I shan't be riding to hounds again."

I saw a flicker of relief in Benedict Kirkby's eyes, and felt I had earned a good mark. Sir Robert did not pursue the subject of hunting, but again talked generally for a little while and then took a watch from his pocket.

"I must be going. You'll all do me the honor of calling at White Lodge once I've settled in, I trust? Bound to be running into one another anyway, since we're neighbors. You've no objection to me walking over your land, Kirkby? I'm a great walker when this damn leg isn't playing me up — oh, forgive me, ladies. Being an old salt is no excuse for salty language."

When Sir Robert had spoken his goodbyes and was about to leave, he paused and said with the air of one not hoping for too much, "I suppose you're not a chess player, Kirkby?"

"Chess?" I could see Benedict Kirkby was concealing his surprise that any man could bother with such a thing when there was hunting to be done or money to be made. "No, I'm afraid not, Sir Robert."

"None of you? Pity. You don't happen to know of any addicts in these parts?"

"I suppose it's possible," Benedict Kirkby said doubtfully. "Am I right in thinking that the vicar's wife and Mrs. Clayton sometimes play together, Prudence, my dear?"

Sir Robert snorted. "Vicar's wife? God forbid. Oh well, it can't be helped."

I said rather timidly, "I've played quite a lot, Uncle Benedict. I used to play with Mr. Galletti almost every evening when we were on the road, but I wasn't very good at it."

"I hardly think Sir Robert would want to play with a novice, Chantal."

"Hold on, Kirkby, hold on. This man Galletti, was he a good player, child?"

"Yes, sir. I think he was very good. Often he'd read a book at the same time, and only glance at the board when it was his turn to move. I managed to draw with him sometimes, but never once beat him."

Sir Robert's eyes lit up. "Sounds a splendid fellow. Suppose you have the black pieces and your opponent starts with a King's Pawn opening, what would you do?"

"Well, there are many defenses, sir —"

"Quite so, but what would *you* do?"

"I'd play the Sicilian Defense."

Again he grinned suddenly. It was strange how this changed his rather stern face and made it seem younger. "You play a fighting game, my dear. I might have expected it." His expression became formal and he turned to look at Uncle Benedict and Aunt Prudence. "I'd esteem it a great favor if you would allow Chantal to visit White Lodge occasionally of an afternoon, and spend an hour or so at chess with me. That's if she so wishes, naturally. She would be properly chaperoned, of course, by my housekeeper, Mrs. Lane." He smiled at Theresa. "Or perhaps this young lady might wish to accompany her and learn the game."

Theresa looked blank. Aunt Prudence gazed appealingly at the head of the family for guidance, as usual. Benedict Kirkby fingered his chin, and I could tell that behind his bland expression his thoughts were racing. Until today I had always thought of him as a strong character, but in the past half hour it had dawned on me that he only seemed so in comparison with the rest of the family. Even with me, he had quelled his usual sarcasm from the day of my arrival, and his manner with Sir Robert had fallen only a little short of obsequious. I knew now that he was a man who in his cold quiet way might bully those beneath him, but would tread warily with those of higher rank, such as Sir Robert.

At this moment he was weighing the social advantages of agreeing to Sir Robert's request. It might be unusual for a young lady to make such visits, but there was nothing incorrect about it, providing she were properly chaperoned. Three times a week Theresa visited a music teacher, driving to Pellridge in the gig, and no question of a chaperon arose. Besides, Sir Robert was a baronet. . . .

"I'm sure Chantal would be delighted," said Benedict Kirkby. "I'll leave you to make whatever arrangements you wish, Sir Robert."

"Very good of you," Sir Robert said

pleasantly, "but let's hear the child speak for herself, shall we?"

I said at once, "I'd be very happy to play chess with you, sir. But please don't expect too much of me."

"Never fear, child. I'm sure your tutor was a better player than I shall ever be, and I rather think you're a good pupil at whatever you set your hand to." He looked at Benedict Kirkby. "I'll send my man over with a note in a day or two, if I may, suggesting a time for our first battle of the chessboard."

"Excellent, Sir Robert. We shall wait to hear from you."

The rest of that day was much happier for me than the earlier part of it had been. My disgrace on the hunting field was forgotten, and Benedict Kirkby almost went out of his way to be pleasant to me. Theresa was apprehensive at first. "Uncle Benedict, I don't have to go and learn chess, do I? I saw a chess set once, and they have all sort of different pieces. I mean, it's not like Snakes and Ladders, is it, Chantal?"

I shook my head. "No, it isn't at all

like that, I'm afraid."

Benedict Kirkby said impatiently, "Of course you won't be going, Theresa. You'd drive the man mad in ten minutes." He looked at me. "If you find that you're a better player than Sir Robert, I suggest you refrain from beating him, Chantal. It would be most inappropriate." I made no answer, and wondered how he could say such a thing.

Aunt Prudence sat with a hand pressed to her chest, eyes closed. "Just fancy!" she breathed. "Chantal is to play chess with Sir Robert Wayman!" She opened her eyes and smiled dreamily. "Oh, I fear this will put Josie Mortinger's nose seriously out of joint."

Next day I took advantage of being in favor for the moment by assuming that I had not been forbidden to exercise the horses, and I had just returned from a half-hour ride on Tamarisk when Gideon arrived. He gave me a smiling greeting as I dismounted.

"Well, young lady, I hear you have a new beau."

"A new —? Oh, you mean Sir Robert?

But how did you know?''

"It's all over the village that the foreign circus girl is a champion chess player who's going to play against the belted earl at White Lodge himself.''

"Oh, stop teasing me.''

"But I enjoy teasing you. Here, let me do that.'' He lifted the saddle from Tamarisk and carried it to the rack. "Have you thought any more about what I said the other day, Chantal?''

"About calling on me officially? No, I — I'm afraid I haven't, Gideon. Please don't think me rude, but it just seems . . . so unreal.''

"It's very real, I assure you.''

"Do you mean . . . well, do you feel you're in love with me?''

"Of course. And I have what your Aunt Prudence would call honorable intentions. Why else would I ask to call upon you?''

"Well, I suppose there couldn't be any other reason. But that's what seems unreal. I mean, the idea of anyone wanting to marry me.''

He laughed. "My poor confused Chantal.''

"I can't *help* being confused!"

"Don't be angry. Do you mind if I ask what you feel towards me?"

"Oh. Well, I like you very much, Gideon. You've been so kind."

"That isn't really the point, Chantal. Never mind. I'll be going away to Weymouth on business for a few days shortly, and taking Belinda with me. I'll ask you again when I come back."

"Gideon, I really don't think I'm likely to fall in love with you as quickly as that," I said apologetically.

"As direct as ever." He laughed. "But you tempt the gods when you say that." He thought for a moment, then suddenly his eyes sparkled challengingly. "Just suppose you came to feel as I feel, Chantal. What would you do if your Uncle Benedict thought me unsuitable and told you to have nothing to do with me?" He picked up my hand and held it gently, the challenging glint still in his eyes. "Would you run away with me?"

I was startled by his words. "Why should Uncle Benedict think that? You're very friendly with him."

"Yes." He released my hand. "But just suppose."

I tried to imagine myself in such a situation. If it occurred, and I defied Benedict Kirkby's wishes, it could only mean running away with Gideon Sumner. Well, I had run away before, but that was different. At last I shook my head. "I don't know, Gideon. I'm hopeless at deciding what I'd do about something that *might* happen."

"Do you feel under a great obligation to Benedict Kirkby?"

"Well . . . not really. He's given me a comfortable home, but that doesn't mean very much to me. I expect I seem ungrateful, but I feel I only owe him whatever it costs to keep me, and I could pay that back, so I suppose if I really wanted to do something, like running away again, then that's what I'd do."

He nodded, his eyes full of merriment, and was about to speak when Harridge and Theresa came into the saddle room. I was relieved to be saved from any further talk on the subject Gideon had so surprisingly raised, for it made me feel nervous and confused.

Two days later I paid my first visit to Sir Robert. In his note to Benedict Kirkby he had said he would send his man with a carriage to drive me to White Lodge. Benedict Kirkby replied that there was no need for Sir Robert to go to such trouble, and that Harridge would bring me; but in the end, and by my own wish, I made my way there on foot. It was a journey of little more than half a mile by the footpath, and since we were neighbors I would be on Wildings land or White Lodge land the whole time. The weather was crisp but fine, and I was glad of the chance to stretch my legs, for since coming to England I had been having no more than a fraction of the daily exercise I had been used to in the circus.

White Lodge was smaller than Wildings, and only two hundred years old, but it was a warm and cozy house with a mellow beauty I found very peaceful. Sir Robert welcomed me warmly, and there was a moment or two when I felt very emotional and near to tears, for now that I looked back it seemed to me that nobody had been truly pleased to see me since the day I had left the circus, except perhaps for Gideon, and he had no doubt been restrained in showing his feelings by the presence of others.

Sir Robert's manservant and housekeeper were introduced to me. Catling was a quiet, soft-spoken man who had been with his master in the Navy. There was an air of self-reliance about him which appealed to me, and I thought how different he was from the civilian servants I had known. Mrs. Lane was a motherly country woman, rather plump and with graying hair.

"Tes happy I am to meet you, Miss Chantal," she said as she took my hat and coat. "And right nice it'll be for Sir Robert there, having someone to play his ol' chess games with, 'stead of fuming and muttering to hisself, tryin' to play both sides at once without cheating."

"You hold your tongue, woman," grunted Sir Robert, taking my arm and leading me to a fine chess table with the pieces set out in readiness. "Sit by the fire and get on with your knitting. And don't click those damn needles while we're trying to concentrate."

"Language, Sir Robert," she said placidly, quite unperturbed. "You just remember there's a young lady present, and behave yourself proper now."

Sir Robert snorted, gave me an apologetic glance, and said, "Sorry, m'dear. That wretched woman brings out the worst in me. Heaven knows why I put up with her. I'll turf her out one of these days, mark my words."

"Bin saying that ten years now, you have, Sir Robert," Mrs. Lane said amiably. "Tes lucky for you I take no notice."

It was clear to me that this sort of exchange was a long-established habit with them. It reminded me of my daily squabbles with Leo, and suddenly I felt at home. For all that, I was very nervous when we began to play, and before thirty minutes passed I had lost the first game in only fourteen moves.

"I'm sorry," I said unhappily. "I'm not a very good opponent for you, sir."

He smiled. "Just nerves. Take white

again and try to restrain your instinct for attack, child. You're too hasty."

The next game lasted a full hour, and as it went on I realized that though Sir Robert was a very good player he was still not up to Mr. Galletti's standard. I concentrated on developing my pieces and striving for a strong position in the center of the board, resisting all impulses for a daring attack. This made me much harder to beat, and when at last I was checkmated Sir Robert sat back with a smile of approval. "Excellent game, and thank you very much, my dear. I think if you'd exchanged Queens when you had the chance ten minutes ago I might have been in some difficulty."

"I did think of it, sir, but I couldn't quite see beyond the next three moves, so I made myself resist the temptation."

He chuckled. "We must try to find the right balance between your natural style and being too cautious." He looked at his watch, then glared at Mrs. Lane. "Good God, woman, it's half past three! Why haven't you brought us tea, hey?"

"Because you always like it at four

o'clock, to be sure."

"Argue, argue, argue! Miss Chantal must leave at four."

"Not on her own, she won't, Sir Robert. It'll be near dark by then."

"Of course it will, my good woman! It's November. No doubt you'll inform me that the days are drawing in next. I shall walk Miss Chantal home myself, and now will you kindly go and fetch tea?"

"Wi' pleasure, Sir Robert. No need to shout, I'm not a passing ship."

I giggled. When she had gone, Sir Robert grinned and flickered an eyelid at me. "Splendid woman, that. Don't know what I'd do without her. Well now, there's no time for another game, so let's chat a while. Will it trouble you if I smoke?"

"Oh, no. Not at all, sir."

"My leg's a little stiff from sitting. Would you mind fetching me that tobacco jar, child? And a pipe — the smaller one at the end of the pipe rack."

As I picked out the pipe I remembered the times I had filled Mr. Galletti's for him, and said on an impulse, "Would you like me to fill it for you?"

"You?" He looked doubtful.

"I often used to do it for Mr. Galletti. He always said I had a gift for packing the tobacco just so."

"Well, by all means let's see. This was your chess friend in the circus?"

"Oh, more than that. He took me into his family, and I lived in their wagon for five years."

He looked at me curiously. "I'd very much like to hear about those days, Chantal."

I hesitated, rubbing the tobacco between my palms. "It's a little difficult, sir. I . . . I lost my family, and ran away rather than be put in a home. Mr. Galletti took me in, and then years later Mr. Kirkby discovered I was a distant relative and managed to have me found and brought home. But he's told me several times he doesn't want me to talk about my past."

"We must respect his wishes, of course," Sir Robert said slowly. "I've no wish to pry into family affairs, but surely he wouldn't object to your telling me about your circus days."

389

I was not too sure, but I had not been expressly forbidden, so I said, "What would you like me to tell you about, sir?"

He waved a hand. "Everything, child. It's a world right outside my experience, but it must surely be a fascinating one. What was your particular job?"

"I was one of the Flying Gallettis." I took the pipe to him, ready filled now. "We performed on the flying trapeze."

"Good God!" He stared at me open-mouthed for a moment, blinked, looked me up and down, then threw back his head and gave a great laugh of sheer delight. "My dear, you're a treasure. Come now, sit down and tell me all about it. Dammit, I've not spent such a pleasant afternoon for years." He shooed Mrs. Lane out as soon as she brought the tea, and I poured for him as I talked, answering question after eager question. When four o'clock came he reluctantly rang the bell for Catling to fetch our coats and hats.

Later, as I walked back to Wildings on his arm in the gathering dusk, he said absently, almost as if thinking aloud,

"That was an excellent pipe. Haven't had one packed for me since Jessica used to do it, long ago." He sighed. "Lord, but you remind me of her . . ."

"Who is Jessica, sir?" I asked. He had not mentioned the name before.

"She was my wife, child."

"Oh. I — I didn't realize . . ."

"Most people take me for a bachelor, but in fact I've been a widower these past twenty years. My dear wife died when she was only twenty-five . . . in Port Said, when I was shore-based there for a year. There's much in you that reminds me of her, Chantal. She had a fine free spirit . . ."

After a little silence, I said, "I'm so sorry you lost her."

"Time heals, thank God, and the happier memories remain. Well, we mustn't talk of long ago. How are you settling into your new life?"

"Well . . . slowly, I'm afraid."

"You know that young couple at Hatch Cottage, I believe?"

"Gideon Sumner and his sister? Yes, it was they who found me for Mr. Kirkby and brought me home."

"Rather odd. Is young Sumner some sort of Sherlock Holmes?"

"Well, no, not exactly. He's a gentleman who . . . oh dear, it's hard to describe. I think he makes a hobby of having adventures, at least that's what Belinda said. Sometimes he does quite dangerous things."

"I wonder what he's doing here in Osburne?"

"Just passing the time, I believe."

"He was the fellow who rode back with you after you headed the fox that day, wasn't he?"

"Oh. You know about that, sir?"

"Catling heard about it in The Bell. Confounded fox-hunting crowd. If I were you I'd take it as an honor to be in disgrace with 'em. Still, young Sumner had the decency to ride home with you. Interested in you, is he?"

If anyone else had asked such a question I would have been embarrassed and perhaps annoyed, but with Sir Robert I did not mind, for in some strange way I felt closer to him than to anyone I had known since leaving the circus. I said, "Yes, he is. He wants to court me officially."

"And how do you feel about that?"

"Well . . . I'm not sure. It all seems unreal to me, and that's what I've told him. I wish I did know how I feel."

"My dear, you'll know well enough when the time comes." He was silent for a moment, then went on, "Will you promise me something?"

"Yes, sir — if it's one I think I can keep." Mr. Galletti had taught me never to make a promise lightly.

Sir Robert said, "If you ever have cause to think you're falling in love with this young man, will you tell me?"

I was puzzled by such a strange request, and a few seconds passed before I said, "Well . . . yes. But I don't really understand why you ask, sir."

He laughed. "My dear, I know it's impertinent, but if I'm to be in danger of losing my new-found chess companion, I want to be forewarned."

When Dixon opened the door of Wildings to us, Benedict Kirkby came across the hall. "Good afternoon, Sir Robert. Will you come in and take a glass of sherry with me?"

"Thank you, my dear fellow, but I've much to do still in White Lodge, so I'll not linger. And thank you also for the pleasure of Chantal's company. She's given me an immensely enjoyable afternoon."

"I'm delighted to hear it."

Sir Robert looked at me. "Could I trespass upon your kindness for another game or two on Thursday, if that's convenient to you?"

"Of course, of course," Benedict Kirkby said quickly. "Chantal will be only too pleased."

Sir Robert continued to look at me, waiting for my reply, and I said, "Yes, I shall very much look forward to it, sir."

During the next three weeks it became an accepted custom that I should visit Sir Robert on Tuesdays, Thursdays, and Saturdays, the days on which the hunt usually met. This made my life at Wildings much happier, for it meant I did not have to accompany Aunt Prudence and Theresa on so many morning calls, and I was also excused from being "at home" with them on these days.

Perhaps because Sir Robert's friendship towards me reflected a little glory upon the Kirkby family, no objection was made to my continuing to use the stables, despite my disgrace as a huntswoman. I usually spent some time there with Harridge each day, and was able to go out riding whenever I wished, often on my own, but sometimes with Theresa or Gideon or both. On two occasions when Gideon was present Sir Robert joined us, riding one of the three horses he had taken over from the Dennisons. He rode well, seemingly untroubled by his stiff leg, but declined all invitations to join the Osburne Hunt.

My visits to White Lodge gave me great pleasure. Now that I was no longer nervous, my chess improved, and I was sometimes able to hold Sir Robert to a draw. We always stopped, even with a game unfinished, at least half an hour before it was time for me to leave. Then I would fill his pipe and we would chat while having tea. I enjoyed this even more than the chess. Sir Robert had many fascinating stories to tell about his years in the Navy, and also liked to set me talking about all that went on in that small, strange, self-contained world of the circus.

I had been looking forward to the time when the Kirkby family would move to their London house for the winter, but now I knew I would be reluctant to go when the day came. One afternoon at White Lodge I spoke of this to Sir Robert, who looked at me in surprise. "Oh, nonsense, young lady. You'll have a splendid time in London. Parties, balls, lovely dresses, handsome young chaps dancing attendance. You should be longing to go."

I gave him his pipe and said, "Well, I was, because I'm rather lonely at Wildings, but it's different now. When we go to London I won't see you again till the spring."

He had struck a match, and sat staring at me until it burnt down, then dropped it with a muttered oath. From where she sat by the fireplace Mrs. Lane said placidly, "Language, Sir Robert."

"Oh, be quiet, woman." He spent a long time lighting his pipe, watching me from under lowered eyebrows, then said at last, "In all my life I've only ever known one other girl who could have said that without being coy or intending to flatter . . . and that was long ago. You're a devilish disconcerting child, Chantal."

I smiled at the thought that anyone could disconcert Sir Robert. "I don't mean to be. It's just that I spoke without thinking. At Wildings I always have to think about what I'm going to say before I say it, but it's different here." I realized I had come close to being disloyal to the Kirkby family, and went on quickly. "It's my own fault. I still haven't grown used to living with ordinary people yet."

He chuckled. "One day you'll have to stop dividing the world into circus folk and ordinary people, Chantal."

In early December I was told that Theresa and I were to have dancing lessons. Aunt Prudence had arranged for a young woman to come from Dorchester three times a week for the next fortnight, to teach us. The lessons were held in the music room, and Uncle Arthur played dance tunes on the piano, wearing an expression of pained resignation.

Miss Fisk acted as male partner for us in turn, and was a good teacher. I had never been to a ball, and was thankful for the chance to practice before we went to London. To my relief I was able to pick up the steps quickly, but Miss Fisk had great difficulty with Theresa. On one occasion Benedict Kirkby came in to watch for a few minutes, and informed Theresa that she danced as if trying to break in a horse, which was cruel but not entirely untrue.

By the time our last lesson was over I felt that at least I would not make a fool of myself when the moment came for my first partner to lead me onto the floor. I would have liked to test the success of my lessons by dancing with a man, and thought that perhaps Gideon Sumner might agree to take a turn round the music room with me, but he and Belinda were in Weymouth at the time of our last lesson, and I could not bring myself to impose an extra ordeal on Uncle Arthur by asking him to play for us.

On a morning in mid-December I went out riding alone. Another letter had arrived from Maria, and I was glad to be by myself. Though I loved to have her letters, I was always a little disturbed for a few days after receiving one, for I still missed her sorely. On my way home I felt an urge to gallop, and put Tamarisk at the long downward slope of a grassy hill. She went beautifully, seeming to revel in it as much as I, and it seemed that the wind in my face was blowing away the cobwebs of homesickness.

At the foot of the hill the ground rose slightly to a broken hedge bordering a rough, little-used lane which lay in a deep cutting. I eased Tamarisk to a canter, then to a trot, and was about to turn back, letting her take the hill at her own pace, when my eyes was caught by a metallic glint at the foot of the hedge some little distance away. I thought it was a gin set to snare a rabbit, and swung down from the saddle. The gin was a cruel device. I had twice found a rabbit in one, and shivered to think of the poor creature's torment.

I walked along by the hedge, determined to spring the gin, then smiled at my own mistake as I found myself looking down at the wire handle of an old bucket, half buried in the hedge. Next moment I jumped with alarm, for a voice spoke clearly, and it seemed to come from beneath my feet.

"Don't be a damn fool, boy!" It was Sir Robert's voice, harsh with anger. Even as I realized that he must be standing in the road below me, another voice spoke.

"I've had enough."

I caught my breath. Martin's voice? It was sharper and colder than I had ever heard it, yet I was sure it was his.

"You're an ungrateful whelp. Let her go."

"No." A single word, cool and quiet, but still with iron in it.

"You'll fail me for the sake of a woman?"

"A lady."

"Hoity-toity! Where's this incomparable lady now?"

"In another country."

"And what's to stop her coming to you, if she wishes?"

"Stone walls and iron bars."

"What?" Sir Robert gave a snort of contempt. "A female jailbird?"

"No."

"Then you're talking in riddles."

"Perhaps I learned that from you, sir."

"You learned everything from me, boy. Will you fail me in seizing the biggest prize of all?"

"Yes. I've been your hunting dog long enough."

"And reveled in it till now. Who is she?"

The other voice softened a little for the first time. "I'll bring her to you one day, then you'll understand. You'll fall at her feet."

"Good God, you talk like a simpering romantic! There's only one game worth playing, and it's being played *here,* boy! Has the wolf turned lapdog?"

"My teeth are still sharp. I go on Friday. You can count on me till then."

"That's no use! We can't make a killing

till the right moment."

"The right moment could come any day."

There was a silence, then Sir Robert's voice said thoughtfully, "Could it, now? You're a crafty young dog, but tight-lipped. Never tell me what you have in mind."

"That's something else I learned from you, sir."

Sir Robert grunted. "All right. You'd better be off. And don't fail me, damn you."

"No promises."

I heard a jingle of harness, and the next moment a small tinker's cart drawn by a donkey came into my view, moving away from me along the sunken lane. The man driving it was in rags, and wore a stained hat with a brim that flopped over his face. I had no way of telling whether or not he was Martin. The cart clattered away along the lane and vanished from my sight. I heard Sir Robert begin to walk, and a few seconds later I saw him as he crossed to the other side of the lane, moving in the opposite direction to the way the cart had taken, stumping along, swinging his stiff leg, and banging his stick on the ground at every step.

Dazedly I turned and walked slowly back to where Tamarisk stood cropping the grass. No more than a minute could have passed since I dismounted, but in that time the world had turned upside down for me, and I was trembling with shock. Until that moment I would have trusted Sir Robert utterly and in every way, but the man I had heard speaking in the sunken lane was not the amiable host I knew at White Lodge.

And then . . . Martin. Was he the man disguised as a tinker, or had my memory of his voice deceived me? In my conversations with Sir Robert I had never mentioned Martin. I had not spoken of him to anyone since that day when Belinda had told me the kind of man Martin Verne was.

I climbed into the saddle, my head whirling. It was impossible to decipher the cryptic conversation. "We can't make a killing till the right moment," Sir Robert had said. Those words could have more than one meaning, but I shivered as I remembered them. And what was "the only game worth playing"? Something tugged at my memory. The second man, whether he was Martin or not, had said, "I've been your hunting dog long enough." Surely that meant *he* must be the wolf-born hound Sir Robert had spoken of that day when he first called at Wildings — a human hound. And what they hunted could only be human quarry. But who? And for what strange purpose?

It was clear they had worked together for a long time, but it seemed this was soon to end, much to Sir Robert's annoyance. I wondered who could be the woman Martin had spoken of, and felt a pang of emotion I would have found hard to describe. Nudging Tamarisk to a walk, I told myself quickly that I did not know for certain the other man was Martin. But I knew one thing . . . whoever he might be, he was no tinker.

That night I lay awake for a long time, feeling almost as lonely as on my first night at Wildings, and wishing I had someone who was close to me to talk to. In the morning I was bad-tempered, and spoke sharply to Harridge when I could not find the cotton head scarf I always left in the stable.

I was on edge because I still had not made up my mind whether to pay my usual visit to Sir Robert next day or to make some excuse. I could not believe that his warm friendliness towards me was a pretense, but neither could I forget the disturbing conversation I had overheard. In the end I thought of his housekeeper, Mrs. Lane, remembering that she had held that position with him for some ten years now. Such a gentle and amiable woman could never have remained with a man who had sinister secrets to hide, I reasoned, and therefore I would try to put yesterday's experience out of my mind, and go to see Sir Robert as usual.

Perhaps this was not a very logical decision, but I was relieved to have made it, and went at once to the stables to tell Harridge I was sorry for having got into such a huff about the head scarf earlier.

After luncheon next day I put on my

gray coat and straw hat for the walk to White Lodge. Aunt Prudence had recently bought me a fur muff, but I had no need for it yet. The weather was still unusually mild for an English December. I made my way at a brisk pace down the footpath, up the hill, then down again to the stream. Here the water was bridged by a plank of oak, long and broad, which saved a detour down the stream and over the culvert. It was as I approached the plank bridge that I heard from far behind me a short shrill whistle. I turned, but saw nobody. Then a black shape broke suddenly from the trees a hundred yards away to my right and began moving down towards me. It was a huge dog, running fast. Even before my eyes had fully focused on it I felt the hairs on the back of my neck bristle and my flesh creep.

I stood still for a moment, annoyed with myself. I was used to all kinds of animals, and had no fear of dogs, but still my heart pounded. The creature had cropped ears, which gave it a menacing appearance, and there was something horribly purposeful about the way in which it was heading straight for me. The next moment I found myself running, possessed by terror, knowing in the marrow of my bones that I was the great hound's quarry.

ELEVEN

Hampered by skirt and coat, I ran across the plank bridge and turned. The hound was no more than fifty paces away. I bent, managed to get my fingers under the end of the plank, and heaved, but it was set fast in the dried mud. I drew in a great breath, summoned every ounce of my energy, and heaved again. Fear must have lent me added strength, for the heavy plank lifted. I staggered sideways and flung the end from me so that it fell into the stream, then stood watching, dry-mouthed and afraid, to see if the powerful black creature would take to water.

It came to a halt on the far bank, eight paces away from me, and seemed to measure the jump, then looked down at the slow-moving water. I knew the stream to be no more than three feet deep here, but the eye could not tell the depth, for the water was muddy. The animal's massive head lifted, jaws agape, tongue lolling between great yellow fangs, and I looked into the eyes of a killer dog.

On the black coat were the mahogany markings of the Rottweiler breed I had seen in Germany, but the tail was not docked short, and there was something of the mastiff strain in the shape of the head, also in the greater size, for this creature stood as high as my hip.

The pointed ears twitched, and he seemed to be waiting. From far away came another sharp whistle, a trilling note and then a lower-pitched one. Like a sheep dog answering a signal, the hound turned and began racing along the bank towards the culvert. I heard a sob of fear break from my lips. In less than thirty seconds the hunter would be upon me.

In the wild jumble of my thoughts there came a darting memory of the red vixen running from the hounds, small yet determined, ready to fight with all her wit and skill until the very end. I was the red vixen now, and in some strange way this thought helped me to take hold of the panic which was rising to engulf me. I was still terrified, but my brain no longer felt frozen. Even so, instinct was quicker than thought, for I found myself tearing off my coat and straw hat before I knew why. I threw them down, watching the black killer as it crossed the culvert and turned towards me again. Then I gathered my skirt and petticoat up to my waist and slithered down into the stream. Unknown to Aunt Prudence, I never wore the long drawers that were part of the wardrobe she had provided, but still used the several *petits caleçons* I had brought with me, washing them through at night and drying them over the radiator in my room. I was truly thankful for this now as I waded thigh-deep through the stream, for clinging wet underwear would have badly encumbered me.

I took one glance back as I scrambled up the bank. My black pursuer slithered to a halt on the far side and began to worry my coat. Then I turned and ran. There were several trees bordering the footpath this side of the stream, and my one hope was to reach a tree I could climb quickly to a sufficient height for safety.

I had covered no more than thirty yards when the whistling sound came again, a double note, short and sharp. Seconds later I heard a great splash behind me, and held back a groan of despair as I realized that this time the hound had been commanded to cross the water. As I ran up the slope I sought frantically for a tree with low branches, but there was not one I could reach in time. Then, just ahead of me, I saw the tall ash. It had no low branches, but there was one which reached out across the path from a bigger bough. The branch was as thick as my wrist, and nine or ten feet above the ground . . . too high for me.

Suddenly my fear fell away and I felt only a raging anger, a fury towards the monstrous killer dog and towards his cold-blooded master who watched from the cover of the woods. The branch was too high for me to reach by leaping from the upslope of the path, but . . .

I passed under it, ran on for ten paces, stopped and turned suddenly, gathered my skirt and petticoat to my thighs again, then started to run back. The black hound was clear of the stream and racing towards me. My eyes swept the path in front of me, saw that it was smooth, then lifted to the branch and fixed upon it with fierce concentration.

I offered up a frantic prayer that my timing would be right, then released my skirt and sprang in the same instant, a forward-lunging leap from the downslope of the path, reaching, reaching desperately . . .

My hands clamped on the branch. Before me I glimpsed the black shape of the hound making its spring. My feet swept forward and up. Something heavy grazed my back. I threw back my head, and my legs circled up and over. Skirt and petticoat fell about my shoulders. Then I was lying horizontally across the branch, balancing on my stomach, staring down at the black brute below, flinching as he sprang again, seeing the great slavering jaws snap together an arm's length below me before he dropped back thwarted to the ground.

I was safe. And now I began to tremble like a fool. I looked up, edged along the branch a few inches, then brought one foot onto it and stood up quickly, grasping another branch above. The hound sprang again, then again. I stared down, hating it with every fiber of my being.

He squatted on powerful haunches and sat watching me with equal hatred. I began to wonder how long I would be trapped here. When I failed to arrive at White Lodge, Sir Robert might send Catling with a note to inquire after me; or perhaps Theresa might ride out this way. New anxiety struck me, and I kept looking first one way then the other, ready to scream a warning to whoever might appear. Suddenly I remembered the hound's hidden master. Suppose he came out from hiding and climbed after me, or flung a heavy stone to bring me down?

I was preparing to climb to the very top of the tall ash when a rider appeared, coming from Wildings. I knew from the jacket and red cravat he wore that it was Gideon Sumner, and at once began to shout at the top of my voice.

"Gideon! Keep away! There's a savage dog here, a killer! Go and fetch Harridge, he's got a shotgun!"

I saw Gideon set heels to his horse and come galloping across the slope of the hill towards me. At the same moment there came a long whistle from the woods on the other side. The hound rose and went racing away in that direction without a backward look. As it vanished into the trees, Gideon's voice spoke below.

"Chantal! Did that creature attack you?"

As I looked down I saw that he was shading his eyes, staring across the pasture. My teeth began to chatter and I stammered, "It was *s-sent* to attack me, Gideon! Someone in those woods was wh-whistling, telling it what to do."

"What?" He turned to stare up at me, and I had never seen such shock and anger in his face before. "Who in God's name would do such a thing?"

"I don't know! Nobody! But somebody *did!*" I was babbling stupidly now, and tried to take a grip on myself. "I'm sorry,

I didn't mean to shout at you, it's only because I was so frightened. Gideon, I'm coming down. Don't look for a moment."

"Wait, Chantal." He backed his horse beneath me, then said, "Come along." I bent, gripped the branch, swung down, and lowered myself into the saddle behind him, hitching up my skirt. "Did you mark where the brute disappeared?" he asked, his voice rough with anger.

"Yes. Just beside that dead bush under the oak."

"Let's go and see."

"All right — but it's a ferocious brute, Gideon."

"I saw it, and I know the sort." His voice was very grim. "They can tear a man's throat in the blink of an eye." He lifted the thick cane he always carried, attached to his wrist by a leather loop when he was mounted. Twisting one end of it, he drew out a slender blade eighteen inches long, and half turned to show me. "I've quite a nasty fang of my own," he said. "Do you want to wait in the tree?"

"No, I'm not afraid now."

"Good girl. Hold on tight."

We went cantering across the pasture to the fringe of woods, slowing as we came to the dead bush. "I rather fancy they've gone," Gideon said, and I caught a hard note of disappointment in his voice. "Take the reins and wait here, Chantal."

He swung a leg forward and over the horse's neck to dismount, and I took the reins as he walked towards the oak, the sword-stick poised in his hand. I watched him circle the dead bush, then he looked about him and said, "They've gone. But the man was here sure enough. Come and look."

I dismounted and led the horse forward. Gideon was crouching now, lifting something on the point of his blade, a blue-and-white cotton head scarf. I jumped with new shock, and Gideon said tautly, "Yes, it's yours, isn't it? He must have used this to give the dog your scent. But how the devil did he lay hands on it?"

My voice trembled as I said, "I — I usually leave it in the stables, but I suppose I could have lost it."

He thrust the scarf in his pocket and crouched again, pointing to something which smoldered slightly on the ground. "Tobacco. The swine knocked his pipe out here." He picked up a crumpled piece of yellow paper with an oily glaze to it. "French tobacco," he murmured as if to himself. "I've seen their seamen in Weymouth with this kind of packet."

"A French seaman?" I echoed wonderingly. "But . . . why would a French seaman come here and send such a dog after me?"

Gideon had stood up and was fingering the packet, staring down at it with eyes like stones. After a moment he shrugged. "It's madness. You haven't had an encounter with any such man during your walks, have you? A man begging, perhaps, and you refused him?"

"No!" I said irritably. "I wouldn't refuse a beggar, and if I did it's hardly a reason for sending his dog to kill me. Why should a seaman have a dog anyway?"

"Some of the ships have guard dogs aboard to keep sneak thieves away when they're in port. I've seen them." He shook his head and tossed the piece of paper away. "He must have been drunk, it's the only answer."

I did not believe that, but I felt suddenly relieved to hear Gideon say it, though I scarcely knew why at that moment. I only knew I did not want to speculate on the mystery any further. I was suddenly aware of feeling cold. I had no coat, my stockings were soaked, and my shoes squelched with water.

Gideon must have seen me shiver, for he said, "Where's your coat and hat?"

"On the other side of the stream. I had to wade across after I'd thrown the plank in, because the hound came over the culvert." He took off his jacket, held it for me to put on, then turned me towards him and rested his hands on my shoulders, looking down at me wonderingly. "God knows how you shifted the plank!"

"I only just managed to. But I'm strong because of my training."

"And then getting up onto that branch . . . it's as well you happened to be Chantal." He put a hand under my chin, tilted my head, and kissed me gently on the lips. It was a good feeling, but I had no time to dwell on it, for he smiled and said, "Come along, I must get you home. Can you mount behind me from the ground?"

"Yes, but I won't, Gideon. I'll hold a stirrup and run, then I won't get chilled. Besides, if Aunt Prudence saw me riding astride in a skirt she'd have a fit."

"She's going to have a fit anyway when she hears what happened."

Ten minutes later we reached Wildings. To my surprise, Benedict Kirkby was the one who showed most agitation on hearing my story. His usual cold and efficient manner deserted him completely, while Aunt Prudence, no less surprisingly, remained calm and rose to the occasion admirably. She at once sent Harridge off in the gig to fetch Sergeant Price from the police station and to call out Dr. Mansfield. Alfred, the footman, was dispatched with a note of explanation to White Lodge, and then I was taken to the fine bathroom used only by the older Kirkbys, where Aunt Prudence left me to take a piping-hot bath for ten minutes before bringing me a warmed nightdress and ushering me into bed. When I remembered how often I had been soaked to the skin during my circus days it all seemed to be a great fuss over nothing, but I felt very grateful to her for her kindness.

Dr. Mansfield came, pronounced me as fit as a cart horse, refused Aunt Prudence's urging to leave me a bottle of medicine, on the grounds that he could find nothing I needed it for, and took his leave. When I was propped up in bed and well wrapped in a dressing gown, Sergeant Price was brought in. He sat looking uncomfortable, never lifting his eyes from his notebook as I told my story again, asked me a few questions, most of which I could not answer, and seemed relieved to withdraw.

Sir Robert, on receiving Aunt Prudence's note, rode over from White Lodge at once to inquire after me and to send his best wishes for my quick recovery. Molly brought me a bowl of hot soup, a cold leg of chicken, and some bread and butter, with good wishes from the servants' hall. When I had eaten, Theresa came and chattered to me until I pretended to be very sleepy, and then at last I was left alone.

I lay with eyes closed, sadly and wearily forcing myself to think the thoughts I had been shutting from my mind. Months ago, in Regensburg, somebody had tried to kill me by partly cutting through the bar of my trapeze. Today I had again come close to death, and at this moment I could not believe that a drunken seaman had been responsible. I did not even try to think why anyone should wish me dead, for I had been through all that before and found it fruitless. But I knew of only one person in the world who had been at hand on both occasions, and that was Martin.

A tear squeezed from under one eyelid and ran down my cheek. Madness, Gideon had said. Perhaps that was it. Martin's brain had been affected by the blow which took his memory. But he had sounded sane enough when speaking with Sir Robert only two days before, and they were working together in some way. Surely they could not both be out of their minds.

Once again I was assuming it was

Martin's voice I had heard in the sunken lane, but I might be wrong. I tried to recapture the sound of that voice, tried to remember what had been said, but now the whole incident seemed unreal, as if it had been a dream. Perhaps this was so, perhaps my own mind had played tricks on me. How could anyone ever tell if that happened? The affair of the trapeze could have been the work of some wild, foolhardy local youth. A wager. He had simply expected one of us to fall into the net. After all, it was against this kind of stupidity that we guarded the circus by night. And perhaps Gideon was right about the ferocious guard dog's attack on me today . . . a dangerous prank by a man too drunk to realize what he was doing.

My thoughts went round and round as I tried to convince myself that nobody wished me dead, and that there were far more plausible reasons for what had happened. Then slowly the thoughts became elusive, my weary mind grew still, and sleep came upon me.

Next morning, to prevent any argument

about my being well enough to get up, I rose early and was first down to breakfast. When the others arrived, Aunt Prudence protested that I should have stayed in bed for a day or two, but I thanked her warmly for taking such good care of me and assured her I was perfectly well.

Benedict Kirkby had recovered his usual calm. He said briskly that there had been enough discussion of the affair by the family last night, and the subject should now be dropped until such time as the police found the man responsible, which he thought very unlikely. I was only too glad to hear him say this, for I had dreaded going over the story again and again.

There was a meet of the Osburne Hunt that morning, the last but one for the Kirkbys, since we would be leaving for London at the weekend. When Benedict Kirkby and Theresa had ridden off I decided to walk down to Hatch Cottage and thank Gideon for his help. It was not until I reached the cottage that I suddenly remembered how he had kissed me, and began to feel a little shy, almost hoping that he would be out with the hunt and that I could simply leave a message with Belinda.

To my surprise the front door was not properly latched, and swung open a little as I lifted the knocker. When nobody answered I pushed the door wide and stepped hesitantly inside. I was about to call Belinda's name when I heard the sound of a muffled sob. "Belinda?" I said hesitantly. There was no response. I moved forward a few paces to where a door opened onto the sitting room. It stood ajar, and I could see a figure sprawled face down on the big sofa, head buried in her arms.

It was Belinda. I recognized the dress she wore, though the room was dark, for the curtains had not yet been drawn back. She sobbed again, a strange choking sound. Alarmed, I pushed the door open and said, "Belinda, it's me. Are you all right?" She jerked to a sitting position, staring at me.

"How did you get in?" Her voice was no more than a whisper, but there was anger in it.

"The door wasn't latched. I'm sorry, I didn't mean to intrude, but then I heard you . . . well, I heard a funny sound and thought you were ill."

"I'm all right." She got to her feet, moved to the window, and drew back the curtains.

I scarcely knew how to go on, and said awkwardly, "I won't stay a moment. Is Gideon here?"

"No. He left for Weymouth again last night. He has some idea of looking for the owner of the dog which attacked you." She did not turn round as she spoke.

I said, "It's very good of him, but he shouldn't leave you alone like this."

"Why not?" Her voice was normal again now. "My brother never treats me as a fragile female, and I wouldn't wish him to."

"Well . . . at least he ought to make sure he leaves the door properly latched at night."

She gave a curious laugh, hard and without humor. "Oh, that wasn't Gideon. It must have been this morning's visitor."

She turned suddenly, and I gasped. One

side of her face was red and swollen, but not from crying. I knew that look, for it was as my own face had looked after Strabo's heavy-handed slapping.

"Belinda! Who did it?"

Her mouth twisted. "Your friend Martin Verne."

"Martin?" My voice shook. "Oh, he couldn't!"

"He was here this morning."

"But . . . but *why?*"

"He wanted me to lend him money. A lot of it. He knows I have money of my own, and he thought he could twist me round his finger, as he used to. When I refused . . ." She shrugged and put a hand tenderly to her cheek. "I think he's out of his mind."

I stood in utter misery and said, "Oh, Belinda, I'm so sorry. It — it's such a dreadful thing to have done."

She shrugged again. "He's gone now, and he won't come back. Please don't speak of this to Gideon."

"Don't —? But you *must* tell him, Belinda!"

"That's the last thing I'll do. He

wouldn't rest till he'd found Martin, and then . . . I don't know what the outcome would be. They're both dangerous men.''

"But surely Gideon will see what's happened to you?"

"He won't be back till tomorrow, and I can get the swelling down by then."

"Well . . . if that's what you want, please let me go and fetch some ice from the fishmonger for you. I'm sure cold compresses would help. And I'll get some witch hazel from the chemist. That's very good, we used it a lot in the circus."

She looked quickly away from me and stood without speaking for what seemed a long time, head lowered. Then at last she said in a low voice. "You're very good Chantal. Yes, will you do that for me? Wait, I'll give you some money."

"No, it's all right, I have some in my purse." I turned to the door. "I'll only be a few minutes, and then I'll stay with you till it's time for luncheon, and help with the cold compresses."

I was glad to be out of the cottage, to hide my distress. Now I knew for certain that Martin had been in Osburne, today at least, and this made it harder for me to doubt that he had been the man I had heard speaking with Sir Robert in the sunken lane only two days before.

I tried to match a memory picture of the Martin I had known with the picture of a man who could beat a woman about the face, a man who could set a killer dog on someone who had been his friend. But the pictures would not match. I tried to stop myself remembering that the Martin I had known was not himself but another man, not Martin Verne, but simply Martin.

During the next few days I could not wait to get away from Osburne, for I felt like a fly trapped in an invisible web, as if I were caught up in some strange mystery which had nothing to do with me. I paid one more visit to Sir Robert before we left, but although he made a great fuss of me in his gruff way I felt ill at ease with him, played two very bad games of chess, and was thankful when it was time to go home.

I saw no more of Gideon and Belinda in

Osburne. Two days after my visit to the cottage, Benedict Kirkby received a note from Gideon saying that he had urgent business abroad and would be leaving next day with Belinda. He sent warmest good wishes to the family, regretted that he and Belinda would be unable to see us during the Christmas festivities, but hoped to be in London towards winter's end.

"How odd," said Aunt Prudence. "I do feel they should have called to say goodbye."

"If they're catching a boat tomorrow they'll have more than enough to do," said Benedict Kirkby. He was in a good humor, and I felt he was pleased that the Sumners were going away, though I could see no reason why he should be.

"All the same, they're a peculiar couple," Aunt Prudence mused. "Very pleasant, of course, but most unconventional. I hardly think it wise for Gideon to take his sister on these trips to foreign parts. Foreigners are known to be *quite* unreliable."

"I doubt that he's taking her into the wilds of Arabia, my dear Prudence. In any event, she probably wouldn't jib at that. She's one of the New Women. They're becoming more independent every day."

"One wonders what the world is coming to," Aunt Prudence sighed, shaking her head. "I had a letter from Lottie Cranmer the other day. Her eldest girl is actually working as a typewriter in a London bank."

I was feeling rather put out by Gideon's behavior myself. He had wanted to court me officially, he had even said that he was in love with me, and only a day or two ago he had kissed me. Yet now he had gone away without a word, except for his note to Benedict Kirkby, and I felt hurt. But within a few moments I was wondering at my own stupidity, for I still had no idea whether I wanted to be courted by Gideon or not.

Three days later we came to London in a snowstorm. Hooves and carriage wheels slipped and slithered in the thick white carpet as we were driven from Waterloo Station to the Kirkby house in Cranmore Square. I had only once been to London before, and had seen little of it then, for it had been the occasion of my ordeal in the solicitor's office. Now I was full of excitement, for despite the snow the city was bustling with life.

As we crossed Waterloo Bridge and turned down the Strand to Trafalgar Square, I kept rubbing the steam of my breath from the window to see all that I could. We made our way along the broad and handsome approach of the Mall to Buckingham Palace, then onto a bustling jam of carriages at Hyde Park Corner, and finally into the gracious tree-lined streets and squares of Belgravia.

The house in Cranmore Square was much smaller than Wildings but very handsome. Dixon had traveled the day before with three of the servants, and all was in readiness for us when we arrived. My excitement was not caused only by the fact of being in London. I felt that I was putting everything behind me and making a new start. All the family was in good spirits, and Theresa and I spent the first two days shopping for Christmas presents with Aunt Prudence, while the servants busied themselves decorating the hall and the drawing room in festive fashion.

We wrapped our presents in pretty paper, wrote cards for each of them, and placed them at the foot of the Christmas tree which had been set up in a great tub in the hall. Among the many greetings which had already arrived for the family there was a letter for me addressed in Maria's hand. I had written to the Galletti family three weeks before, giving them my London address, and had also posted a small Christmas present to each of them — a brooch for Maria, a clasp knife with many useful tools for Leo, and a book on comparative religion for Mr. Galletti, which he had once read about in a newspaper and said he would like to have.

Each one had written to me in the letter, sending Christmas greetings, and Maria had embroidered a Nativity scene on a piece of gold card in colored silk thread. It was very simple, but she had done it beautifully. As soon as I opened the letter I went to my bedroom and sat looking at the card, crying quietly, remembering the Christmases we had spent in the wagon together in winter quarters.

Already Benedict Kirkby and Aunt Prudence were making plans for the New Year. We had several invitations for hunting weekends, and as soon as Christmas was over there would be balls and parties at various London houses. The dates when we would entertain had to be decided, the guest lists drawn up, and the printing of invitation cards put in hand.

Christmas itself was a time of laughter and tears for me, though I was careful to hide the tears. On the Thursday, which was Christmas Eve, we went to the midnight service, slept late next morning, and after breakfast drove to Hyde Park and walked there for a while. The snow had thawed several days before, and the weather was now dull and cloudy, which pleased Theresa and Benedict Kirkby. They hoped it presaged a mild winter, which would give them better sport when the fox-hunting weekends began.

Christmas dinner was a triumph for Mrs. Foster, the cook, and I had never known the family so at ease. Benedict

Kirkby indulged in no sarcasm, and even Adrian forgot his lofty poetical calling and became quite human. Once dinner had been cleared, the whole household gathered by the tree in the hall for the presents to be distributed, including those for the servants, and when this was over the duties of the domestic staff were ended for the day. They would have their own Christmas dinner belowstairs that evening, and we would have a cold supper which had already been prepared, serving ourselves.

Among my presents was one sent by Sir Robert. It was a very beautiful chess set, and with it was a card on which he had written:

My dear Chantal,
Thank you for the many happy hours your visits have given me.
Affectionately,
Robert Wayman

I was glad then that I had left with Mrs. Lane a book of chess problems, a pipe-cleaning tool, and a greeting card to give to Sir Robert for me on Christmas Day.

That evening we enjoyed ourselves playing silly games, and Uncle Arthur surprised me by coming to earth for a while, putting on Adrian's top hat, which was much too small for him, and singing some comical songs at the piano. But often throughout Christmas I would think of my circus family, and these were the moments when I had to rub my eyes and pretend they were watering from mirth.

Three days after Boxing Day another letter came for me, and this was from Mr. Galletti. He wrote:

My dear Chantal,

This is my first letter to you, though I know you receive all news of us from Maria. I have delayed writing until now because I wished to allow time for you to settle down a little before saying what I feel I must say to you.

It is simply this. I know you must miss us as much as we miss you, dear child, but you will be most unwise if you cling to the past. Our ways have separated now, and you have a new road to follow, new bonds to be made with new friends. It is sometimes a part of life, and a hard part, to put all that is familiar behind you and tread a new path. But if you cling to us, to memories of the circus, to memories of Chantal flying on the trapeze in the big top, then you will stand still and achieve nothing.

I hope you will never forget us, dearest Chantal. Please continue to write to us, as Maria and I will write to you. We shall always love and remember you. Perhaps in time to come, when you are firmly set on whatever your new road may be, you will visit us and spend a little time with us, renewing old friendship. But remember, there can be no going back. When Maria is a little older, perhaps she will marry. Leo also. Then they will each become the center of a new family. Perhaps you will marry, perhaps you will become a doctor. Whatever comes to pass, the time of our being together is ended, dear child, and you must try to accept that we made part of a chapter in your life which has now closed. Remember us with love, but do not yearn for us. Let it be a good memory. If we do not yearn for what cannot be, then our memories can be precious treasures indeed.

And now all has been said. This is the first advice I have ever given you, and it will be the last. I give it with my love, and pray that you will be happy.

Arrivederci, mia cara,
Leonardo Galletti

I sat by my bedroom window with a sad heart, reading the letter for the third time, knowing that Mr. Galletti was right and his counsel wise. I did still cling to the past, and so far had not found the strength to remember it without yearning. I would love my circus family until I died, but our ways would be separate. As Mr. Galletti had said, I must settle to my new life and become a part

of it, not looking back with sadness.
I knew in my heart that I had not tried
hard enough yet.

TWELVE

For the next week I was utterly miserable. I did not want to do anything or talk to anybody, and I was thoroughly disagreeable, even towards Theresa. I was not the only one to be out of sorts in this way. With the short-lived spirit of Christmas fading fast, all members of the Kirkby household seemed quickly to return to normal.

I felt as if in a void, without energy or ambition, disgruntled and lackadaisical. It was not until the first ball we attended that my mood changed. I had not wanted to go to the ball, which was being given by the Morton-Coles, but once I was there I suddenly found myself beginning to enjoy the occasion.

I had a very pretty dress, in pale-blue satin, which made me look taller and more elegant than I really was, and now that my hair had grown longer Molly had been able to do it for me in a fashionable style. Within half an hour my program was full, and after the first two dances I had no more fears of stumbling over my partner's feet. It struck me that I might well have better balance and be lighter of foot than most because I had spent years in acrobatic training.

As the evening wore on, my gaiety increased. I found the young men very pleasant, and for mischief I began to copy some of the other girls, fluttering my eyelids coyly when my partners paid me compliments. The music and merriment, the dancing and light-hearted chatter, all combined to take me out of myself. On the way home in our carriage I was still bubbling with excitement and did not feel in the least tired, but next morning, for the first time since I had come to England, I was last down to breakfast.

During the fortnight that followed we attended the theater, the opera, and three more balls. I enjoyed Mr. Barrie's play *Little Mary* at Wyndham's Theatre, and

Cricket on the Hearth at the Garrick, but the Verdi opera disturbed me because it was sung in Italian, and the pantomime at the Drury Lane Theatre had the same effect because it reminded me a little of the circus. After each of these two outings I was very bad-tempered for a while. Most of all I enjoyed the dancing, especially when I found myself with a good partner.

On two or three mornings each week I would go riding in Hyde Park with Theresa and Benedict Kirkby, and during the next month we spent three long weekends at the Templetons' beautiful house in Kent, where Mr. Templeton was Master of the Crowbridge Hunt. It was here that I attended my first Hunt Ball, a splendid occasion, full of color and excitement, where two young men slipped love notes into my hand.

As the days passed I found myself getting on much better with the Kirkby family, particularly with Benedict Kirkby, and I was sure he would have allowed me to ride to hounds again if I had asked, but I still had no wish to do so. In spite of this, I did not find time to be bored during our country weekends, for we were not the only guests. I enjoyed meeting new acquaintances, riding out with a new escort, gossiping with the other young ladies, studying the latest fashions in ladies' magazines, and experimenting with powder and rouge to make myself look prettier.

I was also enjoying the gay life of London, going to the theater, paying and receiving calls, taking tea in one of the famous hotels, shopping in the great emporiums which seemed as full of treasures as Aladdin's Cave, and again having fervent little love notes pressed into my hand by elegant young men at balls. I no longer spoke simply and bluntly in my old manner, but was rapidly learning the art of conversation as practiced by the society in which I now moved.

The circus became a half-remembered dream, and so did my early weeks at Wildings. It was difficult to believe that I had once found time hanging upon my hands, for now there seemed scarcely enough hours in the day to do all that I wanted to, especially as the servants had become slower, more stupid, and more disobliging since our coming to London, and often had to be spoken to sharply. I felt confident now, and sure of myself for the first time since my arrival in England, for at last I had become a part of the new world I had been thrust into only a few months ago.

In the last week of February a letter came to Benedict Kirkby from Gideon Sumner, in Rome, saying that he and Belinda had wintered on the Continent but hoped to return to their London home before the spring. Benedict Kirkby informed the family of this at luncheon one day, but called me to his study later and told me that there was something more in the letter; Gideon had said that on his return he would ask to call upon me officially.

I opened my eyes wide, and pretended surprise as Benedict Kirkby laid the letter down on the desk in front of him and gave me a questioning look. "Well, Chantal . . . what are your feelings in this matter?"

I noticed that he seemed uneasy, almost

nervous, and I hesitated for long moments, trying to decide what I felt. At last I shook my head. "I don't really know, Uncle Benedict."

"I see. You haven't yet met any young man in our circle you would prefer to call on you officially?"

"Well, no. I like several of them, of course, but . . . no, there isn't anybody special."

"That's rather a pity." He put down the letter and plucked at his lower lip in a fidgety manner. "Of course, since I stand virtually as a parent to you, I could simply tell young Sumner that I won't allow him to call on you officially, but I don't wish to do that. I would much prefer to tell him that *you* have declined."

"Oh. Do you mean you don't want it to happen, Uncle Benedict?"

"To be frank, no. He's a very able and engaging young man, but something of a mystery, and certainly he leads a most unconventional life." He tapped the letter. "This is with a view to marriage, Chantal, and I very much doubt that he's suitable."

I was not attracted by the idea of

rejecting Gideon Sumner out of hand, and said, "Perhaps when he speaks to you about it, you could say he must wait because I haven't made up my mind yet?"

Benedict Kirkby smiled. "I would prefer a plain refusal, but never mind. I've noticed that young ladies have a habit of keeping young men dangling on a string, even when they fully intend to cut the string in the end." His smile vanished and again I saw anxiety in his eyes. "Sumner's a man who acts boldly to get what he wants. I'd like your assurance that you won't come to any decision without informing me, Chantal."

"No, of course I won't, Uncle Benedict."

"Well . . . we'll leave it there for the time being."

The following week we heard from Sir Robert Wayman. To our surprise he was in Paris. He had been staying with an old friend in the Diplomatic Service there, but would be returning to London shortly and hoped that he might call upon us then. Aunt Prudence at once wrote to his London address, saying that she hoped he would call as soon as convenient on his return, and inviting him to the ball she was giving at the end of our London stay, just before we left for Osburne.

The daffodils in the parks bloomed to herald the coming of spring, and during the second week of March we had a guest from abroad staying with us at Cranmore Square. This was Baron Joseph Krenner. I had forgotten about the family's Hungarian connection, for it had been mentioned to me only once, and that was by Gideon Sumner, when he first told me about the Kirkby family. Now I was reminded that my grandfather, James Kirkby, had had a brother called Rupert, and I learned that over fifty years ago Rupert had married Eva Krenner, the sister of a Hungarian nobleman who held a position at the embassy in London at that time.

At first it seemed strange to think that the mother of Benedict and Arthur Kirkby had been Hungarian, but it became less so when I learned that she had been sent to school in England at the age of ten and had spent the rest of her life there, so her ways were entirely English. For all that, Benedict Kirkby never spoke of his parentage, and I sensed that he had no wish for it to be generally known that he was partly of foreign descent. Uncle Arthur never spoke of it either, perhaps for no special reason but simply because he rarely spoke of anything.

Baron Joseph Krenner, our visitor, was the son of the Hungarian nobleman who had been Eva's brother, which made him a first cousin of Benedict and Arthur Kirkby. They had seen little of each other over the years, except for short periods when the Baron came to England on business. He had some banking interests here, and also carried out certain transactions for Benedict Kirkby in Europe, especially in the Balkans, where it seemed there were opportunities to make money if one had a close understanding of the highly complicated and swiftly changing political situation.

I gathered all this from half listening to Benedict Kirkby talking at table a few days before our guest arrived, but I had too many important things to think about to pay much attention to such matters. The only point of interest for me was that the Baron lived in a castle above the village of Szigvár, and this was not many miles from Kaposnika, a town where Kayser's Giant Circus had pitched regularly for a week or ten days each year in early summer.

Baron Krenner spoke good English with only a slight accent. He was a man of about fifty, tall and slender, with very short fair hair, vivid blue eyes, and a face which narrowed from a broad brow to a pointed chin. During his visit he spent most of the time with Benedict Kirkby, either closeted in the study or going to visit bankers and brokers and merchants in the City.

My first instinct was to dislike him, but then I found that he showed more interest in me than in the rest of the family, and I was quite flattered. He must have been told that I played chess, for he suggested that we might have a game or two. He was not nearly as good a player as Mr. Galletti, or even Sir Robert, and I could have won most of our games, but diplomatically avoided doing so. At a ball the family attended during his visit I discovered he was so good a dancer that it was a pleasure to be partnered by him.

"I thank you, Chantal," he said, smiling as he led me back to my seat beside Aunt Prudence. "I must not claim you to dance again, for I see that the young men are looking knives at me. One day you must come to my home in Hungary, and learn to dance as we do there. Perhaps my good friend Benedict will bring all the family, yes? That would be most happy, would it not, Mrs. Kirkby?"

"Oh, really, Baron." Aunt Prudence fluttered her fan in agitation. "Such a long journey. Most kind of you, but you must remember that we ladies are more fragile creatures than you men."

He bowed politely. "Of course, dear lady. That which is beautiful is usually fragile. Yet I think Chantal may be an exception. Perhaps Benedict will bring her one day, if she wishes."

"I very much hope so, Baron," I said, giving him a bright smile. "I'm sure I would enjoy it immensely." I did not know whether I meant what I said or not, but this did not trouble me, for I had learned that in polite conversation it was only the words that mattered, not the meaning.

Baron Krenner went back to Hungary at the end of the week, and my life continued on its gay and exciting way. A few days after the Baron's departure, Gideon and Belinda Sumner returned to London and came to visit us. I watched Gideon with interest as we all took tea together, wondering how he would respond when Benedict Kirkby told him I did not wish him to call upon me yet. I was to learn the answer to that the very next morning, and most unpleasantly, when Theresa and I went riding in Rotten Row with Gideon. There came a moment when Theresa had gone off for a final gallop on her own, and I could not resist saying, "Uncle Benedict told me of your letter, Gideon. Have you spoken to him yet?"

He smiled and nodded. "Yes, I had a word with him in the club as soon as I got back." His smile became rueful. "I do wish he hadn't told you about the letter, Chantal."

"Oh? Why not?"

He smoothed the neck of his horse. "Well . . . because I changed my mind. I know that's supposed to be a lady's privilege, but there you are."

My cheeks were scarlet, and for a moment I could not find my tongue, then I said furiously, "You — you sit there and tell me you've *changed your mind?* That's a . . . shocking thing to do! You couldn't be more insulting if you tried!"

"Yes, I could," Gideon said amiably. "But it's no insult, Chantal. I've simply thought things over and decided I'm not the right man for you. I doubt if there's a girl in London that I *am* the right man for, and you're certainly much too nice for a wandering adventurer like me. I'm sorry if you're hurt, but you should really regard my change of mind as a compliment."

"Hurt?" I managed to force a laugh. "Really, Gideon, that's very amusing. I was only annoyed because your manner seemed insulting, but I realize now that I misunderstood you. In fact it's very satisfactory to me not to be troubled by the matter any further."

He nodded, his eyes friendly. "Good. I'm glad you're not angry with me any more. Ah, there's Theresa coming back. Let's go and meet her."

For the rest of the day I was in a very bad mood. It was one thing for me to keep Gideon Sumner dangling on a string, but quite another for him to cut the string before it was attached.

Sir Robert came to London only two days before our final ball. I was pleased when he called to take tea with us, but felt less at ease with him than I had done at Osburne. He seemed different, and I noticed his gaze resting on me curiously once or twice. On the evening of the ball I spent a great deal of time getting ready for the occasion. Molly had become sulky of late, and was not doing my hair satisfactorily, so I had persuaded Aunt Prudence to have a hairdresser come to the house to prepare the ladies' hair. Mine was now long enough to wear swept up on top of my head, and I felt that this style made me look very grand. My dress was of pale-green *soie de Chine,* with a pleated top skirt and angel sleeves.

Theresa wore blue, but though the color suited her she always looked out of place except in riding clothes, and I was secretly pleased by the contrast between us as we stood with the rest of the family to receive our guests. Carriages crowded the road, waiting their turn to draw up to the red carpet which had been laid across the pavement and up the steps to the open front door, with an awning above it.

At nine o'clock the orchestra struck up the first waltz, and soon the floor of the ballroom was full of color and movement. The music competed with the chatter of many voices, long skirts rustled and black coattails swirled. My own program was full in the first few minutes, and even so I had declined several invitations from young men I did not particularly want to dance with.

Gideon Sumner had been among the first half dozen to ask me for a dance, but I had smiled and said coolly, "I'm so sorry, Gideon, you're too late."

He made a grimace of mock sorrow, eyes twinkling. "What a pity. I was afraid I might be. Perhaps I can attend on you when the buffet is served?"

"Thank you, but Tim Forrester and Michael Dean have claimed that office."

"You're sought after by all the handsomest young men, Chantal. I'm not surprised."

I wanted to make an answer that combined modesty with wit, but could not think of one, and was glad when we were interrupted at that moment by Tim Forrester, who gave Gideon a somewhat hostile look. Later, when I saw Aunt Prudence for a few moments, she was much concerned that Sir Robert had not yet arrived.

"It's most odd. He did accept the invitation, didn't he, Chantal?"

"Yes, but I suppose he can't dance because of his stiff leg, Aunt Prudence, so perhaps he's just coming along for an hour or two later."

"Ah yes, that must be it. I do hope so. There are so many of our friends I wish to introduce him to. Oh, here's Michael. Are you having this dance with him? Off you go then, dear."

I danced, chattered, flirted, was brought food and drink from the laden buffet tables, and danced again. It was eleven o'clock when across the room I saw Sir Robert talking with Benedict Kirkby and Aunt Prudence. Cutting short the waltz, and receiving a plaintive look from my partner, I made my way towards him.

Sir Robert was saying, "I trust you won't think me presumptuous to have brought him along with me, Mrs. Kirkby, but —"

"Not at all, not at all, Sir Robert," Aunt Prudence gushed fondly. "A friend of yours is always welcome, and he seemed a very pleasant young man."

I said, "Good evening, Sir Robert. We thought you had forgotten us."

He turned, took my hand, and bowed over it. "I would scarcely do that, my dear. As I was explaining to your Aunt Prudence, I was unavoidably delayed. In any case, for an old codger who can't dance, the last two hours of a ball are the

455

best. Now don't let me keep you. I can see this young fellow with you is fretting to resume.''

We talked for a moment or two longer, and then I returned to the floor. A little later, between dances, I was the center of a small group of young men and young ladies, making them laugh as I told an amusing story of how Theresa had caused chaos in Harrods by knocking over a rack of dresses. Towards the end of the story I seemed to sense that someone was standing behind me, watching, and as I ended the tale I turned.

Martin stood there, only a few paces away, hands tucked under the tails of his coat, looking at me with an expression I could not fathom. I caught my breath with surprise, but recovered quickly and moved towards him, extending my hand gracefully.

''Martin! But how extraordinary!''

''Hallo, Chantal.'' He took my hand, gave me a small smile, then stepped back, tilting his head a little to see me from a different angle, as if not quite sure that he recognized me.

I was inwardly very confused, but I had now learned to hide such feelings behind a calm and polite exterior. "You do remember me, then?" I said.

"Yes. I remember. There was a time when I didn't, after my old memory came back in Regensburg, but the gaps have been filled for me now, piece by piece."

There was so much I might have asked — what he had been doing in Hungary before I found him that day by the stream; if he knew that somebody had cut through the bar of my trapeze the night before he disappeared; whether he knew I had been attacked by a killer dog; whether it was true that he had cruelly beaten Belinda; what "the game" was that I had heard Sir Robert speak of when they met in the sunken road. And a dozen other questions. Once I would have asked them, but I knew better now. Blunt questions were bad manners, and to discuss any matter of importance on a society occasion was quite simply not done.

I gave a little laugh and said, "So you guessed right. Your name was Martin after all."

"Yes. Martin Verne."

"I know. An old friend of yours told me. Belinda Sumner."

"I thought she might have done."

"Have you seen her tonight? She and Gideon are here."

"I imagined they would be. I haven't seen them yet." His eyes narrowed a little in that strange wolf look I had glimpsed before.

I began to flutter my fan, and said, "It's delightful to see you again, Martin, and such a surprise. I had no idea you were on Aunt Prudence's guest list."

"I'm not. I'm more or less a gate crasher," he said, unsmiling. "Sir Robert brought me along."

"Ah, you know Sir Robert?"

"Yes."

That one short word was his only answer. I did not pursue the subject but glanced about the ballroom and said, "Well, I do hope you're going to enjoy yourself. I'm afraid only the wallflowers have any dances left on their programs."

He shook his head as if coming to some private and sorrowful conclusion.

"Wallflowers? Oh, yes. Well . . . that's my penalty for arriving late. I'm sure all the pretty girls are fully booked."

"Never mind." I looked at my program. "I could scratch somebody off my list for you."

After a moment he said, "I suppose you could." For the first time he smiled, but it was a forced smile. "However, I wouldn't wish to make an enemy of the young man you discard."

Before I could decide whether to be annoyed, Gideon Sumner spoke from behind me. "Hallo, Verne." He came forward with Belinda on his arm.

Martin looked at him and said, "Good evening, Sumner." He gave the smallest of bows to Belinda. "Miss Sumner."

Gideon was smiling, but there was tension in the air as the two men stared into each other's eyes. Gideon said, "Chantal told us how you'd met in Hungary. I take it your memory's returned?"

"Oh, yes." Martin's teeth showed for a moment, but there was no humor in his face. "I remember everything now."

Belinda said, "Splendid. Are you busy these days?" Her look was one of cool contempt.

"I have one or two undertakings on hand, Miss Sumner." Martin did not take his eyes from Gideon as he answered.

"Your kind of business tends to be speculative, of course," Gideon said thoughtfully. "I hope you won't take unnecessary risks."

"Thank you, I'll remember your advice." At that moment the next dance began, and Tim Forrester arrived to claim me. I would have put him off, but Martin gave us all a little bow and said, "Will you excuse me, Chantal? Miss Sumner?" He turned away.

I felt bemused and angry, without being quite sure what I was angry about, unless it was the fact that Martin's manner towards me had been so stilted and withdrawn. As we circled the floor I snapped at Tim Forrester, criticizing the way he danced, and when it was over I began to look for Martin again, but could find him nowhere. At last I saw Sir Robert, near one of the long buffet tables, leaning against a pillar with a glass of champagne in his hand. He was alone for a moment, and I hurried towards him.

"Sir Robert, have you seen the friend you brought with you, Martin Verne? You see, we met last summer, when he lost his memory — oh, he must have told you." I gazed impatiently about the crowded ballroom as I spoke. "I had a few words with him just now, but then we were interrupted and I can't seem to find him again."

Sir Robert gave me the same searching, half-puzzled look I had seen in Martin's eyes, then said, "He's left, Chantal."

"Left? But he can't have been here long, and the ball goes on till one o'clock!"

Sir Robert looked down at his glass and swirled the champagne in it. When he spoke his voice seemed a little tired. "He didn't come here to dance, my dear." Sir Robert hesitated, then went on, "He came to look for somebody . . . but she wasn't here."

I stood very still as those simple words sank slowly in. Something within me seemed to bend agonizingly, then snap. The ballroom swung lurchingly about me, as the big top had once seemed to swing when I somersaulted from the trapeze. The noise and the music were suddenly unbearably loud. I put my hands to my ears and closed my eyes. Sir Robert was holding my arm, speaking close to my ear. "Chantal! Are you all right?"

I opened my eyes, shook myself free, and stepped back. My face felt drained of color, and I was trembling. With an enormous effort I said, "I have to go now. Please excuse me."

I could not wait to be alone, but in a corner of my scattered mind I knew that if I disappeared without a word I would soon have Aunt Prudence and Theresa coming to my room to ask what went wrong. Somehow I sought out Aunt Prudence and made another great effort to appear calm and reassuring as I said, "I'm sorry, Aunt Prudence, I don't feel very well. Will you make my excuses if I go to bed?"

"Heavens, you look ill, Chantal! What is it? Do you need a doctor?"

"No, no, please don't worry. I was stupid and drank two glasses of champagne. If I can just go to bed and sleep I'll be quite all right, really, Aunt Prudence. Please don't let anyone disturb me — I mean Theresa, or the servants."

"Nonsense, Chantal. I'll come and see you safely to bed, then arrange for Molly to —"

She was interrupted by Benedict Kirkby, who had come up as we were speaking. He looked at me shrewdly, then smiled and said, "Be quiet and don't fuss, Prudence. The champagne's gone to her head and the best thing she can do is to sleep it off. But let this be a lesson to you, young lady."

"Yes, Uncle Benedict."

I did not remember getting to my room, but once there I put on the gaslight, locked the door, and sat at my dressing table, hands resting limply in my lap, wishing that what ailed me had truly been the champagne. But it was something much worse.

For a long, long time I sat looking at myself in the mirror as if at a stranger, who looked back at me as Sir Robert's words echoed again and again in my ears. *"He came to look for somebody . . . but she wasn't here."*

Those words had been like a sudden great beam of light shining cruelly into my mind, revealing me to myself with a horrifying clarity. Martin Verne had come here tonight looking for Chantal, I knew it in my bones. I had no idea whether he had come for good or ill, but that did not matter to me at this moment. What mattered was that he had not found Chantal. He had found another creature, a different creature who bore her name, the stranger I now saw in the mirror. I was not the Chantal he had known. And to Sir Robert I was not the Chantal he had known at Osburne. Now I understood the puzzled, searching look I had seen in both faces.

Painfully I looked back over the past few months, forcing myself to see the changes in me I had been unaware of. Martin had once called me a red vixen, and meant it as a compliment, but now I had only the worst characteristics of the vixen. Less than an hour ago I had been making people laugh at Theresa's expense by gaily telling the tale of her blundering accident in Harrods. I could recall many similar small and nasty meannesses now, and I shivered to remember them.

Ever since Christmas I had felt that the servants were changing for the worse, seeming slower and more stupid. Now I saw that I was the one who had changed, for I had become more demanding, more irritable and imperious every day. Since coming to London I had not once done my morning prelims, had not once opened my medical textbooks. Even my increased liking for Benedict Kirkby was a miserable discredit to me, for it sprang only from the fact that I had begun to find the sarcastic wit he inflicted on the rest of the family amusing, and had even begun to imitate his manner.

I remembered how I had been quite prepared to keep Gideon Sumner on tenterhooks over the question of calling on me officially, and how furious I had been with him when I found the ground cut from under my feet. Yet this was only the most recent of many shameful memories. When I looked in the mirror I saw a rouged and powdered doll, lazy, selfish, and vain, who thought of nothing but her own pleasure yet found no real happiness in that pleasure. She was a tattler and a gossip who imagined herself a witty conversationalist. It was hard to remember when she had last spoken words which were not empty and insincere.

I must have sat gazing dully into the mirror with shame and disgust for a very long time, only remotely aware that the sounds of the ball had faded and that the house had become quiet. Once somebody tapped softly on my door, but I took no notice. Doubtless it was Aunt Prudence, but she must have thought me asleep and did not tap again. I had grown very cold now, but I did not care. At last I rose from the dressing table, poured cold water into my washbowl, and scrubbed my face clean. I took off my dress and petticoat, my shoes and stockings, and put them tidily away for the first time in many a week. Now I wore only my *petit caleçon* . . . the last remnant of Chantal. I stood before the pier glass which was set on the inside of the wardrobe door, brushing out my hair and studying myself coldly with eyes well practiced in judging a fit and healthy body.

There was flabbiness in my arms, my legs, and especially round my middle. Trying to think sensibly now, I knew it was stupid to expect that I should be as lean and hard as I had been in the circus, for that came only with the long daily exercise my work had demanded. But I was growing spongy from soft living and self-indulgence. Maria would have been horrified to see me, and it would no longer have been a joke for Leo to call me his fat English girl.

I leaned forward, staring, and saw the beginnings of two red spots on my chin. Fat, white, and spotty . . . the echo of those words came back to me from long ago. Chantal was dead, and I had come close to being that hated creature I had known throughout my childhood, who had been called Roberta.

I closed the wardrobe door. Putting my hairbrush down on the dressing table, I took off my *petit caleçon,* put on my nightdress, turned out the light, and got into bed. I could not have slept if I wished, and I had no intention of doing so. But as I lay staring into the darkness I no longer wallowed in the misery of my self-disgust, for I now had the sense to realize that this would be fruitless. Instead I began to plan how to bring Chantal to life again.

On my first day at Wildings I had told Benedict Kirkby that without work to do and something difficult to achieve, I was an unhappy and unpleasant person. Like a fool, I had forgotten that truth, but now I had new and bitter proof of it. I told myself fiercely that I must never again forget, never again slip back. Never.

Tomorrow I would begin a new life. Every morning I would rise early and do my prelims for an hour before taking my bath and going down to breakfast. I would behave decently towards the servants again. It would take some time before they responded, but that did not matter. Only my own behavior mattered. I would never again titter at Benedict

Kirkby's sarcasm, and — I smiled wanly to myself in the darkness — I would even play Snakes and Ladders with Theresa when she asked me.

But above all I would study my medical books, for I was sure that my salvation lay in the difficulties and hard work I should face in becoming a doctor. Our stay in London was over now, and we would be returning to Osburne in a few days. Benedict Kirkby had said that this was the time when he would help me in my ambition, if I was still of the same mind. I had believed him then, but now I was not so sure. He had probably counted on the fact that by the spring I would have become immersed in a completely new way of life, forgetting the foolish ideas I had brought to England with me.

This was something I could put to the test without delay, the very next day. And if Benedict Kirkby demurred, or tried to postpone any definite action again, I would know what to do. Something in my mind seemed to grow hard and fierce, just as it had done all those years ago when a fat, feeble, clumsy girl had vowed to herself that one day she would turn the joke back on her monkey-faced tormentor by flying on the high trapeze.

I did not need Benedict Kirkby. On my first day at Wildings I had told him that if need be I could earn the extra money I should want before I could apply to be a medical student. Now I might have to begin preparing myself for that task.

Somewhere a church clock struck the hour of three. I willed myself to wake at seven, hoped I had not lost this ability, then closed my eyes at last and allowed sleep to come upon me.

THIRTEEN

On a day in May I drew Tamarisk to a halt outside the lofty disused barn, screened by trees, which stood on the edge of White Lodge land. I looked carefully about me, slipped from the saddle, opened the big door, led Tamarisk inside, and tethered her loosely to a cleat in the wall. From under a pile of dusty straw I drew a long thin pole with a hook at one end.

It was dim but not dark in the barn, for light came through a large square opening high up at the far end, where the remains of an old block and pulley hung outside from an arm projecting from the ridgepiece of the gable. There was an open loft at this end of the barn. I climbed the rickety ladder set against it, drew the pole up after me, then reached up into the darkness above the big central crossbeam, groping. The next moment the trapeze hooked under the ridgepiece fell down, swinging on its two well-stretched ropes attached to the crossbeam above.

The bar of the trapeze was a length of seasoned ash, cut from a long-handled shovel, and the ropes were hawser-laid. Immediately after our return to Osburne I had accompanied Theresa into Pellridge for one of her music lessons, and during the two hours I was alone I had bought all I needed from a small oil shop on the outskirts of the little town, had the bar cut from the shovel handle, returned to hide my purchases in the barn, and driven back just in time to meet Theresa as her lesson ended.

The next day I had made grooves in the ends of the bar with a rasp, and fashioned eye splices in my ropes to fit tightly into the grooves. It was a rather primitive trapeze, but good enough for my purpose. When I first began to practice I had been worried that somebody might by chance enter the barn and find me there, but as the weeks passed without cause for alarm I had gradually lost most of my anxiety about being disturbed.

Now I quickly took off my boots and socks, trousers, jacket and blouse, and stood barefoot in one of my practice leotards. I twisted my hair into a tight bun at the nape of my neck and secured it in a tiny net bag I had made. The trapeze hung fifteen feet above the floor. I threw a length of knotted rope over it, gave the double rope a few twists, then gripped it and climbed till I could reach the bar. I threw the rope aside, worked up a steady swing, then circled up onto the trapeze and began some easy exercises to loosen my muscles.

My hope was that by mid-July I would have reached the peak of my abilities again, and also that I would have worked out a good program for the single trapeze. It could never be as exciting as a flying double act, and in some ways called for different skills, more for grace and balance than speed and acrobatics, but I was sure I could compose a performance good enough to win me a place in one of the smaller tenting circuses.

I no longer doubted that I would have

to go through with my plan, for I had spoken to Benedict Kirkby about my future even before leaving London. He had looked taken aback, then said vaguely that we would talk about it later, when we were settled in Wildings again. This was no more than I expected, and I had at once decided to find some way of beginning to practice as soon as possible.

On at least three days in every week I went out with Tamarisk immediately after lunch, having eaten sparingly. For the first half hour I rode, allowing time to digest my small meal. Then I would make for the barn and practice on the trapeze for an hour before putting my clothes on again and riding home.

I did not yet know how I would obtain my own trapeze equipment when the time came, but I had written to Mr. Galletti, telling him my plans and asking his advice. I knew he would not try to deter me, for this was against his philosophy; he had not even tried to deter me from running away as a child of thirteen, once he knew there was no better course for me to take. I had also asked him if Mr.

Kayser could find out from his agent in Paris which circuses would be touring in England that summer, and if both Mr. Galletti and Mr. Kayser would be so truly kind as to give me letters of recommendation. I now waited anxiously for a reply, knowing that letters sent to a traveling circus were not likely to arrive quickly.

Osburne was very quiet after London, and for this I was glad, for it gave me more time to study and practice. I had heard nothing of Gideon and Belinda Sumner, or of Martin Verne. Sir Robert's six-month tenancy of White Lodge had ended, and as far as I knew he had remained in London. I would have missed him sorely if I had not been so busy with all I had to do. It would have been good to sit talking with him again after a game of chess, and to fill a pipe for him. Above all, I wished that we could have met even for a little while, so that he might have seen me as Chantal again, rather than the false and detestable creature he had found in London.

The days grew longer, and the last of the spring blossom was shed from the trees. I had a letter from Mr. Galletti, saying that when the time came he would provide a suitable trapeze for me, shipping it to a London agent who had been recommended by Mr. Kayser's agent in Paris. This man acted for a number of music-hall and circus artists, and would be the best person to help me get an engagement with a circus when I was ready. Mr. Galletti enclosed two glowing letters of recommendation for me, one from Mr. Kayser and one from himself. He also suggested that I should include plenty of ground acrobatics in my training, since it might be possible for the agent to place me with a flying-trapeze act in the same way that I had joined Maria and Leo.

From that moment my confidence grew. If possible, I would try to get a booking with a continental circus, which would return from its tour in England during the late summer and then travel down to southern Europe to take advantage of the shorter winter there. With a year's engagement, and only a brief time on half pay in winter quarters, I could add enough money to my savings to see me through my years as a medical student.

On an afternoon in mid-June I was in the old barn, practicing as usual. I now spent the first quarter of an hour on ground acrobatics, and a further ten minutes setting the trapeze a-swing and diving from the loft to catch it as it came within reach, to keep my sense of timing sharp. I had finished this part of my practice and was now rehearsing the program I had composed for an act on the single trapeze, counting the rhythmic swings in my head as I went through the movements.

One, two, three, circle up. Swallow position, balanced on my stomach, arms extended . . . four swings. Grip the bar, swing down, up and over again into a sitting position. Eight, nine, ten, eleven . . . kiss a hand to the audience, graceful arm movements . . . now, fall back suddenly and hang by the knees. Seventeen, eighteen, nineteen, twenty — *drop* to an ankle grip, with the feet hooked round the ropes . . . twenty-one, twenty-two, twenty-three . . .

My heart turned over, for I saw that the barn door stood open a little, and a figure was framed in the rectangle of bright sunlight, a man in a faded green shirt, a brown jerkin, and brown corduroy trousers, binoculars hanging from one shoulder, hatless, and with a thick stubble of beard. To me he was upside down, and with the light behind him I could not see his face clearly. I doubled forward, snatched at the bar, released my feet, swung away from the man, and pirouetted to face him as I dropped to the floor.

Glaring, half crouched, I must have looked like a creature at bay. The man pushed the door shut behind him and moved forward.

Martin Verne!

If, at that moment, I had thought of the trapeze which had failed me, or the dreadful hound which had hunted me, I might have felt afraid. As it was, I felt only a shock of gladness. He stared at me in astonishment for long seconds, then a sudden grin of wonderment and delight lit his face. He spread his arms and said, "Chantal!"

"Martin! Oh, Martin!" It was as if the long months had never existed and we had been swept back on a magic carpet to that day at the bridge when we had fought the power of the torrent together. Without thought or volition I found myself running towards him, and the next moment I was clasped in his arms. We hugged one another as we had done that day on the riverbank, and I heard him laugh.

He stepped back, his hands on my shoulders, staring at me, eyes sparkling with excitement. "It's you," he said softly. "It really is Chantal."

"Oh, Martin, I hope so," I burst out tearfully. "I was such a horrible creature when you saw me in London. I'm afraid that must be the real me, and I'll have to work all my life at being Chantal."

At first it was as if he had not heard me. Putting a hand gently to my face, he turned my head to one side, then to the other, studying me intently. At last he gave a little sigh, as if he had found what he wanted. "It will be worth it, my little red vixen."

I suddenly realized I was wearing only my leotard, and gave a shaky laugh, for with Martin it did not matter. He had seen me like this daily. "Thank goodness it was you, Martin. If anyone else had found me, they'd think I ought to be locked up."

He glanced at the trapeze. "Chantal, what on earth are you doing? Or rather — *why?*"

"I'll tell you in a minute, but I'd better get dressed. Oh, and you must bring your horse inside."

"I'm on foot. It's less conspicuous. I've just walked across country from Marling."

I pulled the net from my hair, drew on my riding trousers, sat down to put on my socks, and said, "Why, Martin? Why do you need to be inconspicuous?"

He gave a little shrug. "It's something of a habit."

"Yes." I looked at him sharply, remembering the roughly dressed man in the tinker's cart. "Why did you come here?"

"You remind me of a girl I once met

by a stream in Hungary. She was very direct, too."

"You couldn't answer questions then because you'd lost your memory, but you can now."

He picked up my blouse and held it for me to put on. "I came because I wanted to try, just once more, to find Chantal . . . not that strange girl in London." He turned me towards him. "I watched you lead your horse in here," he touched the binoculars, "and when you didn't come out after fifteen minutes, I made my way down through the woods to find you."

In silence I buttoned my blouse and put on my jacket, then climbed the ladder and used the long pole to hook the trapeze up high in the dark shadows of the gable. My thoughts were busy while I did this, and when I came down I said, "I'm glad you found me. I want to talk to you, Martin. Come and sit down."

He followed me to an old wooden trough which lay upturned in a corner of the barn, and seated himself beside me. I turned a little to look at him and said, "What happened that day in Regensburg,

481

when you disappeared?''

He half smiled. ''While I was in the town I saw something that hit me like a thunderbolt, and suddenly my whole mind turned over, the past coming up into the light, and everything that had happened since losing my memory going down into the darkness.''

''What was it you saw, Martin?''

He shrugged. ''I wasn't sure at the time, and it doesn't matter anyway. Suddenly I knew who I was, but I didn't know where I was, or how I came to be wearing the clothes I had on. The last thing I remembered was what I had been doing just before I was hit on the head and thrown in the river.''

''What had you been doing? When I found you, you *felt* it was something illegal.''

He thought for a moment, then said, ''Yes, I'm afraid so. But let's not talk about that now.''

''When did you remember about the circus again, Martin?''

''Not until much later. In March. Something happened to remind me of you.

Then I remembered, not all at once, but piece by piece."

"But you were in Osburne long before that, even before Christmas. I heard you talking with Sir Robert in the sunken lane, when you were dressed as a tinker."

He looked startled. "Did you now? Why didn't you speak to me?"

"I couldn't. I was eavesdropping by accident, and besides . . ." I shrugged impatiently. "Well, that doesn't matter. But you must have known I was there in Osburne. Sir Robert would have told you about a girl called Chantal who played chess with him, and then you would surely remember."

He smiled wryly and shook his head. "Sir Robert didn't mention you. I wasn't seeing him for social gossip. It was I who first spoke your name to him, when I came back to London the day before the ball the Kirkbys gave. My memory of you had come back by then, and I told him of my days with the circus, and of Chantal. That was when he told me you'd been a neighbor of his in Osburne all winter."

I stared. "But . . . it's such an

extraordinary coincidence."

"It seems so, Chantal." Martin rubbed his chin. "But it isn't really."

"Why do you say that?"

He gestured vaguely. "I think there are threads that link everything together."

"What threads?"

"Well . . . that's a dangerous subject. I'd rather not go into it now."

"Dangerous for you?"

"Perhaps."

There was a little silence, and at last I said, "Martin, that day in the sunken lane you told Sir Robert about . . . about a lady in another country. A prisoner, I think, though it wasn't easy to understand. But she seemed very important to you. Who is she?"

I caught a look of alarm, almost of fear, in his eyes. Then it was gone, and he smiled. "I was speaking in riddles that day. She's a statuette, in a museum. Very precious."

His strange answer roused suspicions I did not want to think about. I sat with my hand clasped between my knees and said unhappily, "I hate all this mystery. It's hard for me to know what to think, what to believe, or who to trust." I looked at him. "Martin, did you know that the night before you disappeared in Regensburg somebody cut partly through the bar of my trapeze, and it broke under my weight?"

I saw shock in his face, then it became impassive and he seemed to be looking through me. Long moments passed before he said very quietly, "What happened?"

"I was lucky. When it broke I was thrown sideways, but I managed to fall just inside the edge of the net."

"Do you know who did it?"

"No, Martin. We never found out. We couldn't think why anybody would want to harm me."

Another silence. His eyes focused on me again, and he said in the same quiet voice, "Do you think perhaps I was responsible, Chantal?"

I looked away. "Somebody asked that same question, because you'd disappeared. But I couldn't believe you'd do anything to hurt me, unless . . ." I hesitated.

"Unless what?"

I turned to put my hand on his. "Unless you did it without knowing, because you'd been affected by that blow on the head."

His eyes widened, then narrowed almost to slits. Before he could answer I went on, "And something else happened just before Christmas, soon after I'd heard you talking with Sir Robert. Somebody set a great brute of a dog onto me, a killer dog. I only escaped by swinging up into a tree."

His hand turned beneath mine and closed round my fingers. "Somebody?"

"I don't know who. He was hiding in the woods and controlling the dog by whistling."

"And you thought it might be me again, having another fit of insanity?" His voice was strangely gentle, and I felt suddenly confused and ashamed.

"It . . . it crossed my mind," I said miserably. "Oh, Martin, I don't know what to think about anything. I know you're an adventurer and you've committed crimes. Belinda told me all about you. I try not to think of it because I can't bear it. I just try to think of you the way you were that day when we were in the river together, freeing the logjam under the bridge."

"Belinda told you all about me?"

"Yes. And then the day after the dog tried to kill me I saw her with her face all swollen, and she told me how you'd wanted to borrow money, and hit her when she refused."

He did not answer at once, but sat with that same look of concentration on his face, like a man trying to work out a difficult sum in his head. At last he said slowly, "You say this was the day after the affair with the dog?"

"Yes. The next morning."

"I see."

I waited many seconds before I said, "Aren't you going to tell me it wasn't so, Martin?"

He thought for a moment, then shook his head. "No, I'm not going to deny it." My heart slumped and I felt my eyes fill with tears. Martin drew in a deep breath, his look of concentration vanished, and he gave me a whimsical smile. "Shall I tell you something strange, Chantal? You believe, or at least half believe, that I've

487

tried to harm you, even to take your life, either because I'm mad or bad. Yet when you first saw me today you hugged me, and now you're sitting alone with me in this barn, holding my hand, with nobody knowing you're here, and you don't seem in the least afraid."

For a moment I was startled. What Martin had said was true, yet the strangeness of it had not crossed my mind till now. I said, "No, I'm not afraid of you, Martin. I expect that's stupid. I ought to be."

He gave an odd, sad little laugh. "No. Good or bad, sane or mad, I'd never harm you, Chantal. Your instinct knows that, even if your head doesn't." He pressed my hand, then stood up and paced across the barn, his hands behind his back, head bent in thought. I sat feeling drained and empty. After a few moments he said, "Has anything else happened to you, Chantal? I mean, anything dangerous?"

I thought back over the months in London, and shook my head wearily. "No."

He paced across the barn again and came to a halt in front of me. Taking my hands, he drew me to my feet and looked down into my face. "I have to go away for a little while. A few weeks, perhaps, I can't be sure. But when I come back, we'll talk again."

"Talk? What is there to talk about, Martin?" I said dully.

He smiled. "Oh, many things. I think with any luck you might even be able to reform me. You wouldn't want me to go on being a criminal all my life, would you?"

"Don't make fun of me, please, Martin."

"If anything, I'm making fun of myself." He glanced at the roof where the trapeze was hidden. "You still haven't told me why you were practicing."

"I want to find work in a small circus. I need to save some more money before I can afford to become a medical student."

He showed no surprise, but gave a little nod as if this was the answer he expected, and said, "How soon will you be ready?"

"In about another month. There's an

agent in London who'll try to place me. Mr. Galletti says he doesn't think it will be difficult."

"I'm sure he's right. But will you do something for me, Chantal?"

"What is it?"

"Don't leave Osburne until I come back."

"But . . . why?"

"I can't tell you yet."

"Oh, Martin, don't ask me to make a promise like that. I *must* go on with my plans. I'm afraid that if I stop I — I might change again."

He enfolded my hands in his own and said gently, "Will you give me four weeks? Will you meet me here four weeks from today?"

That would not delay my plans, for I had not expected to run away from Wildings before then. I said, "All right, Martin. Four weeks." I took my wristwatch from my pocket, looked at it, and began to fasten it on my wrist. "I must go now. I'm late already."

"We'd better not leave together. I'll wait a few minutes. Let me see if the coast's clear." He went to the barn door, eased it open a little, peered warily out, then turned to beckon me, pushing the door wider as I led Tamarisk to it.

I paused to look at him, a confusion of feelings stirring within me, and said, "Oh, I wish I knew where you were going, and why."

He regarded me soberly. "It's nothing criminal this time, Chantal. Trust me." He took my hand and touched my fingers to his lips. Then I led Tamarisk out into the sunshine, and the barn door swung to behind me. The woods were quiet, and there was nobody in sight as I mounted and began to ride along the narrow track bordering the pasture where the barn stood. Perhaps I had known too many emotions in the past half hour, for now I simply felt numb.

Four weeks. I wondered if Martin would come back then, and what he would have to tell me. I did not know that in little more than half that time I was to break the promise I had just made him.

For the next ten days nothing disturbed the pattern of life I had established since our return from London. Early each morning, before ringing for my bath, I spent a full hour doing my prelims, and it was only fear of the noise I would make that prevented me practicing ground acrobatics in my bedroom. Every afternoon that I was free, I went secretly to the barn and worked hard at polishing my performance.

On the eleventh day I had left the barn and was riding homewards when I saw Harridge cantering towards me. He reined in his horse and touched his cap. "I was just comin' a-looking for you, Miss Chantal. Master zent word to find you."

I was thankful Harridge had not come seeking me earlier, and said, "It must be something urgent. Did he tell you what it is, Harridge?"

"No, miss. But that Mr. Sumner's in the study with 'im, Albert sez."

"Oh. And Miss Sumner?"

"She be 'ere too, talking with Mrs. Kirkby."

"Well, we'd better hurry along."

Ten minutes later, still in my riding clothes, I tapped on the door and entered Benedict Kirkby's study. Gideon, lounging in a chair, rose to greet me with a smile, his eyebrows lifting in surprise.

"Hallo, Chantal. My word, you look very different from when I last saw you."

I gave him an apologetic smile, remembering how badly I had behaved. "I hope so, Gideon. How are you? It's nice to see you again."

Benedict Kirkby said, "Sit down, Chantal. I have something very important to say to you." I obeyed, trying to hide my nervousness and wondering if my secret activities had been discovered, but he continued, "This will no doubt be a shock, but I'm sure you will take it calmly. Now, do you remember that your mother's name appeared in the casualty list of passengers who were lost when the *Tiberia* sank in the Ionian Sea, in the spring of 1897?"

I was startled, for I had never dreamt that this subject would ever be raised again, and I clasped my hands together in my lap in case they began to tremble. "I

493

didn't know all the details, Uncle Benedict. I only knew she was lost at sea. I think the solicitor, Mr. Blythe, showed me a casualty list, but I — I was in something of a daze, and I can't remember much now."

"That's very natural. However, the facts are as I just stated." He opened a folder on his desk and took out a half sheet of newspaper. "This is from *The Times,* and you will see that it's dated May 15, 1897. Will you please read the item on the right, which I've marked with a cross?"

I took the cutting, and at once saw a cross in black ink against a column of print a few inches long.

REMARKABLE ESCAPE BY *TIBERIA* SURVIVORS

Our Correspondent in Rome reports that on May 9th a life raft from the ill-fated passenger ship Tiberia *was sighted near Augusta, on the east coast of Sicily, by local fishermen. On the raft, in dire straits from exposure and thirst, were two passengers earlier reported lost in the disaster, a Mr. John Furnival and a Dr. Elizabeth Martin. They had been afloat at the mercy of the sea for twelve days —*

The words danced before my eyes. When I lifted my head, Benedict Kirkby seemed to be a long way away, as if I were looking at him through the wrong end of a telescope, and there was a buzzing sound in my ears. I shook my head, and heard the air come sighing from my lungs as I let out the breath I had unconsciously held.

"My mother?" I whispered. "Elizabeth Martin?"

"She evidently chose to use her maiden name professionally," said Benedict Kirkby.

"*Dr.* Elizabeth Martin?"

He smiled his rubbery smile. "She is a Doctor of Medicine. It seems the same ambition runs in the family. But please finish reading the item, my dear."

I looked down, but my eyes were full of tears. "I — I can't see properly."

"Well, you can study it later. Briefly,

your mother and this Mr. Furnival were afloat for twelve days with no food and very little water, so their final deliverance was something of a miracle. They were taken to a hospital in Siracusa, and five days later, when the *Times* correspondent visited them, they were recovering from their ordeal. It seems they had little to say about it, except to confirm that it was a freak wave of giant proportions which caused the *Tiberia* to sink. This was already known from other survivors, who had escaped in lifeboats and been picked up."

Benedict Kirkby continued speaking but I heard no more, for my head seemed filled with darting sparks of light. For five years I had wronged my mother in my thoughts, wronged her dreadfully. And when at last I learned the truth about her marriage and about my birth, I believed her to be dead, so that I could have no hope of finding her and asking her forgiveness. But now . . .

I cried out suddenly, interrupting Benedict Kirkby. "Oh, it — it's almost too wonderful to believe! When did you find out, Uncle Benedict?''

''Several months ago. It was —''

''Several *months?*'' I stared in shocked astonishment.

Gideon laughed. ''It would have been foolish to tell you at once, Chantal. At first we knew only that Elizabeth Martin had survived the foundering of the *Tiberia,* but that happened seven years ago. It seemed prudent to make sure she was still alive before telling you, and perhaps raising false hopes. I'm sure you would agree that patience isn't your greatest virtue.''

''Yes, yes, I see. Oh please, where is she, Gideon?''

''Not in England, but you'll see her very shortly. Now be a good girl, dry your eyes, blow your nose, and listen to your Uncle Benedict.''

''Yes. I'm sorry.'' I made a great effort to steady myself as I obeyed.

Benedict Kirkby leaned back in his chair and put his fingers together. ''We have Gideon to thank for the discovery,'' he said. ''When he was in Rome earlier this year he attended a number of functions held by the English community there, and made the acquaintance of the *Times* correspondent. In the course of conversation the *Tiberia* disaster was mentioned, and then this remarkable business emerged." He gestured to the newspaper cutting I had laid on the desk, and shrugged. "I may well have read the item myself at the time, but the name of Elizabeth Martin meant nothing to me then, so I had no cause to remember it."

I did not care how the discovery had been made. All I could think of was that my mother was alive and soon I would see her. I said in a wavering voice, "Does my mother know about me? I mean, does she know it was really the other baby who died?"

"She does now," said Gideon. "I told her, of course."

"You've *seen* her? Seen her yourself?"

"Yes. I was with her a few days ago, in Hungary."

"In Hungary? But how —? Oh, that doesn't matter! Tell me what she's like, Gideon! What did she say when you told her about me? Did she seem happy?

Couldn't you have brought her back with you?"

"Please, Chantal, one thing at a time." Gideon lifted a hand, smiling as he spoke.

"I'm sorry. It's just that I'm so excited." I was almost gabbling now. "It's so strange, I think I shall be a little afraid to meet her, in case she . . . well, in case she might be disappointed."

"Let me answer some of your questions, Chantal," Gideon said quietly. "Your mother is a very handsome woman, and I'm sure you'll be proud of her. You're unlike her in looks, but very much like her in other ways. When she learned that her baby had lived, and was a young woman now, and when I told her all that I knew of your story, she wept tears of happiness. And I would say she is a woman who hasn't shed tears for many years. Oddly enough she expressed the same fear you spoke of just now . . . that you might be disappointed in her."

Benedict Kirkby cleared his throat. "You may wonder why it took so long to find her, Chantal. The simple fact is that when your mother qualified as a doctor, seven years after you were born, she devoted herself to medical work in less fortunate countries. She has served with mission hospitals in primitive parts of East Africa and in Egypt, with the Red Cross in South Africa during the war, and with nursing orders of nuns in Jordan, Greece, and the slums of Naples. Such a person is by no means easy to find."

I looked at Gideon through a blur of tears and said, "I'm so grateful to you."

He spread his hands and made a wry grimace. "But I didn't find her, Chantal. I tried for weeks, through medical associations and the like, but I failed. Do you remember Baron Krenner, your uncle's Hungarian cousin, who visited England earlier this year? It was he who found her."

Benedict Kirkby said, "I told him of our search when he was with us in London, and this letter from him arrived ten days ago." He took three thick, creamy sheets of writing paper from his file, and as he handed them to me I saw that there was a coat of arms embossed on the top sheet. The letter began without preamble.

My dear Benedict,

I have found Elizabeth Martin! How strange it is that while you have been seeking diligently without success, I should have discovered her in the ordinary course of my affairs.

As you know, some two years ago I established a small hospital in Szigvár for the benefit of my tenants and their families. We have only one doctor, and although he is very capable we sometimes have to send a patient to Budapest for major surgery. Last week Dr. Brandt took a young girl patient there. On his return he mentioned to me that in the same ward he had encountered an Englishwoman who was recovering from an injury caused by a carriage wheel passing over her foot. They had talked together (in German) and Brandt learned that she had been with the Red Cross medical group which was sent to give aid following the disaster of the Karakose earthquake in Turkey. Returning to the Red Cross headquarters in Switzerland, she had broken her journey in Budapest, and it was here that the accident occurred.

Brandt imagined she was a nurse, but then learned that in fact she was a doctor. When I asked her name, he said it had not been mentioned! After the first exchange he had simply called her "Doctor." However, he judged her to be in her early forties, which would be the age of Elizabeth Martin, and since I felt that there cannot be so many Englishwoman doctors in the world, I could not resist taking the train to Budapest next day.

And that, my dear Benedict, is how I found Elizabeth Martin! I hasten to say that I have told her nothing yet, and for a very good reason. She will not be able to make a long journey for several weeks, and I felt it would be cruel to tell her of Chantal, her daughter, until you had made whatever arrangements you think best to bring them together as soon as possible.

Please write at once and tell me what you wish me to do. I am of course entirely at your service.

Yours ever,
Joseph Krenner

As I raised my eyes from the letter Benedict Kirkby said, "I thought it best to enlist Gideon's services once again. A woman in your mother's situation, discovering that the baby she believed to have died at birth is alive, and now almost nineteen years old . . ." He smiled and shook his head. "She would have a hundred questions to ask, and I felt that perhaps Gideon knew you and your story better than anyone. Also, he happened to be in Vienna, so I sent him a long telegram there. He went at once to Szigvár, then accompanied Baron Krenner to the hospital in Budapest."

I looked at Gideon and said anxiously, "Is my mother's foot badly hurt?"

He gave me a reassuring smile. "I understand it was quite a severe injury, but she's well satisfied with the way it's mending. We arranged for her to be discharged from the hospital, and she's now at Szigvár Castle, Baron Krenner's home, under the care of Dr. Brandt. I left her only two days ago."

Benedict Kirkby took the letter from me, placed it neatly in the file, and said, "Gideon reached London late last night, and telephoned me at once. After discussing the matter with him, I felt that we could give you the good news today without trying your patience too greatly."

I felt almost sick with excitement, and drew a deep breath to steady myself. "Uncle Benedict, do you mean I can go to see her soon?"

His lips stretched in a brief smile. "My dear, I don't think this household could contain you if you had to wait. That is why we have delayed telling you anything until now. I'm sure you'll be pleased to know that the necessary travel arrangements have been made, and that you leave tomorrow. It's the wrong time of week for catching the Orient Express, so you will be making overnight stops at

Stuttgart and Vienna, which will be less tiring, I hope. Gideon and Belinda have very kindly agreed to escort you on your journey."

An overwhelming wonder and happiness swept me, yet I dared not try to thank him, for I knew that if I spoke I would burst into tears. I hoped he would see in my face the enormous gratitude I felt, but he sat looking down at the desk, his face strangely pale, and on his forehead a gleam of perspiration. For a moment I had the foolish fancy that he could not bring himself to look at me.

Gideon rose and strolled idly across to the shelves of curios. "I think Chantal might run along now," he said. "She'll have to think about getting her trunk packed with whatever she wants to take, and we can talk again later, when she's had time to absorb the shock and feel a little more composed."

Benedict Kirkby did not move or speak. I looked at Gideon. He had picked up the woven black wristlet from among the curios and stood swinging it idly on one finger, looking at it with interest. I had not thought about that strange and sinister object for months, but now the sight of it brought back memories of old Solange and her garbled prophecies. *The day when the lost ones stand face to face shall be heavy with fear . . .*

My mother and I would soon stand face to face, and we had been lost to one another all my life. For a moment I felt a chill of foreboding, then thrust it angrily away. I would not have my joy marred by the vague mutterings of a fortuneteller.

Benedict Kirkby darted a glance at Gideon from under lowered lids, then he started, and his face twitched strangely before he looked down at the desk again.

"Yes. Of course," he said at last, his voice low. "Leave us now, Chantal."

FOURTEEN

It was a curious sensation to be traveling back across Europe by the way I had come less than a year before. I tried to seem outwardly calm, but my first joy and excitement had now been replaced by a turmoil of emotions. Most of all I felt nervous.

Until now my mother had been a shadowy figure to me, someone of whom I had no memories and would never see. But now I could think of her as a real person, existing, living, breathing, feeling. I wanted her to love me, but had a great fear that the long years had made an unbridgeable gap between us, and that she would see me as the stranger I was. I told myself that the ties of blood were too strong for this, but knew I was trying to deceive myself. I could not have loved Mr.

Galletti and Maria and Leo more if they had been my own family; yet for the Kirkbys, a branch of my true family, I had never felt deep affection.

If I had been allowed any choice I would have preferred to make this journey on my own, for I could neither talk about all that went on in my mind nor concentrate on anything else, and so for the most part I was silent. This was ungracious, but Gideon and Belinda Sumner seemed to understand my distraction, and left me to my thoughts. In fact, we had reached our first overnight stop, at Stuttgart, before I remembered with guilty shame that I had not yet thanked them for their kindness in escorting me.

When I apologized, Gideon brushed it aside with a wave of his hand. "Our pleasure, Chantal. It's all at your Uncle Benedict's expense, you know."

"Yes, and I'm so grateful to him, but you've just made the journey from Hungary, and now you're traveling back with only a day's rest in between."

Belinda laughed. "Traveling is almost a

hobby with Gideon. He enjoys it. And in any case, he always likes to complete a task once he's begun it."

As I prepared for bed in the hotel that night I found in my handbag a letter from Maria. It had arrived by the morning post, but in all the hustle and bustle of our departure I had forgotten it. I now saw to my surprise that the letter had been posted in Rumania two weeks ago. It was not the delay that surprised me, for the postal service in many parts of the Balkans was slow, but the fact that Kayser's Giant Circus was touring this area so early in the year. Evidently they had made some changes in their usual bookings.

The letter was six pages long, for Maria usually spread the writing of her letters over several days, and it contained all the gossip I loved to hear about happenings in the circus and my special friends there. Towards the end I learned that Mr. Kayser now had a partner, and it seemed that this had eased his difficult financial situation. Also, the route of the tour had been somewhat changed, so that there would not be so many short stops in small places where we could only hope to fill the big top for a few days.

At the time of writing she was unsure of the exact itinerary for the summer, but had written out a provisional one which Mr. Kayser had provided for her. She went on to say that I must practice very hard on the trapeze, because if the new partnership made the circus more profitable, then her grandfather hoped he might persuade Mr. Kayser to let me rejoin the Flying Gallettis for a year, so that I could earn the money I needed. My delight at this news was tempered only by the fact that all my plans were in chaos, and I could not think beyond the time of meeting my mother.

I looked at the provisional itinerary, and my heart jumped. The circus would be pitching near Kaposnika for two weeks, as usual, on its way to Budapest. Kaposnika was only a few miles from Baron Krenner's home in Szigvár, and I saw that if the provisional dates had been correct it would mean that the circus was there at this moment, having arrived three days ago.

I felt almost dizzy with excitement, for the thought of being able to introduce my adopted family to my real mother seemed almost too wonderful to be true. Of all people in the world, Mr. Galletti would surely speak well of me, and that would help to make my mother like me.

I could have danced with joy, and was glad Belinda had a separate room, for she would have thought me mad if she had seen me give vent to my feelings. I was half undressed, wearing only my shift and my *petit caleçon*. Throwing off the shift, I skipped exuberantly to the middle of the room and threw two back somersaults, one after the other, trying to land as lightly as Maria always landed, then dived onto the bed and hugged the pillow with delight, half laughing, half crying. It seemed that suddenly my life had been touched with golden sunshine.

We spent the next night in Vienna, and at noon the following day arrived in Budapest, where we had a short wait before boarding a local train to Kaposnika, the nearest railway station to Szigvár. At three o'clock, when we alighted, a large and very ornate carriage was waiting for us, with two servants to take charge of our luggage. And there, outside the station, I saw our circus posters.

I had been reluctant to speak of the circus since reading Maria's letter, for fear that the itinerary had been changed, and now I could not speak of it, could scarcely speak at all, for my mouth was dry and my throat seemed to have a great lump in it. I was vaguely aware that Gideon and Belinda exchanged a glance at sight of the posters, but he simply shrugged and made no remark.

The journey to Szigvár took well over an hour, for soon after leaving Kaposnika the road became steep and narrow as it wound upwards between slopes of evergreen forest. We passed through three villages, and came at last to the larger village of Szigvár. The castle stood above it, almost half a mile away beyond a thick belt of trees. Only the turrets could be seen from the village, and we had to travel a broad stony track between the trees before I had my first full view of

Baron Krenner's home.

It was not the great medieval castle I had imagined, but a miniature palace of gray stone which the centuries had mellowed. A slender staircase turret rose at each end of the façade, where three rows of embrasured windows reflected the afternoon sun. Above the parapet lifted a roof of slate with a shallow pitch.

Our carriage passed through the gateway in the high and crenelated outer wall, and I glimpsed a man staring through the window of the small gatehouse just within. A cobbled drive led to a wide apron of flagstones in front of a portico with four pillars, and as the carriage halted by the broad stone steps I saw two liveried servants waiting. The heavy doors stood open and Baron Krenner himself was coming from the arched doorway to greet us. My teeth were chattering as one of the servants handed me down from the carriage. Now that the moment I longed for had come, I was almost dreading it.

"Well done, Mr. Sumner," the Baron said, shaking hands with Gideon. "I assume all has gone well?''

"Perfectly." Gideon smiled as he spoke, and indicated me with the short cane he carried looped on his wrist as usual. "Here she is, my dear Baron, safe and sound. Elizabeth Martin's daughter — or rather Elizabeth Kirkby's daughter.''

Baron Krenner glanced at me. "Good afternoon, Chantal.'' He bowed over Belinda's hand. "Miss Sumner, a pleasure to see you again. Please come in, you must be tired after your long journey.''

I felt an odd sense of being shut out, as if I had suddenly become a stranger. They were all three moving into the paneled hall, the Baron saying something about the usual room having been prepared if they wished to rest. I hurried alongside them and said anxiously, "Sir, my mother — where is she, please?''

The Baron smiled. "You will see her in an hour, child, when she returns from the hospital in Szigvár.'' He snapped his fingers and a fair-haired girl in a heavily beaded blouse with embroidered skirt and white apron came forward. "Anna will show you to your room. I am sure you wish to tidy yourself and look your best before meeting your mother."

I nodded dumbly, trying to swallow my disappointment at this delay, and ashamed to have forgotten that my mother was still having attention at the Baron's own small hospital for her injured foot.

My room was on the third floor, and on the eastern side of the castle. Five minutes later I was unpacking my trunk and trying to talk with Anna, the maid, who had no English and only a few words of German. With much pointing and sign language I gathered from her that *"Gnädige Frau Doktor"* had a room on the same floor but on the western side of the castle, and that she would be returning soon.

Anna seemed a friendly girl, but I noticed that she kept looking at me with a kind of furtive awe, as if I were a curiosity who roused her sympathy. I made clear to her that I would do my own unpacking, but as soon as I was alone I began to wish I had not sent her away, for a nameless feeling of unease began to stir within me. I could have given no sensible reason for it. Baron Krenner's welcome had perhaps been less warm and friendly than I had expected, and it seemed to me that Gideon and Belinda had ignored me from the moment of our arrival. But perhaps in Hungary it was bad manners to show emotion in front of servants.

I tried to push my foreboding aside, and concentrated on the simple task of unpacking. I had brought with me only two dresses for evening wear, and two for day wear, together with a skirt and some blouses, for I had no wish to play the peacock here, in front of my mother, as I had done during those shameful months in London. Nobody could love a creature like that, but I hope fervently that my mother might find something to love in me as Chantal. I had packed my riding clothes, and all that I had brought with me to England from the circus, including my moccasin shoes. To anybody else this might have seemed stupid, but to me my circus clothes were symbols, reminding me that I could be either Chantal, with few virtues, or a fat, white, spotty, and spiteful creature with no virtues at all.

While I was hanging up my clothes

Anna brought hot water in a big copper jug. When she had left I stripped off my clothes, washed my hands and face, then sponged my body to cleanse the sweat of travel from it before putting on fresh underwear and another dress, a simple cream-colored day dress with a pale-brown jabot.

As I brushed my hair I kept darting from the mirror to the window, hoping at least to hear the sound of a carriage bringing my mother home, for even when I opened the window and leaned out as far as possible through the embrasure I could not see the forecourt of the castle. After completing my toilet I tried to contain my restlessness by examining the bedroom. This did not take long. It was a lofty room, and the bed was a huge four-poster, but the furnishing was sparse compared to an English bedroom.

I thought I might write a short letter to Maria, to be delivered by hand, but there was no sign of pen and ink. Trying to be calm, I stood looking out of the open window, across a bailey of cobbles in which a few small lawns and flower beds had been laid, and it was then, for the first time, that I remembered with a little shock my promise to Martin Verne. I had said that I would not leave Wildings for four weeks, and now I was here in Hungary, a thousand miles away. Yet it was a promise I could not have kept, even if I had remembered it. Martin would surely understand . . . if he ever came to learn what had happened. It dawned on me that I could not be sure he would keep our rendezvous, and for all I knew we might never meet again. The thought brought a curious ache to my chest.

There came a tap on the door and I almost ran across the room, calling, *"Herein!"*

It was Baron Krenner. He looked at me for a moment with an air of remote interest and said, "Your mother has returned and is waiting for you, Chantal. She has her own sitting room. I am sure you will both prefer to be left alone for this first meeting."

"Yes. Yes. Thank you." Those were the only words I could manage. As if in a dream I walked beside him along the corridor, down two flights of stairs, then across a small hall and along a wider corridor to a door at the end. He knocked, opened the door without waiting for a reply, and stood aside for me to enter as he said, "We shall see you at dinner. By then your mother will have told you all you need to know."

It was not until later that I took in his words and understood their meaning. With my heart thumping and legs feeling as if they belonged to somebody else, I walked slowly into the room and heard the door close behind me. It was a room smaller than my bedroom, again sparsely furnished by English standards, but with some womanly touches — a vase of flowers, some dainty cushion covers, a sewing box, an embroidered screen hiding the fire grate.

She stood by the window, in a gray dress, her hands clasped in front of her, facing me. At first her features were a blur, and I saw only that she had dark-brown hair drawn loosely back in a short thick plait at the nape of her neck. She seemed tall, but then I realized that this was a false impression, given by the slenderness of her body, the erectness of her stance, and the long column of her neck.

I had rehearsed many different greetings in my mind, but now I could find no words. I moved closer, and still neither of us spoke. My vision cleared and I saw her face. It did not match the picture I had made in my imagination during the past two days, for she was not beautiful as my daydream had made her; but this was a real face, while the face in my daydream had been as unreal as a fairy tale.

A broad brow set above large gray eyes. Small ears and nose. A large mouth. A complexion too weathered by sun and fresh air to be fashionable. A few frown lines in the center of the brow. Little crow's-feet at the corners of the eyes. A firmly rounded chin. But all this conveyed nothing of the character and spirit dwelling in that face. Its quietness was the quietness of strength, and the eyes were those of one who had walked through many a dark valley without flinching.

Even so, I caught a hint of fear in her

gaze now, and saw that her hands were clenched so tightly together that the knuckles showed white. Slowly my numbed mind grasped the fact that at this moment she was as nervous as I. She smiled hesitantly, and I glimpsed even white teeth as she said, "I'm so frightened that you won't like me, Chantal." Her voice was soft and a little unsteady, but it had a mellow lilt that reminded me of Maria speaking Italian.

I said in a hoarse whisper, "I've been afraid, too." My fingers hurt, and I found my own hands were clenched hard. I wanted to say a thousand things, but all that emerged was, "Do you mind about my name?"

"Chantal? It's beautiful." She drew in a deep breath. "I didn't give you a name. I mean, didn't give a name to the baby I thought was you. I wasn't well, and it was all over before . . ." She made a small helpless gesture. "Can you forgive me?"

"Forgive you?" Distress rose within me. "No, please don't say that. I'm the one to be forgiven. I thought such dreadful things of you."

She put out her hands and I grasped them. They were small, strong hands, much like my own. Now I saw that my first impression had been wrong. She was beautiful, far more beautiful than my fairy-tale imaginings had made her, for they had been empty of life. Though the eyes were wise with experience, they were still youthful, and though tropical sun had laid tiny lines on her face, the flesh was still firm.

I found myself in a difficulty I had not thought about before, and said apologetically, "Please, what shall I call you? I know it's usually Mamma, but . . . oh, I don't know. It doesn't feel right."

She studied me, still nervous but half smiling now. "Yes. I don't think you're a Mamma girl. Could it be Mother?"

"Yes. Yes, please."

Now I saw that the dress she wore was almost threadbare in places and had been carefully mended many times, but before I could wonder about this she said, "It's going to take a little while for us to know each other, Chantal. We shall have to be patient."

"Yes. Oh, I'm a fool! You mustn't keep standing with your bad foot." I drew her carefully towards the deep curved sofa covered in dark-blue velvet.

"My foot?" She seemed not to understand.

"They told me how you'd been hurt by a carriage wheel running over it. Is it better now . . . Mother?" I used the word for the first time, and felt a wave of happiness as we sat down, turning a little to face each other, still holding hands.

Something almost like anger flickered for a moment in her eyes, and then was gone. "Yes," she answered quietly. "My foot isn't troubling me. We'll talk about all that later. Now let me look at you."

She took my face between her hands, turning it a little this way and then the other, as Martin had done not long ago in the barn. Her hand moved to touch my hair. "Dear God," she said softly at last, "you're so like my John, so like your father."

It was then, just when I thought I had safely passed the danger of tears, that I began to cry. She gathered me to her, and

I half lay with my head on her breast, making very little noise, yet shaking with sobs as I wept with happiness for this moment, and with sorrow for all the wasted years.

"Let the tears come, darling, let them come. It's better so," she whispered, and I felt the warmth of her own tears as one fell upon my brow. I do not know how long the fit of weeping lasted, but when at last it subsided I felt as if a thousand anxieties had been lifted from me. There was a time of dreaminess, of a great content . . . and the next thing I knew I was waking from a kind of sleep, still in her embrace.

I sat up slowly, trying to gather my wits. "Oh . . . I'm sorry, Mother. Was I asleep long?"

"Only ten minutes. The happiest ten minutes I've known since you were born." She smiled as she spoke, and seemed free from tension now, as I was myself, yet I thought I glimpsed something somber in her eyes.

I said, "There's so much to ask you. I hardly know where to begin."

"We've so much to ask each other, my dearest . . . all that's happened to both of us in nineteen long years. I know it can't be told in an hour or even a month, but I hope you'll be patient with your own questions, and tell me something of yourself first. I know so little about you." She leaned forward and pressed her cheek to mine. When she drew back, her eyes were sparkling with laughter. "Is it true that when you were thirteen you ran away and joined a circus?"

I nodded, responding to her smile. "Yes. That was after I discovered I wasn't Roberta Armitage at all. Oh, I'm so glad you didn't know me then, Mother. I was fat and spotty and just dreadful in every way . . ."

For almost an hour I talked with scarcely a pause, and even then it was only for my mother to ask another question. I told of my childhood, of the day when I had learned I was a changeling, and of my years in the circus with Mr. Galletti and Maria and Leo. I did not spare myself concerning recent events, but confessed that in London I had slipped back for a time to my old selfish and spiteful ways without realizing it, until my eyes had been suddenly opened.

I had never known anyone listen so intently. My mother's eyes scarcely left my face, and as my sketchy story was told her own face was alive with response, laughter and sorrow, excitement and pity, mischief and concern. At last, when my throat was dry with talking, she rose and poured me a glass of water from a carafe.

"Sip it, dearest, then suck this lozenge." She stood looking down at me, hands folded in front of her, but loosely now, and said, "How John would have loved you."

I shook my head and sighed. "I must have told it badly, Mother. I'm not a very lovable person."

"Didn't Mr. Galletti and his family love you?"

"Oh, yes, they did. But that was different, because in the circus I managed to do something they thought well of. It's really the only thing I can be a little proud to have done, I suppose. Besides, they weren't ordinary people."

"Neither was your father, Chantal dear." She gazed wistfully into space for long moments, then collected herself and looked at the watch on her wrist.

I said, "Shouldn't you rest your foot, Mother? Gideon said it had been quite a serious injury."

She sat down again and put her hand on mine, looking down with a little frown. Slowly the gentleness and humor left her face, and I saw the muscles of her jaw twitch. "It's my turn to talk now, I'm afraid," she said at last. "I've delayed because I didn't want to spoil our moment of coming together. But what I have to tell you is . . . shocking beyond all words." She lifted her head and looked at me with steady eyes. "Thank God you're Chantal, your father's daughter."

I stared at her, puzzled and disturbed. "What is it, Mother?"

She drew in a deep breath, and her hand tightened on mine. "My foot was never hurt," she said in a flat voice. "That was a trick to bring you here. I was never in hospital in Budapest. I've been here in Joseph Krenner's castle for over a year now, ever since Benedict Kirkby and Gideon Sumner discovered that I was legally married to John Kirkby. I'm a prisoner here, Chantal. And you're to be a prisoner here, too."

She stopped speaking, and the room was heavy with silence. For one terrifying moment I wondered if she had lost her reason, but the very quietness of her sorrow as she watched me belied this. I felt stunned and winded, as I had felt that day when my trapeze broke and I bounced from the net to the beaten ground of the ring. Now I made the same huge effort to gather my wits and be calm, despite the host of questions that clogged my mind.

"Prisoners? But *why,* Mother?"

She half smiled, but without humor, and her eyes were angry. "So it hasn't occurred to you, either. We're two of a kind, it seems."

"What hasn't occurred?"

"That my John, your father, was the son and direct heir of James Kirkby. But when the time came for the will to be proved, nobody knew that John had left a wife and child." I tried to think clearly, but found it hard to remember what Gideon Sumner had told me about the Kirkby family connections that day in Ingolstadt.

"The whole of the Kirkby fortune was willed to John," my mother went on. "There was a provision that if he died before his father, then the inheritance would pass to his wife, if he were married, and to his children, if any, in certain proportions. So you and I were the heirs, Chantal dear." She shook her head impatiently. "I neither knew nor cared, for I didn't know my baby had lived, and I wanted nothing for myself."

I said wonderingly, "You mean . . . it *didn't* belong to Benedict and Arthur Kirkby?"

"Oh, they believed so. Old James made no new will when John died. Perhaps the heart went out of him, for he only lived a few months. And since there were no further provisions in the will, the inheritance automatically passed to his nephews, Benedict and Arthur."

"They were . . . wait, let me think. They were the sons of his brother, Rupert, and the Hungarian lady?"

"Yes. Eva, sister of Baron Krenner's father."

I pressed my fingers to my temples. "You said Benedict and Arthur believed the inheritance was rightfully theirs at the time?"

My mother nodded. "So did the solicitors involved. You see, my darling, nobody knew that John had married me, except his two naval friends who attended the wedding. When he died, and when I lost my baby as I thought, I simply wanted to cut myself off completely. I wrote to his friends, asking them not to reveal our marriage."

Many small events which had puzzled me in the past began to come together now in my mind, and I shivered as a chill ran through me. "Mother . . . are you saying that a year ago, when Benedict Kirkby discovered that you were alive and had been legally married, he was so frightened of losing the Kirkby fortune that he . . . he set out to make sure you could never claim it?"

"Yes, darling." She spoke reluctantly.

"I'm afraid there's no doubt of it. At least, I gather it was Benedict rather than his brother. I've never met either of them."

"It would be Benedict," I whispered. "Uncle Arthur couldn't have known, he's just a dreamer. But Benedict loves money more than anything except hunting, and he *needs* a lot of money for that." I tried to think, to make a clear pattern from my jumbled thoughts. "Then . . . Baron Krenner and Gideon Sumner must be in league with Benedict Kirkby?"

"Oh, yes." My mother's voice was tight. "Gideon Sumner, with those merry eyes and that wonderful charm . . . he's been part of it from the beginning." She looked at me with pain in her fine gray eyes. "I've seen much wickedness in the world, Chantal, but I truly believe that Gideon Sumner is the most evil man I've ever met . . . though there's little to choose between him and Joseph Krenner."

I flinched with shock, then stood up and moved restlessly across the room to the window. Outside, the early-evening sun still shone, the sky was blue and the trees wore their summer greenery. I looked out upon a world that seemed normal. But within the room, dark shadows grew longer with the cruel and terrible story my mother was unfolding. I still knew only a little of it, still found myself groping confusedly to unravel the threads, but a huge anger was beginning to rise up within me as I thought of what had been done to her. With an effort I held it in check and said in a strained voice, "What do you know of Gideon, Mother?"

"Many things." She made a grimace of disgust. "He talks quite freely to Krenner at table, even when I'm present. I know that it was he who killed a man called von Dreyer with a bomb last summer. I know he caused the death by drowning of a young solicitor called Quillan, because the poor man knew that you and I were entitled to the Kirkby inheritance." Her voice shook suddenly and became almost ugly with passion. "I know that it was he who tried to kill *you,* my darling, only a few weeks after the von Dreyer murder."

"Me?" I turned to stare at her. "You — you mean when the trapeze broke? But

that was in Regensburg, and he didn't find me till two weeks later, in Ingolstadt! Besides, he could never have passed the guards and climbed to the trapeze in darkness —"

"It was in Regensburg that he discovered you," my mother broke in gently. "Do you remember one of the circus workers being found drowned in a trough there one morning?"

"Hans? Yes, but . . . oh! Did *Hans* do it?"

"Gideon Sumner bribed him to do something to your trapeze that night. And when it was done he knocked the man insensible and put him in the trough to drown. Krenner told me the story only a few days ago, with great amusement."

"It's so hard to believe," I whispered. "If Gideon could do that, why didn't he try again later?"

"Because he decided you might be more profitable to him alive." Again her voice shook with anger.

"But how? Oh! You mean by marrying me? But it can't be so, Mother! He couldn't be a murderer and a criminal without Belinda knowing, and surely no sister could be fond of a brother who did such dreadful things."

My mother sighed. "She isn't his sister, my precious, neither is she fond of him. Belinda is his woman, his mistress, and she has the misfortune to be wildly in love with that evil man." She gave a sad little shrug. "Or perhaps it's the wickedness in him that she can't resist. There are such women."

I looked about me, struggling to absorb this new shock. It seemed that ever since leaving the circus I had lived amid a web of lies and deceit; and danger, too, for now I realized that there had been those who had strong reason to wish me dead. Yet still I could not grasp the whole truth of it, for there was so much that seemed to make little sense.

I moved to the sofa and sat down again. My mother said in a shaky voice, "Dear Chantal, I'm so sorry I can't spare you all this horror."

"Don't be upset, Mother. I want to know." I took her hand and held it between my own. "Besides, we're together now, and that's the most important thing." I managed to smile. "It's funny, I wanted to ask you so many things, especially about your work, and how you became a doctor, but first we'll have to find a way to escape. I'm sure it won't be difficult, not with the two of us."

She looked down. "I'm guarded every moment of the day, Chantal, and so will you be. Even when I go to the little hospital each day, two men go with me."

"There really is a hospital?"

"Yes, in the village."

"Couldn't you secretly give a letter to one of the patients to post? A letter to the British Ambassador?"

"You don't understand, darling. Krenner's word is law on his own estates, and the tenants are loyal to him. He treats them well, on the whole. A Hungarian peasant simply could not conceive of doing something for a foreigner against his master's orders. Besides, it's just a twenty-bed hospital and most of the patients are children."

"But the other doctor — Dr. Brandt?"

"Who? Oh, the man in the story they

concocted to bring you out here. He doesn't exist." She gave a weary little smile. "One night last year I tried to escape from my window with a rope of sheets —"

"Mother, you might have killed yourself!"

"No, dear." A spark of laughter briefly touched her eyes. "I haven't been on a trapeze, but I've led a very active life in some strange parts of the world. There was a time when I paddled ten miles in a dugout canoe on my daily rounds for months on end, so I'm quite agile." The spark faded. "However, they caught me. A guard with a lantern circles the castle every hour, and he saw the sheets. I could never have traveled far anyway, on foot or by horse. Krenner's estates spread for miles, and even if I could get to a police station they wouldn't help me. He's put it about that the unfortunate English lady doctor, who is so good with the children in his hospital, sometimes has a nervous disorder and imagines that she's a prisoner, held here against her will."

In the past half hour I had known many

shocks, but in some part of my half-numbed mind I had felt that we could never be held prisoner in Castle Szigvár for long. It was only now I began to realize, with growing fear, that the Baron held us in an iron grip extending far beyond the castle walls. A new and even more frightening thought came suddenly to my mind, and I said slowly, "It would be safer for them all if we were both . . . dead."

"Yes." My mother spoke calmly. "And I'm sure we would be, if it wasn't for the fact that there's no honor among thieves. You have to understand that each man has been working in his own interest. Benedict Kirkby feared losing his fortune. Baron Krenner had speculated heavily and was in debt, so he sought a way to prise large loans from his English cousin. And Gideon Sumner had even bigger ideas." I shook my head, uncomprehending, and she went on. "It's best if I tell you all I know of the story, dearest. God knows this is a terrible way to spend our first hours together, but there's no help for it."

I slipped to the floor, my legs curled

beneath me, and leaned against her, taking her hand and drawing it across my shoulder. "Yes. Please tell me. I'll feel better when I know everything."

My mother began to speak, rather quickly and without emotion, as if she had rehearsed the story in her mind in readiness for this moment. "It began when a young lawyer came to Benedict with a memorandum and papers to prove that John Kirkby had been legally married to a woman called Elizabeth Martin, and that their child had not died at birth, but was the girl called Roberta Armitage who had run away from Farleigh Hall. As far as Mr. Quillan, the young lawyer, could ascertain, there was no record that either of us had died. Benedict was horrified to learn that there were possibly two people, somewhere in the world, who might one day discover that they were entitled to his fortune. He told his cousin, Baron Krenner, who recommended employing Gideon Sumner to deal with the situation. Krenner had hired Sumner's services several times, and knew the kind of man he was. . . ."

And so the hunt for my mother had begun. It had taken a long time, but Gideon and Belinda Sumner found her at last, working in a Neapolitan convent hospital. Gideon had said nothing of the past, but pretended to be representing Baron Krenner, of the Red Cross, who was urgently seeking a woman doctor to take charge of the small hospital for children he had recently established in Szigvár.

And there she found herself a prisoner.

"I learned the truth then," my mother said quietly. "Those evil men told me with pride, not shame. At first I could scarcely believe it, but soon I began to wonder why they hadn't simply done away with me. I can only give Gideon Sumner's answer to that. He said that Benedict Kirkby is a weak man who had simply given him instructions to take whatever steps were necessary to make sure I could never claim the Kirkby fortune."

I lifted my head. "But, Mother . . . that could mean anything."

"Yes, even my death. But the death of an unknown person holds no reality for some. Perhaps Benedict Kirkby hoped to achieve that end without putting it into words. But Krenner wanted me alive, as a threat to hold over Benedict, and this suited Gideon Sumner well, for he was paid by both men and could play one against the other." She closed her eyes for a moment. "His next task was to find you, Chantal, if you still lived, to make sure that *you* could never claim your father's inheritance."

"That was when he tried to do away with me in Regensburg?" I was long past feeling shock now, and could speak as calmly as my mother.

"Yes. But he failed, thank God, and then he had a new idea. He would take you home to England, to the Kirkby family. Benedict would be horrified when he received the telegram telling him to expect you, but there was little he could do about it, for he was afraid Gideon would put all the evidence about your birth and the Kirkby inheritance in the hands of a solicitor."

"It's so strange," I said slowly. "They always seemed good friends."

"These men wear masks, my darling."

"Yes." I remembered old Solange's words . . . *the actors wear masks.*

"Gideon Sumner planned to let you settle in, and then to court you and marry you. In that way he would be able to lay hands on the Kirkby fortune by claiming it for his wife."

"Yes," I said heavily. "He once asked whether I would run away with him if Benedict refused to let him court me. But later he said he'd changed his mind."

"That was Belinda's doing. She had no fancy for him to take a wife."

I remembered the day when I walked from the stables with Belinda, and she had spoken about the pain of loving a man without a conscience, a thief, a trickster, and a hireling. She had named Martin Verne, but now I knew this was a lie, for he was not the man she loved. My heart jumped a little . . . perhaps everything she had told me of Martin Verne was untrue of him, but true of Gideon Sumner!

My mother cupped her hand upon my cheek as I sat by her knee. "I think his plan to marry you would have failed anyway," she said in a low voice. "Perhaps he realized it was so, and in any event he dared not risk Belinda turning against him. In the end he wrung the best out of the situation by making Benedict pay heavily to have you taken away from England and brought here, to Castle Szigvár, to be a prisoner with me."

There was a long silence in the room. I was thinking that this could not be the end of the story, for it was surely impossible to keep us prisoners here forever, yet it seemed equally impossible that Joseph Krenner would ever set us free.

I said, "Suppose you signed something to say you gave up your claim to the Kirkby inheritance?"

"My precious, I've never wanted it, and I offered to renounce my claim long ago. But these men are quite unable to believe anyone would give up such wealth."

Ugly thoughts began to stir in my mind. Matters could not rest as they were for long. Joseph Krenner and Gideon Sumner would try to outwit each other if the prize were big enough. As if reading my thoughts, my mother said in a whisper, "I wasn't going to tell you this so soon, but you're very strong, Chantal, and you give me strength. I believe Krenner plans to use *you* to make me marry him."

My spine turned to ice, and a haze blurred my eyes. Though I sat like a child at my mother's knee, I did not feel like a child. With a terrible ferocity I felt protective. The red vixen . . .

My mind spun. Half-remembered things whirled as if in a kaleidoscope, then settled in a startling new pattern. *Martin Verne!* He had come from the east when I found him that day, which meant he must have been somewhere in the area of Kaposnika. And the word "doctor" had stirred a chord in his lost memory. I recalled his words in the sunken lane near Wildings, when he had spoken cryptically of a woman in another country, and Sir Robert had asked what prevented her coming to him. *"Stone walls and iron bars . . ."* he had replied.

How many women were held behind stone walls and iron bars? I turned to look up into troubled gray eyes. "Mother, do you know a man named Martin Verne?"

I saw her catch her breath, then she leaned forward, a look of wonder and tenderness lighting her eyes. "Martin? Oh, I can scarcely believe it! Do you really know my dear Martin?"

Before I could answer there came a sharp tap on the door. I rose quickly to my feet as my mother whispered, "Krenner. We'll talk again later. Do as I do, darling." She stood up and turned to face the door, very erect, hands folded in front of her, face coldly impassive. I took up the same position beside her as she called brusquely, "Yes?"

The door opened. Joseph Krenner studied us for a moment, then said, "We are about to dine, Elizabeth. I take it you have explained certain matters to your daughter?"

My mother inclined her head. The Baron shrugged. "I hope that to have her company may help you feel less stubborn and hostile."

My mother said nothing. I could not see her face, but I felt she was gazing through him as if he did not exist, and schooled myself to do the same. He waited several seconds, looking from one to the other of us, then gave a short angry laugh, stepped aside, and gestured for us to precede him.

FIFTEEN

The lamps had been lit in the dining hall.
In the center stood a long table with
ornately carved legs. Rugs were scattered
on the floor, and the paneled walls were
hung with portraits, ancient weapons, and
trophies of the chase. From above the
fireplace a wolf's head mounted on a
block of polished wood grinned down
upon the hall.

Gideon Sumner and Belinda were seated
facing each other at the far end of the
table, talking and laughing together.
Gideon rose as we entered and said,
smiling, "Good evening, Dr. Martin.
Good evening, Chantal." Belinda put her
head on one side and gave us a whimsical
look. My mother ignored them and moved
to a place at the foot of the table,
touching my arm to guide me to the seat

on her right. Joseph Krenner moved to his place at the head of the table, between Gideon and Belinda.

"Elizabeth still speaks to me only when obliged to," he said with an amused air, "and this usually arises from matters concerning the hospital. Let us hope she may become more reasonable now that you have reunited her with her daughter, my dear Gideon."

"Chantal will be a great help," Gideon said cheerfully. "She's slow-witted and quick-tempered, but I'm sure she'll come to realize that she's no longer at Wildings, with only a sheep in wolf's clothing like Benedict to deal with."

I could not prevent myself looking at him. It was only a brief glance, but enough to stain my mind with a picture that was to linger for many a day. He was smiling, and his eyes held the same merry twinkle I had remarked when I first saw him in Ingolstadt. But now there was a difference. Perhaps it lay only in my own eye, yet it was as definite as the changing color of shot silk when turned to catch light from a new angle. The smile and the merriment were not false, but now held a quality that frightened me. In a gallery in Florence I had once seen a huge painting of a scene in hell. Smiling imps and devils were doing vile things to the wraiths of the dead, and the horror of it was that their pleasure in this seemed almost absentminded, without spite or hatred. I had shivered at their soulless inhumanity then as I shivered now.

I heard Belinda give a little gurgling chuckle as Gideon Sumner finished speaking, and I looked quickly away. Copying my mother, I seated myself, folded my hands on my lap, and stared down at the cutlery in front of me. The next hour was the strangest I had ever spent at table. Two footmen served us from a huge trolley, another poured white wine into our glasses. Baron Krenner, Gideon, and Belinda talked together, sometimes about political parties and groupings in the Austro-Hungarian Empire, sometimes about business affairs which meant nothing to me. Much of their talk was cryptic, but I gathered that the Baron was alarmed at the way in which the authorities in Vienna were slowly breaking down the feudal power of the old Hungarian nobility, and was disgruntled that the assassination of von Dreyer had not achieved what he hoped for.

I listened with only half an ear, for I was wondering about Martin Verne, and trying to think how my mother and I could escape, but a great tiredness had descended upon me now. It was as much as I could do to watch my mother from the corner of my eye and follow her example. She ate the food that was served, and though I had little appetite I made myself do the same. Her glass of wine remained untouched. Sometimes she caught my eye and gave a little smile, but she did not speak.

As coffee was served, Baron Krenner looked down the table and raised his glass. "Shall we drink to your reunion with your lost daughter, my dear Elizabeth?"

My mother stirred her coffee as if unaware of his presence, and again he gave the short angry laugh I had heard before. "She has yet to drink wine at my table, Gideon, or to wear the fine dresses

I have provided."

Gideon Sumner smiled. "You must persevere, Baron, you must persevere." He looked at me. "Even in the most obstinate woman there's a weak spot to be found."

Five minutes later my mother stood up, and I followed suit. She looked down the table and said, "May we withdraw?"

Baron Krenner waved a hand. "As you please."

"May my daughter accompany me during my duties at the hospital tomorrow?"

He shrugged. "Have you explained to her that any attempt to deprive us of her company would hurt me deeply, and would also be quite fruitless?"

"Yes."

"Then I have no objection, my dear Elizabeth. Anna will come to take her to her bedroom in an hour."

My mother slipped a hand under my arm and we walked side by side from the dining hall. No word was spoken until we were in her sitting room again with the door closed, then she put a hand to her brow and gave a sigh of relief, looking at me with a wan smile. "Such an ordeal for you, my dearest. I'm sorry."

I held back tears and said, "Have you really endured this alone, for over a year?"

"I'm used to being alone." She spoke as one stating a simple fact, then excitement lit her face and she took my hand. "Come and sit down. I want to hear about Martin."

"Oh, Mother, so do I. Everything I know of him is a mystery or . . . things I've been told. Do you really know him well?"

She leaned back on the sofa, a warm glow in her eyes.

"We first came together seven years ago, when he was little more than twenty. I've seen him only five or six times since then, but when two people spend twelve days adrift on a tiny raft, they come to know each other well."

"*On a raft?* But . . . but that was someone else!" The name from the newspaper cutting came back to me. "Furnival. John Furnival."

"Yes. I understand that's one of the names he sometimes uses." She shook her head. "I do worry about that boy and the things he does."

My tiredness vanished, and I said eagerly, "Tell me about the raft."

She linked her hands round her knee and gazed distantly at the fireplace screen. "It happened at night," she said quietly, "and the ship sank very quickly. I discovered later that some people managed to scramble into lifeboats, but I found myself drifting alone in the life belt I was wearing. I'd hurt my head, and I was afraid of passing out, and turning face down." She paused, remembering. "Then this young man appeared beside me. He was a good swimmer, and he held me so that I floated on my back. Later we bumped into this empty raft in the darkness. . . ."

It had been daylight when at last she woke from her stupor, and they were alone, drifting in a heavy sea mist. It was not until then she discovered that the young man with her had two broken ribs. She had torn strips from her skirt to strap his chest, and found a water bottle clipped between the slats of the raft. Then the long ordeal began.

"It was so strange . . . I'd noticed him aboard ship. He was traveling alone, a quiet young man, older than his years, very wary and watchful. I thought him unfriendly, but he was quite different on the raft, so grateful to me for caring for him, Chantal, so gentle and thoughtful. We were blistered by the sun during the day, and shivered together in the cold night winds, but I never heard him complain. He used to try to cheat over the ration of water we allowed ourselves, so that there would be more for me. Night and morning I used to spread out our clothes for an hour to catch dew, and wring a few drops of grimy water from them. Once it rained . . . and we stored almost half a pint of water that day." Her eyes grew somber. "We would have died without each other. He always said that I kept him alive, but the reverse was just as true. He could always manage a smile and a little joke. So young . . . but so much older than his years. I learned his real name early on, before it became too difficult to talk." She smiled. "He used to call me Dr. Elizabeth because he said it would be too confusing to have a Martin and a Dr. Martin aboard."

By the ninth day they had given up hope, though neither would confess it. At dawn on the twelfth day they found themselves only a few miles from land, and two hours later a Sicilian fishing boat picked them up. They were gaunt and wasted, with sores on their faces and bodies. But they were alive.

I sat silent for a long time when my mother ended her story, imagining the horror of those endless days when they had waited for death. It was little wonder that a bond had been forged between them in that time. At last I said, "Was it while you were on the raft together that he told you about himself?"

"Yes, little by little, and I learned more later." She looked at me. "Do you know about his guardian?" I shook my head. "Well, I've never discovered his name, but Martin was orphaned as a small boy in Hong Kong, and this naval man took charge of him and brought him up. He went to a boarding school in England, and —"

"Naval man!" I exclaimed. "Was it Sir Robert Wayman?"

"I don't know, darling. Who is he?"

"Well . . . I know he's connected with Martin. I'll explain later, Mother, but what happened after you were saved by the fishermen?"

"There isn't much more to tell. When we were discharged from the hospital we went our separate ways, but Martin asked me to write to him in London sometimes, to give him my news and let him know where I was. I suppose we wrote to each other about twice a year, but there were times when he would suddenly appear, quite unexpectedly. He'd come perhaps a thousand miles just to see me for a day or two. It happened in Asmara once, and in Nairobi, Vienna, and Naples . . . it was always such a lovely surprise."

"Do you know what he is, Mother?" I asked. "Do you know what he does?" I was sure I knew the answer now, sure that Belinda had reversed the true roles of

Gideon Sumner and Martin Verne.

My mother frowned. "That guardian should be ashamed of himself. He seems to have an obsession about criminals who are clever enough to escape the law, and he brought that boy up to be a trained . . ." She groped for a suitable word.

"Hunting dog?"

She gave me a startled look. "Yes, I suppose so. Martin seemed to regard it as an exciting game, tracking down some dangerous scoundrel and finding evidence to bring him to book." She looked troubled. "I hate to think of the risks he runs for this wretched guardian."

I said slowly, "I believe that may have changed. Was it in Naples you last saw him, Mother?"

"No. I saw him here in Castle Szigvár last year, a few hours before Gideon Sumner arrived for the von Dreyer business."

"Ah. I thought somehow Martin must know you were a prisoner here. Did you speak with him?"

"No." She looked at me doubtfully.

"He didn't see me, and I don't think he can possibly know I'm here, darling."

"Tell me what happened."

"One day I was told that Baron Krenner was entertaining a businessman from Rumania to dinner, so I would be served dinner in my room that evening. I'm never allowed to speak to anyone from outside, of course." She gestured towards the curtained french windows. "I was on the little terrace later, and saw them walking below. I even heard them talking. The visitor was Martin, and he was speaking in German. I suppose he was posing as a Rumanian to account for any foreign accent." She bit her lip and frowned, a little mannerism I had noticed before. "I was going to call to him, but then I realized I would be exposing him as an impostor, and that would be very dangerous."

"You thought he was on one of his hunting missions, and Baron Krenner was his quarry?"

"Yes. I knew Krenner was behind the assassination of von Dreyer."

"I think Gideon Sumner was his quarry,

557

but it doesn't matter. What did you do?"

"While they were at dinner I went to the coach house and put a folded note on the seat of the coach that would take him to the station, telling him I was a prisoner here. I knew he would recognize my writing, and hoped he would find the note." She gave a wry smile. "It was weeks before I could bring myself to accept that I'd hoped in vain. I'm sure he would have found a way to help me."

I said, "He did find the note, Mother, he must have. He knew you were a prisoner here, and I'm almost sure he came back that very night. I don't really know what happened, but perhaps he was so anxious that he became careless, or perhaps Gideon Sumner caught a glimpse of him — I think they're old enemies. But I'm sure Martin was caught trying to save you . . . and they left him for dead."

"Dear God, no!" She stared at me in horror.

"He was hit on the head, stripped, and thrown in a river to drown," I said, holding her hand. "They put a woven black wristlet on him, a mark to show that it was the work of the Brotherhood of the Wolf."

"You *know* about that?"

"A man in the circus told me. He was from a Hungarian village. Is Baron Krenner one of the leaders?"

My mother nodded slowly. "Yes. I thought that was why Martin was hunting him. But, Chantal, how can you know what happened?"

"Because I found Martin a few days later. He was traveling on foot like a tramp, in stolen clothes, and he'd lost his memory."

She bowed her head and put her hands over her face, weeping silently. "My fault . . . my fault. That poor boy."

I put my arm about her. "Mother, it's all right now. He's well again and his memory has come back. I saw him in England a little more than two weeks ago, and I'm sure he's planning to save you!"

She lowered her hands and gazed at me from bewildered eyes. "Does he . . . does he know you're my daughter?"

"I'm not sure, but I think so. And I think he didn't tell me of you because he knows what an impulsive fool I am, and he was afraid I might do something stupid and dangerous if I knew the truth. When I asked him about something I'd overheard, about a lady who was a prisoner in another country, he looked alarmed and then said he had been speaking of a statuette in a museum.''

My mother took a handkerchief from her sleeve and dabbed her eyes. A smile touched her lips and she said, ''I think he must know you very well, my darling. You'd probably have run away to find me on your own. Now tell me how you first found him wandering with amnesia.''

Quickly I told of that meeting by the stream, and how Martin had spent several weeks with the circus before disappearing in Regensburg. I now thought it likely that he had caught sight of Gideon and Belinda there, and it was this which had jolted his memory into its first awakening. I told how I had overheard his conversation with Sir Robert in the sunken lane, and how he had appeared on the night of the last ball at the Kirkby house in London.

''He came to look for me, but I . . . I

wasn't the girl he remembered, Mother. Then he went away, and I didn't see him again till two weeks ago.'' I went on quickly to explain how Martin had found me practicing in the barn.

My mother said, "Why do you think he came to look for you? Twice?"

"I don't know, Mother. He didn't say."

She smiled. "Perhaps he had fallen in love with Chantal?"

"Oh!" I was startled. "I don't think it could be that."

She studied me. "Do you like him?"

"Yes." I remembered how happy I had been with him during those weeks last summer. "Yes, I like him very much. I tried not to think about him for a long time, because I believed he was a bad man after Belinda lied to me about him."

My mother was still smiling. "Think about all the other young men you've met. Try to picture them." She was silent for a few moments. "Now think about Martin. Does it feel different?"

Slowly I put a hand to my lips and turned to look at her, wide-eyed.

Something warm and golden seemed to be expanding inside me, as if a key had been turned and a door opened. I whispered, "Oh! Oh, dear. How did you guess, Mother? I — I didn't even know myself."

"Something comes into your eyes when you speak of him, my precious."

There was a little tap on the door, and a voice called in German, "It is Anna, Frau Doktor. I am to take the Fräulein to her room now."

My mother stood up and called, "Come in, Anna." She moved to a worn leather case on a side table as the girl entered. "You've crowded a year of emotion into a few hours, my poor darling, and you'll be too tired to sleep." She came towards me and put a small phial in my hands. "Take ten drops in a little water just before you get into bed, and you'll rest well."

"Will you do the same?"

"Yes, I promise." She put out her arms. "Good night . . ." Her voice broke and she caught me in a fierce embrace. As I hugged her I whispered, "Good night, Mother. Be happy. It's all going to come right, now we're together."

Fifteen minutes later I lay in bed, staring up into the darkness. In a few short hours almost all that had mystified me over the past year had been explained, and the fragments of a grim and shameful story had been put together. In the same few hours I had met my lost mother, and discovered that I loved Martin Verne. My body was limp and my spirit felt bruised from so many shocks, so many conflicting emotions. I had no doubt that my mother and I would sooner or later be in danger of our lives, but at this moment I was untroubled by fear, perhaps because I felt the danger was not imminent.

An awareness of Martin lay curled within me, a warm, wondering sensation shot through with little sparks of strange excitement, but this was held in some remote part of my being, was something that would truly awaken in time to come. I was thinking of my mother, and with a joy that no danger could extinguish. I pictured her now, as she had sat at table. The shabbiness of her dress had not diminished her. The evil menace of our captors had not cowed her. To me she had shone like a jewel in a pigsty, for the quality of her presence made Gideon Sumner and Joseph Krenner seem the animals they were.

I felt so proud of her that tears came to my eyes. All my earlier fears of meeting her were gone now, for I knew that she loved me. After the first few minutes we had ceased to be strangers, and by the evening's end we had become even closer than many mothers and daughters who had spent twenty years under the same roof, for the very nature of our plight had forged rare and powerful bonds between us.

I was glad she had wept only a little, had not smothered me with sentiment. Dreamily it occurred to me that we both had a fiery spirit, and though hers was more controlled, we might easily come to dispute over some difference of opinion. I smiled in the darkness. That would not matter. I had sometimes argued fiercely with Maria, but we had never ceased to love each other.

With an effort I tried to put my mind to thoughts of escape, but it was then that the medicine I had taken began to exert its grip upon me, and I fell into a deep, dreamless sleep.

At seven o'clock next morning, my mind refreshed and strangely calm, I was leaning across the broad sill of my window, studying the wall which fell to the courtyard below. I had already discovered that my door was locked or bolted on the outside. My window was not in view from the gatehouse, and as I peered down I could see deep crevices where the ancient mortar had been weathered away between the great stone blocks of which the castle was built. Even in darkness I could climb down that wall with little difficulty, and without leaving a rope of sheets to tell the tale of my going.

My mother had said that to escape from the castle was not enough. Baron Krenner's arm was long, for in every village would be two or three men owing allegiance to the Brotherhood of the Wolf, and it was doubtful that we would be truly safe from recapture anywhere in Hungary, unless we could reach a safe haven.

I had the uneasy feeling that the British Embassy in the Austro-Hungarian Empire was far away in Vienna. There might be a consulate in Budapest, but I did not know where, and doubted that we could ever reach Budapest before being caught. But there was one haven which lay very close at this moment. Kayser's Giant Circus was pitched only a few miles away, outside Kaposnika, and there we would be among friends. I decided that my biggest problem was to bring about my mother's escape from her room without leaving any sign of her going, for it was this which had betrayed her before.

Half an hour later, with the problem still unsolved, I tugged the bell pull. Five minutes passed, then I heard a man's voice as the door was unlocked, and the next moment a maid I had not seen before entered the room. She spoke better German than Anna, and I had no difficulty in making her understand that I wanted hot water for my bath, and then wished to take breakfast with my mother before leaving for the hospital with her.

It was wonderful to greet my mother again, an hour later, when I was shown to the breakfast room. She wore a dark skirt and a white blouse with short sleeves, both garments much mended. We took breakfast alone, for Baron Krenner and his guests were not yet about, and though we spoke little because a footman was present I felt a sense of warmth and belonging that made me very happy.

Two men rode beside the carriage which took us to the hospital. One was an amiable young man who wished us a pleasant good morning, the other a dour fellow with suspicious eyes. As he mounted his horse the sleeve of his jacket slipped back, and I saw on his wrist the woven band of black leather I had come to know and fear.

The hospital was a small, single-storied building on the outskirts of the village. There were two wards, a laundry, an office, a consulting room, and an operating table. Few of the beds had mattresses. Water had to be carried from a pump, and the lavatories were buckets which were carried away to be emptied twice daily. There were only two local girls for all nursing duties, and the stock of medicines was meager.

When I wondered how anything could be achieved in such a place my mother smiled. "I've practiced most of my medicine in tents or native-built huts, Chantal. This is luxury. I've found that if you keep a patient clean and rested, with fresh air to breathe, nature does more healing than medicine." She made a wry face. "I try to avoid surgery, because the facilities are so poor, but at least I've had a great deal of experience under worse conditions, so when an operation has to be done I just say my prayers and do the best I can."

During the short ride in the carriage I had told of my own ambition to become a medical student, and how I had been working towards this by studying books and helping Mr. Brunner during my circus days. My mother had looked radiant with delight, and hugged my arm as we sat side by side, saying that she would begin teaching me at once.

In the hospital that morning I saw my

mother in a new light, as a doctor, and my admiration for her grew still more. She had learned enough Hungarian to be able to talk with the children, and spent more time in this way than in medical examination and prescribing treatment. In these activities she was very light-handed, very quick and decisive. I was now wearing a spare overall she had found for me, and was helping in such small ways as holding a kidney bowl, mixing a draught under her instruction, or distracting a child while she renewed a bandage. Watching her hands at work fascinated me. I felt I had never seen such capable hands.

I learned that both her parents had died in an influenza epidemic soon after I was born, and with the small legacy left to her she had set out to follow her father's profession by becoming a doctor. The fact that he had been a medical practitioner helped a little, and after passing the necessary Arts Examination she had managed to secure a place as a medical student at the London School of Medicine for Women, where the renowned Elizabeth

Garrett Anderson was dean.

There she had obtained her degree in 1892, but by then her money was exhausted, and since she could not afford to set up a practice in England, she had begun her career by taking a position in India, in a hospital endowed by one of the Indian princes. From that times on she had wandered the world, going wherever she felt her help was most needed, but rarely staying in one place for more than six months.

"I'm afraid I'm a restless person," she said as we sat for a few minutes with a cup of dark, sweet coffee in her office. "I became lonely without work to do, and even so I seem to need some fresh task every so often. It would have been different if my John had lived, but . . ." She gave me a quick warm smile. "Perhaps it will be different now I have you."

"When we're free, Mother." I kept my voice low. "Everything will be different then."

She darted a glance at the open door and gave a warning shake of her head.

"Not now, dear," she whispered. "Don't speak of escape except when we're quite alone."

We returned to the castle for luncheon, and found the atmosphere at table very strained. It was clear that Gideon Sumner and Baron Krenner had fallen out. Gideon seemed amused, but the Baron was grim and silent, making curt replies to Belinda's attempts at lighthearted conversation. I could not help feeling pleased to catch the look of anxiety in her eyes, though I had an uneasy feeling that whatever breach had occurred might not augur well for us.

We spent the afternoon at the hospital, took tea in my mother's sitting room, then walked in the castle grounds for a while, talking in turn as we began to fill in a few of the many gaps in the brief stories we had so far told each other. But as we walked I was studying the castle, the gatehouse, and the outer wall. When we were on the western side I interrupted my mother to whisper quickly, "Which is your window, Mother? No, don't point, just tell me."

"The third floor, fifth from the right." Her voice became anxious. "Chantal, what are you thinking of?"

"Please don't worry. I'll tell you after dinner this evening, in your room." As we turned I glanced up and marked the position of the window, to the left of a buttress.

An hour later, when we came down to dinner, the atmosphere had undergone a remarkable change. Baron Krenner and his guests were in high humor and on the best of terms again. I did not like it, and sensed the same uneasiness in my mother, but we sat wooden-faced and silent throughout the meal, as we had done the night before. I rarely suffered from a headache, but I had one now, a strange tight feeling like a band clamped about my brain. There seemed too little air, and I found myself breathing deeply as if my lungs lacked oxygen.

When we had finished coffee my mother stood up, as before, and said in the expressionless voice she used with Baron Krenner, "May we withdraw?"

He grinned. "Certainly, my dear. Oh,

but first we have a little news which I'm sure will interest you. A young man named Martin Verne is lurking somewhere in this area. We do not quite know where, but we do know that he has made careful plans to deprive me of your company."

I stood still, my heart hammering. My mother had lost a little color, but she still stared remotely over Baron Krenner's head. He went on, "I thought we had dealt with Mr. Verne last year, but apparently he survived. Now he plans a rather dramatic rescue by seizing your carriage as you return from the hospital the day after tomorrow, and has bribed several worthy fellows to assist him."

Belinda was watching me with spite in her eyes. She said, "He's a fool. They took his money and came straight to Baron Krenner with the story."

Gideon Sumner leaned back in his chair and laughed. "Verne doesn't know yet that Chantal's here. I'll look forward to telling him, when we nab him. Remember how he looked when he was searching for her at the ball, Lindy? I think poor Martin is quite besotted with Kirkby's changeling." Still smiling, he came forward on his chair and slapped his hand down hard on the table, as if swatting a fly. "By God, this is a lucky chance for us. That fellow's been on my heels a damn sight too long already."

My head felt as if it would split, and the room wavered about me. I heard my mother say in the same flat voice, "May we withdraw?"

I felt her take my arm, and forced myself to walk steadily beside her as we left the dining hall. The moment we were alone in her room she turned to me, white-faced. "Dear God, they'll kill him!"

"Yes." I put my hands to my head. "But if we can escape first, *tonight,* there'll be a hue and cry and he's bound to hear of it, wherever he's hiding!"

A spark of hope flared in her eyes, then died. She started to shake her head, but stopped and looked at me wonderingly for long seconds. At last she gave a little nod of decision, drew me to the fireplace on the far side of the room, put her hands on my shoulders, and stared at me again, with a look in which trust and confidence shone through her anxiety.

"How shall we do it?" she whispered.

I knew she had put her faith in me, and I felt as if some precious treasure had been placed in my hands. The confusion that clouded my mind fell away, and I said, "Mother, you climbed down a rope of sheets from your window once. Can you do it again?"

"Yes." She gave a shaky laugh. "I'll be better at it this time."

Though my head still throbbed, everything was sharp and clear in my mind now. I said quickly, "Twist the sheets well, tie a knot every foot or so. Use a reef knot for joining the sheets, as you do for a sling or a bandage. You may have to tear them in half lengthwise to make a long enough rope. At midnight, open your window a little and watch for the guard making his rounds. When he's been gone five minutes, lower your rope and come down. I'll be waiting for you."

A hint of doubt crept into her gaze. "But, Chantal, he'll see the sheets within an hour, when he comes round again. Yours and mine —"

"No. I won't have to use sheets, and as soon as you're down I'll climb up and untie yours."

Her eyes widened. "Can you do that? Can you really do it?"

"Yes, truly."

She laughed a little tremulously, then again she gave that small decisive nod. "What else must I do?"

"Did you go out by the gatehouse or postern before?"

"The gatehouse. The postern's locked, but the man in the gatehouse would only see us if he happened to be looking out of that little window." She hesitated. "Chantal dear . . . what then? We've nowhere safe to go."

"But we have, Mother — the circus! It's only just beyond Kaposnika, so we can reach it on foot by dawn."

She caught her breath. "The circus? Your own friends?"

"Yes, Mother, yes!"

For a moment she seemed scarcely able to take it in, then her face was suddenly lit with hope and joy. She turned quickly, moved to her sewing box, and took out a pair of scissors. As I watched she picked up the dark skirt she had brought down from her room to mend, and began to slit it up the middle.

"Mother, what on earth . . . ?"

"I'll make it into a divided skirt for tonight!" Her whispering voice was full of excitement and she looked even younger than when I had first seen her. "Help me, Chantal. You hem and stitch one side while I do the other."

I did not care about the pulsing of my head. Close to foolish laughter, close to foolish tears, I began to thread a needle. "I'm so bad at sewing, you'll be ashamed of me. Maria was always scolding me about my sewing."

"How it looks won't matter. Sit here, Chantal, then we can work together. Now, tell me about Maria."

SIXTEEN

The storm broke at eleven. Even through the thick leaded panes of my window I saw the glare of the first huge flash of lightning from the east, and five seconds later the thunderclap bellowed over Szigvár. Then came the rain. When I eased the window open an inch or two I could hear the first big spots hitting the cobbles of the bailey, and within minutes there was a deluge.

Again and again the sky was ripped by jagged light, and the thunder settled to an almost continuous roar. Water began to pour from the stone spouts of the roof. Even as I watched, the band clamped about my skull loosened and the ache in my head faded. I knew now that it had been caused by the gathering storm. For ten minutes I stood peering out through the narrow gap, then saw the pale glow of a storm lantern moving along the path between the flower beds. Despite the storm, the gatehouse guard was doing his hourly duty.

I closed the window and sat on my bed in the darkness, hardly knowing whether to be glad or sorry about the storm. Certainly it meant that nobody was likely to be looking out of a window, and when the time came for us to pass the gatehouse the teeming rain and darkness would help to cloak us, but wet stone would make my climb down the wall more hazardous, and I wondered how my mother would manage her descent with rain hammering down upon her. I comforted myself with the thought that there was still an hour to wait. The rain might ease before then, and at least there was no wind to drive it into our faces or pluck at us as we descended the castle walls.

I was wearing my riding trousers and a shirt of Leo's I had brought with me from the circus and never worn since. My feet were bare, my hair drawn back and tied in a tight roll at the nape of my neck. Beside me on the bed lay my jacket and my moccasins. I was ready, and there was nothing to do now but wait.

The storm seemed to be moving in a circle. Slowly the thunder drew closer, then receded. I thought of the circus. On a night like this, few of our people would be in bed. Strabo, Rama Singh, and the other animal men would be with their beasts, soothing and calming them. Tentmen would be busy round the big top, adjusting the great guy ropes. Others would be digging trenches to carry away water and prevent flooding. Mr. McLeod would be protecting his traction engine and his cable. Mr. Albertini and his grooms would be with the horses. It was hard to believe that all my circus friends were so close, only a few miles away. . . .

The hour dragged slowly by. It was not until I struck a match for the fifth time to look at my watch that the hands stood at midnight. I put on my jacket, hung my moccasins about my neck, and again opened the window an inch or two. The rain still fell straight and hard, but the storm center had moved away a little.

Every minute or so a brilliant glare lit the sky and was later followed by a roll of thunder, but I saw no lightning flash now.

Ten minutes passed, and I was in a fury of impatience when at last I saw the glow of the storm lantern again. It moved slowly across the eastern bailey, and in a sudden flash of brightness I saw the man himself, a dark figure hunched in a long cloak, and with what looked like a sou'wester pulled well down on his head. It was a measure of Baron Krenner's grip on his followers that the man was stolidly doing his duty on such a night.

As soon as the lantern disappeared round the corner of the castle wall I climbed out on the broad sill and pushed the window shut behind me. Carefully I reached down to test the slipperiness of the stone, and was relieved to find that it was not as bad as I had feared. I turned and slid over the edge, groping with my toes for the crevice between the courses. In ten seconds my hair was plastered to my head, and my jacket and trousers soaked through. To my right, a gush of water fell from a spout above. I had to climb by feel alone, for I could see nothing, but this did not distress me. My hands were strong, I had trusted them for years, and I had long ago lost all fear of heights.

As I edged my way down I moved sideways, to pass between two windows of the next floor. Once lightning flared, and I froze against the wall for long seconds before moving on again. Grope with one foot . . . find a niche. Seek with a hand . . . a shallow crevice here, a fingertip hold. Test carefully. Now the other foot . . . the other hand.

I could not measure time, but the climb could have taken me little more than three minutes, for when I had put on my moccasins and hurried along the wall to peer round the northwest corner, the guard with his lantern was just disappearing beyond the angle of the tower on his way back to the gatehouse. Hugging the wall, I ran to stand below my mother's window. I had misjudged my timing, for if she followed my instructions it would be five minutes before she began her escape. I hesitated, then turned to the wall, kicked off my moccasins, and began to climb, feeling that at least this would save a few minutes later. The ascent went more swiftly, as I had expected, for it was easier to find a crevice by groping up with a hand than down with a foot. Two minutes later I was crouched on the broad sill of the embrasure, tapping on the window. It opened, and I saw the pale shape of my mother's face in the darkness. She said softly, "Dear God in heaven!"

"I came up to help you through the window, Mother. That's the awkward part." I had to whisper loudly for my voice to be heard above the hissing rain. "Are you ready?"

"Yes. Here's the sheet rope, darling. I've tied it firmly to the bed." She passed something bulky through the window, her medical bag, with the end of the twisted sheets knotted to its handle.

"Mother, you can't take this!"

"I must dear, I'm never without it."

"But we've miles to walk!"

"I'll manage, really."

I held back a half-hysterical giggle as

583

the madness of the moment struck me. I was crouched forty feet above the ground, soaked to the skin, and having my first argument with my new-found mother. Without another word I took the bag and began to lower it to the ground. When the knotted sheet went slack, I moved in through the open window and said, "Now, Mother. Try to clamp a knot between your feet whenever you can."

"Yes, Chantal. Don't be angry with me about the bag."

"I'm not, truly. Hurry now."

She was surprisingly nimble as she threw back her cloak and slipped quickly onto the sill, turning in readiness to lower herself. I whispered, "Don't catch your fingers between the rope and the edge. Wait, I'll hold one hand till you've got a grip lower down. Now try to grip with your feet. Ready . . . ?"

I leaned out of the window with my heart in my mouth, watching her rain-beaten shape move slowly down. She vanished into the darkness, and after what seemed an age I felt the rope go slack. I allowed time for her to untie the case, then drew in the knotted sheets, crawled onto the sill, pushed the window shut behind me, and once again began to grope my way cautiously down the wall, aware that my toes were becoming sore.

Five minutes later we were huddled by the gatehouse, a pale-yellow light gleaming from the small window above our heads. Only a few paces away stood the great wooden gates of the castle. They were closed now, but a smaller door was set in one of them, a heavy key jutting from its lock. We had now to pass through that door unseen, and I would have dearly loved to peer through the window, to see if the guard was dozing, before we began to cross that dangerous patch of ground between the gatehouse and the door. But I did not dare.

The rain had dwindled and almost stopped, in the abrupt way of storm rain, and everywhere seemed a little lighter than before. When I twisted my head to look up, I saw a silvery line edging the great bank of cloud that now covered only half the sky, and to the south the stars were clear and bright. If the clouds were moving, they might soon unveil the moon, so there was no time to be lost.

I put my lips to my mother's ear and whispered, "Wait here till I've opened the door, then come as quietly as you can." I saw her nod, and moved to the gates, my moccasins making no sound. Warily I gripped the key and tried to turn it, but it moved only a little way. A surge of alarm swept through me. I bit my lip and used more strength, but in vain. Then I pulled . . . and the door swung open. It had not been locked.

I turned and beckoned my mother. She came towards me clutching her doctor's bag in one hand. I urged her through the door, then followed and closed it gingerly behind me. We stood beneath a great stone arch, twelve feet in depth, with the gates set on the inner side of it. A lantern hung from a hook in the center of the span. Once beyond the arch we would quickly be lost in the darkness of the track leading down through the trees.

I started to take the bag from my mother, but she shook her head. Deciding that we could argue about that later, I put a hand on her arm and we began to move forward, only to freeze with shock. A tall man in a cloak and mackintosh hat had suddenly rounded the abutment, stopping short, staring at us open-mouthed. I recognized him as the dour man with the wolf badge who had been one of our escort between the castle and the hospital. Half stunned with despair, I realized that he was the gatehouse guard tonight, and must have stepped outside for some reason unknown to us. That was why the door had not been locked.

For a moment we all stood as if rooted, and perhaps it was the quick responses I had learned in the circus that helped me to be first to recover. I croaked urgently, *"Run, Mother, run! I'll catch up!"* As I spoke I took two quick strides forward and flung myself at the man's straddled legs, twining myself about his knees, clutching with arms and legs like a monkey, wrenching frantically.

I had the wild hope that I might tumble him over backwards, knocking the wind out of him for a few moments, but though he swayed and staggered a little he did not fall. A powerful hand reached down and took me by the back of the neck. I tried to sink my teeth in his leg, but my head was jerked away. Then, incredibly, in the moment when hope had vanished, I heard the sound of a sharp impact, a grunt, and the brutal hand went suddenly slack as the man crumpled forward and fell full length.

I lay on my back, his legs resting heavily across me, and pushed an unresisting knee away from my face. I saw my mother standing with her medical bag gripped in both hands and swung back over her shoulder, as if about to strike. But she had not struck. She was rigid as stone, and staring in unbelief. My eyes turned to follow her gaze, and I saw the head of a man above me, half obscured by a bar of shadow thrown by some part of the lantern's framework, so that only his upper face was visible. The eyes were narrowed. The head was turned and cocked a little as if to listen, alert as a wolf, and beyond lay the stars that form Orion, framing that head as I had seen it framed with strange premonition on a summer's evening a year ago.

I croaked, "Martin . . . !"

His head turned. He darted a glance down at me, then bent quickly and hauled me to my feet. Now I saw that he wore rough peasant clothes and had a stubble of beard, with straggling sideboards which reached up to join his tangled hair. He stood looking at me with an almost angry glare, rubbing the knuckles of his fist as if they were bruised, and whispered, "My God, I thought you were in England!"

I said stupidly, "Well, I'm not."

My mother lowered the bag to her side and said in a voice that shook, "Martin, you were betrayed, and we were so afraid for you."

"The betrayal was my own doing." His teeth showed in a grin. He moved quickly to her, took her hand and touched it briefly to his lips. "Dr. Elizabeth. I'm sorry I've been so long." He turned, knelt beside the unconscious guard, rolled him face upwards, then tilted the head back. "Hold him so, Chantal." I knelt and obeyed. Martin took a phial from a pocket of his ragged jacket and uncapped it, then slid a finger into a corner of the man's mouth to open his lips.

My mother crouched beside him and said, "Give it to me, dear." She took the phial, tilted the man's head back a little more, and poured the contents up one nostril. "There. That way he won't choke and spit it out."

Martin nodded gravely. "I'll bear it in mind another time."

I smelled a powerful odor, like garlic, and my mother said, "Paraldehyde, Martin?"

"Yes. A hundred and twenty minims."

"He'll sleep for hours. You must put him in the gatehouse, he can't be left lying in the open."

Martin started to say something, then shrugged and made a smiling grimace. He pulled the guard to a kneeling position, then with a quick movement hauled him upright and bent to catch the toppling figure across his shoulders. "Open the door, Chantal," he said quietly, "and wait here, both of you."

I understood now why the gatehouse guard had gone prowling outside. Martin had lured him out, perhaps by some deliberately suspicious noise, so that the door would be opened and the man disposed of for the time being. A minute later Martin returned, took us each by an arm, and murmured, "Now we'll go." As we passed out from under the arch I saw a rucksack lying against the abutment, and whispered to draw his attention to it. He shook his head. "Ropes and climbing irons. I don't need them now. Give me your bag, Dr. Elizabeth, and no more talking for a little while, please."

Halfway along the track which led through the belt of trees surrounding the castle, he turned and led us between two hawthorns into a glade. There stood a pony harnessed to a small two-wheeled cart with a pile of brushwood and old sacks beside it. "There's room for two, I think," he said briskly. "Lie on the mattress I've laid on the bottom of the cart, and I'll cover you with brush and sacks."

As he helped my mother into the back of the cart I said, "Will you make for the circus, Martin?"

"I shall now. That's a stroke of luck I hadn't counted on. We'll be skirting the villages, but don't worry about anyone becoming curious. I'm known for miles around as Moonlight Jan, the mad tinker."

I had a hundred questions to ask, but bit them back and wriggled onto the ancient mattress beside my mother. Soon we were jogging at a steady pace along the track. I could feel my mother moving, fumbling with her bag, and after much wrestling in the darkness she thrust something into my hands. A small flask.

"It's brandy, dear," she whispered. "Take a few little sips to keep the cold out. Your clothes are soaked."

It was hard to remove the cap and get the flask to my lips without spilling the brandy as we jolted along, and again I had to struggle against a foolish fit of the giggles. I did not feel cold, for I was warmed by a great glow of joy and relief from within. Martin was here, and the heavy burden of responsibility had been lifted from my shoulders. I choked as the brandy touched my throat, then sipped again more cautiously, and felt a new warmth kindle inside me.

The jolting eased, the wheels no longer rattled, and I guessed that we had turned from the road and were passing along a grassy track through woods. Huddled in darkness, swaying with the movement of the cart, I felt a dreamy sensation creep over me. Nothing seemed real. It was absurd to think that I had been climbing a rain-swept castle wall less than twenty minutes ago, or that in another few hours we would be safely within the little world of the circus. This was not a small cart, with Martin at the reins in the guise of a tinker . . . it was the Galletti living wagon, trundling along the road to our next pitch, and I was drowsing in my narrow bunk. . . .

I woke to find myself in Martin's arms as he carried me from the cart to a small log hut in a forest clearing. It was still night, but in the hut a lamp was lit and a fire was burning under a crude chimney.

I said dazedly, "I'm all right, Martin. Where are we? How long have I slept?"

My mother stood by the fire, smiling at me as Martin set me down. "Only an hour," he said, and turned to close the door. "This was an abandoned charcoal burner's hut, and it's been my home for the last six months, except for two short trips to England."

I stared about me, bewildered. "But . . . why aren't we going straight to the circus?"

"The river's in spate and there's a bridge down, so we have to take a long loop round." He put his hands on my still damp hair and smoothed them down to my cheeks, smiling. "I don't want you to arrive there with pneumonia, and I've spent weeks making every preparation I could think of. Don't worry, you're safe here." Without taking his eyes from me he went on, "Dr. Elizabeth, will you wrap her in a blanket and start drying her clothes while I attend to the pony?"

"Yes, Martin dear."

"Are your own clothes wet?"

"Just my cloak and the bottom of my skirts, but they'll soon dry."

He nodded, still looking at me steadily.

"I've hot soup and bread ready. We'll move on our way in half an hour. Dr. Elizabeth, do you know I love this green-eyed daughter of yours?"

"I hoped you might, Martin. Now I can see it."

He moved his hands to my shoulders, drew me towards him, and kissed me gently on the lips. I put my arms round him and rested my cheek against his chest. "Martin . . . I'm so happy." I meant it with every fiber of my being.

He gave a quick glad laugh. "Ah, Chantal . . . now I think I know how it feels to fly on a trapeze."

Five minutes later I sat curled on the floor by the fire, wrapped in a blanket and eating a bowl of soup and a wedge of coarse bread. My mother sat with Martin on a roughly made settle, and as we ate we listened to his tale.

I had guessed right in thinking that his lost memory had first been startled to wakefulness when he caught a glimpse of Gideon Sumner and Belinda in Regensburg; but in that moment, as I already knew, his new memories had vanished, and the old had not fully returned. He had no recollection of anything since setting out for Hungary on a mission to trap Gideon Sumner, and so he had taken a room in a cheap lodging house and sent a telegram to Sir Robert. Five days later he was in England, and under medical care.

When the doctors pronounced him physically in good health, and said that his memory would gradually return, he had made ready to take up the trail of Gideon Sumner again. It was a matter of waiting for Gideon to make a new move, and trying to catch him in some act of villainy, but since he seemed settled in Osburne for a while, Sir Robert himself had rented White Lodge and taken over the task of surveillance.

It was in December that Martin's memory of my mother suddenly returned, bringing back all that had happened in Szigvár — when he had found her note, tried to rescue her, and been left for dead by Baron Krenner's hirelings. That memory had sent him posthaste to Osburne, to meet Sir Robert and tell him that he would be his hunting dog no longer.

"I knew I would have to be very careful," Martin said, gazing into the fire. "I knew Krenner had many watchful eyes in his service. So I came into Hungary from Poland, as a lone gypsy tinker, to account for speaking the language poorly. I traveled all the villages for twenty miles around Szigvár, making myself known, then set up home in this hut. And often at night I'd go out with my cart, driving through a village, shouting for knives to grind and pots to mend." He laughed. "I've had many a rotten cabbage and suchlike thrown at me, but soon everybody knew of Moonlight Jan, the mad tinker."

In this way he had created a person who could come and go as he pleased, by day or night, without rousing suspicion, and all the time he was studying the castle, noting how it was guarded, pretending to doze in his cart near the hospital, watching the carriage and escort which brought my mother back and forth. He well knew that it was one thing to snatch her from Baron Krenner, but another to carry her safely out of Hungary and beyond Krenner's long reach.

In the end he had decided to take her eastwards, to the Rumanian border, as this was the least likely escape route, and he had summoned his patience to wait until June for the attempt, so that they would have fair weather for journeying through the Transylvanian Alps. He had explored the route, seeking out places where they could rest and eat — a cave, a mountain hut, an outhouse on a farm, anywhere to lie hidden overnight. And he had bought peasant clothes ready for my mother to wear on the journey.

On a day towards the end of March he had been plying his tinker's trade outside the hospital, peering from under the floppy wide brim of the stained old hat he always wore, watching as my mother made her way to the waiting carriage. A child had climbed on the step of the coach, and Baron Krenner's man had struck him. . . .

I saw my mother give a little start as she remembered. Martin said quietly, "I was only a few paces away when you rounded on the man, Dr. Elizabeth. I saw your face . . . and in the same instant I saw Chantal in you." He looked from my mother to me. "You're not alike in features. But the manner, the turn of the head, the flash in the eyes . . . they were all Chantal, just as I'd seen her one day in the circus, protecting her friend Maria."

He smiled, leaned forward, and reached down his hand for me to take. "That was when the long gap was filled at last, my sweetheart. I remembered Chantal, the circus, the day of the logjam in the river, everything. And I was stunned, thunderstruck. I scarcely remember making my way home to this hovel, and as the hours went by I began to wonder if my imagination had played a trick on me . . ."

There were weeks to go before the rescue he had planned, and so he had left Szigvár, shaved off his beard, and set out to find me. From Mr. Kayser's agent in Paris he learned that I had left the circus months ago, and was in England. He had made for London, called first on his guardian, Sir Robert, and there learned that we had been neighbors and good friends in Osburne, and that Sir Robert would be attending the Kirkby ball at Cranmore Square next day.

The Kirkby ball. I winced and said, "Don't talk about that, Martin. I hate to remember."

He laughed gently. "It's past now. I couldn't see your mother in you that night, but I couldn't see Chantal, either. So while I was waiting a few days for my beard to grow a little, I began making inquiries about Elizabeth Martin and the Kirkbys, and the circus girl who had become one of the family." He shrugged. "After a few hours at Somerset House, looking at marriage certificates and wills, the truth began to show. I found that Elizabeth Martin had been married to John Kirkby and borne a child which had died after two days. But I was sure now that she hadn't died."

Martin took a watch from his pocket and looked at it. "Sir Robert has a passion for mysteries, so I left him to carry on while I returned here. He managed to trace Albert Minchin from the address on your birth certificate, Chantal, and then everything became clear . . . well, almost everything. I still can't fathom who set that killer dog on you, for Benedict Kirkby wouldn't have the nerve, and Gideon Sumner wanted you alive."

My mother drew a quick breath and said, "Killer dog?"

Martin nodded grimly. "Yes, but Chantal can tell you of that another time. When I came back here I planned to snatch you from Castle Szigvár at the dark of the new moon, in June, Dr. Elizabeth. All my preparations were made. I couldn't climb the castle wall, but I could climb the corner of one of the towers, using irons on my legs, and I was going to come down to your window from the roof, on a rope."

My mother wrinkled her brow. "Oh . . . was that when I fell ill with colic?"

"Yes. I heard about it in the village, and I had to postpone my plans till you were quite well again. It was very hard to wait, so I made another brief visit to England, to see Chantal once more. It only takes forty hours if you catch the

Orient." His smile as he looked at me made me feel suddenly weak with love, and my heart raced. He said, "And this time I found her, found Chantal."

I remembered those moments in the barn, and said, "But you let me go on thinking you were a bad man, Martin! And you didn't tell me about my mother."

"My sweetheart, I didn't dare. As things stood, I felt you were safe, but if you'd known the truth and stormed in to confront Benedict Kirkby with it, I don't know what might have happened. Better for you to go on thinking me a scoundrel for a little longer."

There was a silence, then my mother said, "Martin, we thought you'd been betrayed. Krenner said you had bribed some men to help you seize my carriage *tomorrow.*"

He grinned. "A precaution, Dr. Elizabeth. That man Sumner has a sharp instinct, and could well wonder what I might be up to, so I gave him something to focus his attention. I bribed a fellow from Tomsár, ten miles away, to carry that tale to Krenner."

Martin looked at his watch again. "Time for us to go. I'll harness the pony while you get dressed."

Three hours later, lying snug and dry beside my mother under the brushwood and sacks, I felt the cart come to a halt. A moment later Martin was standing by the side of it, close to my head, pretending to make the load more secure with a piece of rope.

He whispered, "We're just entering Kaposnika, and it's getting light. There's no way round because of the flooding, and a lot of people are about, clearing up damage. I can see half a dozen of Krenner's men lurking near the station, so I think your escape's been discovered. Don't worry if you hear me shouting. Everyone's used to the mad tinker."

He took the reins and we began to move again. Soon I heard sounds of activity, and people calling to one another as they worked. From the splashing of our wheels we seemed to be moving through several inches of water. Then Martin began to howl. My mother told me later that he was crying out in broken Hungarian, "Mend your kettles! Sharpen your knives! Cheap! Cheap! Make way for Moonlight Jan, tinker to the Emperor himself. Pots and pans, scissors and knives . . . !"

The people of Kaposnika had no time for a crazed foreign tinker, shouting his trade at dawn on a day when their town had been ravaged by a storm. We heard cries of anger and derision, and a soft thud or two as a few missiles were flung at the cart. I was excited, but no longer afraid, and with every moment my love for Martin grew, warmed by the exhilarating impudence of the charade he was acting out now.

Slowly we trundled through the half-flooded town, and all became quiet again as we took the road out on the far side. Now we were mounting a hill, and I could hear the clumping of Martin's boots. He had left the driving seat and was walking beside the pony to lighten its load. At last the wheels sank in soft turf and the cart slowed to a halt. The brushwood and sacks were flung aside. Martin's face looked down in the gray light of dawn, his teeth showing in a grin of mischievous delight. "We're home," he said.

I sat up, remembering the site from past years. There stood the big top, a few of the roof panels ripped by the storm. There lay the wagons, ranged in their usual order. Some of the sideshow tents had been damaged, and the field of grass had been churned to mud. Only a few people were about, and I knew that most would be snatching a few hours' sleep after the battle against the storm in the early hours. I could see Captain Lefevre speaking with a group of tentmen, pointing, giving instructions. As I looked towards my old living wagon, the door opened and Mr. Galletti emerged, pulling on his working jacket and glancing up at the sky.

It came home to me then, as a reality, that my mother and I were free. A wave of joy and relief swept me, and as Martin plucked me from the cart and set me on my feet, the tears ran down my face.

"Safe, Chantal!" he said jubilantly, and turned to help my mother down. She looked about her wonderingly, then closed her eyes and drew in a deep breath of morning air, the first she had taken in freedom for a long year.

I hugged her, babbling almost incoherently. "It's all right, Mother, it's over, and there's Mr. Galletti, oh you must come and meet him, and Maria, oh she's so lovely, and she'll squeal with surprise, I wonder if she's awake yet —"

"The gray-haired gentleman by the wagon is staring," my mother broke in. "You'd better run and greet him, Chantal."

"Yes . . . yes. Oh, Martin, bring my mother." I turned and began to run towards the wagon, waving and calling, laughing through my tears as I saw Mr. Galletti put a hand to his head, unable to believe his eyes as I drew near.

My heart was singing as I told myself over and over again that we were safe now. All danger was past, and the nightmare had ended. We were still in Hungary, still within Baron Krenner's estates, and Gideon Sumner would tell him that we must surely have fled to the circus. But all this no longer mattered, for now we were amid a hundred friends and he could never dare try to touch us.

I did not know then what such a man could do when driven to near insanity by fear, rage, and frustration.

SEVENTEEN

Two hours later Maria and I sat side by side in the dining tent, an arm about each other. Mr. Kayser sat at the end of the table between Martin and my mother, and Mr. Galletti was facing me. Sammy had provided us with a good breakfast, and I had felt very proud as I introduced my mother to the circus folk with us in the dining tent. They had gone about their work now, and Mr. Kayser had joined us ten minutes ago, listening quietly while Martin gave him a brief account of our story.

Maria turned to flash her dark eyes at me and whispered, "I told you, Chantal, I *said* Martin was an English milord who had fallen in love with you!"

"He isn't an English milord, *carissima,* and he hadn't fallen in love with me.

That happened later."

"Poof! It is the same thing. I knew it —"

"Shhh! I want to listen."

Mr. Kayser was saying with his heavy accent, ". . . and you will be zafe here, Dr. Elizabeth, be sure of that." His face darkened. "If any man comes to take you from us he will be lucky to escape a horsewhipping, baron or no baron. My people have great respect for women, and you would not be turned away even if you were a ztranger. But you are not. You are Chantal's mother, and so it is our happy pleasure to welcome you."

My mother said, "You're very kind, Mr. Kayser." She looked tired, but there was a brightness in her eyes and her voice was warm and happy.

"When will you be moving, sir?" Martin asked.

"Tomorrow. Business is finished here after the storm. Today we dry out and mend. Tomorrow we strike the tent and move." He smiled suddenly. "You must tell your peculiar story to my partner when he returns from Kaposnika."

"Your . . . ? Oh, your partner. Yes." Martin looked a little baffled, but I remembered Maria had told me in her letter that Mr. Kayser had a partner now.

"He has gone to meet a man from Vienna, but the train has been delayed, of course," said Mr. Kayser. I scarcely heard the last words, for I was rising to my feet, staring stupidly down the tent to where the canvas flap of the door had been thrown back and two men had entered. One was a stranger to me, a fair man in a waterproof cloak thrown back from a neat dark suit, galoshes on his feet, and carrying a document case. The other wore a fisherman's jersey beneath a rumpled dark-blue jacket, with the ends of his trousers tucked into Wellington boots. This man I knew, for it was Sir Robert Wayman.

"Come in, come in, Hauptmann, my dear fellow," he was saying. "We're a bit topsy-turvy after the storm, but I'm sure you'll understand. Ah, here are the unexpected visitors Leo was telling me about just now. Excuse me."

He marched forward briskly despite his

limp. "My dear Chantal, how are you, child?" He took both my hands and bent to kiss my cheek. "You look as if you'd been dragged through a wet hedge, but enjoyed it."

"Sir Robert . . . whatever are you doing here?" I said dazedly.

"Hasn't anyone told you yet?" Sir Robert waved a hand proudly and chuckled. "I've been Paul Kayser's partner since January. How about that, hey?"

"You?"

"Why not?" He shot a glowering glance at Martin, who stood looking as bewildered as I. "When my wolf-born hound deserted me for his own pursuits I remembered all those grand stories of yours. Went to see Paul Kayser at his winter quarters, and bought a half share in the circus. A man needs an interest to keep him lively, you know."

I began to laugh, and tried hard to suppress it. Sir Robert glared. "No mockery, young lady. I'm pretty much of a sleeping partner, but I've spent a good few weeks on the road these six months past, and I'm learning the ropes."

Mr. Kayser said, smiling, "He is too modest. We have done very goot business by his suggestions."

"Never had such fun." Sir Robert looked at his partner. "Paul, will you take care of Herr Hauptmann for me? He's been traveling all night, and he's wet and hungry. Perhaps he could have a bite and a nap in our quarters while I talk to my friends."

"Of course." Mr. Kayser rose and moved to shake hands with the stranger. "A pleasure to meet you, Herr Hauptmann. Will you come with me?"

As the tent flap closed behind them Sir Robert turned scowling upon Martin. "Why the devil didn't you tell me what you were up to?"

Martin had recovered from his surprise, and smiled with an untroubled air. "I wasn't on your business, sir, it was personal. I wasn't after Sumner or Krenner. All I cared about was Dr. Elizabeth. But how did you find out?"

"By putting two and two together," Sir Robert grunted. "I uncovered the Kirkby story for you, and then you vanished without a word. Independent young whelp. But it wasn't hard to work out that Elizabeth Martin must be *your* Dr. Elizabeth Martin. And since Benedict Kirkby had his talons on her fortune, I reasoned that if anyone was holding her prisoner it had to be cousin Krenner." He smiled a little grimly. "That's when I thought it a good idea to enjoy one of my little spells with the circus here in Kaposnika."

His hand on my arm, he moved to where my mother sat watching him with the cool and appraising look I had seen her wear in the hospital. "Chantal, my dear," he said in a quiet, almost apologetic voice, "be so kind as to introduce me to your mother."

My mother rose and stood very erect as I said, "Mother, this is Sir Robert Wayman."

She hesitated, then put out her hand. Sir Robert took her fingers and bowed. "Your very humble servant, Dr. Elizabeth. I first heard of you from Martin, years ago. I know and love your daughter. I shall never have a greater privilege than to meet you."

"I have somewhat harder words for you, sir," my mother said sharply. "How could you use that boy as you have done all these years, sending him into danger to satisfy your own obsession?"

Sir Robert blinked, but continued to hold my mother's hand. "Why I — I scarcely knew what else to do with the young devil, ma'am. He was a wild boy, and it seemed as well to channel his bent for adventure to a useful purpose."

"Nonsense! You used him as a — a hunting dog."

Sir Robert grimaced ruefully. "In a sense, ma'am. You use my own words, and they sound harsh. But the boy and I have long had a way of speaking roughly with each other, as men sometimes do when there's a good liking between them. We understand each other well, I assure you."

Martin said, "It's true, Dr. Elizabeth —"

"Be quiet, Martin." She did not take her eyes from Sir Robert. "Your guardian should be ashamed of himself."

"I am, ma'am, I am indeed, if you say so." Sir Robert spoke meekly, though I saw a twinkle in his eye. "But I've not neglected more important things betweentimes. I've made the young wretch study the business of merchant banking. Six months in every year, without fail, in the firm of which I'm a partner."

"I find that a very small mitigation of your offense, sir." My mother's voice was still cool, but I thought I heard a hint of uncertainty in it now. Martin caught my eye, and winked. He was clearly much entertained by this reprimanding of his guardian. I put my hand quickly to my mouth, but though my mother was still gazing at Sir Robert she said sharply, "Stop sniggering, children!"

Martin straightened his face, and I tried to look contrite. Sir Robert said cheerfully, "See how quickly they get out of hand if you're not strict with 'em, ma'am? Well, I do hope you'll find it in your to forgive me my sins. All men are fools, and some worse than others." He paused, and his face grew sober. When he spoke again his voice was very quiet. "But

I must say one thing to you. Not long ago, Martin told me that one day he would bring you to me . . . and I'd fall at your feet. I beg leave to say that he was right, ma'am."

My mother flushed, then gave a nervous laugh. "I — I think you must be a great flatterer, Sir Robert."

He sighed, then smiled. "No, ma'am. I'm a crusty fellow by nature, your daughter will vouch for that. You do me an injustice there."

"Then I must apologize."

Sir Robert moved a little to take her arm in his. "You've a kind heart, ma'am. I'll escort you to old Solange's wagon now, if I may. She has a spare bed, and I'm sure you must be very tired."

"A little. But so are Chantal and Martin."

Sir Robert chuckled. "Maria will carry Chantal off and keep her awake with ceaseless chatter, and Martin knows the circus well enough to find his own bed. Come, Dr. Elizabeth."

As soon as they had gone Maria danced across the grimy duckboards. "Did you see? He has fallen in love with her, Chantal! Oh, isn't that exciting?"

I laughed, and tugged her hair. "You're as bad as ever with your romancing, Maria."

Mr. Galletti tapped his chest. "Your mother is beautiful from within, Chantal." Smiling, he took out his pipe and pouch. "And now, before you go to bed, I would like to smoke a pipe, if you have not lost your old skill."

I slept for two hours that morning, woke refreshed, and then set about making myself useful. It was almost as if I had never been away. Our circus people were not given to making a fuss. I had gone away, and now I had come back. They greeted me placidly, asked no questions, and simply absorbed me into their community again as one of them.

As the morning wore on I met them all, Strabo and Pepe, Gustave and Violette, Mr. Brunner, Old Sven and the little Khalaf boys. I took a cup of coffee with old Solange, talking in whispers so that we should not disturb my mother. Later, when she woke and had made her toilet, I introduced her to Mr. Brunner. There had been several injuries during the storm, and he was more than thankful to have her skill and experience in the little casualty tent.

No matter what I was doing I was possessed every moment by such an exuberant happiness that I felt it must be shining like an aura around me. I had Martin and my mother, and the world was wonderful. Soon after one o'clock my mother joined the rest of us in the dining tent for a meal of Sammy's stew, and I saw my own radiance reflected in her. Already she seemed at home with everybody, and I realized that this company was no stranger than many others she had known during her years as a doctor.

During the afternoon I was called to Mr. Kayser's office wagon. Sir Robert and Herr Hauptmann were there with him. "Sit down, my dear," Sir Robert said. "We won't keep you long, but we'd like you to write out a statement. Martin and your mother have already done so."

I was puzzled. "What sort of statement, sir?"

"Well, Herr Hauptmann is an acquaintance of mine and is also a high official in the Police Department in Vienna. They've been trying to root out this secret Brotherhood of the Wolf for a long time, and now we can at least give them the proof they need to take action against Krenner."

Herr Hauptmann smiled and said, "Your mother's statement of all she has learned during her captivity is perhaps more than enough, but your own evidence of the past few days will also be useful."

I performed the task rather hurriedly, feeling that at the moment it was more important to get the circus to rights in readiness for tomorrow's move, and half an hour later I was working in the stables again with Martin. He had shaved now, and we had stopped for a moment to kiss when Sir Robert came limping in. Martin laughed, and kept an arm about me as he said, "You might have cleared your throat loudly, sir —" He broke off, for there was a bleak, almost haggard look on Sir Robert's face.

"Bad trouble," he said abruptly. "That woman of Sumner's arrived ten minutes ago in a shocking state. She says Sumner's dead."

"Dead?" I was startled, but found it strange that Sir Robert seemed so deeply disturbed. "How did it happen, sir?"

"Apparently he quarreled with Krenner this morning after your escape was discovered. Sumner wanted to cut and run. All right for him, but this is Krenner's country, so *he* had nowhere to run to. He called Sumner a traitor, and threatened him, the damn fool." Sir Robert sniffed angrily. "Sumner threatened back. Produced a hidden sword of some sort, and said he'd run anyone through who tried to stop him. Krenner went half out of his mind and there was a scuffle in which he got a cut on his face." Hands in pockets, Sir Robert shrugged. "Sumner and his woman were in the coach house, about to take a carriage, when Krenner appeared with a shotgun. Loosed off both barrels into Sumner at point-blank range."

I shuddered. Martin ran a hand slowly through his hair and said, "Well . . . when thieves fall out there's usually bloodshed. I'm not going to mourn Sumner's passing."

"Nor I," Sir Robert said brusquely. "But the woman says Krenner's raising a horde of men to march on the circus and raze it to the ground. And he'll make sure that neither Dr. Elizabeth nor Chantal nor you will survive to tell the tale."

There was complete silence in the stables, and I felt suddenly very cold. "But . . . he can't!" I whispered at last. "How can he make men do such a thing?"

Sir Robert sighed. "It's quite easy, my dear. He needs only a couple of dozen ringleaders, men bound to him by the oath of the Brotherhood. They'll be scouring the villages and Kaposnika now, telling wild tales."

I saw Martin nod grimly, and I said, "Oh, I don't understand! What tales?"

"Anything to rouse a mob against the circus." Sir Robert's voice was hard. "Sumner's woman heard Krenner instructing his men. The circus elephant instructing his men. The circus elephant broke loose during the storm and trampled six children to death in Kaposnika. The circus damned the river to avoid being flooded, and turned the waters down upon the town. The circus king poles drew the lightning that damaged the church. Men from the circus have been looting in the villages and brutalizing the women." He shrugged. "At a time like this, with damage and disorder everywhere, no tale is too absurd to be believed, and even decent people seek something on which to vent their anger."

My heart sank, for I knew his words were true. I had seen for myself, when the alarm bell rang that evening outside Seville, how a crowd of individuals could become a mob, a single entity filled with mindless hate. In Seville they had attacked us for no better reason than that they had been thwarted in attacking their true target. Here they would be constantly urged on and inflamed by Krenner's men and their wild stories.

Martin said, "We'll have to get the women and children away before the mob arrives."

I shook my head. "They won't go, Martin. Never."

His mouth tightened. "Then we'll have to find three or four men as an escort to get you and your mother out of the way."

"You're wasting your breath," Sir Robert growled before I could answer. "Good God, boy, can you imagine Chantal leaving Maria and all her other friends? Or Dr. Elizabeth leaving Chantal? Dammit, she's already organizing a casualty station in the dining tent."

Martin's head tilted, and I saw the look of the wolf. "In that case," he said softly, "there's only one thing left."

"Yes." Sir Robert spoke coolly now, his eyes speculative. "We can hope for nothing from the Kaposnika police; there's only a handful of them anyway, and they're busy with storm damage. Hauptmann's ridden off to the Army post at Nagyeny, but we'll be lucky to see any troops before nightfall, and I fancy it will all be over by then." He turned. "You'd better come and see this wretched woman, my dear."

As we made our way to Mr. Kayser's

office wagon, my hand clutching Martin's, I saw tentmen driving in stakes and setting up a wire fence across the field. Others were busy with teams of horses, hauling wagons into position to form a barrier round the animal enclosure. On one side our site was bordered by the river. It was not broad, but it was in spate from the storm rain and could be held by only a few defenders. I looked slowly round the rest of our perimeter, and my throat went dry as I wondered how many men Baron Krenner would be able to muster.

Belinda sat huddled on a chair, her dress torn, her hair bedraggled, eyes swollen with weeping. Mr. Kayser was at his desk, tight-lipped. My mother stood mixing something in a half tumbler of water. As we entered she said, "Drink this, Belinda. It will help a little."

Belinda lashed out to knock the tumbler to the floor, and a little of the liquid was spilled as my mother moved her hand quickly away. She set the tumbler down on the desk and said, "I'll go back to my duties, Mr. Kayser. I'm desperately sorry to have brought this trouble upon you."

Mr. Kayser shook his head. "I beg you not to blame yourself, Dr. Elizabeth."

Belinda saw me, and her eyes grew huge and wild. "It's *her* fault!" she cried shrilly, pointing with a trembling hand. "He's dead! And it's *her* doing!"

Martin moved forward and stood looking down at her. After a moment he said coldly, "When the mob comes, Krenner won't spare *you,* Belinda, so if you know what his plans are you'd do well to tell us."

She stared up at him, and fear crept slowly into her red-rimmed eyes. "I don't know . . ." she muttered hoarsely. "Wait . . . he said he would use a small mob first, to make you — no, I can't remember."

"To make us spread out round the perimeter?"

"Yes . . . yes, that was it. And then the rest would strike up the slope in a mass."

Sir Robert said quietly, "Well done, boy."

A thought came to me from nowhere, and I said, "Was it you who took my head scarf and paid a man to set that dog on me, Belinda?''

Her mouth twisted, and hatred burned in her eyes. ''Gideon knew,'' she whispered. ''I warned him I'd see you dead before I'd let him marry you. He knew I'd paid that Frenchman from Weymouth, that's why he beat me.'' She put a hand to her cheek. ''But I didn't care. It stopped him. He knew I meant what I'd said and it stopped him.'' Her voice rose again. ''I only wish the brute had killed you that day!''

Mr. Kayser rubbed his chin and stood up. ''I'll have Strabo take charge of that one,'' he said, jerking a thumb at Belinda. ''He can put her in a cage for all I care. What now, Robert?''

Sir Robert grimaced. ''I'd be more at home in a skirmish at sea, but at least I've learned a little from the Marines.'' He looked at Martin. ''And that young pup isn't quite the fool he looks. Come along, my boy, we'll get hold of Captain Lefevre and have a council of war.''

Martin nodded. His eyes were distant, and his face a little pale. He looked at my mother, looked at me, put a hand gently on my shoulder for a moment, then turned and followed Sir Robert out of the wagon. My mother came to me, shaking her head as I began to speak. "It's all right, Chantal, there's no need to reassure me." She managed a little smile. "I've been through something like this twice before, in Africa."

I could find no words, and took her hands. She said, "Will you fetch Maria? I'd like to have you two helping me in the casualty tent."

I had forgotten Belinda, and we were going out of the door when Mr. Kayser said, "And send Strabo to me at once, Chantal, if you please."

It was soon after six o'clock when our men first caught sight of them, a straggling group of peasants, some fifty strong, moving up the slope towards us, shouting abuse, brandishing cudgels, long staves, and heavy-buckled belts. If Belinda was right, others would now be moving along the river and through the woods, closing about us, while the main body remained hidden beyond the rise below where the river turned.

For an hour an eerie silence had hung over the circus as we waited. Our perimeter was triangular now. The river and the wire fence formed two sides, and the shorter third side was the line where the woods began. Strabo alone guarded the river line, but at intervals of twenty paces along the bank a heavy stake had been driven into the ground, and attached to each stake by a long chain was one of his five Himalayan bears.

The line of the woods was also lightly guarded by a dozen men with long poles. A network of wire had been strung between the trees and interlaced with bundles of cut fire thorn to make a vicious hedge. The traction engine stood connected to our water wagon so that powerful jets from three hoses could be turned on any attackers trying to breach the hedge.

Forty men lined the wire fence, armed with pick handles or cudgels cut from the trees. Old Sven and his helpers had been working furiously at their benches, and each of the forty men carried a makeshift shield, fashioned from planking cut from the circus seats. The children had been busy, scouring the ground for a hundred yards around, carrying away every stone and rock which might be used as a missile. These now stood in piles behind our second line of defense, which was a barrier made from the tiers of circus seats piled one on another.

In the center of the triangle stood the big top, the animal enclosure hedged by our wagons, and the dining tent, which was now our casualty station. What Sir Robert called with grim humor our reserve division was under the command of Captain Lefevre. It consisted of twenty active young men, Leo among them, who could move swiftly to any point where danger threatened. The women and children were gathered in the big top, near the entrance, as they had been that day in Seville, armed with stanchions and heavy tent pegs. There was little chatter or excitement, even among the children. Every soul in the circus knew that the mob to be launched against us would come with fire, smashing, wrecking, burning until our little world of tents and wagons lay in ashes. Homes and livelihood, perhaps even life and limb were at stake, and the mood was one of dour and bitter determination.

I had helped my mother and Mr. Brunner to make all preparations we could in the casualty station, and now I stood in the doorway with Maria and Mr. Galletti, my heart in my throat as Leo called to us that the first of the attackers were coming. Through a gap in the high barrier of seats I glimpsed Martin and Sir Robert as they moved along the line of men at the wire.

Strangely, although I felt taut with fear, I had none for myself. It was as if no place was left for it because I had too many others to fear for. There was Maria beside me, an elfin figure in shirt and trousers; there was Mr. Galletti, frail and gray, his eyes haunted as he fidgeted with his empty pipe; there was my mother, my wonderful new-found mother. I turned to look into the tent, and saw her standing with a finger to her lips, looking at the instruments and bandages she had set out, then darting a glance at the two big dixies of water simmering on the stove.

I had visions of my fiery little Maria rushing off with Leo and his group when they were called, and said, "Stay close to me, *piccina*. Don't you dare leave my side. Whatever happens, stay close to me."

She sniffed, her eyes flashed dangerously, and she swung the tent peg in her hand. "I'm going to, silly."

I remembered how she had flung herself at Strabo that day, and my stomach clenched with fear. The next moment there came a great shout from many throats and I heard a sudden clacking and thudding as cudgel met cudgel or crashed down on a wooden shield. Captain Lefevre stood by the gap in the barrier smoking a thin cigar, Leo beside him. Leo kept turning his head to shout to us, but we could hear nothing above the growing noise.

Beside me, Maria was hopping from foot to foot with the agony of not knowing what was happening, and I felt the same unbearable anxiety. Mr. Galletti said, "It is better to know how it runs, until we become too busy. You may go and see, children."

Ten seconds later Maria and I were

crouched beside Leo. I caught my breath as I saw the two lines of men battling across the wire fence. It was a brutal and horrible scene. A man staggered back with blood pouring from his brow, I heard cries and groans as cudgels swung and fell, and above it all rose the growling roar of the mob.

Another man reeled back from the fence, his shirt afire from a flaming torch thrust at him. I saw Martin appear from nowhere, fling the man to the ground and smother the flames with his jacket. Captain Lefevre gestured, and at once four of the young men darted out to carry in the injured. I took Maria's hand and said through chattering teeth, "We must go and help my mother now, Maria."

"Yes."

As I tore my eyes away I saw the fence begin to sway at one point, and next moment Captain Lefevre was leading his reserve in a dash to that part of the line. I caught a glimpse of the river to my left as we ran back to the tent. A group of men had reached the far bank, but not one had attempted the crossing. Strabo stood with a hand on the head of one of his bears, waving a pick handle and jeering.

Within the next few minutes half a dozen men were brought into the casualty tent, and I was too busy helping my mother cleanse and stitch and splint to think about anything else. Then Martin appeared, sweating and cold-eyed, a graze on his cheek but otherwise unhurt.

"There's a lull," he said tersely. "They probed the woods, then gave up there, and we've beaten them back at the fence. The main attack comes next. Dr. Elizabeth, can you spare Chantal?"

"Why do you want her, Martin?" My mother did not look up from the head she was bandaging as she spoke.

"Because she has very sharp eyes. I'm sure Krenner will be out there somewhere, and I want Chantal to help me pick him out from the crowd." His chin came up and his eyes narrowed. "If we can make a surprise sortie at the right moment, and lay hands on Krenner, the mob will have lost both its heart and its head."

My mother nodded. "Go along, darling. Maria, will you hold this splint on the finger, just so? Mr. Galletti, I think you must start cutting up another sheet for bandages."

Two minutes later I lay on top of the barrier of seats beside Martin, gazing down the slope with rising horror. A great crowd of at least two hundred moved steadily up towards the sagging fence where our men waited, fewer than thirty of them now. Sir Robert limped briskly up and down the line, calling in a loud hoarse voice, "Be steady now, gentlemen. All's safe behind you, so keep your eyes front, and hold fast till you hear the signal. Captain Lefevre! Two men to fill this gap here, please."

Martin said, "When you've watched for a while, you'll find you can spot some of the ringleaders urging them on. But I can't see Krenner. I'll swear he's here, to make sure the job's finished, but —"

"There, Martin, *there!*" I pointed as I cried out. "At the back, with the red scarf on his head!"

"You're sure? That fellow's dressed like the rest except for the scarf."

"It's him, Martin, I know it is — I can

tell by the way he moves."

"Good girl." There was a note of exultance in his voice. "That headdress will pick him out for us when the time comes —"

He broke off. The mob was surging forward with a howl that made my blood run cold. It seemed they must sweep through our thinly spread defense as if breaking a cobweb. But when those in front were yet thirty paces from the fence a whistle sounded, and a fusillade of stones hurled by Captain Lefevre's men came soaring from behind our barrier, passing high over the heads of the defenders and dropping upon the crowd beyond. The ranks wavered, but though the onrush of the mob was slowed it could not be halted.

Seconds later came the jarring crash as attackers and defenders met at the fence, and still the shower of stones fell among the rearmost of Krenner's followers. I saw Sir Robert looking this way and that, watching the whole line. Minute by minute the weight of the mob grew, and the fence began to sway dangerously.

Martin touched my arm. "Down, sweetheart. Back to the tent." As we scrambled down I caught a last glimpse of Sir Robert raising the whistle to his lips. The instant it shrilled, our men broke from the struggle and ran for the gaps in the barrier, dragging three or four of our injured. Halfway to the tent I looked back. While the mob was beating down the abandoned fence, our men had gathered behind the barrier. Sir Robert was there near one of the gaps, watching. Martin and Captain Lefevre were hustling the men into position along the whole line of the piled tiers of seats.

Sir Robert blew his whistle again, and the circus men threw their weight against the barrier, thrusting, levering with their poles and cudgels. It swayed, toppled, then the whole length of it fell with a crash upon the foremost of the charging mob. The next moment Captain Lefevre's reserve raced out on one flank and struck in a close-packed wedge, driving into the chaos. A sudden outcry and a great splashing sound made me jerk my head round. The fire wagon had been withdrawn from the edge of the woods, and the full force of three hoses was battering at the mob from the other side. Shrieks, yells, groans, and the din of battle rose to a terrifying crescendo.

I tore my eyes from the scene and ran for the tent. There were more than twenty injured now, four of them unconscious. One man was writhing in pain, and Mr. Brunner was holding him while my mother filled a hypodermic needle. Mr. Galletti had just made a sling to support the splinted forearm of Old Sven. He had scarcely tied the knot when Sven picked up his cudgel and went limping out to rejoin the struggle. Maria called, "Chantal, come quickly!" She was kneeling over a tentman who lay on a blanket, her arms spattered red as she tried to stop the bleeding from a gash in his thigh.

I ran to her and dropped to my knees, groping for the pressure point. "A thick dressing on the wound, Maria — good, now keep pressing hard." I turned my head. "Mother! As quickly as you can, please."

Maria panted, "How does it go?"

"We're holding them. It's all right." I wished I could have believed myself. The ugly roar of the battle seemed very close, and it seemed to me that we might be overrun at any moment.

My mother knelt beside us. "Let me see, Maria. Ah, it's not arterial bleeding. Lift his leg . . . a little higher. So." She began to bandage deftly. "What is his name?"

"It's Marcel, signora."

"Don't worry, Marcel." My mother smiled reassuringly. "You'll spend a few days in bed, and limp for a week or two, but it's nothing serious." She flicked a glance at me. "Do the women and children know how things are going? They must be told, Chantal. It's horrible for them to wait and wonder."

"Mr. Kayser is seeing to that himself, Mother. He won't let anyone else decide when to . . . to send them in."

I saw her bite her lip, but she gave a quick nod and said, "He's right. But God grant it doesn't come to that."

I lifted my head, listening. It seemed

that the noise outside was dwindling a little, and moving further away. Two minutes later Mr. Kayser appeared, his face drawn with anxiety. "We have beaten them back," he said. "It is over for the moment."

Maria and I looked at each other, then at Mr. Kayser. I said, "For the moment, sir?"

"Martin says Krenner and his wolves will rally them to come once more." He shrugged wearily. "We are outnumbered, and have no barriers left now. I do not know what will happen."

My mother completed her bandage and lowered Marcel's leg gently. "What does Sir Robert say?" she asked.

"We are to gather in front of the big top now. Every man who can still stand."

"And the women?"

He looked at her with haggard eyes. "If need be, yes. Excuse me, Dr. Elizabeth, I must go to them now."

My mother stood in silence for a while, looking round the tent. For the moment we had done all that could be done. She bent to take up the pick handle which lay beside Marcel. The cool look had vanished, and in her eyes was something quite different now, a hard anger. "I will protect my patients!" she said hotly.

Maria ran to collect her tent peg, and I picked up an iron stanchion brought in by one of the injured. Together we moved to stand outside the tent doorway. Without a word, Mr. Galletti and Mr. Brunner joined us. Again an eerie quietness had fallen. Down the slope of the hill I could see the mob gathering as Baron Krenner's men moved among them, whipping up their fury for a new attack. I picked out the Baron himself, still wearing the red head scarf.

It seemed that the battle had been raging for hours, yet the sun had not moved far in the sky. In front of us, and a little to our right, all the circus men had gathered in three straggling ranks. Strabo was there now, swinging a length of heavy chain in his hand, and the men guarding the woods had been withdrawn to help face this last assault.

My heart sank, for we seemed so few, even allowing for the injured. Surely there should be more, many more. My eyes sought Martin and Sir Robert, but I could not find them. Behind the circus men, in the entrance to the big top, Mr. Kayser stood in front of the women gathered there. I saw Solange leaning on a staff she carried.

A shout from below ripped the silence, and the mob began to move, a dark ugly mass rippling over the green slope like some misshapen animal. Closer it came, and closer. A great fear swept over me, and I set my teeth.

They were no more than thirty paces from our front when I heard a thudding of hooves to the left. My head snapped round, and I gasped. A close-packed wedge of some twenty men on horseback came galloping from the woods, riding hard, each swinging a cudgel. I knew the men, I knew the horses, for every groom from our stables was there, and half our mounts. Mr. Albertini was at the head of the wedge, with Martin and Sir Robert following close on his left and right. I saw Sir Robert's game leg sticking out stiffly as he rode. Behind them came the grooms, and the best riders among the rest of the circus folk.

The wedge struck against the flank of the mob and drove into it like an ax splitting wood. An uproar of yells and curses filled the air. Above the noise I heard Sir Robert's voice bellowing, "Hold formation! Hold the wedge!" I saw the cudgel whirling in his hand.

Even as the mob reeled under the impact there came a dreadful screaming sound from our right, and this was familiar, too, for it was the sound of Sunbeam "singing." She came lumbering towards the other flank of the mob, trunk lifted, squealing like a hundred pigs. Everyone in the circus knew that Sunbeam was quite incapable of hurting any human, and that her "singing" was part of her performance. But the mob did not know.

Men began to break away and run. The whole mass of the mob wavered and split. I saw Mr. Albertini turning and gathering his horsemen for a new charge. This time they drove straight towards the rear of the disintegrating mob, where a head in a red scarf stood out clearly, and in the same moment a great roar rose from the ranks of our circus men as they hurled themselves forward.

For perhaps a minute all was wild confusion, but I saw that more and more of Krenner's people were breaking away, throwing down their weapons and taking to their heels. Suddenly Martin came surging towards us on his horse, leaning to one side, dragging something with him. It was a man, his heels trailing, the collar of his jacket twisted in Martin's hand, a red scarf wrapped about his head.

His face was purple as he fell half strangled at our feet. "It was Krenner sure enough," Martin panted. "Don't let him go!" He whirled his horse and spurred back into the fray. Choking, Krenner tugged frantically at his collar and started to sit up. Before anyone could stop her, Maria darted forward and cracked her tent peg down hard on his head. "That will stop him going!" she exclaimed as he fell back, stunned.

My mother put a hand to her mouth. "You . . . you really shouldn't have done that, dear," she said uncertainly. "Mr.

Brunner, will you help us take him inside, please?"

"A moment, Doctor," said Mr. Brunner. "Look."

We all turned, and in that moment I saw that the dreadful struggle was over. The mob was dissolving, scattering. Little groups of men, and men on their own, were running down the slope, spreading out, disappearing into the straggle of trees which bordered the road, and perhaps emerging fearfully at last from the madness which had possessed them for the past hour.

The last of the fighting died quickly. Here and there a few men simply drew back, looked about them, then turned and began to trudge heavily away. There was no pursuit. Some two dozen lay injured on the ground, more Hungarians than circus folk. Some of our men sank to their haunches, panting, nursing bruises and wounds, looking about them dazedly as they slowly grasped the fact that all was over. The women came running from the big top to aid their men. Sir Robert limped towards us, leading his horse, a trickle of blood running down his face. He halted in front of my mother, looking very tired, and said, "It seems . . ." He paused for breath. "It seems we've survived, ma'am."

"Yes." She looked about her and grimaced. "An ugly business, Robert."

"Ugly indeed, my dear. Most of the poor devils were simple dupes. But a mob is a mob. They would have destroyed us."

"Yes." She took his face in her hands to examine the cut on his head. "You may need a stitch. Will you please give orders for all the injured to be brought in? I mean Krenner's people as well, knaves and dupes alike."

"Of course."

I saw Martin hobbling towards us, and ran forward. "Martin, are you hurt?"

He laughed. "A bruise on the thigh, no more." His face sobered. Gently he gathered me in his arms and held me as if he would never let me go, his cheek pressed to mine. "When are you going to marry me, Chantal?" he whispered. "We've been engaged for hours now, and I hate long engagements."

I felt tears of happiness of my cheeks, and turned my head to kiss him. "Tomorrow. The next day. As soon as we can. Martin, will you mind if I still want to study medicine?"

"I'd mind if you didn't. We'll take a house in London near your medical school."

Maria was tugging at my skirt. "Chantal, your mother says you'll have to stop kissing him for a little while, there's so much to do."

"All right, Maria, I'm coming."

At dusk Herr Hauptmann arrived with a troop of soldiers and three policemen. He and the policemen left within an hour, taking Baron Krenner with them, a gray-faced empty shell of a man with a bandaged head. The soldier remained to guard the circus throughout that night and the following day, when we would be taking down the big top and setting off for our next booking — at Budapest, three days' journey away. There would be much damage to be made good before our next performance, and perhaps there would be a change in the program if any of the performers had been hurt, but I knew Kayser's Giant Circus would open on the appointed day, for this was our pride.

We worked till well past midnight, clearing debris, repairing damage, and tending the injured, and it was only as I fell asleep in my old bed next to Maria that I thought fleetingly of Belinda. But by morning she had disappeared, perhaps fearing that she also might be taken by the police. Whatever the reason, it was a relief to be rid of her, and I was never to see or hear of her again.

We stayed with Kayser's Giant Circus throughout the three-week booking at Budapest, for there was no pressing urgency to leave. Sir Robert wanted to be sure that all was well with his new enterprise before returning to England, and I was sure he also wished to remain with my mother, who would not leave until her patients had been nursed back to health. For me those weeks were the happiest I had ever known, for I was with Martin, and we knew that we loved each other; we were together in the small world where we had first met, among the best friends we could ever hope to know, and with us was my much-loved mother, who had long ago won Martin's heart, even before she had won mine.

When the subject of the Kirkby inheritance came up, my mother dealt with it briskly. "Let them keep it. My John expected to be disinherited when his father learned of our marriage, and he didn't care. Besides, I've better things to do than wrangle over money."

"My dear Elizabeth," said Sir Robert patiently, "I ask you to think of Chantal, and what might have happened to her if that dog Benedict had had his way. He must be made to *pay*. Now, I'm quite a wealthy fellow, and I'd be delighted to see Chantal through medical school, but —"

"I'll see to that myself, thank you, sir," Martin broke in stiffly.

I said, "But I've saved up money of my own."

"Be quiet, children." My mother half closed an eye at us and turned to Sir Robert. "You see? In different ways we all disagree with you, Robert."

He looked hopefully from one to the

other of us and made an appealing gesture. "Please. Oh, please let me tackle that whey-faced fox chaser. It's the principle of the thing! He must have heard enough by now to frighten him out of his wits, and I can't bear to miss making him dance like a monkey on hot coals. I promise you, I'll take ten thousand off Benedict Kirkby for Chantal, and have him babbling grateful thanks." He put his hand on my mother's. "I'll hunt no more scoundrels, but let this be my one last piece of devilment, dear Elizabeth. Then I promise to turn over a new leaf."

My mother began to laugh.

On our last night before returning to London, I put on the spangled costume of the trapeze artist again. This had been Martin's notion, for he longed to have my mother and Sir Robert see me as he had first known me, as Chantal of the Flying Gallettis, and there would not be another chance.

I had needed no persuading. For two weeks I had secretly rehearsed our old act with Leo and Maria, under the guidance of Mr. Galletti, and at last the moment came when we stood in the mounting place behind the great curtain, waiting to make our entrance. Martin had asked my mother to join him in watching this last show before leaving, which meant that Sir Robert would certainly be there, since he spent every possible moment in her company.

As the liberty horses came cantering out, Leo grinned at me. "Don't knock me off the trapeze, fat English girl."

"Just make sure you don't drop me, monkey face."

"Sir Robert is booking an English tour for us in the autumn," said Maria, skipping from foot to foot. "So we'll be able to see you again very soon, Chantal!"

"I know. And he's arranging the bookings so that you can be my bridesmaid, *piccina*."

Leo gave a groan of mock anguish. Maria, torn between delight and indignation, had no time to decide whether to hug me or stamp on Leo's feet, for the ringmaster was already bellowing his announcement. In another moment we were skipping into the ring, smiling, making our bow, and running to climb the rope ladders.

I saw my mother and Sir Robert sitting in a ringside seat, their faces blank with astonishment and perhaps even alarm as they recognized me. I waved, and blew a kiss to Martin, who sat beside my mother with a huge grin of pride.

We climbed quickly to our little platforms. I heard the blare of the band and saw the familiar haze of upturned faces below. It came to me that for my mother and Sir Robert, for Martin and myself, this was a time of ending, the closing of a chapter. Sir Robert and Martin had already run their last quarry to earth. For my mother it was the end of lonely wandering, and for me it was the end of flying in the big top. But a new beginning waited for each of us, a beginning rich with love and promise.

I was filled with a measureless joy as I focused my concentration, gripped my trapeze, and glanced from the corner of my eye at Maria. The band began to play the familiar music for our twin act on the side-by-side trapezes, and somewhere within me I offered up the coming display of my small but hard-won talent as a thanksgiving.

Maria smiled at me, giving a little nod, and together we launched ourselves across the dome of the big top.